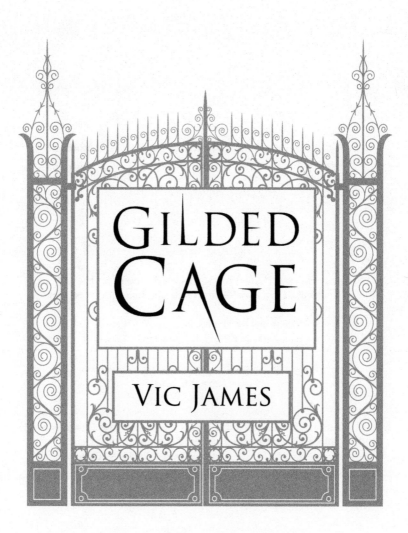

# GILDED CAGE

## VIC JAMES

DEL REY BOOKS

NEW YORK

*Gilded Cage* is a work of fiction. Names, characters, places, and incidents either are the product of the author's imagination or are used fictitiously. Any resemblance to actual persons, living or dead, events, or locales is entirely coincidental.

Published in the United States by Del Rey, an imprint of Random House, a division of Penguin Random House LLC, New York.

DEL REY and the HOUSE colophon are registered trademarks of Penguin Random House LLC.

LIBRARY OF CONGRESS CATALOGING-IN-PUBLICATION DATA
Names: James, Vic, author.
Title: Gilded cage / Vic James.
Description: New York : Del Rey, 2017.
Identifiers: LCCN 2016022954 (print) | LCCN 2016031572 (ebook) |
ISBN 9780425284155 (hardback) | ISBN 9780425284131 (ebook)
Subjects: LCSH: Aristocracy (Social class)—England—Fiction. |
BISAC: FICTION / Fantasy / Contemporary. | FICTION / Fantasy /
General. | GSAFD: Fantasy fiction.
Classification: LCC PR6110.A493 G55 2017 (print) | LCC PR6110.A493 (ebook) |
DDC 823/.92—dc23
LC record available at https://lccn.loc.gov/2016022954

Printed in the United States of America on acid-free paper

randomhousebooks.com

9  8  7  6  5  4  3  2  1

First Edition

Book design by Christopher M. Zucker

*For Mum.*
*Thank you for everything, especially the library books.*

# LEAH

She heard the motorbike first, then the galloping horse—two distant points of noise in the darkness, converging on her as she ran.

Apart from her boots striking the ground, Leah wasn't making a sound, and neither was the baby she held close. But their pursuers didn't need to hear them to find them. The only place she could run to was Kyneston's perimeter wall, and the only hope of escape once she got there was the infant bundled in her arms, her daughter, Libby.

The moon was alternately covered and revealed by high, rapid clouds, but the faint radiance of the wall shone steadily along the horizon. It was like the streak of hallway light beneath a bedroom door, comforting children waking from nightmares.

Was that what her life at Kyneston had become: a nightmare? It had once seemed to fulfill all of her dreams.

The roar of the bike engine was closer now and the thudding hooves had fallen behind. Her pursuers could only be Gavar and Jenner. Both were way off to the left, bearing down in a line that headed straight for her. But Leah had reached the wall first.

She slumped against it for a moment's relief. One hand rested on the ancient masonry as she dragged in a breath. The wall felt cool beneath her fingers. It was slick with moisture and furred with moss, jarring with the illusion of warmth from the unnaturally glowing brickwork. But that was the power of Skill for you. There was nothing natural about this place or the people that lived here.

Time to go.

"Please, my darling. Please," Leah whispered to her child, pulling aside the edge of the blanket she'd knitted and kissing Libby's silky head.

The baby fussed as Leah gently untangled an arm and took her small hand. Chest heaving with terror as much as exertion, Leah leaned on the wall and pressed her baby's palm to it.

Where the tiny fingers touched the weather-beaten brick, a greater brightness bloomed beneath them. As Leah watched, the luminescence spread, flowing through the mortar between the bricks. It was weak, but visible nonetheless. And—there!— the light jumped and climbed upward, stronger now, becoming firmer, sharper. It took on outlines: an upright, then an arch. The gate.

From the darkness came a mechanical snarl. The motorbike engine being choked off. Dying.

Then another, closer sound broke into the night: a leisurely hand clap. Leah recoiled as if it had been an actual slap.

Someone was waiting there. And as the tall, slender figure stepped into the spilling light, she saw that, of course, it was him. Silyen. The youngest of the three Jardine brothers, but not the least. He brought them into Kyneston, all those serving their days, and it was his Skill that kept them here on his family's estate. How could she have imagined he'd let her escape?

The slow applause stopped. One of the boy's narrow, nail-bitten hands gestured at the vaulting ironwork.

"Be my guest," Silyen said, as if inviting mother and child in for tea. "I won't try and stop you. I'm rather fascinated to see what little Libby is capable of. You know I have . . . certain theories."

Leah's heart was pounding. He was the last one of them that she'd trust. The very last. Still, she had to take the offered chance, even if it was no more than a cat momentarily lifting its paw off a mouse's back.

She studied his face as if moonlight and Skill-light might reveal the truth of his intentions. And as Silyen met her eye for perhaps the very first time, Leah thought she glimpsed something. Was it curiosity? He wanted to see if Libby could open the gate. If she could, maybe he would let them both through. Purely for the satisfaction of seeing it—and just perhaps to spite his eldest brother.

"Thank you," she said, in little more than a whisper. *"Sapere aude?"*

" 'Dare to know' indeed. If you dare, I will know."

Silyen smiled. Leah knew better than to mistake it for compassion or kindness.

She stepped forward and pressed Libby's hand to the faintly outlined gate, and beneath the baby's sticky fingers it blazed. Like molten metal flooding a casting mold, it bloomed with brilliant life: an efflorescence of ironwork, leaves, and fantastical birds, all topped with the entwined *P* and *J*. It looked exactly as it had that day, four years before, when Leah arrived at Kyneston and it had swung open to admit her. Just as it had looked, no doubt, hundreds of years ago when it was first created.

But the gate remained shut. In desperation, Leah grabbed one of the wrought-iron vines and pulled with all her strength. Libby began to wail loudly. But the din no longer mattered, Leah thought with dull hopelessness. They wouldn't be leaving Kyneston Estate tonight.

"Ah, how interesting," Silyen murmured. "Your child— that is, my brother's child—has the blood to wake the gate, but not the Skill to command it. Unless, perhaps, she's trying to tell you she doesn't want to leave her family."

"You're not Libby's family," Leah spat, roused to fury by her fear, hugging her baby more tightly. Her fingers cramped from struggling with the unyielding metal. "Not Gavar, not any of y—"

A shot rang out and Leah fell to the ground, crying aloud. Pain raced through her body as fast and bright as the light through the gate.

Gavar walked over unhurriedly and stood above her where she lay, tears leaking from her eyes. She had once loved this man: Kyneston's heir, Libby's father. The gun was in his hand.

"I warned you," Gavar Jardine said. "No one steals what's mine."

Leah didn't look at him. She turned her head, resting her cheek against the cold ground, and fixed her gaze instead on the blanketed bundle lying a few feet away. Libby was howling with hurt and outrage. Leah yearned to touch and soothe her daughter, but for some reason her arm no longer had the strength to reach even that short distance.

Hooves clattered to a halt nearby. A horse whickered and two booted heels hit the ground. And here came Jenner, the middle brother. The only one who might intend good, but who was powerless to act.

"What are you doing, Gavar?" he shouted. "She's not some animal you can just shoot. Is she hurt?"

As if in answer, Leah let out a keening sound that died in an airless gasp. Jenner hurried to kneel beside her and she felt him wipe the tears from her eyes. His fingers were gentle against her face.

"I'm sorry," he told her. "So sorry."

In the dimness that gathered around her, which the shining gate did nothing to dispel, she saw Gavar tuck his gun beneath his coat before bending low and gathering up their daughter.

Silyen walked past, toward the great house. As he went, Gavar turned his back and hunched over Libby protectively. Leah could only hope he would be a kinder father than he had been a lover.

"Silyen!" she heard Jenner call. He sounded distant, as if he stood in the Kyneston Pale calling across the lake, although she could still feel his palm cradling her cheek. "Silyen, wait! Can't you do anything?"

"You know how it works," came the response, so faint that

Leah wondered if she had imagined it. "No one can bring back the dead. Not even me."

"She's not . . ."

But maybe Jenner trailed off. And Gavar had surely hushed Libby. And the gate must have faded away, its Skill-light extinguished, because everything went quiet and dark.

# ONE

# LUKE

It was an unusually hot weekend in mid-June and sweat pooled along Luke Hadley's spine as he lay on his stomach on a blanket in the front yard. He was staring blankly at a spread of textbooks. The screaming was distracting, and had been going on for a while now.

If it had been Abigail trying to revise, Daisy and her pals would never have been allowed to make such a racket. But Mum had inexplicably gone into overdrive for Daisy's birthday, which had turned into the party of the century. Luke's little sis and her friends were careering round behind the house shrieking at the tops of their voices, while some unforgivably awful C-pop boyband blared through the living room window.

Luke stuffed his earbuds in as deep as they'd go without rupturing anything, and turned up the volume on his own music. It didn't work. The catchy beat of "Happy Panda" was backed by the delirious vocals of ten-year-old girls massacring the Chinese language. Moaning, he let his face fall forward onto the books spread out on the grass in front of him. He knew who he'd be blaming when he failed History and Citizenship.

Beside him, her own exams long since completed, Abi was lost in one of her favorite trashy novels. Luke gave it the side-eye and cringed at the title: *Her Master's Slave*. She was nearly finished, and had another pastel-covered horror lined up. *The Heir's Temptation*. How someone as smart as his big sister could read such rubbish was beyond him.

Still, at least it kept her distracted. Uncharacteristically, Abi hadn't nagged him once about revision, even though this term's tests were the most important until he finished school in two years' time. He turned back to the mock exam paper. The words swam before his eyes.

*Describe the Equal Revolution of 1642 and explain how it led to the Slavedays Compact. Analyze the role of (i) Charles I, the Last King, (ii) Lycus Parva, the Regicide, and (iii) Cadmus Parva-Jardine, the Pure-in-Heart.*

Luke grunted in disgust and rolled onto his back. Those stupid Equal names seemed designed to confuse. And who really cared why the slavedays had begun, hundreds of years ago? All that mattered was that they'd never ended. Everyone in Britain except the Equals—the Skilled aristocrats—still had to give up a decade of their life. Those years were spent confined to one of the grim slavetowns that shadowed every major city, with no pay and no respite.

Movement caught his eye and he sat up, scenting distraction. A stranger had walked up the driveway and was peering through the windows of Dad's car. This wasn't unusual. Luke jumped up and went over.

"Brilliant, isn't it?" he told the guy. "It's an Austin-Healey, more than fifty years old. My dad restored it. He's a mechanic. But I helped. It took us more than a year. I could probably do most of it myself now, he's taught me so much."

"Is that right? Well, I reckon you'll be sorry to see it go, then."

"See it go?" Luke was nonplussed. "It's not going anywhere."

"Eh? But this is the address in the advert."

"Can I help?" Abi had appeared at Luke's shoulder. She nudged him gently. "You get back to your revision, little bro. I'll handle this."

Luke was about to tell her not to bother, that the man had made a mistake, when a stampede of small girls hurtled around the house and thundered toward them.

"Daisy!" Abi yelled repressively. "You're not to play round the front. I don't want anyone tearing into the road and getting run over."

Daisy trotted over to join them. She wore a large orange badge with a sparkly "10" on it, and a sash across her chest bearing the words "Birthday Girl."

"Honestly." Daisy folded her arms. "It was only for a minute, Abi."

The man who'd come about the car was looking at Daisy intently. He'd better not be some kind of pervert.

"Birthday girl, is it?" he said, reading the sash. "You're ten? I see . . ."

His face went funny for a moment, with some expression Luke couldn't work out. Then he looked at the three of them standing there. It wasn't a threatening look, but it made Luke put his arm around his little sis and draw her closer.

"Tell you what," the man said. "I'll give your dad a call some other time. You enjoy your party, young lady. Have your fun while you can."

He nodded at Daisy, then turned and ambled off down the driveway.

"Weird," said Daisy expansively. Then she gave a whoop and led her pals in a prancing, cheering conga back round the rear of the house.

"Weird" was the word, Luke thought. In fact, the entire day had felt not quite right.

But it wasn't until he lay awake in bed that night that it all came together. Selling the car. The fuss over Daisy's birthday. The suspicious absence of nagging over his own exam revision.

When he heard hushed conversation floating up from the kitchen, and padded downstairs to find his parents and Abi sitting at the table studying paperwork, Luke knew he was right.

"When were you planning on telling me and Daisy?" he said from the doorway, deriving a grim satisfaction from their confusion. "At least you let the poor kid blow out the candles on her cake before your big reveal. 'Happy birthday, darling. Mummy and Daddy have a surprise: they're abandoning you to do their slavedays.'"

The three of them looked back at him in silence. On the tabletop, Dad's hand reached for Mum's. Parental solidarity— never a good sign.

"So what's the plan? That Abi's going to look after me and Daisy? How will she do that when she's at med school?"

"Sit down, Luke."

Dad was an easygoing man, but his voice was unusually firm. That was the first alarm.

Then as he stepped into the room, Luke noticed the documents Abi was hastily shuffling into a pile. A suspiciously large pile. The uppermost sheet bore Daisy's date of birth.

Understanding slid into Luke's brain and lodged its sharp point there.

"It's not just you, is it?" he croaked. "It's all of us. Now that Daisy's turned ten, it's legal. You're taking us with you. We're all going to do our slavedays."

He could hardly say the last word. It stole the breath from his chest.

In an instant, the slavedays had gone from being a dull exam question to the next decade of Luke's life. Ripped away from everyone and everything he knew. Sent to Manchester's filthy, unforgiving slavetown, Millmoor.

"You know what they say." Luke was unsure whether he was berating his parents or begging them. " 'Do your slavedays too old, you'll never get through them. Do your slavedays too young, you'll never get over them.' What part of that don't you understand? Nobody does days at my age, let alone Daisy's."

"It's not a decision your mother and I have taken lightly," Dad replied, keeping his voice steady.

"We only want the best for you all," Mum said. "And we believe this is it. You're too young to appreciate it now, but life is different for those who've done their days. It gives you opportunities—better opportunities than your father and I had."

Luke knew what she meant. You weren't a full citizen until you'd completed your slavedays, and only citizens could hold certain jobs, own a house, or travel abroad. But jobs and houses were unimaginably far off, and ten years of servitude in exchange for a few weeks of foreign holidays didn't seem much of a trade.

His parents' reasonableness knifed Luke with betrayal. This wasn't something his parents just got to choose, like new curtains for the living room. This was Luke's life. About which they'd made a huge decision without consulting him.

Though they had, apparently, consulted Abi.

"As she's eighteen," Dad said, following Luke's gaze, "Abigail is of age to make up her own mind. And obviously your mum and I are delighted that she's decided to come with us. In fact, she's done rather more than that."

Dad put his arm round Abi's shoulders and squeezed proudly. What had the girl wonder done now?

"Are you serious?" Luke asked his sister. "You've been offered places at three different medical schools, and you're turning them down to spend the next decade saying *nin hao* every five minutes in Millmoor's Bank of China call center? Or maybe they'll put you in the textiles factory. Or the meatpacking plant."

"Cool it, little bro," Abi said. "I've deferred my offers. And I'm not going to Millmoor. None of us are. Do what Dad says: sit down, and I'll explain."

Still furious, but desperate to know how you could do days without going to Millmoor, Luke complied. And he listened with a mixture of admiration and horror as Abi told him what she'd done.

It was insane. It was terrifying.

It was still slavedays, and because he was under eighteen it wasn't like Luke had a choice one way or the other. His parents could take him wherever they wanted.

But at least they weren't taking him to the hellhole that was Millmoor.

Mum and Dad told Daisy the next morning, and she accepted the news with a stoicism that made Luke ashamed. For the first time, he allowed himself to think that maybe his parents' plan was the right one, and that they'd all get through their days just fine, as a family.

A few days later, once it had all sunk in, he told his best friend, Simon. Si let out a low whistle at the big reveal.

"There's a department within the Labor Allocation Bureau called Estates Services, where the Equals go for their house-slaves," Luke said. "Abi made an application for us there. We're being sent south to Kyneston."

"Even I've heard of Kyneston." Si was incredulous. "That's the Jardines. The top of the lot. Lord Jardine is the scary dude who was Chancellor when we were little. What on earth do they want you for?"

"I've no idea," Luke admitted.

The paperwork had detailed roles for Mum, Dad, and Abi: as the estate nurse, Kyneston's vehicle mechanic, and something secretarial. But no assignment was specified for Luke or

Daisy—presumably because they were minors, Abi explained. They might not have a particular job, but simply be required to do tasks on an as-needed basis.

Luke had caught himself imagining what those things could be. Scrubbing the mansion's gold-plated toilets, perhaps? Or how about waiting on the Equals at dinner, hair combed and white gloves on, spooning peas from a silver tureen? None of it appealed.

"And Daisy," Si continued. "What use do the Jardines have for a kid that little? What use have they got for a nurse, come to that? I thought the Equals used their Skill to heal themselves."

Luke thought the same, but Abi, ever willing to clarify and correct, pointed out that nobody really knew what the Equals could do with their Skill, which was why it was particularly exciting to be going to an estate. Daisy had nodded so hard in agreement it was a wonder her head hadn't fallen off. Luke doubted even the Equals could fix that.

The summer crawled by. Some time mid-July, Luke thumped downstairs to find a realtor showing prospective tenants around the house. Soon after, the hallway filled up with boxes so their possessions could be taken to storage.

Early August, he went into town with a few friends from the school soccer team and broke the not-so-happy news. There had been shock, sympathy, and the suggestion of a valedictory visit to a pub where the barman was known to be a poor judge of age. But in the end, they'd just kicked a ball around in the park.

They hadn't made plans to meet up again.

With twelve days to go, the bloke who'd turned up asking

about the car came back. Luke watched his father hand over the keys and had to turn away, blinking. He was not going to start crying over a car, of all things.

But he knew it wasn't the vehicle he was mourning, so much as what it represented. Bye-bye, driving lessons in the fall. So long, independence. Won't be seeing you in a hurry, best years of my life.

Abi tried to cheer him up, but a few days later it was his turn to see her silhouetted in the kitchen doorway, her head bowed and shoulders shaking. She held a torn envelope in her hand. It was her exam results. He'd forgotten all about them.

At first he thought she hadn't achieved the grades she had hoped for. But when he hugged her, Abi showed him the slip of paper. Perfect marks, confirming her admission to every university to which she'd applied. Luke realized then how much his big sister was giving up by coming with them.

Departure Day minus two was an open house for friends and family to say their farewells, and Mum and Dad threw a sub-dued party that evening. Luke spent the day hunkered down with the console and his favorite games, because there'd be no more of those, either, where they were going. (How did slaves entertain themselves at Kyneston? Playing charades round the piano? Or maybe there was no downtime. Maybe you worked until you dropped, then slept, then got up and did it all over again, every day for a decade.)

Then the day itself arrived, sunny and beautiful, of course.

Luke sat on the garden wall, watching his family going about its last bits of business. Mum had emptied the fridge and gone to the neighbors with an offering of leftovers. Dad was drop-ping off a final box of essentials with a friend a few streets away, who would take it to the storage depot to join the rest of the family's possessions.

The girls sunbathed on the grass, Daisy pestering her sister with questions and repeating back the answers.

"Lord Whittam Jardine, Lady Thalia, Heir Gavar," Daisy parroted. "Jenner. And I can't remember that last one. His name's too silly."

"You're halfway there," said Abi, smiling. "It's Silyen—that's *Sill*-yun. He's the youngest, somewhere between me and Luke. There's no Jardine as little as you. And it's Jar-*deen* and *Kye*-neston, like 'lie.' They won't want to hear our northern vowels down south."

Daisy rolled her eyes and threw herself back down on the grass. Abi stretched out her long legs and tucked the bottom of her T-shirt underneath her bra to catch some sun. Luke devoutly hoped she wouldn't be doing that at Kyneston.

"I'm gonna miss that fit sister of yours," Si said in Luke's ear, startling him. Luke turned to look at his friend, who'd come to see him off. "You make sure your lords and masters don't go getting any funny ideas about their entitlements."

"I dunno," Luke muttered. "You've seen the books she reads. I reckon it might be them that need protecting."

Simon laughed. They exchanged an awkward shoulder-bump and backslap, but Luke stayed sitting on the wall, Si standing on the pavement.

"I hear the Equal girls are hot," he said, elbowing Luke.

"Got that on good authority, have you?"

"Hey, at least you'll get to see some girls. My uncle Jim says all the workplaces are single sex at Millmoor, so the only women you hang out with are your own family. It's a right dump, that place."

Si spat expressively. "Jimmy got back from there a few weeks ago. We've not told anyone yet, because he's not leaving the house and doesn't want folk coming round. He's a broken man. I mean, literally. He was in an accident and now his arm—"

Simon folded up one elbow and flapped his wrist. The effect was ridiculous, but Luke didn't feel like laughing.

"He got hit by a forklift or something. He's not said much about it. In fact, he hardly says anything at all. He's my da's little brother but he looks about ten years older. Nah, I'm staying out of Millmoor as long as I can, and I reckon you've scored a right cushy number."

Si looked up and down the street. Looked anywhere but at Luke.

His best friend had run out of things to say, Luke realized. They'd hung out together for nearly twelve years, playing, pranking, and copying homework off each other since their first week at primary school. And all that ended here.

"Don't go thinking those Equals are folk like us," Si said, with one last effort at conversation. "They're not. They're freaks. I still remember our field trip to that parliament of theirs, that House of Light. The guide banging on about what a masterpiece it was, all built by Skill, but it gave me the creeps. You remember those windows? Dunno what was going on inside, but it didn't look like 'inside' any place I've ever seen. Yeah, you watch yourself. And that sister of yours."

Si managed a halfhearted wink at Abi, and Luke cringed. His friend was a complete liability.

Luke wouldn't see him for an entire decade.

Abi wouldn't hear Si's innuendos ever again, because he'd probably be married with kids by the time they all made it back to Manchester. He'd have a job. New friends. He'd be making his way in the world. Everything that made up Luke's universe right now would be gone, fast-forwarded ten years, while Luke himself had stayed still.

The unfairness of it all made him suddenly, violently furious, and Luke smashed his hand down on the wall so hard he took the skin off his palm. As he yelped, Si finally looked at him, and Luke saw pity in his eyes.

"Awright, then," Si said. "I'll be off. You have a quick ten years."

Luke watched him go, the last part of his old life, walking away round the corner and out of sight.

Then, because there was nothing else left to do, he went and joined his sisters, stretching out on the lawn in the sun. Daisy lolled against him, her head resting heavily on his ribs as he breathed in and out. He closed his eyes and listened to the noise of the TV from the house on the other side; the rumble of traffic from the main road; birdsong; Mum telling Dad that she wasn't sure whether she'd packed enough sandwiches for the five-hour journey to Kyneston.

Something small crawled out of the grass and crept across his neck until he swatted it. Luke wondered if he could sleep away the next ten years, like someone in a fairy tale, and wake to find that his days were over and done with.

Then Dad's voice, officious, and Mum saying, "Get up, kids. It's time."

The Jardines hadn't sent a chauffeur-driven Rolls for them,

of course. Just a plain old silver-gray sedan. Dad was showing their papers to its driver, a woman whose sweater was embroidered with "LAB," the Labor Allocation Bureau's initials.

"Five of you?" the lady was saying, frowning at the documents. "I've only got four names here."

Mum stepped forward, wearing her most reassuring face.

"Well, our youngest, Daisy, wasn't quite ten when we did the paperwork, but she is now, which is probably—"

"Daisy? Nope, I've got her down." The woman read from the top sheet on her clipboard. "Hadley—Steven, Jacqueline, Abigail, and Daisy. Collection: 11 A.M. from 28 Hawthornden Road, Manchester. Destination: Kyneston Estate, Hampshire."

"What?"

Mum snatched the clipboard, Abi craning over her shoulder to look at it.

Anxiety and a mad kind of hope knotted their fingers in Luke's guts and pulled in opposite directions. The paperwork had been botched up. He had a reprieve. Maybe he wouldn't have to do his days at all.

Another vehicle turned into the street, a bulky black minivan with an insignia blazoned across the hood. They all knew that symbol, and the words curled underneath: *"Labore et honore."* Millmoor's town motto.

"Ah, my colleagues," said the woman, visibly relieved. "I'm sure they'll be able to clarify."

"Look," Abi whispered fiercely to Mum, pointing to something in the papers.

The van pulled up in front of the house and a thickset man, hair buzzed almost to his scalp, got out. He wasn't wearing the LAB outfit, but something that looked more like a police uniform. A truncheon hung from his utility belt and knocked against his leg as he walked over.

"Luke Hadley?" he said, stopping in front of Luke. "Guess that's you, sonny. Grab your bag, we've got another four to pick up."

"What does this mean?" Abi asked the LAB woman, thrusting the clipboard at her.

Several sheets were curled back and Luke recognized the face in the photo now uppermost as his own. The page was scored by a thick red line, with two words stamped across it.

"What does it mean?" The woman laughed nervously. "Well, 'Surplus: reassign' explains itself, surely? Kyneston Estate has been unable to find any useful activity for your brother, so his file was returned to us for reassignment. As an unqualified solo male, there's really only one option."

Anxiety had won the tug-of-war, and was hauling Luke's guts out length by length, helped along by fear. He wasn't needed at Kyneston. They were taking him to Millmoor.

"No," he said, backing away. "No, there's been a mistake. We're a family."

Dad stepped protectively in front of him. "My son comes with us."

"The paperwork says otherwise," the LAB woman piped up.

"Stuff your paperwork," Mum snarled.

And then it all happened horribly quickly. When the uniformed guy from Millmoor reached round Dad to grab Luke's arm, Dad swung a fist at his face. It connected with the man's jaw and he swore, stumbling backward, his hands scrabbling at his belt.

They all saw the truncheon come down and Daisy screamed.

The baton whacked Dad round the side of the head, and he fell to his knees on the driveway, groaning. Blood trickled from his temple, reddening the little patch where his hair was going gray. Mum gasped and knelt beside him, checking the injury.

"You animal!" she yelled. "Blunt-force trauma can kill if the brain swells."

Daisy burst into tears. Luke wrapped his arms around her, pressing her face against his side and holding her tight.

"I'll report you," said Abi, jabbing a finger at the Millmoor man. She peered at the name emblazoned on his uniform. "Who do you think you are, Mr. Kessler? You can't just assault people."

"How right you are, young lady." Kessler's lips drew back across a wide, teeth-filled grin. "But I'm afraid that as of 11 A.M."—he checked his watch ostentatiously, rotating his wrist outward so they could all see the dial, which showed 11:07— "you all began your slavedays and entered a state of legal non-personhood. You are now chattels of the state. To explain for the little one here," he said, looking at Daisy, "this means that you are no longer 'people' and have no rights at all. *At. All.*"

Abi gasped and Mum made a low moan, pressing her hand to her mouth.

"Yes," the man continued, with that thin-lipped smile. "People don't tend to think about that when they're making their arrangements. Particularly not when they think they're something special, too good to slave alongside the rest of us. So you have a choice."

His hand went to the belt and unclipped something. It looked like a child's drawing of a gun: blocky and intimidating.

"This fires fifty thousand volts and can incapacitate each one of you. Then we load you into the car, along with your bags. You four in there, and you"—he pointed to Luke, then to the van—"in there. Or you can all just get in the correct vehicle. Simple."

You could appeal these sorts of things, couldn't you?

Abi had got them all into Kyneston. She'd be able to get him out of Millmoor. Of course she would. She'd wear down the labor bureau by force of paperwork alone.

Luke couldn't let anyone else in his family get hurt.

He loosened his arms from around Daisy and gave her a gentle push away.

"Luke, no!" his little sis yelled, trying to cling more tightly.

"Here's what we'll do, Dozy," Luke told her, kneeling down and wiping the tears from her cheeks. "I'm going to Millmoor. You are going to Kyneston, where you'll be so super-special-amazing that when you tell them you've got a brother who's even more awesome, who somehow got left behind, they will send their private jet to come and fetch me. You understand?"

Daisy looked too traumatized to speak, but she nodded.

"Mum, Dad, don't worry." Dad made a choking noise and Mum broke out in noisy sobs as he embraced them both. "It's just for now."

He couldn't keep up this act much longer. If he didn't get in that van quickly, he'd completely lose it. He felt empty inside, just bitter black terror washing around like dregs in the bottom of his stomach.

"I'll see you all soon," he said, with a confidence he didn't feel.

Then he picked up his duffel bag and turned toward the mini-van.

"Aren't you the little hero," sneered Kessler, slamming open the vehicle side. "I'm weeping here. Get in, Hadley E-1031, and let's get going."

The baton hit Luke hard between the shoulder blades and he sprawled forward. He had the presence of mind to pull up his feet before the door banged shut, then was thrown back against the seat legs as the van pulled away.

Facedown on the filthy vehicle floor, pressed against strangers' stinking boots, Luke didn't see how anything could be more awful than what had just happened.

Millmoor would prove him wrong.

# TWO

# SILYEN

Early September sunlight streamed through the oriel window of Kyneston's Small Solar, throwing a thick golden cloth over the breakfast table. It turned the silverware arrayed in front of Silyen Jardine into a constellation of stars. The fruit bowl in the center, a dazzling sun, was piled high with pears. They were freshly cut from the trees in Aunt Euterpe's garden. He pulled the dish toward him and selected a russet-and-green specimen.

With a sharp, ivory-handled knife, he cut into the pear. It was ripe and he watched the juice bleed out onto the plate before wiping his fingers.

Before he even reached for his coffee cup, the footman who stood one pace behind and to his left was pouring a steaming black stream into it from a burnished pot. Gavar, his eldest brother, may once have blacked a house-slave's eye for bringing him burnt toast, but the staff were quickest of all to serve the Young Master. Silyen found this fact gratifying. That it incensed Gavar was a bonus.

As usual, however, Silyen and his mother, Lady Thalia, were the only people in the Small Solar at this hour. As was also customary, there were at least half a dozen slaves going to and fro with the breakfast things. He watched them absently. So much bustle, all of it so unnecessary.

And today Mama was adding yet more to their number.

"An entire family?" he said, sensing that some comment was expected of him. "Really?"

Staffing was Jenner's domain. Their mother believed it was important to give his middle brother a sense of usefulness and value within the family. Silyen suspected that Jenner knew all too well how his family truly regarded him. He'd have to be stupid not to, as well as Skilless.

Across the table, Mama was nibbling a brioche as she leafed through some sheets bearing the Labor Allocation Bureau letterhead.

"The woman is the reason the bureau sent us their papers. She's a nurse with extensive experience of long-term care, so she'll take over looking after your aunt. The man is handy with vehicles and restores classic cars, so he can fix up some of those wrecks your father and Gavar insist on collecting. And they're just starting their days, not coming from one of the slavetowns, so they won't"—she paused, searching for the right phrase— "won't have picked up any faulty notions."

"Won't have learned to hate us, you mean." Silyen looked at his mother with dark eyes just like hers, from under the dark curling hair that was also characteristic of his maternal ancestors, the Parvas. "You said it was a family, so what about the children?"

Lady Thalia waved dismissively, causing one of the maids to step forward for instructions before realizing her mistake and stepping back again. The slaves that trailed around after the Jardines performed this tiresome dance of servility many times daily.

"Well, there's a clever girl of eighteen. Jenner's been asking for extra help in the Family Office, so I'm assigning her to him."

"Eighteen? Are you going to tell them what happened to the last girl who came to Kyneston at eighteen to do her days?"

His mother's immaculate makeup hid any rising color, but Silyen saw the documents flutter in her hand.

"You shouldn't speak like that. I could cry right now when I think of that poor girl. Such a terrible accident—and for it to have been your brother that shot her. He's still distraught. I believe he loved her very much, foolish infatuation though it was. That dear little baby without a mother or a family."

Silyen's lips twitched. It was just as well Gavar wasn't present to hear that disavowal of his child. The infant had grudgingly been permitted the Jardine surname—there was no denying her parentage, after all. Her shock of copper-colored hair proclaimed her clear kinship to Gavar and their father, Whittam. But the child had no other privileges of blood.

"I'm thinking these nice people could look after it," his mother continued.

Ordinarily, Silyen took a lively interest in his eldest brother's illegitimate child. Though slave-born bastards weren't unheard of among the great families, they were usually cast out along with the offending mother. Fortunately, Leah's death had prevented that from happening with little Libby, giving Silyen the opportunity to study her at close quarters.

As the child wasn't born to two Equal parents, the laws of heredity deemed she would be Skilless. But you never knew. Silyen was intrigued by what had happened at the gate the night Leah had tried to run. And curious things had happened at Kyneston before—like Jenner's lack of Skill, despite his parents' impeccable pedigree.

Libby's childcare arrangements, however, interested Silyen rather less. He had other things on his mind today.

Soon, the Chancellor would arrive at Kyneston: Winterbourne Zelston himself. Zelston was coming to visit Mama's sister, to whom he had been engaged in their youth. They still were engaged, presumably, as Zelston was both too in love and too guilty to break it off. But Aunt Euterpe was in no position to walk down the aisle. For the last twenty-five years she had been in no position to do anything at all, apart from breathe and sleep.

Well, Silyen had some news about that to share. Zelston would find this visit memorable.

Impatience burned within him. His leg was jiggling beneath the table and he pressed his palm down on his knee to still it. On days like this, Silyen could feel his Skill thrumming through him, seeking an outlet. Channeling Skill was akin to playing the violin. That moment when the strings' vibrations burst forth as music: exquisite, irresistible music. He ached to use it.

He didn't understand how his family could go through life seemingly untroubled by this constant need. Did not understand how Jenner, without Skill, could bear to live at all.

"They look like honest, dependable people," Mother was saying, dabbing crumbs from her mouth without smearing her lipstick. "They arrive around four o'clock, so you'll be needed. Jenner will get them settled in. Here, take a look."

She slid a photograph across the polished walnut expanse of the breakfast table. It showed five people on a windswept English beach. A middle-aged man with receding hair and a proud smile had his arm around a trim woman in a zip-up top. In front of them stood a small girl, freckled and pulling a face at the camera. Flanking the trio were two older children. There was a tall girl with long sandy hair twisted into a braid, caught in the act of deciding whether or not to smile, and a blond boy, embarrassed and grinning.

The older girl didn't look like Gavar's type, which was a relief. The boy earned a second glance. He appeared to be around Silyen's age, which raised interesting possibilities.

"How old is the son?"

"Nearly seventeen, I think. But he's not coming. I simply couldn't think of a thing he could usefully do. And, you know, boys of that age can be so difficult and disruptive. Not you, though, my darling. Never you."

Lady Thalia raised her tiny teacup in a salute to her favorite son—albeit there wasn't much competition. Silyen smiled back serenely. It was frustrating, though, that the boy was not coming. Perhaps one of his sisters would prove suitable instead.

"I can't imagine there's anything the youngest can usefully do, either."

"I quite agree. But Jenner insisted. He wanted the whole family, said we couldn't split up parents and children. So I met him halfway and said we'd take the little girl, but not the boy.

He still wasn't happy, but he knows my word is final. I worry that because of the way he is, he identifies overly much with these sorts of people. It's not something your father and I wish to encourage."

Jenner's unfortunate deficiency and inappropriate sympathy for the commoners was another well-worn topic of conversation, so Silyen transferred his attention back to the pear on his plate. Its dissection was almost complete when the doorbell jangled from the hallway beyond, horribly echoed by a strangled howl.

Great-Aunt Hypatia must have brought her pet. As Silyen listened, the howl gave way to low whining. It would be a mercy to kill the creature one of these days—though it might be more amusing to set it free.

"That'll be the Chancellor and your great-aunt," said Lady Thalia, quickly checking her appearance in a silver cream jug before rising. "Your father's got her down to talk about Gavar's wedding. When she heard Winterbourne was coming here, too, she invited herself into his state car for the journey. Only Hypatia would inveigle a lift from the most powerful man in the land."

Their visitors waited just inside Kyneston's carved oak door. Chancellor Winterbourne Zelston cut a stately figure, while Great-Aunt Hypatia was resplendent in fox furs, every one from an animal she'd hunted herself. A third filthy shape lay between them, its thin sides heaving. It scratched occasionally, as if at fleas, though more likely at the sores that badged its protruding ribs. Its nails were untrimmed and curled under, scrabbling against the smooth flagstones.

"Lord Chancellor," Lady Thalia said, dropping a curtsey.

As the Chancellor nodded acknowledgment, sunlight from the vast windows of the Great Hall caught the beads ornamenting the neat cornrows of his hair, casting bright spangles across Kyneston's walls. Silyen suspected the man had long cultivated the art of positioning himself for such effects.

Zelston clasped Lady Thalia's hand, platinum rings gleaming on his dark fingers. An immaculate starched white cuff peeped out beneath the rich black fabric of his coat. His dress suggested a man of absolutes. But his politics were less clear-cut. Father, the previous incumbent of the Chancellor's Chair, would issue frequent dinner-table diatribes on its current occupant's shortcomings.

"It's an honor to be back at Kyneston," Zelston murmured. "I regret that parliamentary business has kept me away so long. I have missed my visits."

"And my sister Euterpe has missed you," Mama replied. "I am sure of it, though we cannot truly know. Please do go through to her."

The Chancellor wasted no time. He issued a clipped "Good day" to Great-Aunt Hypatia, then strode toward the inner recesses of the house. Silyen pushed off from the wall to follow him, stepping carefully over the quivering creature. He gave his great-aunt her customary greeting, which is to say none at all.

The Chancellor needed no directions as they passed through the wide passageway lined with Jardine and Parva family portraits. He had been visiting Kyneston since before Silyen was born.

At the end of the passage were two doors. The left revealed a plainly painted room containing an ebony piano, a spinet, and shelves packed with scores. Silyen's music room, where he practiced rather more than music.

Zelston, of course, ignored it. He reached for the familiar handle of the second, closed door, then paused and turned. Against his dark skin, the man's eyes appeared bloodshot. Had he wept when he'd read Silyen's letter?

"If you have lied to me," Zelston said hoarsely, "I will break you."

Silyen suppressed a smirk. This was more like it.

The Chancellor's eyes searched his face, looking for—what? Fear? Indignation? Falsity? Silyen was silent, inviting him to take a good look. Zelston grunted, then opened the door.

Almost nothing in Aunt Euterpe's chamber had changed during Silyen's lifetime—including the woman who occupied it. She lay in the wide white bed, her long hair brushed out across the pillows. Her eyes were closed, and her breathing was steady and even.

The room's latticed windows were kept latched open. They overlooked a small formal garden. The tops of tall hollyhocks and bobbing agapanthus brushed the sill, and wisteria wound around the casement as if trying to pull the great house down. Beyond was the orchard. Pear trees were espaliered against the red-brick wall, limbs spread as carefully as those of a knife thrower's assistant.

A side table held an array of bottles and a porcelain ewer and basin. Beside the table was a single straight-backed chair. Zelston lowered himself heavily into it, as if his body were the most burdensome thing in the world. The covers were drawn up to the sleeper's chest, and one nightgowned arm lay on top of the bedcovers. As Silyen watched, the Chancellor seized the exposed pale hand between both of his and held it tighter than any nurse would have permitted.

"You received my letter, then," he told Zelston's bowed head. "You know what I'm offering. And you know my price."

"Your price is too high," the Chancellor replied, not releasing Aunt Euterpe's hand. "We have nothing to discuss."

The man's vehemence told Silyen everything he needed to know.

"Oh, please," he said mildly, walking round the bed to stand in Zelston's line of sight. "There's nothing you wouldn't give for this, and we both know it."

"It'd cost me my position," said the Chancellor, condescending to meet Silyen's gaze. "Did your father put you up to this? He can't take the Chancellorship a second time, you know."

Silyen shrugged. "Which is the greater tragedy: a lost career or a lost love? You strike me as a better man than that. I'm sure my aunt thought so."

The room was still. The only sound was a buzzing, then the audible knock of a pollen-drugged bee against the window-pane.

"She's lain like this for twenty-five years," said Zelston. "Since the day Orpen Mote burned to the ground. I've tried to bring her out of it; your mother has tried, and even your father. Those most Skilled at mindwork have attempted it, and failed. And you stand there, a seventeen-year-old boy, and tell me that you can do it. Why should I believe you?"

"Because I've been where she is. All I need do is lead her back."

"And where is she?"

"You know that." Silyen smiled. It was his mother's smile—which meant that it was Aunt Euterpe's, too, given the close family resemblance. Zelston must hate that. "She's right where you left her."

Zelston surged from the chair, which fell to the ground with a bang loud enough to wake the dead—though not, of course, the woman in the bed. He grabbed the worn velvet lapels of Silyen's riding jacket, which was an unanticipated development. Silyen heard the fabric tear. He was overdue a new jacket anyway. The Chancellor's breath was hot on his face.

"You are vile," the man spat. "The monstrous child of a monstrous father."

Zelston thrust Silyen back against the casement, and the rattle of his skull hitting the leaded glass sent birds startling from the trees.

"I'm the only one who can give you your heart's desire," said Silyen, annoyed at how reedy his voice sounded, though a man's fist around your windpipe would do that. "And I don't ask for much in return."

The Chancellor made a noise of revulsion and released his grip. As Silyen straightened his ripped collar with dignity, the older man spoke.

"The Chancellor's Proposal allows me, each year, to set one new law before our parliament for discussion at the three Great Debates. And you ask that this year I abuse that prerogative by proposing the abolition of the slavedays, the foundation of our country's social order. I know that a handful among our Equals believe that the days are somehow wrong, and not merely the natural order of things. But I would never have thought you one of them.

"You must know that such a Proposal would never pass. Not even your own father and brother would vote for it. Them least of all. And such a Proposal wouldn't merely ruin me—it risks ruining the country. If word gets out to the commoners, who knows what might happen? It could shatter Britain's peace.

"I will give you anything within my power. I can have one of the childless appoint you their heir. As heir of an estate, then lord, you'd have a seat of your own in parliament and a shot at the Chancellorship one day—something you'll never achieve as Lord Jardine's third son. But this makes no sense. No sense at all."

Silyen looked at the man in front of him. Zelston's dark face was shiny with sweat, his immaculate white silk cravat askew. It was remarkable how much emotion the Chancellor was displaying. Was that a politician's habit, all for show? Or were some people really subject to such constant storms of feeling? Gavar was, Silyen supposed. It must be exhausting.

He gestured to the overturned chair by the bedside and it flipped back onto four legs. Gratifyingly, Zelston took the cue and sat down. The Chancellor bowed his head and ran his fingers along his knotted braids. His posture suggested prayer. Though praying for what, or to whom, Silyen couldn't imagine.

"Here's a question for you, Chancellor: what is Skill?"

He knew that Zelston had been a lawyer. This was before his elder sister's early death elevated him from spare to heir, at which point an unsuspected political ambition revealed itself. Lawyers liked questions—and even more, they liked supplying smart answers.

Zelston looked up warily from between his fingers and obliged. He used the taxonomy devised by scholars centuries ago. "It's an ability, origin unknown, manifesting in a very small fraction of the population and passed down through our bloodlines. Some talents are universal, such as restoration— that is, healing. Others, such as alteration, persuasion, perception, and infliction, manifest in differing degrees from person to person."

"Magic, you could say?" Silyen offered.

He watched the Chancellor wince. It was an unfashionable word, but Silyen thought it a good one. How dry and ill-defined those traditional categories were. Skill was not a parceling up of small talents. It was a radiance that lit the veins of every Equal.

But he needed to speak to the Chancellor in a language the man understood: that of politics.

"Perhaps you could say that Skill is what separates us"—he pointed to himself and Zelston—"from them." He indicated the window, beyond which two garden-slaves were grumbling about apple weevils. "But tell me this: when was the last time you used your Skill, beyond healing a paper cut when opening a letter, or exercising a little persuasion in political matters? When did you last use your Skill to actually do anything?"

"We have slaves to do things," Zelston said dismissively. "The whole purpose of the slavedays is to free us to govern. And you want to dismantle this system?"

"But many countries are governed by commoners: France, where the people rose up against the Skilled aristocracy and slaughtered them in the streets of Paris. Or China, where our kind retired to mountain monasteries long ago. Or the Union

States of America, which deems us enemy aliens and bars us from their 'Land of the Free,' though their cousins in the Confederate States live as we do. Government is not what defines us, Chancellor. Nor is power. Nor wealth. Skill is what defines us. The slavedays have made us forget that."

Zelston stared at him, then rubbed his eyes. He showed all the signs of a man about to give in. Despite his fine words about the country's peace, he was going to toss it all away for a chance to regain the lost love of his youth. It was almost admirable, if one were inclined to admire such things. Silyen was not.

"And you think this Proposal will somehow remind us?"

"I think it will help," Silyen said.

Which was true, as far as it went.

Zelston let his hooded gaze drop to Aunt Euterpe's face, then reached out and stroked her hair.

"Very well. I will lay this Proposal before parliament. We will debate it at Esterby Castle, and then at Grendelsham. And when the Third Debate comes to Kyneston in the spring, you will keep your side of the bargain. Euterpe will be restored to me before I call the vote. Which will go against you. Now get out of my sight."

Silyen dropped a shallow bow and couldn't resist a taunting knock of boot heels as he came to attention. He turned before he left the room:

"Oh, milord Chancellor? You couldn't have laid a finger on me just now if I had not permitted it."

He shut the door behind him.

Silyen went into the adjacent music room. Only the piano would suffice right now—would be big enough and loud enough to drown out just a little of the endless roar of his Skill inside him.

He folded back the instrument lid. As he poised his fingers over the keyboard, he heard, in the next room, Chancellor Winterbourne Zelston begin to cry.

# THREE

# ABI

They had sat numbly in the car, speaking only to rage, sob, or—in Abi's case—to offer plan after plan of how she was going to get Luke's assignment to Millmoor overturned. Dad was quiet, and Mum made the driver pull over while she checked him for concussion. Her reassuring verdict calmed Daisy down, and allowed Abi to focus on her brother. For the remainder of the journey, Luke was the sole thought in her head.

Until they reached the wall.

"That's Kyneston on the left now," said the Labor Allocation Bureau woman at the wheel. She had been silent the entire journey, after making it plain that it was above her pay grade to comment on the morning's disaster.

"It's the oldest and the longest wall in the country: eight

million bricks. Most of the Equals didn't bother enclosing everything, just the house and immediate grounds. But not the Parva-Jardines. They did the woods, the whole lot. You see it?"

Despite herself, Abi's attention shifted. She buzzed down the car window, as if that would somehow bring her closer to the ribbon of brick that wound around the lush green fields, wrapping up England's landscape like a present—to be opened by the Equals only.

"It's not very high," she said in surprise. "I always thought the walls would be much taller than that. It doesn't look like it could keep deer in, let alone slaves."

The woman gave a short, barking laugh, as if she'd told a good joke. "It keeps them in all right. But it's not the bricks that take care of that. Not even the Equals themselves can get into or out of that place, except when the Young Master lets them."

"The Young Master?"

That must be the youngest Jardine son: Silyen.

Abi knew that Skill was woven into most of the estate walls—a legacy of Black Billy's Revolt of 1802. That had begun when a blacksmith led an army of laborers against their lords at Ide, and ended with the smith being tortured to death using monstrous implements he had first been Skillfully compelled to forge. Immediately after, the Equals had begun raising walls around their estates. It was said that some of the most powerful families additionally had gatekeepers, to maintain the centuries-old layers of defensive Skill. And the Jardines were the most powerful of all—the Founding Family.

Were the gatekeeper stories true? And if they were, Silyen

Jardine—just seventeen years old—was surely an odd choice for such a responsibility. A bit like entrusting Luke with the sole key to the house, Abi thought, only to feel the sharp stab of her brother's absence once more.

Meanwhile, the LAB woman, mortifyingly, had misinterpreted Abi's curiosity. "Don't you be getting interested in the Young Master, my girl. From what I hear, the boy's a strange one, even among them lot. Never seen in a car; goes everywhere on horseback."

Abi flushed. She caught the woman's eye in the rearview mirror and saw something unexpected there: concern.

"No, don't you get interested in any of them. That's the only safe way for folks like us. You see nothing, you hear nothing, and you do your job. People see these estates as a soft option, but I've heard stories that'd freeze your blood. When my time comes, Millmoor will be good enough for me, among my own kind."

Abi sat back in her seat, cross and embarrassed. Who in their right mind would prefer a slavetown to this lush, open countryside? The air on her face through the open car window was fresh and sweet. No, she'd made the right choice in getting her family to Kyneston, she was sure of it. And she'd ensure Luke made it here, too.

The car's wheels crunched over stones as it pulled onto the side of the road. There was nothing special about the spot, just more road and wall, same as there had been for the past ten minutes. Kyneston Estate must be huge.

"Here we are," the LAB woman said. "Out you hop, and good luck. We're half an hour early, but I could use the head start to get back up north. I'm sure that after all the effort you made to get here, you wouldn't be thinking of disappearing."

"But there's nothing here," said Abi. "What are we supposed to do, just wait? Will someone come and get us?"

"I don't know any more than you do, love. My instructions were to get the four of you here for 4 P.M. This is the spot. The GPS says so."

"Well, the GPS must be wrong."

But the woman was having none of it. She was back to being a functionary, just following orders. There was no point arguing, so Abi opened her door, helped Daisy out, then went to the car's trunk and started hauling out their bags.

"Have a quick ten years," the driver said.

Then she closed the vehicle windows so quickly you'd think the air was poisoned. Gravel flew from beneath the tires as the car turned and sped off.

Mum slumped down on the small heap of their possessions, the fight temporarily gone out of her. Dad stood beside her, staring into the distance, still smarting with humiliation and impotence at his failure to rescue his son. At least Abi hoped that was it, rather than delayed concussion. Either way, they had both better snap out of it soon, or the Jardines would take one look and send the lot of them to Millmoor to join Luke.

Daisy settled into the clipped grass verge, making a chain of her namesake flower. Abi told her not to wander into the road, and got a do-you-think-I'm-stupid look for her pains. Checking her watch, she decided there'd be time for a brief exploration. Ten minutes to jog in the direction they'd been traveling, with the same time to get back, still gave her ten minutes' grace before 4 P.M.

It proved an unrewarding exercise. The wall continued, low and featureless, exactly like the section they'd driven along.

When it was time to turn, she paused to inspect the brickwork and was startled to discover that it gave off a faint radiance. It was barely perceptible in sunlight, but at night the wall would glow.

Abi worked up the courage to touch it. Her hand recoiled of its own accord—she'd been expecting something like an electric shock, she realized, but nothing had happened. Bolder, she brushed her fingers against the old mottled brickwork. But the wall appeared to be perfectly normal, apart from the dim luminescence. Was that Skill? Abi wondered if she could climb over, but this probably wasn't the best moment to attempt it.

She made it back to her family with time to spare, relieved to see that her parents were finally making some kind of small talk. The remaining minutes were spent helping Daisy with her flower chain. Abi looped it round her sister's neck. Let their new masters see she was only a little kid and should be treated as such.

"Horses!" said Daisy, hearing the muffled clop of shod hooves and eagerly looking up and down the road.

"Not here," said Abi. "They're on grass, on the other side of the wall. It must be someone coming."

Was it the Young Master, who went everywhere on horseback?

She climbed to her feet and the four of them stood together, facing the wall.

Which is stupid, thought Abi, because there's nothing there apart from solid bricks. Unless they're going to blast a hole in it—or fly over.

But she couldn't make herself smile at the ludicrous image, because the truth was she had no idea what the Equals could do. Nobody did. You just saw them on the TV or the internet, or in celebrity magazines. They looked like everyone else, to be honest. Groomed and gorgeous, of course, but all that took was money, not Skill.

Information on the Equals' true abilities didn't exist. Apart from the famous stories of the Equal Revolution—Lycus the Regicide's unnatural killing of King Charles, and Cadmus Parva-Jardine's Great Demonstration when he built the House of Light—history textbooks banged on about affairs of state, not Skill. In her favorite novels, hot male Equals blew up Ferraris and mind-controlled bad guys, but Abi was hardly going to put much store by their accuracy.

The best clues were news reports from the handful of countries that, like Great Britain, were ruled by the Skilled. Such as Japan, where the entire country's cherry trees burst into blossom in a single instant every spring, in a public display of the Imperial Family's power. In the Philippines, Skilled priests regularly repelled dangerous weather systems that threatened their islands. What were Britain's Equals capable of? Abi wasn't sure.

But she was about to find out. A mixture of excitement and apprehension closed up her throat. This was what she'd postponed her future to discover. Could it possibly be worth it?

Then it happened almost too fast for astonishment. Daisy squealed.

Directly in front of the Hadleys a gate appeared. The ornamental ironwork was a gilded riot of cleverly wrought birds and flowers. It reared up to twice the height of the wall and gleamed with a strange, intense light. Through its elegant, open tracery, two male figures on horseback were now visible.

With a start, Abi realized that they were both close to her

own age. One wore a navy-blue cable-knit sweater and sat upright on a beautiful chestnut horse. His hair was the same rich
russet—the famous Jardine coloring—and his face was open
and handsome. The other horse was an unremarkable all-black
animal. Its rider sported muddy black jeans and creased tan riding boots. His jacket lapel was ripped and flapped loose. Surely
the redhead was the Young Master, and the other a favored
slave, perhaps a groom.

But the black horse's rider was the first to urge his mount
toward them. He flicked his fingers carelessly and the massive
gates began to swing open. The two horsemen passed beneath
the entwined initials that surmounted the arch: the Parva-
Jardine family monogram. It seemed to Abi that the top of the
*P* tenderly kissed the *J,* and the curve of the *J* embraced the *P.*

The scruffy young rider swung a leg over his saddle and
dropped lightly to the ground. He handed up the reins to his
companion and walked to where the Hadleys stood. Abi felt
the power crackle off him like static, lifting the hairs along her
arms and neck, and knew instantly that she'd got it all wrong.

This boy, not the other, was the Young Master.

He didn't look like much. Around the same age as Luke, he
was taller than her brother, but skinnier. Badly in need of a
haircut. But dread squeezed Abi's insides as he approached.

He stopped in front of her father. Dad opened and closed his
mouth in silence, clearly unnerved.

The boy reached out a hand and touched Dad's shoulder. It
looked like the gentlest of gestures, but Steve Hadley crumpled
slightly as if he'd been winded, and a soft groan escaped his
mouth. The Young Master's expression was almost bored, but

beneath the mess of hair Abi saw his eyes narrow in concentration. What was he doing?

Daisy stood next in their makeshift line. Abi felt proud of her little sister's fearlessness as the boy brought his hand down even more lightly, and Daisy blinked and swayed like a flower in the breeze. Mum, when touched, merely ducked her head and winced.

Then Silyen Jardine stood before Abi, and she swallowed as he reached out . . .

. . . and it was like the giddy pull of standing in a high place and looking down; like the queasy surge of terror after shoplifting just that once for a dare. It was the millisecond after downing an unwise triple shot of Sambuca on her eighteenth birthday; the stunned joy of opening her exam results in the kitchen that day, before she remembered she'd be doing her days, not going to university. Her heart raced madly—then stopped, for just an instant.

She was suddenly cold to her core, and felt naked in a way that had nothing to do with clothes. It was as though something had carefully turned her inside out and inspected everything she contained. Then, finding nothing of use or interest, had put her back exactly the way she had been—to outward appearances, at any rate.

When the boy's hand lifted from her shoulder, Abi shuddered and thought she might be sick.

The Young Master was already back in the saddle, exchanging brief words with the second horseman before kicking into a canter away through the gate. Abi wasn't sorry to see him go. The labor bureau woman's words came back to her, about her preference for her "own kind." Neither Abi nor her family were among their own kind anymore.

The second rider came toward them, leading his glossy chestnut horse.

"You must be the Hadleys," he said with a smile. "I'm Jenner Jardine. You're very welcome to my family's estate."

"Are you nicer than that other one?" asked Daisy.

Abi wanted the ground to swallow her up, even as her mother's face blanched. But astonishingly, the young man before them simply laughed.

"I try to be," he said. "And I'm sorry for what you just experienced. It's unpleasant, but necessary. I do ask Silyen to at least warn people, but he never does. He says he finds their reactions interesting."

"It was horrid," said Daisy. "Why don't you do it, then maybe it wouldn't be so bad?"

Abi wanted to put her hands over her sister's mouth before anything even more ill-advised came out.

"I can't," was the unexpected response. "I mean, none of us could do it quite like Silyen, but I can't do it at all. I possess as much Skill as you do, Daisy Hadley. I presume you are Daisy," he added gallantly, "unless you are Abigail, and a little on the small side for your age, while this tall young Daisy here . . ."

Jenner Jardine turned to Abi, while Daisy spluttered and giggled and assured him that no, no, he had them the right way round.

Abi had been going to apologize to the Kyneston scion for Daisy's big mouth. And she had intended to ask him what he meant about having no Skill, because they all had Skill, all the Equals.

But her words died behind her lips when she looked at Jenner Jardine. Not from a distance on his horse, or with one eye on her indiscreet little sis, but properly at him.

He had warm brown eyes and coppery hair. His face was dusted all over with freckles, and though his mouth was wider than usual in a man, it was balanced by strong cheekbones. Abi took in all these details, yet none of them really registered. She felt giddy again. Felt naked again.

But none of it was due to Skill. And it didn't leave her cold. No, not cold at all.

Jenner was looking at her oddly, and Abigail realized she had been staring. Her cheeks scorched.

A wash of shame, heavy and humiliating, broke over her. She stood before this man not as the bright, quick, passably attractive girl she knew herself to be, but as a slave. That seemed to Abi, in that moment, the worst and cruelest thing the slavedays could possibly do. It could take away everything that made you who you were. Then place you in front of someone whom, under wholly different circumstances, you might let yourself love and who might even have loved you back.

Jenner's words were kind, but she shouldn't delude herself. He was an Equal. And despite his inexplicable claim to be Skilless, he was a Jardine. He would never see Abi for who she truly was. It was as that Millmoor brute had said: to the Equals they were all simply chattels, things to be used—or rejected as useless.

Her humiliation burned away in a flare of anger and guilt about her little brother. It was Abi's carefully crafted plan that had exposed Luke to the pitiless judgment of the Jardines. His banishment to Millmoor was all her fault. She shook her head, dizzied by the force of this realization.

"Are you all right?"

There was a firm hand grasping her elbow. Jenner. Then an arm around her shoulder. Her father. The hand let go.

"Skill can affect people sometimes," Jenner said. "If you've never been exposed to it, you need to acclimatize. It's strongest with Silyen around, but you might feel it again when my father and older brother return from London. Let's get you all to your cottage. I've put you over in the Row; you'll like it."

Jenner led the way. He didn't get back on his horse, but walked alongside them. Dad hefted his and Abi's bags onto his shoulders, while Mum swung hers and Daisy's, one in each hand. Daisy scampered back and forth, admiring the horse and peppering Jenner with questions about it. Abi walked by herself, off to one side, trying to make sense of everything that was roiling through her.

"Oh!" Daisy's exclamation was so loud that the small group stopped, alarmed. "Look," she said, pointing back the way they had come. "It's gone. Is it invisible?"

Where the shining gate had been was a single, unbroken expanse of wall. The Hadleys stared.

"You were right with 'gone,' " Jenner said, coaxing his horse to a stop. "The gate only exists when one of my family calls it into being, and it can be summoned anywhere along the wall. That's why there's no driveway and no roads inside the estate. It's also why my father keeps busting the suspension on the classic cars he loves so much, and why Sil and I prefer to get around on horseback. Gavar takes his motorbike. The gate can only be opened by Skill, though. That's why just now . . ."

He trailed off.

"Why are you telling us?" said Abi. "Isn't that sort of stuff, I don't know, a state secret or something?"

Jenner fiddled with his horse's bridle, pausing before replying. "Kyneston isn't always an easy place to be. Sometimes people think about trying to leave." He turned to Abi. "My brother told me that before we arrived, when you were still on the other side, you did a bit of exploring. No, don't worry"—for panic had wrapped its fingers tightly round Abi's throat and squeezed—"you didn't do anything wrong. But just . . . try not to be too interested in things. It's easier that way."

He sounded subdued, and Abi suspected he wasn't talking generally, but recalling something specific and distressing. Was it ridiculous of her to want to comfort him?

It was ridiculous.

"Try not to be too interested?" she said, a touch sharply. "Isn't your family motto '*Sapere aude*,' 'Dare to know'?"

"Trust me," Jenner said, those brown eyes on hers. "There are some things it's better not to know."

He turned away, and they all walked on in silence. It was around a quarter of an hour later—Abi could see from Daisy's face that she was about to do the "Are we there yet?" thing—when the ground sloped upward to a small rise. And as they crested the top, what she saw stole her breath.

Kyneston.

She'd seen pictures of it, of course: in books, on the TV, and online. Seat of the Founding Family. Once the home of Cadmus Parva-Jardine, Cadmus the Pure-in-Heart, peacemaker and chief architect of the Slavedays Compact.

The pre-Revolutionary part of Kyneston was built of pale, honeyed stone. Three stories high with soaring windows, it was topped with a small dome and edged with a parapet crowded with statuary.

But the rest of it shone almost too brightly to bear. From the main body of the house, two great glass wings stretched out, each as wide again as the original frontage. These had been Skill-forged by Cadmus, just as he had raised the House of Light, seat of the Equals' parliament. In the low afternoon sunshine, the two wings were like greenhouses filled with exotic blooms of fire and light. Abi first shaded her eyes, then had to look away entirely.

"It's beautiful," said Daisy. "And very shiny. Do you live there?"

"Yes," said Jenner Jardine. "It is, and I do."

He was smiling, genuinely pleased at Daisy's pleasure. He loves this place, Abi realized. Although if what he had said about the gate and his lack of Skill was true, he was as much a prisoner here as they were.

"Look," said the young Equal, directing Daisy's gaze to a petite female figure appearing from behind a topiary hedge. "There's my mother, Lady Thalia. She and I look after the house and grounds. She does everything Skillful, and I take care of the rest."

"And who's that?" asked Daisy as a second person appeared.

Then she gasped, a hurt, shocked little sound that made Abi fleetingly wonder if Jenner had pinched her.

Abi glanced at where Daisy was looking, at the second figure now emerging from the hedge line. It was another woman, her hair a steely coif, her shoulders mantled in what looked like dozens of fox furs. A leash was wrapped around one gloved hand.

And at the end of that leash, crouched on all fours and naked, was a man.

# FOUR

# LUKE

Through the scratched and grimy van window, Luke saw Mill-moor squatting under a cloud of its own making. He slid back the tiny pane for a better look, but it didn't make much differ-ence. The muck wasn't on the glass. It was in the air itself. The light was pallid and unclean.

They were a twenty-minute drive from home, but even back in Manchester you could taste Millmoor when the wind blew in the wrong direction. Sometimes it was an acrid chemical stink from the industrial zone. Other days, the whiff was foul and rotting, from the meat-processing plant. If you were really unlucky and the breeze was strong, it was a gut-churning cock-tail of both. On those days, Mum would keep all the windows shut.

There'd be no shutting out Millmoor now. The road dipped and rose, and there was the slavetown again, twice as large, filling the horizon. Chimneys lanced the sky, poking cruelly at a sagging belly of smog. A distant flare stack hemorrhaged flame.

The van was waved through an outer sentry ring, then stopped at a second checkpoint, where they all got out. A blank-eyed young soldier with a gun strapped conspicuously across his chest asked Luke his name.

"Luke Hadley," he replied, but the final syllable came out as a gasp as Kessler's baton drove into his midriff.

"You are Hadley E-1031," the man barked. "Now tell him your name."

"Hadley E-1031," Luke repeated, stunned by more than just the pain of the blow.

From the checkpoint they filed across the parking lot of a vehicle depot. On the other side was a low, wide building faced with grubby white plastic—a medical center.

"I'm really not looking forward to this," said one of the blokes who'd arrived with Luke, an overweight guy, pale and stubbly. "It's gotta be the worst thing."

"What is it?" Luke asked.

"Didn't you read the booklet?" the man said. "Blimey, don't you know nothing about this place, kiddo?"

"I'm not supposed to be here," Luke muttered, realizing not quite in time that this wasn't the best thing to say.

"That's right," said Kessler, who was there again, his baton prodding Luke forward. "Hadley E-1031 here thinks he's too good for the likes of you. He thinks he should be down south, mixing with his Equals. He thinks there's *been a mistake*."

He mimicked Luke's words, making them sound prissy and girlish, and the pasty guy laughed, all sympathy gone.

The "worst thing" was pretty sick-making, but Luke already

had a hunch that Millmoor would throw a few things his way to rival it. A nurse rolled up his sleeve, prodded the skin of his forearm, then picked up what looked like a staple gun. Except it didn't shoot out just one needle, but stabbed a dozen of them deep into Luke's flesh. When the device lifted away, there was a neat matrix of welling blood. Kessler wasn't around, so Luke risked a question.

"It's your ID chip, pet," the nurse replied. "Sits nice and deep in the meat. So they know where you are."

She bandaged a square of gauze over his arm, then scanned it with a small rectangular wand. Luke couldn't see the readout panel, but he heard it beep and saw a green flash.

"That's you done. Here, have one of these." The woman pulled a small jar of sweets from a drawer in her nursing station. "I usually keep them for the little kids, but I reckon you deserve one. Only sixteen, and here without your family. I didn't think that was allowed."

Luke took one, thinking of his little sister as he did so. Daisy's skinny arm would barely be big enough for the chip gun. He would have watched over her night and day in this place. He knew Abi would do the same in Kyneston.

From the med center, Kessler herded them on foot through Millmoor's streets. There were no vehicles other than trundling buses and gleaming jeeps blazoned with the slavetown's insignia and "Security" written in vivid crimson. Uniformed men stood on street corners, palms fondling the handles of their batons and the butts of their stun guns. Everyone else wore shapeless tunics and jumpsuits and walked with their heads down. It was difficult to discern either age or gender.

Even when Luke succeeded in catching someone's glance, they turned away quickly. He couldn't believe this place. Mancunians were a feisty bunch—how was it possible they could be this cowed? However long he spent in Millmoor, Luke swore, he was never going to stop looking people in the eye.

His new home was a six-bed dormitory in a looming prefab block. A row of coveralls hung on pegs like shriveled skins, as if Millmoor had sucked the substance out of the bodies that wore them. In one of the beds a figure tossed and turned, a blanket pulled over his head to block out the light. He was presumably a night-shift worker, because Luke doubted they took kindly to sickies in Millmoor. The air smelled stale and sharp. Too much sweat, not enough soap, as Mum would say.

He dumped his duffel on the bed with a bare mattress, and tore open the envelope on the locker beside it. It was his assignment. The components shed in the Machine Park's Zone D. Shifts: Monday to Saturday, 8 A.M. to 6 P.M. Start date: September 3. Tomorrow. He stared at the paper in disbelief.

This afternoon was all the freedom he had left until Sunday came round, another six days away. Where was the Machine Park? How did he get there? Where could he get something to eat? He thought longingly of the sandwiches Mum had made, carefully preparing everyone's favorites. The girls would be scoffing theirs right now, halfway to Kyneston. He devoutly hoped that whatever was waiting for them at the end of their journey was better than what he'd found here.

A caretaker sat in a dark cubbyhole by the dorm-block entrance—an old guy who must have come in at fifty-five as a last ditcher, delaying his days to the final moment. He obligingly sketched a rudimentary map. Armed with that, and a few vague memories from films they'd been shown in Citizenship classes, Luke headed out. He could feel each alveolus in his lungs contract in protest as he stepped into the smog-choked street.

Millmoor was the country's oldest slavetown, as old as industry itself. No sooner had some genius developed manufacturing machinery than the Equals had put people to backbreaking work slaving on it. Up until then, the slavedays had resembled feudalism, everyone doing days under their local lord as farm laborers, craftspeople, or house-slaves. Illustrations in school textbooks contrived to make it appear almost cozy—grateful peasants in candlelit cottages, clustered outside the Skill-glowing wall of a great estate. But for three hundred years, the reality had been Millmoor and the slavetowns that sprang up in its likeness, shadowing each of Britain's cities.

Luke checked the map. The old geezer had drawn something resembling a dart board, circular and quartered. The heart of Millmoor was its administration hub; ringing that were the residential blocks. Beyond them, the industrial zones: the Machine Park, the Comms Zone (hangar after hangar of call centers, which they'd walked past on the way in), the meatpacking district, and the old quarter—those earliest mills and loom sheds. The caretaker had crosshatched that, explaining that it was derelict.

Luke's dorm block was in West, while the Park (Luke doubted it had a duck pond and "Keep off the grass" signs) was over East, so he set off in what he hoped was the right direction. But the streets became a warren, branching again, and he was soon hopelessly lost.

He'd turned in to a dead-end maze of courtyards round the back of several run-down accommodation blocks. A rusty plaque on the wall said "East 1-11-11," which was precisely less than no help at all. Then he spotted two guys chatting at the far end of the courtyard, by an arched array of heating ducts and ventilation shafts. Maintenance men. They'd tell him the way out.

But something stopped him calling to them. They weren't talking to each other. They were speaking to a third person, hidden behind the wall of their backs, who must be caught between them, the ducts, and the moldering building. Luke crept closer.

". . . know you've got some," the larger of the two men was saying. "I've seen you bringing it round. The old cow quits her moaning for a while after you stop by, which is great, but a few vials of morphine for our personal use would be even better. So hand it over."

Had he stumbled on some kind of black-market deal? Luke was about to creep away when the other guy shifted, and he glimpsed the person they were talking to. It was a girl—and from the birdlike look of her, she was barely older than Daisy.

His feet glued themselves to the ground. He wouldn't be going anywhere until he'd got the kid away from these creeps twice her size.

"I've not got nothing I'm giving you," the girl said fiercely. "Other than this."

And as Luke's brain was still working through a plan, she darted at one of the men and he cried out.

"Bitch has got a knife," he yelled, as the other guy swung a massive fist at the girl—and connected with empty air.

Luke saw her. She'd dropped to the ground and was squirming on her stomach into the tiny space beneath a duct, intending to slip out the other side. The man she'd injured crouched down and thrust fingers into the gap, hunting for a piece of her to grab. The other had worked out that the only way he'd reach her was by doubling back and round, so he turned and charged—right toward Luke.

Obeying instinct, Luke crouched, then snatched blindly as the bloke ran past. The handful of rough fabric was pulled instantly from his grasp as the guy went down, and Luke toppled backward.

Small fingers dug into his armpits, hauling him up.

"C'mon."

The girl took off, frizzy hair flying, as the guy she'd cut looked up and snarled, blood dripping from his hand. Luke didn't stop to think.

He'd never been more grateful for all those weekend soccer training sessions he'd spent shivering in his shorts in the rain, because the kid was fast. She fled down alleys and ginnels, slipping between buildings, leaping over broken bricks and gutted rubbish sacks that bled sloppy detritus across the pavement.

"Upsie," yelled the girl as they hurtled down what looked like a dead end. She threw herself at the wall at the far end, her fingers finding handholds too small for Luke to see. He resorted to a running jump, nearly smacked his face against the brick, felt his toes scrabble, and reached desperately for the top, hauling himself over.

The girl was waiting on the other side, hands on her hips, narrow chest barely rising and falling despite the exertion.

"Easy, tiger," she said. "We lost 'em about seven streets ago."

"Who the hell were they?" Luke asked, panting, with his shoulders slumped. "What did they want from you? Well, I heard that bit. Morphine. But you're how old—eleven? Twelve? What are you doing with morphine?"

The girl snorted derisively. "Thirteen, actually. And it's none of your business. Though there's a woman in that block who's gonna have a rough few days now until I can get the Doc to her."

"The Doc?"

"I woulda got out of there just fine, but thanks for trying. It's not everyone would risk making an enemy of those two, so you're either very brave or very stupid. Which is it?"

Her muddy brown eyes assessed him. "Ach, it's neither. You're just very new." She let out a throaty cackle, sounding older than her years. "Welcome to Millmoor. What's your name?"

"Hadley E-1031. And I arrived today. How did you know that?"

"Got the Skill, ain't I?" the girl said, pointing two fingers at her forehead and waggling them mysteriously. "Nah, nah, I'm joking. Your bandage. You just been chipped. And none of those numbers—what's your name, really?"

"Luke." He held out a hand in his best nice-to-meet-you fashion. Mum would be so proud.

"Renie," the girl said, with an amused look at his outstretched hand. Luke withdrew it. Millmoor probably wasn't big on manners. "Rhymes with 'genie.' Grants wishes and that. Well, you look after yourself, Luke Hadley. Have a quick ten years."

"Wait. Wait!" he called out as she turned. "I was trying to

get somewhere: Machine Park Zone D, the components shed. It's my workplace. Do you know where it is?"

"Zone D? You poor bastard." Renie's pinched features softened momentarily. "Yeah, that's it. Kinda hard to miss."

She pointed away over the accommodation-block roofs to an immense scaffold-framed building. It seemed to house nothing but fire that clawed at every window to get out. All around, like stakes penning a monster, tall chimneys vented dense black smoke. It was, Luke realized with horror, the source of the roar and clangor that was audible even here, several streets away.

"Good luck. You'll need it in there."

Renie-Rhymes-with-Genie tipped her chin in a small salute and trotted off. The gloom that pooled at street level in Millmoor swallowed her up.

It turned out that a bus ran from the West dorms over to the Machine Park, so the following morning, dressed in the jumpsuit and boots he'd found by his bed, Luke was at the gate to Zone D in good time.

Abi had once shown him an illustration of the Kyneston gate—just a sketch, as there were no photographs. It was a twirly wrought-iron monstrosity. His family would be on the other side of it now. Luke had lain awake for hours thinking about them, hoping his parents weren't eating themselves up with guilt and worry. Hoping Abi was working on a plan to get him back. Hoping that whatever use the Jardines had for Daisy was something decent and not degrading. (They couldn't make little kids sweep chimneys nowadays, could they?)

Zone D's gate was different: a steel arch inset with a scanning strip that registered the chips of each slave passing through. He took a deep breath and stepped forward. As his ID tag flashed along the gate's display, a strong-built man with a weak-jawed face introduced himself as Williams L-4770, Luke's co-worker.

"What's your real name?" Luke asked.

Williams bared his protruding teeth in what looked like fear and said nothing. He led Luke deep into the industrial zone. They passed through one cavernous brick building after another, crossed massive loading bays, and skirted the fiery heart of the foundry. The noise grew worse the deeper they went, as if everything that was loudest in the world had been gathered together under one roof. From the building ahead came a din that was as much sensation as sound, the earth-shaking stamping of a violent giant.

"Components shed," Williams L-4770 mouthed.

And wasn't it the final humiliation, Luke thought, that cleaning Kyneston's toilets suddenly seemed like the cushiest life imaginable?

Their workstation was a complex array of hoists suspended from a gantry that transferred newly cast components from the heavy press (the source of the thumping) into and then out of the preliminary finishing machine. Williams's briefing was thorough and entirely mimed. His enactment of the fate of his previous partner—spine crushed when a slipped chain block swung a turbine into him like a giant wrecking ball—struck Luke as excessively realistic. Their jumpsuits and chafing work boots offered no protection at all.

It wasn't only the noise that made them communicate silently. The work was so arduous that every breath Luke took was used up powering his muscles. When the call came from

Kyneston, he'd walk out of Millmoor with the physique of a superhero from those banned Union American movies. Assuming he didn't fall foul of the machinery, in which case he wouldn't be walking at all.

There were two breaks: a hasty lunch in a canteen that served up the unappetizing with a side order of the inedible, and a ten-minute tools-down in the afternoon. At shift's end on that first day, every limb trembling with exhaustion, Luke crept out of the components shed and toward the bus stop. Back at the dorm, desperate equally for food and sleep, he limped up the stairs to the skanky communal kitchen. He'd need to eat to give him strength to get through the next day.

"Luke?"

He turned from the cupboard he was searching for a tin of something that he might know how to cook—or even open— and saw a face he dimly recognized.

"O'Connor B-780," the guy said, just as Luke's failure to remember his name was getting embarrassing. "I mean, Ryan. I was a few years above you at Henshall Academy. Started my days straight after."

"Sorry," Luke mumbled. "Of course I remember you. I only arrived yesterday. Still adjusting."

"No worries," said Ryan. "No wonder you're all over the place. Here, I'll fix us both something."

Luke would have eaten his own socks by that point, so he fell on the beans on toast that Ryan put in front of him. He was happy to let Ryan talk—though it turned out there wasn't much to say about two years of days. His former schoolmate was considering converting to the military route: three years of labor followed by seven years of conscripted service as a "mauler," then a minimum of ten years enlisted. As a mauler you were still a slave and didn't get pay or benefits, but you did get a head start in your career in the forces.

"Only downside," said Ryan, around a forkful of beans, "is that the maulers get all the most dangerous assignments. No compensation payable if you get injured or killed, you see."

As downsides went, Luke thought that wasn't insignificant. He didn't mention Kyneston, remembering Kessler's taunting and the reaction of the men he'd arrived with. But he had to offer small talk about something, so he told Ryan about the girl he'd met, the one delivering medicine. Ryan frowned.

"Morphine? That doesn't sound right. There's no way a kid that age would have access to it. She must have stolen it, been trading it. You should report her."

"Report her?"

"Safest thing," said Ryan. "Security here is fierce. Infringements are slapped on you for the smallest thing, and bigger violations add years onto your days. For serious offenses, there's slavelife. Apparently lifer camps make this place look like a palatial estate. But it goes both ways. If you flag up something dodgy, it buys you favor with Security."

Luke thought that through. He was pretty sure the girl hadn't been selling the drug. It had sounded more like she was delivering it to someone who really needed it. And while Ryan's account of how Millmoor worked made a fair amount of sense, it also sounded a lot like snitching at school.

"So where did you see her?" Ryan asked.

In his memory, Luke clearly saw the rusted sign screwed to the wall, the word "East" and the row of five 1s.

"No idea, I'm afraid," he said. "It was my first day. Barely know where I am right now, though I do know that my bed is a couple of floors up. Thanks for the feast, but I'm going to turn in. See you around."

He pushed back his chair and left. And despite the million and one thoughts churning in his head, Luke was asleep the minute his head hit the thin, lumpy pillow.

On Wednesday he got up and did it all over again. And Thursday. And Friday. On Saturday, he ate his congealed horror of a lunch in record time and was using the remainder of his break to poke around a corner of Zone D he hadn't seen before (dirty and noisy, like every other corner he'd investigated so far) when a voice spoke from the shadows.

"How's it goin', Luke Hadley?"

As far as Luke was aware, only four people in Millmoor knew his name, and only one of them was a girl.

"How did you get in here?" he asked Renie, who was wedged into the corner behind a toolshed. "More important, why did you get in?"

"Shopping trip," said Renie. "And social call. Came to see how you was getting on. Well, you still got all your limbs, so you're doing awright."

She tipped her head back and gave that inappropriately husky laugh. It sounded like she smoked fifty a day. Or like she'd lived her whole life in Millmoor, breathing the tar that passed for air here.

"Shopping? What, for a new turbine?"

"Nothin' so fancy." Renie grinned, and pulled her tunic up a few inches to reveal what must have been yards of cabling wrapped round her middle. It was red-and-white striped—the fine, super-high-strength variety. (It was amazing how fast you learned about cables in a week of trusting your life to them.)

So she did steal stuff. Was Ryan right about her?

"But that's not the main thing. I'm here to ask your help. Reckon you owe me for getting you out of that tricky spot in East-1."

Luke spluttered, but Renie carried right on. "One of your workmates' kids got her glasses smashed last week. Girl's blind as a mole, but she don't need to see properly for her packing job over in Ag-Fac, and things like specs ain't high on the priority list in Millmoor. Anyway—ta-da! Will you be my delivery boy?"

She produced a flat plastic case from her back pocket and held it out. Luke opened it. A pair of glasses. He took out the little cloth they were wrapped in and felt around for any secret compartments that might contain drugs. But it was just a hard plastic shell.

"Suspicious, ain't ya?" Renie said. "That's good. Now, will you take 'em?"

"What's this all about?" Luke asked. "Because you're the world's most unlikely fairy godmother, and I don't believe for a minute you're supposed to have that cabling. I may have only just arrived, but I'm not entirely stupid."

"I don't think you're stupid. I think you're someone who'd do a good turn for another and be glad to. Millmoor changes people, Luke Hadley. But what most folk never realize is that you get to choose how."

Luke hesitated, curling his fingers round the small case. It had assumed a strange and disproportionate weight.

He slid it into the trouser pocket of his jumpsuit. Renie bared her gappy teeth in a grin and Luke couldn't help smiling back.

She reeled off delivery instructions before twirling on one toe and fading back into the shadows.

"Tell 'im compliments of the Doc," her voice rasped. Then she was gone.

# FIVE

# BOUDA

The House of Light—or the New Palace of Westminster, seat of the Parliament of Equals—was four centuries old. Yet it stood as ageless and unblemished as the day it was made.

As their chauffeured Rolls pulled in beneath the Last King's Gate, Bouda Matravers craned past her papa's ample form to admire it. Its crenellated spires were as lofty as a French cathedral, and its gilded roof glittered like a Russian palace. But only those familiar with it noticed these details. Tourists and field-tripping students gawped at the House's walls, each a sheer and seamless expanse of glass.

Inside was the debating chamber that housed eight tiered ranks of twinned seats, four hundred in total. Here the lord or lady of each estate sat, with their heir beside them. Bouda was one of those heirs. But no one on the outside peering in would ever see them.

That was because the House of Light's windows looked onto a different place entirely: a shining world, in which nothing could be clearly distinguished. The more curious fact—witnessed only by the Equal parliamentarians and the dozen commoner parliamentary observers permitted to enter the chamber—was that the view through the windows was exactly the same on the inside. On whichever side of the glass you stood, that eerie, incandescent realm lay on the other.

Cadmus Parva-Jardine had known what he was doing when he Skillfully raised up this building from nothing on that day in 1642, Bouda thought, as she swung her legs out of the car. The Great Demonstration, history called it. Commoners often misunderstood the term, thinking it a mere exhibition of the man's incredible Skill—a show of strength. But Bouda knew it to be far more than that. The House of Light demonstrated the glory, the justice, and the sublime inevitability of Equal rule.

Nothing expressed that rule better than today's special date in the parliamentary calendar. Excitement fluttered within her as she steered her father, Lord Lytchett Matravers, inside the House and through spacious corridors hung with red silk. Papa was unsteady on his feet. Her sister, Dina, had put him on some kind of healthy eating plan again. However, Bouda suspected that the glasses of tomato juice Daddy had drunk at breakfast had actually been Bloody Marys, and strong ones.

But then, it was Proposal Day, so perhaps a little celebration was warranted.

The very first Chancellor's Proposal had been made by Cadmus. It had established Britain as a republic, governed in perpetuity by the Skilled. In the centuries since then, the annual Proposals had ranged from the sensible—such as 1882's suspension of the legal rights of commoners during their slave-days—to the sensational. Chief among the latter was the 1789 "Proposal of Ruin." This had urged Britain's Equals to obliterate the city of Paris and crush the revolution of French commoners against their Skilled masters. That had been narrowly defeated—an unforgivable act of cowardice, in Bouda's opinion.

The first Proposal she heard and voted upon had been Lord Whittam Jardine's last. That was seven years ago, at the end of his decade-long incumbency as Chancellor. He had unsurprisingly proposed removing the one-term restriction upon the office.

Bouda had been just eighteen and newly installed as Appledurham's heir. But her sights were already firmly set on a match with Gavar Jardine, so Bouda had supported the Proposal. Her father did likewise. (Daddy had never been able to refuse her or Dina anything.) The vote went against Whittam. But Bouda had eventually achieved her goal, and was now engaged to Kyneston's heir.

It wasn't Gavar himself that she wanted, though. That fact wasn't lost on Bouda as she caught sight of her fiancé. She and her father passed through the great Skill-bound doors to the debating chamber, and she felt the wards tingle across her skin. Gavar stood straight ahead, beneath the marble statue of his ancestor Cadmus.

He was as handsome as any girl might wish, but his skin was blotchy with anger and his mouth set in a petulant sneer. Beside him was his father. Both men were tall and auburn-haired, their shoulders squared back. But where Gavar's emotions were plain in his face, his father's expression gave away nothing at all.

All Bouda could tell from their watchful posture was that they weren't happy, and that they were waiting for someone.

For her, she realized as Lord Jardine caught her eye.

Cold trickled through her. What was wrong? She was so close now to her prize of marriage into the Founding Family that she didn't know what she'd do if thwarted.

She swiftly sorted through the possibilities. Nothing had happened that she knew of that might jeopardize the alliance. She hadn't woken up one day ugly or Skilless, nor had her father's vast wealth vanished. Indeed, the only stumbling block on their way to the altar had been provided by Gavar, in the form of a bastard child sired on some slavegirl. Bouda's affront at the brat's existence had been surpassed only by the fury of Lord Jardine, but she had contained her emotions. Her future father-in-law had been impressed with Bouda's cool response to the whole distasteful episode.

She nodded an acknowledgment to them, then looked around the chamber. Thankfully, Lord Rix, who was Daddy's best friend and her and DiDi's godfather, was waiting over by the Matravers seats. He could keep Daddy entertained with his usual convoluted anecdotes about racehorses. She waved at Rixy and gave her papa a kiss on the cheek, a whispered "Be with you in a minute," and a gentle shove in the right direction.

Then she hurried to hear what Whittam and Gavar had to tell her.

It was nothing she could ever have expected.

"You can't be serious?" she hissed.

"Silyen informed me of it only last night," said her future father-in-law. While he spoke, Gavar was watching the chamber to see if they were noticed, but only Rix was looking their way, concern plain in his face. "While buttering a bread roll at dinner, as casual as you like. I assure you, it was as much of a surprise to me as it appears to be to you."

"Appears to be?" Bouda didn't care for the insinuation in those words. But she couldn't make sense of what Lord Jardine had just told her.

"Silyen has bargained with the Chancellor, using Euterpe Parva—and he's asked Zelston to Propose *abolition*? We'll be a laughingstock if this gets out. How could you let it happen?"

"*I* let it happen?" Whittam's eyes were flat and assessing. "You are quite certain your sister has nothing to do with this?"

"My sister?"

And there, thought Bouda, was the one aspect of her life she couldn't control: her daft, darling sister, Bodina. Dina was a fashionista, a party girl, and prone to handing wads of Daddy's cash to ridiculous causes such as animal rescue, international poverty relief—and abolition.

It said much for Bodina's naivety that the money she was so happy to spend was derived entirely from slavery. The Matravers fortune was maintained by Daddy's BB brand, named for his daughters. It churned out electrical goods by the million for export to the Far East. It was said that half the homes in China were equipped with BB hair dryers, foot spas, rice cookers, and kettles. BB's use of slave labor—the corporation had factories in several slavetowns—was what kept prices competitive.

It was a source of fond exasperation for Bouda that despite her sister's scruples about slavery, Bodina was perfectly willing to live off its proceeds. With her love of travel and couture, DiDi burned through cash.

"Why on earth would Silyen do something at Dina's behest? They barely know each other."

Whittam's face twisted; he had no answer for that. So this was pure speculation. Relief flooded through Bouda. Her arrangement with the Jardines wouldn't be ending today, over this.

"Your sister is attractive." The lord of Kyneston shrugged. "She has a certain nubile charm that might turn a boy's head."

"If you think that would have any effect on him, my lord, then you plainly don't know your youngest son at all."

At his father's side, Gavar gave a vulgar snort. Bouda and her husband-to-be might have little in common, but one thing they could agree on was their dislike of Silyen.

"No," she pressed, indignation rising at her future father-in-law's blatant attempt to shift the blame for Silyen's outrageous act from his family to hers. "All Bodina thinks about right now is her heartbreak, and the next party to help her get over it. You need to look closer to home for an explanation. It was only a matter of time: Jenner, a Skilless abomination; Gavar, father to a slave-born brat; and now Silyen, an abolitionist. Congratulations, your sons are quite the set."

And she really shouldn't have said that. Coolness and control at all times, Bouda.

An angry flush bloomed above the salamander-printed neckerchief at Lord Whittam's throat, and crept up his face. Gavar's fists had clenched. These Jardine men and their touchpaper tempers.

"I apologize unreservedly," she said, ducking her head and baring her neck submissively. "Forgive me."

She gave it a few moments for her sincerity to sink in, then looked up and met Whittam's eyes. Beside him, Gavar looked fit to throttle her, but to her great relief his father's face was composed.

"You apologize like a true politician, Bouda," he said, after a pause in which Bouda was quite sure she did not breathe at all. "Promptly and prettily. One day, you may find that's not enough, but for now it will suffice. We will discuss this later, once we are sure that my youngest son's words were not some jest in remarkably poor taste. Come, Gavar."

He turned and Gavar trailed after him to Kyneston's twinned seat in the center of the first tier. It was directly opposite the carved majesty of the Chancellor's Chair. The old joke ran that this gave the Jardines the shortest possible distance to walk to their preferred seat in the House.

Lord Whittam intended for Gavar to sit there one day. Bouda knew that her wealth made her an acceptable bride. But in their arrogance, it hadn't occurred to the Jardines to wonder why Bouda herself might seek such a match.

She took a calming breath and made her way to the Appledurham estate seat at the center of the second tier, right behind the Jardines. Its prominent position had been secured through hard work, not heritage. None of Bouda's ancestors had been present the day the House of Light rose shimmering from the ashes of the royal Palace of Westminster.

No, Bouda's family fortunes were of more recent date. A couple of centuries ago Harding Matravers, heir of an impecunious and obscure line, had decided to put his derided Skill for weatherwork to good use. He scandalized the genteel Equal society of the day by taking to the seas as captain of a cargo ship, only to sail back from the Indies an obscenely wealthy man. No one had raised a murmur when he did it again the very next season.

By the third year, half the great families of Britain were in his debt, and soon after, a loan default meant the Matravers seat in the seventh tier had been traded for one far better situated, whose spendthrift lord had offered it as collateral.

Even after all this time, the taint of trade hung about the Matravers name. There was only one thing that would expunge it, Bouda thought.

Her glance darted down over the Jardine father and son, and lit on the angular shape of the Chancellor's Chair. The shallow, high-backed seat was borne upon four carved lions. A shattered stone was lodged beneath it: the old coronation stone of the kings of England. Lycus the Regicide had broken it in two. This had been the throne of the Last King—the sole object spared in Cadmus's incineration of Westminster Palace.

In the centuries since the Great Demonstration, no woman had ever sat there.

Bouda intended to be the first.

Reaching the seat where her father sprawled, fingers locked across his claret velvet waistcoat, Bouda bent and kissed his cheek, prodding him lightly in the stomach. Lord Lytchett tossed back his mane of ivory hair and hauled himself upright to make room for his darling girl. She slipped easily through the narrow space and into the heir's chair on his left.

As Bouda sat, smoothing her dress, a thunderous sound echoed through the high chamber. It was the ceremonial mace, striking the outside of the thick oak doors. The doors opened only for those qualified by blood and Skill: lords, ladies, and their heirs. Not even Silyen, for all his supposed gifts, would be able just to walk in here. But Cadmus had created a provision— one long overdue for reform, Bouda thought—for a dozen commoners to witness parliamentary proceedings.

"Who seeks admittance?" quavered ancient Hengist Occold, the Elder of the House, in a voice that didn't seem loud enough to be heard on the other side.

"The Commons of Great Britain most humbly seeks admit- tance among its Equals," came the formal response, in a clear female voice.

The old man's hands worked in the air with surprising deft- ness, and the doors swung open to admit a group of people.

Outwardly, there was nothing to distinguish the twelve well-dressed newcomers from those who filled the chamber. But these were merely the OPs, the Observers of Parliament. Voteless. UnSkilled. Commoners. Not, Bouda thought, that you'd know it from the way that bitch Dawson, their Speaker, was decked out in the height of Shanghai fashion.

Rebecca Dawson, a dark-haired woman in her fifties, led her group to their allotted place: the back bench along the west side of the chamber. It was opposite the tiers of estate seats and behind the Chancellor's Chair. She held herself perfectly up- right, despite wearing towering Brazilian heels. The Speaker and Bodina could probably spend hours talking about shoes, Bouda thought. Shoes and abolition. Both equally pointless topics.

As the OPs settled themselves the air thrummed again, to trumpets heralding the Chancellor's approach. The sound thrilled Bouda as much now as it had the very first time she'd heard it. The current, unworthy incumbent of that great office swept into the chamber, and with a final gesture from the Elder of the House, the doors closed.

Bathed in coruscating light that streamed through the south-end window from the shimmering world beyond, the black-and-white figure of Winterbourne Zelston ascended the steps to the chair. He unclasped his heavy ermine and velvet robe and swept it into the waiting hands of the Child of the House, the youngest heir present.

The Chancellor sat. Parliament was in session.

Before the Proposal came the regular business. Usually Bouda took a keen interest in the routine affairs of state, but today she was distracted by thoughts of the coming announcement.

Down on the chamber floor Dawson was up on her hind legs, yapping away. She was objecting to a perfectly logical scheme to assist the long-term unemployed by returning them to slavery for twelve months' respite. So Bouda tuned her out and gave the matter further thought. Could Silyen really do as he had promised, and revive Euterpe Parva? Could Zelston still love the woman so much that he would risk his position with such an insane Proposal?

And this was hardest of all to understand: why, given that the Proposal would surely fail, would Silyen ask for it?

She turned over what she knew of the boy, and to her surprise found that it wasn't much. Silyen was rarely present at Kyneston's social events—the garden parties, the hunts, or Lady Thalia's interminable chamber opera evenings. He would occasionally turn up for family dinners, eating sparingly and offering sly, barbed remarks. These were usually at the expense of his eldest brother, and Bouda had to repress her urge to laugh. The family all maintained that Silyen was powerfully Skillful, but Bouda had never seen any direct evidence.

Although there had been moments. Feelings. She'd never been able to put her finger on one, but sometimes at Kyneston she'd experienced small sensations of wrongness. Conversations that she couldn't clearly remember. Objects that didn't feel entirely right in her hand. Even the taste of the air felt off sometimes, static and heavy.

She usually put it down to Gavar's generosity with the contents of his father's wine cellar. She'd even wondered if it was due to the charge crackling through Kyneston's vast Skill-forged wings.

But she couldn't be sure.

When the recess bell sounded, Daddy levered himself up to head for the Members' Parlor and its cake trolley. His disappearance gave Bouda the opportunity to have a long-overdue conversation. She looked for her quarry. Sure enough, Lady Armeria Tresco was there, in the farthest row of seats. Alone.

The Tresco seat in the chamber matched the location of their estate of Highwithel: peripheral. Had Highwithel's heir not broken her sister's heart, Bouda might one day have found herself a frequent visitor. She was glad this was no longer likely. The Tresco estate was an island at the heart of an archipelago: the Scillies. They were the southernmost point of the British Isles, off the tip of Cornwall. Beyond Land's End.

That was quite the best place for feckless Heir Meilyr and his ghastly mother. If only they'd stay there.

Lady Tresco looked up as Bouda approached. She had been rifling through a worn leather handbag. Possibly for a hairbrush, given the woman's disheveled appearance—though then again, it seemed unlikely she owned one.

Armeria gave Bouda a pleasant smile, closed her bag, and placed it on the adjoining heir's chair. The conspicuously empty heir's chair.

"Meilyr's still not with you, I see," Bouda said. "Any word from your prodigal son?"

"None, I'm afraid," replied the older woman. "Believe me, your sister would be the first to know. But he's been gone more than six months now. Bodina must be over the worst of her disappointment, I hope?"

"Oh, yes," said Bouda. "Quite over it. He could long since be back at Highwithel for all she cares. I was only asking on my own account, as I'll be sending out the wedding invitations soon. Just the one for the Trescos, then?"

"You never know," said Lady Tresco unhelpfully. "So that's happening soon, is it? Congratulations. Your star really is rising."

"Thank you." It was an automatic response. "And yes, at Kyneston in March, after the Third Proposal Debate and the vote."

"The Third Debate? How fitting for such a politic union. Well, I shall see you before then at Esterby for the First."

And with that, Armeria Tresco retrieved her handbag and recommended sorting through it.

Bouda stood there a moment, astonished. Had she just been dismissed? It appeared that she had. At least no one had seen it happen. But still. She felt her cheeks flame as she turned away and descended to the second tier. She would look as florid as dear Papa.

At least she'd gleaned a little information for Dina. Or rather, had no news—which was most definitely good news, in Bouda's opinion. Her little sister's passion for Meilyr Tresco had been quite genuine, but sorely misplaced. Meilyr was an affable creature, but of the same absurd political persuasion as his mother, and Bouda held him chiefly responsible for filling Di-Di's head with abolitionist enthusiasm.

Even the way he'd broken things off with Dina had been vague and unsatisfactory. He'd simply told poor DiDi that he wanted to go and "find himself," her heartbroken sister had confided. With Meilyr out of the picture, a more suitable husband could be found for her. Dina needed someone solid and reliable, who understood the family's interests. Bouda had a few possibilities in mind.

Papa was back at their seat, an emergency, napkin-wrapped slice of cake tucked into the corner of his chair. Greedy Daddy! She pinched his cheek indulgently and whispered in his ear.

"From what I heard from Lord Jardine earlier, this could be interesting."

Then the trumpets again; the Chancellor again. The chamber fell expectantly quiet.

Zelston walked to the chair, but remained standing. His expression was grim, and clutched in his hand was a single-sheet order paper. He launched straight in.

"It is my prerogative as Chancellor to introduce for the House's consideration a Proposal of my choosing. You will all be aware that a Chancellor's introduction of a Proposal does not necessarily signify that he supports it. It may simply be a matter that he believes merits discussion. That is the case with my Proposal today."

This disavowal brought jeers and catcalls from some of the more troublesome Members. "What an endorsement!" yelled one, from his place on the sixth tier. "Why'd you bother, then?" mocked another, from somewhere rather closer to the seat of power.

The Chancellor didn't dignify them with a response. He looked around the chamber, level and composed, though Bouda saw the paper tremble in his hand.

"At the conclusion of this session the Silence will be laid upon all Observers, and the Quiet accepted by all Members."

There were murmurs of surprise and displeasure from the assembled Equals. Bouda sat forward in her seat, tense and excited. She had never seen the two ancient acts of Silence and Quiet bestowed publicly.

Of course, to call it "Silence" was misleading. The act didn't really silence a person; it hid their own memories from them. It was forbidden to lay the Silence on one's Equals—though practice obviously couldn't count, Bouda had long ago decided, or how would anyone ever master it? All Chancellors had to be able to perform it, so from childhood Bouda had practiced on her sister. Darling DiDi hadn't minded.

The only permitted use of the Silence was within the House of Light, when it was laid upon commoners—the Observers. They were sometimes privy to Proposals or other business deemed too sensitive, too incendiary, to become common knowledge. Once the Chancellor had bestowed the Silence, the OPs would remember nothing of his Proposal until he lifted it again.

The parliamentarians themselves, the Equals, would accept the Quiet. This was a lesser act, but still effective. You retained your memories, but could not speak of or otherwise share them with those outside the sanctioned group—in this case, the Members of Parliament. Rumor had it that many a family secret was protected by hereditary Quiet.

Speaker Dawson looked like she wanted to protest. Bouda rolled her eyes. Historically, of course, the Silence had been used in ways that were perhaps less than desirable. Possibly it still was. Gavar and his pals had acquired a reputation at Oxford for parties attended by commoner girls that guests found strangely unmemorable the following day. But here in the House of Light, both acts were perfectly legitimate.

The Chancellor stood impassive until the hubbub had died down. Then he took a final look at the order sheet in his hand, as if he couldn't quite believe what was written there.

Bouda watched eagerly, one hand pressed to her mouth. Even her father had hauled himself upright and was listening with interest.

Zelston spoke.

"I Propose the abolition, entire and immediate, of the slave-days."

# SIX

# LUKE

It was amazing how much you could do in ten minutes.

Luke checked his watch—a cheap plastic thing stamped with the gaudy BB logo, Millmoor standard issue for all slaves—then slid into the shadows on the side of the hangar and upped his speed to a jog. Although tools-down was brief, the movement of workers throughout the Machine Park made it the perfect opportunity for all sorts of activities best conducted unnoticed.

He'd learned that, and a lot more, under Renie's tutelage. After he'd delivered the glasses for her, the kid had come back a few days later with another request. Then another. And Luke found that no matter how bone-meltingly knackered he was after his shifts in the components shed, he could draw on some last reserves to accomplish what she asked.

"I'm pretty sure I've worked off any favor you think I owe," he'd told her after taking some bits to fix a busted air-conditioning unit in a skanky block over in West, where the residents' pleas for repairs had gone unheard and people were developing breathing problems. Breathing the air inside the building had been like sucking an exhaust pipe. Luke thought he'd coughed up a bit of lung just making the delivery.

"'Course you have." She grinned gappily. "Now you're doing it 'cause you like it."

And Luke had found that he was.

As far as he could see, Renie-Rhymes-with-Genie was indeed in the business of granting wishes. Or not wishes so much as simple, everyday needs that Luke couldn't believe weren't being met by Millmoor's authorities. Yes, she was operating outside official channels. But Renie sourced a lot of her info on what folk needed from a Millmoor doctor, which must make it halfway legit. And for all Ryan's warnings, it surely wasn't as though they'd slap you with slavelife for taking people medicine, books, and food.

He'd reached the canteen. Six and a half minutes remaining. Three to find what he needed, then three and a half to get back to Williams at their workstation.

Luke had laughed when Renie had issued his latest task—liberating food from the Zone D stores. He could just about choke down the canteen's offerings without hurling. Surely the only ones to benefit from him taking the stuff would be the Zone D workers who no longer had to eat it.

"It's got extra calories and protein," she'd explained. "To keep you heavy-labor guys going. You should see what people get fed in the other zones. Just as nasty, but only half as filling. An' you know the junk in the dorm kitchens. People get scurvy in here, Luke. I'm not kidding."

Luke had wondered about Renie herself. Even for a thirteen-year-old she was tiny—scrawny and hollow-cheeked. Her dark skin didn't hide the even darker circles round her eyes. She looked malnourished in a way that shouldn't be possible in Britain today. Had she come to Millmoor aged ten? Was this what three years of life here had done to her?

And as he had many times in the month since their separation, Luke gave silent thanks that none of his family was here in this nightmarish place. Especially not Daisy.

He ducked into the storeroom. The shelves rose above his head. Each was labeled, but not arranged in any obvious system. There were so many boxes, so many cartons. He jogged along one row, looking up and down, scanning the labels.

Then he slammed forward against the shelf edge as something smashed into the back of his skull.

Luke crumpled to the floor, half blind with pain. Had something fallen on him from a high shelf behind?

A steel toecap dug under his shoulder blade and turned him over.

The strip of fluorescent ceiling light threw off throbbing coronas. One of them formed a queasy, technicolor halo around the head of the figure that stood over him. Luke blinked to try to steady his vision. What he saw wasn't an improvement.

"Taking a little stroll, Hadley E-1031?"

The boot nudged beneath his chin. Luke's gaze followed the leg up to a barrel chest, a bull neck, a square head crowned with writhing light.

Luke's very own angel of pain: Kessler.

"Feeling peckish, were we?" Kessler continued, looking around the shelves in the food store. "Are we not feeding you to your satisfaction here in Millmoor, E-1031? Disappointed you're not eating roast swan with your betters at Kyneston?"

The tip of his baton thrust deep into the soft space beneath Luke's ribs. Work in Zone D had been layering muscle onto Luke's abdomen, but it was inadequate defense against Kessler's jabs. The baton angled up, probing—the man's grasp of anatomy was as good as Mum's—and thrust again, and Luke's body jackknifed as he curled onto his side and coughed up the lumpy remains of breakfast.

Luke moaned, and wiped sticky strings from his mouth with the cuff of his jumpsuit. Even that small movement made his head yammer with hurt. He remembered Mum crouching over Dad on the driveway. What had she yelled out? Something about blunt force. He closed his eyes.

"I hope you've not been stealing anything, E-1031," Kessler continued. "Because Millmoor doesn't approve of stealing. Years on your days, that can be. I'll check, shall I?"

Rough hands pawed at Luke's limbs, patting down the coveralls, tugging at pockets. Just when he thought it was over, the guard pincered Luke's chin between finger and thumb, forcing his mouth open.

"I like to do a thorough job," Kessler said, thrusting the index and middle fingers of his other hand into Luke's mouth. Luke gagged, and as saliva welled in his mouth he tasted soap and sharp antiseptic. Were Kessler's hands the only clean thing in Millmoor?

Kessler pulled out his fingers and wiped them down the

front of Luke's jumpsuit. "Looks like you've been a good boy, E-1031. But it was careless of you to trip and fall while moving around the Machine Park. That can be dangerous in a place like this."

"Trip?" Luke croaked, anger welling up as nausea ebbed. "You hit me, you bastard." He coughed, hoping for a bit of bile to take away the taste of Kessler in his mouth.

"You tripped," repeated Kessler. "Clearly you need a little lesson on being more careful in future."

The baton reared up, light flaring along its length.

It can kill, Luke remembered in an instant. Blunt-force trauma can kill if the brain swells.

But the blow struck lower. Luke heard something—several things—crack, and gasped. He inhaled knives. Saw needles.

Blacked out.

When he came to, the antiseptic smell was still there. But when he opened his eyes, Kessler was nowhere to be seen. Luke had been dumped in a chair in the corner of what looked like a medical waiting room.

The core of his body was one jagged mass of pain, as if all his organs had been taken out and replaced by broken glass. He leaned forward unsteadily and threw up again on the floor. There wasn't much of it this time, and it was pinkish. Spotted with red. It was hard to breathe.

"How did this happen?"

A voice nearby. Low. Angry.

A shape squatted down at Luke's side and a palm reached up to his forehead. Luke cringed away, but there was nowhere to go.

The touch was cool, the hand gentle, and Luke let his head sag forward against it with a sob of relief.

"I'm Dr. Jackson, and I want you to try and stand," the voice said. "Don't think about it hurting, and maybe it won't. Come with me."

And unbelievably, Luke found that he could. Leaning on the medic's white-coated arm, moving as if someone had just added a zero onto his age, he shuffled down the corridor. The doctor led him into a small room and directed him to lean against a gurney.

"I'm going to take a look at you. I'll be as careful as I can. May I?"

He gestured toward the buttons on Luke's coveralls, and Luke nodded. He studied the man, to distract himself from the agony that was surely coming. The medic had a short-sided haircut and a neat beard. His face was tanned, and laughter lines at the corner of his eyes stood out pale against his skin. "Jackson J-3646" was embroidered in blue on the breast pocket of his coat. He looked almost too young to be a doctor.

He must have started his days straight after uni, Luke decided. Abi had told him that wasn't unheard of among medical graduates with more ambition than scruples. You'd be thrown in at the deep end in the slavetowns and acquire loads of experience, with nobody minding too much about any mistakes.

But this guy knew what he was doing. His hands carefully lifted Luke's hair for a look at his skull, then lightly pulled up his T-shirt. With each press of fingers, Luke anticipated a detonation of agony, but all that came was a dull throbbing.

"Let me guess," the doctor said, letting the cotton drop back over Luke's middle. "Workplace accident. You tripped and fell. Right onto something shaped like, oh, a Security baton?"

Startled, Luke glanced at the doctor's face. Was this a trap? Careful, Luke.

Maybe this Jackson was Kessler's pal. Did the smiling medic patch up all the Security man's "little lessons," keeping them hush?

"Workplace accident," Luke agreed. Jackson frowned.

"Of course it was. And I'll tell you what: it's not nearly as bad as it must feel. I think you hit your head on the way down, which sent your neural pathways into a state of hypersensitivity. But it's nothing I can't fix with some heavy-duty analgesics. Wait a sec."

Jackson turned away to rummage in a mirror-fronted cabinet.

The doc was right: Luke already felt much better than he had on coming round in the waiting room. He'd thought Kessler had pulverized a few of his ribs, but when he risked a look at his midriff, all he could see was livid bruising. That made sense, in a twisted sort of way. Kessler couldn't go around beating people half to death. Slaves might be chattels of the state, but that didn't mean sadistic Security guards could just break them. Kessler must have known exactly what he was doing, landing every blow for maximum agony and minimum actual injury.

Jackson turned back with a fat tub of ointment. As he smeared it lightly across Luke's abdomen, the last of the pain lifted away. Luke wanted to cry with relief, and spluttered his thanks.

"No problem," said Jackson, straightening up and looking Luke in the eye. "Least I could do for the friend of a friend."

And there went Luke's heart again, leaping against his not-busted-after-all rib cage. What did the doc mean? Luke didn't have any friends in Millmoor, just a mute work partner, a former school acquaintance, and a barely teenage taskmaster.

The doc.

*The* doc. The one who knew stuff. Who ran Renie's show.

"A friend? Would that be, uh, one of your younger patients? A girl?"

Jackson laughed, a low, reassuring sound. "Renie's never been a patient of mine. She's got more lives than a cat, that girl. You could throw her off a roof and she'd land feetfirst. Looking after you today is the least I could do, after all you've done for us, Luke Hadley."

Luke flushed at the unexpected praise. "I've not done much. Nothing that anyone else wouldn't do."

"That's not quite true, I'm afraid," said Jackson. "There aren't many that see this place for what it truly is. Even fewer who realize that the slavedays aren't an inevitable part of normal life, but a brutal violation of freedom and dignity, perpetrated by the Equals."

Luke stared at the doctor. Was that what Luke thought? He wasn't sure. He'd dreaded his slavedays—still did dread the decade stretching ahead. He both resented and envied the Equals. He hated Millmoor, and the cruelties and indignities he saw here every day. But just like Abi and the rest of the family, Luke had never questioned the fact that he'd have to do days eventually.

"I shouldn't get heavy," said Jackson, sensing his confusion. "You've had a wretched time of it this afternoon. Go back to your dorm and rest. But there are a few others like Renie and me, and we get together occasionally as the Millmoor Games and Social Club. If you fancy joining us, we'd be glad to see you. Renie can tell you when."

With that, Jackson opened the door and yelled down the corridor for his next patient.

To his astonishment Luke woke the following morning pain-free, with only yellowing bruises to show where Kessler had laid into him. Which was good, because he had a job to do. During tools-down, he went straight to the canteen storeroom. Kessler wouldn't be expecting him back so soon—if at all. He filled his jumpsuit pockets with as many packets as he could conceal. That night, he went to the rendezvous spot arranged with Renie for the previous evening, planning to cache the food there. But she was waiting for him.

"Knew you'd come tonight," she said, snapping some definitely-not-Millmoor-approved gum in her mouth. "Doc said that if you showed, I was to tell you that the next club meeting's this Sunday. See me by Gate 9 of the South vehicle repair yard, 11 A.M."

She stuffed the pilfered food inside her hoodie and melted back into the gloom.

"Wait!" Luke hissed. "This club. What did Jackson mean— games and social? What do you do, really?"

The girl's face reappeared, bobbing disembodied in the drizzle of light from a lamppost.

"Chess. Scrabble." She shrugged. "We had Clue, but it got taken off us for being subversive. Bumping off poshos in a mansion, and it could have been one of the servants what dunnit."

At Luke's disappointed expression, she threw back her head and cackled.

"Only joking. You'll find out soon enough. And remember: no one will make you play. We may have chosen you, but you have to choose the game."

Then she was gone.

Luke lay awake in the dorm that night, thinking about his family, and about Doc Jackson's club. His whole life he had been surrounded by the noise of his sisters and parents, a sound so familiar that it went as unnoticed as breathing—until it wasn't there anymore. So he sometimes just talked to them anyway. Which wasn't weird at all.

He'd hear nothing from them until December at the earliest, once he'd been here three months and the customary restriction period on outside communication for all new slaves had passed. And it wasn't as though he could tell them about the club in a letter anyway. So a one-sided conversation inside his head would have to do.

What would they make of how he'd spent his first weeks in Millmoor, and his plan to go with Renie on Sunday? Because he was pretty sure the club's activities were nothing to do with board games.

"Forget about it, son," Dad would counsel from under the hood of the Austin-Healey, hand held out for a wrench. "Keep your head down. Just get on with your work."

"Don't go getting into trouble," he could hear Mum say. And Abi would surely remind him that he knew nothing about these people he was getting mixed up with.

Daisy might think it rather cool. She'd never been one for doing what she was told. (Though Luke hoped she was being more obedient at Kyneston.) Would Millmoor have turned Daisy into a Renie, streetwise and defiant?

Luke saw that it came down to a single question: was getting involved with the club worth risking another thrashing from Kessler—or worse? Possibly even endangering his transfer to Kyneston?

Mum and Dad would say no, without a moment's hesitation. But they hadn't been here and seen what life was like in this place. It wasn't up to Mum and Dad anymore, he realized. It was as Renie had promised: the choice was his.

That realization didn't help him sleep.

On Sunday morning, Luke reached the vehicle depot half an hour early. He prowled around the wire fence, curious. There was a row of Security 4x4s raised on hydraulic jacks, to be worked on from below. He knew what Dad would have said about that: it was incredibly unsafe without axle stands, too. Were the authorities who ran Millmoor that ignorant, or did they simply not care about the people who slaved here?

Or was it something worse? Were Millmoor's many accidents—like what happened to Simon's uncle Jimmy, or the man who used to do Luke's job—more than just negligent one-offs? Perhaps they were part of how slavetowns operated. Risky work and harsh living conditions would keep people focused on themselves and their own challenges, unable to see the bigger picture.

Is that what Doc Jackson had been trying to say?

Was Luke beginning to see Millmoor for what it truly was?

Renie materialized at Luke's elbow. Her nod of approval at

seeing him scoping out the depot turned into a grin when he explained how he'd fixed up a car with Dad.

"It's not like I'll get much chance to use what I know in here," Luke said ruefully. "I'm seventeen next month. I should have been learning to drive. I already can drive, sort of. But I won't be getting behind a wheel or under a hood anytime soon."

"Never say never, Luke Hadley," Renie retorted, jaw working furiously at some gum. "C'mon. Let's get you introduced to the club."

Luke switched on his mental satnav to try to remember the route, but after fifteen minutes he was lost as they took shortcuts and nipped through buildings and courtyards, making it impossible to keep track of roads followed and corners turned. Did Renie not trust him with the location of the meeting?

"Scenic route?" he asked, a little sharply.

"Least-amount-of-surveillance route," she replied, still hurrying ahead. Soon after, she ducked beneath the half-lowered shutter of a warehouse freight entrance and headed for a door set into the wall of the cavernous space inside.

Luke didn't even have time to run a hand through his hair and plaster on his best how-do-you-do face. He needn't have worried. The Millmoor Games and Social Club appeared to be half a dozen people in some back room.

They were seated in outsize black-mesh office chairs around a wheeled desk littered with cans of soda and an empty fruit bowl. It was like the judging panel of the world's crummiest TV talent show.

There were two gray-haired women who must be last-ditchers; they looked old even by ditcher standards, well into their sixties. A skinny guy was swiveling his chair with nervous energy. A shaven-headed black bloke sat next to a petite woman with a ponytail and a wan complexion. Were they Renie's parents? But she gave them no special acknowledgment. Then Doc Jackson. Beside him: two empty seats.

"Hello, Luke," said the doctor. "Welcome to the Millmoor Games and Social Club."

The others introduced themselves: Hilda and Tilda, Asif, Oswald—"Call me Oz"—and Jessica. The two women with matching names were sisters, but Oz and Jessica didn't claim Renie.

"And this is Luke Hadley," said Jackson, slapping a reassuring hand on his shoulder as he sat down. Despite the frankly odd assortment of people, Luke felt a buzz of excitement.

"So you've already seen how we socialize, Luke," the Doc said, smiling. "Things like the food and the air-con parts, that's the small stuff we do every day. It's not only essentials. A book or some music, or a love letter from outside that hasn't been read first by a censor—anything from out there that makes life in here more bearable, we're on it.

"But though that's all important, none of it changes anything. And changing things is what the club is all about, Luke. It's the game we play. Let us show you."

Luke nodded, tense but intrigued.

"If you decide you don't want to play, we'll understand," Jackson continued. "But if that's the case, we ask that you don't mention the club or its activities to anyone. Jessica, why don't you go first and show Luke how we roll."

It turned out the fruit bowl wasn't empty, because Jessica

reached into it and drew out a small, folded square of paper. She frowned at it.

"Honestly, Jack, your handwriting is terrible."

Jackson held up both hands. "What can I say? I'm a doctor."

"It's a good one, though," Jessica continued, reading from the paper. " 'Identify and destroy Security evidence on charges against Evans N-2228.' I'll take Hilda and Oz: her for the identifying, him for the destroying."

She looked up at Oz. They might not be Renie's parents, Luke decided, but they had a thing going on, which was kind of sweet.

"Tell us more, Doc," rumbled Oz.

Jackson laced his fingers together, suddenly businesslike. "Barry Evans lost a hand in an accident at the poultry-processing plant. He'd been telling his supervisor for ages that the equipment was faulty, but nothing was done. The day he gets out of hospital, he goes in during the nighttime shutdown and smashes the place half to bits. No one saw him, but they caught him on camera and they're going to slap him with slavelife. Find the footage, delete it. Make sure it's off any backup servers. And if they've anything else incriminating, make sure that disappears, too."

The two women looked at each other and Hilda smacked her hand on the tabletop. Was it enthusiasm for their task? Disgust at what had happened to Evans? Luke couldn't tell. In fact, he could hardly believe what he'd just heard, but the draw had already moved on and Tilda was reaching into the bowl. She hooted as she unfolded the paper she had selected.

" 'Live interview with ABC AM'—is that the Aussie radio

people, Doc?—'at 11:15 P.M. Tuesday, about conditions inside British slavetowns.' Asif, you do the talking, and I'll get us a secure line out through NoBird."

"Excellent," said Jackson. "You'll do a great job. Which means there's one game left this week."

The room fell quiet. Asif quit swiveling his chair, silencing its squeak; Renie even stopped chewing her gum. The seven people in the room all looked at Luke.

No pressure.

"You need to know," said Jackson, turning squarely to him, "that what we do has consequences. The penalty for the things we've just discussed could be many more years of days. But we do them because we believe that the consequences for everyone else, if we don't, will be much greater.

"I'd like you to join us, Luke. I think you could do great things for the club. But only you can choose whether or not to play. There aren't any winners in our game—not till it all ends. And the opponent never changes."

Luke eyed the fruit bowl, which sat in front of Tilda. A single square of paper, folded to the size of a thumbnail, lay at the bottom.

He looked back at Jackson, wiped his sweating palms down both legs of his coveralls, then steadied them on the edge of the desk.

He'd always enjoyed games. This one was worth playing.

He reached out to the bowl.

# SEVEN

# ABI

Daisy was thrilled with her job at Kyneston. Even Mum and Dad had come to accept it, once they'd seen that their youngest daughter could cope.

But in Abi's humble opinion, it wouldn't end well.

Abi had been the first to see the crib, when Jenner had shown them around their cottage. She'd asked what it was doing there—in the third bedroom that should have been Luke's.

Jenner had looked sheepish, and promised to explain when he briefed them on their assignments the next day. When he walked into their kitchen that morning, Abi got up to clear everything off the table, because otherwise there'd be no stopping Daisy cramming more toast into her mouth. It was imperative they make the best possible impression if they were to get Luke back quickly.

She didn't trust herself to return to her seat, given that Jenner had taken the empty chair next to it. Instead, Abi hovered by the sink as he began to talk. Her parents' assignments were exactly what Abi had hoped for when she'd filled out the forms for Estates Services. Mum would be nursing a lady up at the great house and seeing to the slaves. Dad would take care of Lord Whittam's vintage car collection and maintain the other estate vehicles.

"And I think you'll be perfect as Kyneston's administration assistant," Jenner had said, looking right at Abi with that lovely smile. "I hope that doesn't sound undemanding for someone as bright as you. It really isn't. I took over the Family Office myself when I left university last year, and you wouldn't believe how much there is to be dealt with. I need someone I can rely on to ensure that happens."

Abi went bright red. She'd be working alongside him. It was a nightmare and a dream wrapped up in one thrilling but super-awkward parcel, bow-tied and with a gift tag saying "crush." She saw Daisy snigger and sent her a ferocious glare.

Then Daisy's assignment stole everyone's attention away—Abi's included.

Daisy would be looking after a baby. One born to a girl who'd been a slave here on the estate. She had been inappropriately involved with his eldest brother, Jenner had explained, but had tragically died in an accident a few months ago.

They all had lots of questions, but it was clear Jenner didn't want to talk about it. He said "That's all I can tell you" a bit crossly, and Abi mouthed "Shut up" in Daisy's direction.

Soon after, Heir Gavar had turned up. The expression on his face was furious, as if he'd come to accuse them of stealing something. He was even taller than his brothers and big, wide across the shoulders. The baby had looked very small, lying along the crook of his arm, but she was sleeping peacefully and Gavar held her so carefully you'd think she was a porcelain doll.

"That's the kid?" he'd said to Jenner, pointing at Daisy. "You're joking, right? She's still a baby herself."

"Don't start," Jenner said wearily. "You know how it's got to be."

The heir muttered something crude and Dad pushed his chair back as if he was going to tell him off for swearing, before thinking better of it. Poor Daisy looked like she might die of fright.

Gavar called her over with a curt "Come here," but Daisy was too petrified to obey.

"Go on," Mum had said, nudging her gently. "He's not going to eat you."

And Abi's heart swelled with pride as her little sis did the bravest thing ever and walked over to stand in front of Gavar Jardine. He looked at Daisy like his eyes might burn holes in her.

"This is my daughter, Libby," the heir said, angling his arm slightly. The baby was adorable, with round rosy cheeks, curling coppery hair, and long dark lashes.

"She is the most important thing in my life, and now she is the most important thing in yours. You must be with her at all times, and when I am at Kyneston I will come and find you every day. I'll know where you are. You are to talk to her—proper talk, not stupid chatter. Play with her. Show her things. Her mother was an intelligent woman, and she is an intelligent child. You are to address her as 'Miss Jardine' at all times. If any harm comes to her, you and your family will pay for it. Do you understand?"

"Yes," said Daisy, nodding her head emphatically. Then, "Yes, sir."

"Good," said Gavar.

He held out the baby.

In the week that followed, Daisy became more confident at handling her tiny charge. And Abi did a bit of sleuthing to find out more about Libby Jardine and her mother.

She discovered that one of the older kitchen-slaves had looked after the baby before the Hadleys arrived. She was a kindly sort, and proved talkative when Abi dropped by on the pretext of a pantry inventory.

"The bairn's real name is Liberty," she said, shaking her head. "Her mother chose it. She was a good girl, Leah was, and very much in love with Heir Gavar. But when she found out she was pregnant, they had a falling-out and he was cruel to her. So she called the little one that to have a dig at him, to rub it in that she was just a slave.

"He wanted the mite to have some high and fancy name like they all do—an Amelia or Cecilia or Eustacia or some such— but his parents wouldn't hear of it. They didn't like 'Liberty,' either, of course. Lord Jardine said it was 'in poor taste.' So it was Lady Thalia, bless her, who hit on the solution, and the little darling's been Libby ever since.

"They don't regard her as one of them, you see. No Skill— though her mum was convinced she did have it. Poor girl. I think she was all muddled at the end. It's impossible, of course; everyone knows that. That's why Libby's looked after by the likes of us, instead of up at the big house. But Heir Gavar loves her something fierce."

And wasn't that the truth.

None of them knew when Gavar might turn up to see his daughter. He would suddenly loom over them in the cottage kitchen, while Daisy was spooning mush into Libby's sticky mouth and crooning nursery rhymes. Gazing out of Kyneston's office window, Abi would often glimpse him striding toward the lake, where Daisy had taken Libby to look at the ducks.

As she hurried through the service corridors one day, Abi heard Gavar roaring furiously about disrespect to his daughter. Fearing the worst, Abi diverted toward the formal front of the house, ready to throw herself between him and Daisy. But as she opened the concealed door, she saw a particularly snooty parlor-slave cowering against a tapestry, a pile of fresh linen crumpled at her feet. Gavar jabbed a meaty finger into the woman's face. His other hand was protectively on Daisy's shoulder, resting on the harness she used to carry Libby.

"And apologize to Miss Hadley," Gavar snarled. "Even if you see her alone she will be going about the service of my child. You get out of her way, not the other way around. Now say it."

"I . . . I'm sorry, Miss Hadley," the maid stammered. "I won't do it again."

Gavar grunted, and Daisy tipped her head in acknowledgment like a diminutive queen. Astonished, Abi shut the door silently and returned to her errand.

The most startling thing happened the following week. They'd not yet been at Kyneston a month and the four of them were sitting down to dinner. Daisy was uncharacteristically

glum—even when Mum opened the oven and produced a surprise treat: apple crumble.

"What's up, puppy?" Dad asked.

Daisy sniffed theatrically and wiped her nose with the back
of her wrist.

"I miss Gavar," she said, her voice small. "I'm going to go
and check on Libby."

And just as Mum put the baking dish down in front of her,
Daisy stood and disappeared upstairs.

The three of them looked at one another, bewildered.

"Where's Heir Gavar?" Mum asked after a moment.

Abi sighed and dished herself some dessert. "He and Lord
Jardine have gone up north," she said. "To Esterby Castle. It's
the First Debate—you know, when they discuss the Chancellor's Proposal. There's one in the autumn, one midwinter, then
the Third Debate is here at Kyneston in the spring.

"Jenner says they usually talk about the Proposals a lot, all
the family, but that his dad and Gavar have been tight-lipped
this year. Silyen's mixed up in it, too, but I don't get how. Jenner says his father claims the Proposal is so ridiculous it's not
even worth discussing. I don't think he believes him, though."

"Jenner says this, Jenner says that," Dad said. "Are both my
girls going doolally over these Jardine boys?" His words were
teasing, but his face was grim.

"You watch yourself, young lady," Mum said.

Any retort would have kicked off an almighty family shouting match, so Abi bit her lip. Her parents were being ridiculous. She barely mentioned Jenner.

No, Daisy was the one they should be worried about. Heir
Gavar might be charismatic but he was a brute, all swagger and

shout, displeased with everyone and everything except his daughter.

And there was something even worse. Estate gossip held that he was responsible for the death of Libby's mother, Leah. She had been shot accidentally when Gavar was out hunting one night.

Why would Leah have been roaming the grounds after dark? Abi couldn't construct any convincing scenario.

Which led to one inescapable question: had it really been an accident?

At any rate, it couldn't be safe for Daisy to spend so much time with Kyneston's heir. All her initial fear of him had been replaced by a kind of worshipful adoration. But she was only ten, and while she was doing brilliantly minding Libby, surely at some point she'd slip up or make a mistake. Then how would Gavar react? No, it was too risky. Abi would have to see if Jenner could get Daisy assigned to some other task.

With this thought, guilt welled up inside Abi again. She was no nearer to getting Luke transferred from Millmoor. The first few times she'd dropped her brother into conversation with Jenner, he had made no comment and she'd thought him simply preoccupied. But on the third occasion, he'd turned to her with regret plain in those kind brown eyes.

"I'm very sorry, Abigail, but there was a good reason why your brother couldn't come to Kyneston, and that reason still stands. Please don't ask me again."

Then he shut himself off, just as he had the day they arrived and again when they'd first asked about Libby.

His words were soft, but the refusal hit Abi hard. She had to keep asking. The thought of Luke stuck in Millmoor and at the mercy of people like that brutish guard for another few months was awful. That he might never join them was unthinkable. Luke, being the only boy, might fancy himself his sisters' protector, but Abi was the eldest. Looking out for her siblings was her responsibility.

Whatever that "good reason" was, she'd have to discover it. Overcome it.

In the meantime, there was Daisy to think about.

The next morning was a Saturday, and though the weather had turned chilly now it was late September, the day was sunny and gorgeous. Abi found her sister changing the baby and suggested a walk in the estate woods. It would be the perfect opportunity to give her a gentle talking-to about her attachment to both Libby and her father.

"We can show Libby the foliage and kick some leaves around," she told Daisy. "Babies like color and noise, they stimulate their brains."

"Gavar would like that," her sister said approvingly, as Abi tried not to roll her eyes. "But I'd better go and find her hat and mittens."

The woods were every bit as beautiful close up as they had appeared from a distance. By the lake was a showy miniature temple. (Follies had become fashionable among the Equals a few centuries ago, because clearly having an enormous house wasn't ostentatious enough.) Then the trees began, and stretched as far as the eye could see. Kyneston Estate really was as vast as it had seemed that first day.

Abi led the way in beneath the branches, her boots rustling through the deep leaf-fall. Sunlight filtered through the tree canopy, making the already colorful foliage vivid and bright, like stained glass cast by someone who liked only the first half of the rainbow.

"This one is red," said Daisy, stooping to pick up a leaf and presenting it to Libby, who promptly dropped it. "And this one is orange."

Farther ahead was a tall, triangular tree that was perfectly yellow. Abi bent to root in the leaf-fall for a nice specimen to show Libby.

Her hand hit something solid yet yielding. Furry.

Backing away, she grabbed Daisy and shoved her little sis and the baby behind her, toward the tree's sturdy trunk.

What an idiot she'd been! There could be anything in these woods. So what if there weren't supposed to be wolves or bears in England anymore. There weren't supposed to be naked men on leashes, either, but Lady Hypatia had brought one to Kyneston.

But nothing erupted from the forest floor. No slavering fangs snapped at them; no claws knifed through the air toward them. Nothing.

Abi waited. Her hands trembled.

Nothing.

Why wasn't the creature moving? She'd whacked it hard enough to wake anything—even Luke.

Hardly believing what she was doing, she crept back to the pile of leaves. Holding her breath, she slowly reached one hand down and felt it.

Coarse fur. But cool to the touch. And still. You didn't have to be a med student to work out what that meant.

Emboldened, Abi brushed away the rest of the leaves. The creature—she soon saw it was a deer—never stirred. The eyes were wide open and filmed over. It was dead.

But how? There were no injuries or signs of sickness. The corpse looked perfect in every way. The fur was still thick and glossy. It didn't even smell.

In fact, the odor here was pleasant: sweet and fragrant. Abi lifted her head and looked about, sniffing. She saw the source and smelled it at the same time.

A short way off, in a glade open to the sky, stood a tree. A cherry, judging from the profusion of pink blossoms. Its branches bent down to the forest floor under their weight. In the crisp autumn air, the scent was unmistakable.

The sight was mesmerizing. Abi moved toward it and sensed Daisy following. She put her palms out and brushed them over the blossoms, luxuriating in the dense flowers. At her side, Daisy had taken off Libby's mittens and was encouraging her to touch them, too.

"It's so pretty," Daisy cooed to the baby. "Isn't it pretty?"

Except it was also, some part of Abi's brain belatedly told her, very wrong. It was late September. Autumn. Not spring, when these flowers usually bloomed.

She felt a sudden chill that had nothing to do with any breeze. The deer was dead, but didn't look it. The tree was alive and blossoming when it shouldn't be.

"Okay, sweetie," she told Libby, gently moving the branch back out of reach and shooting Daisy a trust-me-on-this-one look. "We're going to go now. We'll have our picnic back by the big house."

She only saw him when she turned.

He was sitting on the ground several yards away, legs stretched out in front of him and his back propped up against a tree trunk. His hair was tangled, and he'd raked it back from his face, which looked thin and tired. But his eyes were bright with curiosity as he watched them. The Young Master.

For a moment he said nothing, and neither did she. Then he jumped to his feet, a smooth, quick motion, and strolled over to where they stood. He reached out and offered a finger to Libby, who seized it and started gnawing enthusiastically. Abi felt Daisy shift uneasily beside her. She plainly wanted to step away, but was unable to do so without breaking that contact.

"Do you like my tree?" said Silyen Jardine.

"Your tree?" said Abi, stupidly.

"Yes." He smiled and it was bright and cold as the day. "Or, to be more accurate, my experiment. From the noise you made just now, I'm guessing you found my other one, too. This is prettier, though, isn't it?"

He reached out his free hand and fingered the petals thoughtfully.

"The dead deer," said Daisy indignantly. "That was you?"

"Death. Life," said Silyen, waggling his finger in his niece's gummy mouth as she blew bubbles around it. "The usual party tricks. Little Libby here was my inspiration, actually. Or rather, her mother was, when Gavar shot her and she died right there in front of us. There was nothing I could do, which was . . . intriguing. I don't like problems I can't solve. I'm sure you know what I mean, Abigail."

It gave Abi the creeps hearing him say her name like that.

But the words before it held her attention. Silyen had seen Gavar shoot, and Leah die. It didn't sound much like a hunting accident.

"What?" Daisy had gone alarmingly pink. "Not Gavar. He wouldn't. He loved Libby's mummy. He's told me so."

"Coming to his defense? Gavar's way with the ladies is legendary, but I never knew it started so young. Your sister knows I'm telling the truth, though."

"Abi?" Daisy was shrill.

Abi gritted her teeth. She had wanted to introduce her sister gently to the idea that Gavar Jardine might not be a hero. Not with this shocking knowledge. Daisy hadn't even known he was involved in Libby's mother's death—let alone Silyen's rather more dramatic version of events.

"We'll discuss it later," she said. "We were just heading back anyway. So if you'll excuse us, Master Silyen."

She ducked her head and made to pull Daisy away, but Silyen Jardine wasn't done with them yet.

"Tell me," he said, withdrawing his finger from Libby's grasp and eyeing her speculatively. "Does she ever do anything . . . special? Unusual?"

"Skillful, you mean?" said Daisy. "No. She's just a baby."

"Oh, that doesn't stop us." He smiled. "If anything, babies' Skill is much more noticeable, because it's more uncontrolled. Apparently Gavar used to shatter plates if our mother tried to feed him anything other than mashed banana. Twenty-three years and he's barely changed."

"I don't believe a word you say about him," said Daisy. "You're just jealous because he's the heir."

Please, thought Abi. Please, let us just get out of these woods in one piece, away from dead animals, Silyen Jardine's party tricks, and Daisy's lack of any self-preservation instincts whatsoever.

But Silyen merely shrugged and turned away, his gaze returning to the tree. He reached out to a branch and shook it, just as Daisy had done, and watched the petals shower to the ground. He frowned.

He removed his hand but the petals kept falling, faster and faster, whole flowers dropping off, entire and perfect, until all three of them stood ankle deep. The scent rose up from the woodland floor in an overpowering wave of sweetness. On the branches, green shoots appeared, pushed out, and unfurled. Soon the tree was covered in leaves, as thick and full as the flowers had been. Despite her desire to flee just moments before, Abi was fixed to the spot as if she'd put down roots herself.

The leaves began to curl up. The tree lost its vibrancy as they shriveled; yellowed; fell. Dead leaves piled on top of the flowers.

Soon the tree was entirely bare. Black and skeletal, it reached long fingers down to the ground to trail sadly among its fallen beauty and vigor, as if yearning to gather it all back in again.

Silyen Jardine said nothing. Daisy said nothing. Baby Libby kicked her legs and gurgled.

Silyen cocked his head, as if listening for something. "My father and brother are back," he said, turning to them. "Gavar's desperate to see his daughter again. He'll come straight to you. It'd be better if he didn't find you with me. That's the most direct way out."

He pointed across the glade, indicating a route between two great oak trees. Neither of them needed telling twice.

Daisy set off at a pace, early fallen acorns crunching under her feet and Libby's soft-booted heels knocking against her middle. Abi followed. She didn't look round, not at the Young Master, the dead cherry tree, or the woods beyond where the deer lay lifeless and still. She emerged from the treeline blinking in the full glare of the sunshine. Her heart was pounding, as if she'd just had a narrow escape, though from what exactly she couldn't have said.

When they were past the temple grotto, Abi heard the faint roar of a motorbike. Daisy clapped her hands with excitement and Abi cringed. She never knew people actually did that.

More to the point, how could Daisy still be so stoked to see Gavar, now she knew what had happened to Libby's poor mother?

The bike surged into view and slashed to a halt, gouging grass into mud. The heir kicked his bike to a stand and hurried over.

"You're a long way from the house," he said to Daisy sternly. Abi might as well not have been there.

Gavar wore the fierce expression that made house-slaves wet themselves in terror, but her little sister simply grinned.

"We're wrapped up warm and have everything we need," she told him, undoing the clasps on the harness and handing Libby to her father. Gavar doted on the baby for a few moments, rubbing her nose against his and making her laugh. Then he looked at Daisy and his expression was almost gentle.

"I missed her while I was away," he said. "But I knew she'd be safe with you. Let's go sit by the lake and you can tell me what you've been up to."

He tucked Libby against his chest and laid a hand on Daisy's shoulder, steering her toward a bench by the water's edge.

"You," he said, over his shoulder, not bothering to look. "Get the bike to the garage."

Abi scowled as he walked off, secure in the knowledge that whatever else Skill did, it didn't give you eyes in the back of your head.

The bike was a nightmare, an incomprehensible lump of metal reeking of petrol and hot leather. She didn't have a clue how to get it moving. Luke would have known.

"Brilliant idea!" she heard Daisy sigh, with dreamy approval.

Abi turned to see what Gavar the Marvelous was doing now. On the lake a long, shallow keelboat was gliding across the water. On the far shore, the doors of the boathouse where it was usually kept stood open. The oars were shipped, lying inside along the length of the hull. There was no one in the boat and no visible means of propulsion. It was heading straight to where Daisy, Gavar, and the baby sat, as if drawn on a string like a toy.

Held upright by her father, Libby kneaded her small feet into his thigh and smacked her hands together.

The boat made a faint plashing noise as it moved smoothly forward. Disturbed, a moorhen gargled and scudded away. Everything else was quiet and still. So Abi heard Heir Gavar's next words very distinctly.

"I'm not doing anything."

Abi stiffened, one hand clenched uselessly around the bike's handlebars. She scanned the wood's edge for any sign of Silyen. She couldn't see anything, but that didn't mean he wasn't there, plotting mischief. There were only rooks, circling.

The prow thudded softly into the bank, right in front of the bench. There was a faint clatter of wood as the oars rolled with the impact. Then the boat swung until the whole length of it rested alongside the bank.

It was possible—just—that the boat might have slipped its mooring in the boathouse and drifted across the lake. But this movement was unnatural. Deliberate.

Abi heard Gavar's next words, full of wonder and pride— and just a touch of disbelief.

"It's not me, Daisy. It's her."

Squirming in her father's grasp, Libby Jardine giggled.

# EIGHT

# LUKE

From his perch high up on the roof parapet, Luke could see right across Millmoor. No one would be charging tourists ten quid to admire the view anytime soon.

What stood out wasn't the shape or size of the slavetown, but its color—or rather, the lack of it. Everything had a drab, drained look, especially now as dusk mildewed the sky. Partly that was because it was all built of concrete and metal. Partly it was because any sunshine simply zapped the air pollution into perma-smog. But mostly, he'd come to realize, it was inside your head.

Frankly, it wasn't the setting he would have picked for his seventeenth birthday. Nor were this evening's activities what he would have planned for his big day, either.

But as he sat there, waiting for Renie and trying to ignore the fear and excitement knotting his gut, Luke thought there was nothing he'd rather be doing than playing Doc Jackson's game. With every day that passed, he saw more clearly the injustice of the slavedays and the resilience of those enduring them.

"Always look at the people, not at the mass," Jackson had told him. "A face, not the crowd. Look at the world, not at the ground. Every little detail you see is a victory."

So as he kicked his heels on the rooftop, Luke tried doing just that. He looked out over the low-rise office buildings that surrounded him, toward the residential high-rises beyond. He picked out a potted plant silhouetted on a windowsill; a towel in bright soccer team colors hanging over a door. In the yellow light of a dormitory stairwell, a couple were snogging up against the wall. He let his eyes move swiftly on. A girl sat by a window, reading. That made him think of his sisters—she looked about Daisy's age, and Abi was rarely without a book in her hand.

Would he be up here on the roof now if his family were in Millmoor with him? Luke wasn't sure. It was one thing to risk yourself, but another to endanger those you love by your actions.

And he'd seen a surprising amount of action in the month since he'd reached into the club's fruit bowl, all of it fitted around his backbreaking work in Zone D. Luckily, the guys who shared his dorm had different shift patterns, so coming and going at all hours went unremarked. When it was your turn to sleep, you just pulled the thin blankets over your head, wrapped the lumpy pillow round your ears, and tried to ignore it all.

In fact, ignoring things was a talent every Millmoor resident acquired. And Luke had realized that worked to the advantage of the slavetown's authorities. You weren't so likely to look out for others if you felt your own survival depended on looking out for yourself.

Well, no one could ignore what he and Renie were about to do.

A low whistle startled Luke so violently he nearly fell off his perch, and he swore. Behind him, Renie let out a noise for which the word "cackle" was surely invented.

"Wotchit," she said. "Falling ten stories ain't the best way to celebrate, birthday boy."

Luke swiveled to glare at her, swinging his legs back over into safety.

"Very funny," he said. "Ha-ha. I've got what I need—have you?"

He kicked at the bundle coiled at his feet. It was a length of rope ending in a cat's cradle of webbing and oval metal clips. He'd nicked the rig from a shed round the back of the casting plant. The Zone D maintenance teams used them to clean inside some of the larger machines. He and Renie had a different use for it tonight.

"I got my necessaries right here," said Renie, patting the bulging pocket on the front of her hoodie, which rattled. "Lemme have a look at that rope. You'd better remember your knots, boy scout."

"And you'd better remember your letters," retorted Luke, nettled by her need to check on him. "You did spend long enough at school to learn the alphabet, I presume?"

"Yee-owch," said Renie, sticking her middle finger up. "I ain't never been to school. But yeah, I can write three measly letters."

"Never been to school?" said Luke, incredulous. "Is that even possible? Didn't the council come and find you?"

"What council?" said the girl, holding on to Luke's sleeve with one hand and leaning cautiously over the edge to scan the streets below. "Ain't no councils in here, is there?"

"What?"

Luke tried to puzzle through the possibilities, but none of them quite fitted.

"Long story," said Renie. "Tell you later, if you doesn't drop me. But now it's time to go. This way."

She disappeared across the roof, cat-footed and sure. Luke slung the rope over his shoulder and followed. He could barely make out where he was going, which was unnerving—though maybe it was better not to see the drop. The sky was darkening by the minute. It wasn't that late in the afternoon, but it was early November and darkness was closing in fast.

As it was a Sunday, the administration district was deserted. Slaves weren't trusted to work in the MADhouse—the nickname given to the headquarters of Millmoor Administration. The staff were all free employees, recruited from distant parts of the country so there'd be no risk of favoritism. They left the slavetown at the end of each day, and the offices were locked on weekends. Security patrolled, but Renie knew their movements. She and Jackson had timed this perfectly.

"Oof!"

Luke had run straight into Renie's back, and she had every right to look annoyed, given the precariousness of their footing. They'd passed from the relative safety of the roof onto a narrow grate walkway that joined the building to its neighbor. There was no handrail, just a low metal lip along each side.

"Keep your mind on the game," Renie scolded, sounding more like Mum than any thirteen-year-old had a right to. Then she relented; he must have looked pretty shamefaced. "Not bein' mean. Just, we can't ever afford to clock off, you know? Not till a thing's done."

"No," said Luke. "It won't happen again, I'm sorry—and for saying what I did earlier. I'm a bit petrified, to be honest."

"S'okay," Renie said, her pinched features softening a bit. "Me too. This is a biggie."

She pointed into the gloom ahead. "Here we go. This top floor is the Overseer's Office, for the Overbitch, an' then all her cronies beneath her. That's where I'll go down. Do a bit of re-decorating."

Renie turned and spat expressively over the side of the walkway, then headed for the spot she'd indicated. Luke followed, careful to keep two paces behind, no more, no less.

What had Renie meant about having no schooling? How had she acquired her intimate knowledge of every corner of Millmoor? Could she really have been here for years? That would explain a lot, not least her feral ways and scrawny size.

She'd helped the Doc give the briefing earlier, describing in detail how Luke could make his way up to the rooftop without being seen. She'd outlined the route Oz and Jessica would take, too. They were way across on the other side of Millmoor, near the vehicle depot. Asif and Jackson were at the largest call-center complex. How were they all getting on? he wondered.

But no, mustn't get distracted.

Focus, Luke.

Renie was waiting for him, jiggling up and down on the balls of her feet. The thing in her pocket gave a muffled rattle.

The roof here had no parapet, just an edging that came up to about knee height. If he lost his footing, it wouldn't be enough to stop him going over.

He pulled the rope bundle from his shoulder, laid it out on the concrete, and started sorting through it. When he asked her, Renie stepped into the harness without demurring. It was far too big, of course, but he tightened what straps he could until she was cradled in it well enough. He'd spotted a good anchor point for his end of the rope—some sort of maintenance hatch in the roof. The MADhouse occupants presumably never had to wait to get their air-con fixed if the filter busted.

And then for the knots he'd carefully learned. There was a figure-eight follow-through to secure Renie's harness, with the loop at his end so he could control her descent. He tugged the lines he'd laid down and practiced paying out the rope to make sure everything flowed smoothly. Next he ran his hands along the edge of the building, checking for anything that might snag or fray the rope. Renie watched him.

"Very thorough," she said approvingly. "You're getting good at this, I can see."

Luke grinned back, running a hand over his fuzzy scalp—some bloke in the dorm had had a go at it with electric clippers a few days ago. Mum would have freaked at the result, but Luke thought it looked sharp.

"Can't be dropping you, can I? Not even the Doc would be able to scrape you back together."

"Don't be so sure." Renie checked her watch. "Come on, kiddo, it's time."

He was going to protest at being called "kiddo" by a thirteen-year-old, but Renie avoided any retort by stepping backward off the roof.

Luke staggered as the rope went taut. But it held. His heart was banging away beneath his ribs: should-have-done-another-check-did-I-anchor-it-firmly-enough-what-if-the-knot's-loose-what-if—

"More!" Renie's voice floated up from the darkness below. "Three yards. Slowly."

Luke paid out the rope, little by little. From over the edge came a rattle as Renie drew the canister from her pocket and shook it. He heard the pop of the plastic lid coming off, then the hiss as she sprayed the letter as large as she could make it. Luke wondered what color paint she'd purloined. Something neon would be good. Or red, like blood. He imagined it dripping slowly down the building. Yeah, nice effect.

"Lower!" Renie called.

Luke shifted to feed out more rope, wincing as it scraped along the roof edge. Again, he heard the whir of the ball bearings and the hiss of propellant gas. He felt their connection flex as Renie twisted her body. The rope dug into his palm, but didn't cut, and when she called up he paid out one final length. Renie was fifteen yards down, and despite her sparrow weight the tension through the cord was unbelievable.

The third letter. He heard a huff of effort as the girl strained to draw it in one long, smooth shape. Then the plastic cap snapped back in place. The smell of wet paint and aerosol drifted up from the darkness, tickling his nose.

"Up!" he heard.

He braced his foot against the edge and prepared to heave the deadweight that was Renie back up and onto the roof. Oz would easily manage Jessica, but he wondered if the Doc and Asif had tossed a coin to decide who did the heavy lifting in their team.

Of course not. No coins in Millmoor. Just one more bizarre thing about life here, he thought, as he grunted and hauled. No cash. He used to wonder at the stories in his mum's magazines about women who bankrupted themselves shortly after finishing their days. They emptied their savings accounts from their lives before and blew it on handbags, shoes, junk like that. He thought he understood their madness a bit better now.

He understood a lot of things better now. He'd just turned seventeen, but he felt at least ten years older.

But age wasn't the only alteration on his mind as he stood there, steadily moving hand over hand on the rope until he saw Renie's fingers scrabbling at the roof edge. He was getting stronger, his muscles harder. Who knew that all it took to get ripped was a steady diet of canteen cuisine and some serious slave labor? It was a winning combination, albeit not one likely to catch on.

Millmoor was changing him, inside and out. And he remembered Renie's words when he'd done his first job for her: *Millmoor changes people. But you get to choose how.*

"Awright!" the girl said as he grabbed both her hands and lifted her up bodily. He lowered her to the safety of the roof and she crouched there a moment, wiping her face with the flat of her palm.

"Let's get back to base," she said. "I wanna hear from Jackson exactly why we've all been kindly giving a paint job to Millmoor's prettiest landmarks."

She stepped out of the harness and they were off. Back across the walkway, down the fire escape, into the dank-smelling service stairwell, and out.

The street lighting was intermittent and dim, but Renie knew where all the lampposts were. As they rounded each corner they were always on the unlit side of the street. She kept up a mumbling, sarcastic commentary like the world's least tippable tour guide: shortcuts here, CCTV cameras there. But it wasn't Millmoor Luke was curious about.

"How do you know all this?" he asked her. "How long have you been here? Kids can't start days until they're ten, and then only accompanied by their parents. Yours must have brought you, but you never mention them."

Even as the words left his mouth, an awful thought occurred and he kicked himself. What if Renie's parents were dead, both killed in some terrible accident?

But it was somehow even worse than that.

Renie's jaw stopped its urgent working of the gum in her mouth. When she turned to Luke her expression was ferocious. He was glad the darkness half hid it.

"All that stuff," she said, hunching her shoulders, hands deep in her pocket. "That's the rules they tell you about. The rules for people like you. Ain't the rules for all of us.

"Me mam and da was decent folk, and they tried to do their best for us kids. Mam was young—she'd been your age when she had the first of us. And Da didn't have much education to speak of. But they loved each other, and me an' my brothers. Da provided for us all the best way he could. It just weren't a way the police exactly approved of.

"Stuff would turn up at home, nice stuff he'd nicked. Mam would tell us not to touch it in case we broke it so it couldn't be sold. We moved around a lot, so he never got noticed too much in one place, I guess. But someone musta noticed eventually. I was about six when we was all rounded up." She trailed off and stared ahead into the gloom, as if looking for her family among the pooling shadows.

"Didn't know what happened to any of 'em until Asif helped me look up my records one time when we was on a game. Da got sent to one of the lifer places; my brothers, Mam, and me was parceled out all over. I came to Millmoor. Used to live in a block with a few other oo-moos—that's kids," she added, seeing Luke's blank look. "Unaccompanied Minors Under Sixteen. Sounds cute, right? It weren't. I ran away about two years ago. Fended for myself; never got caught. I hid out in the old part of town, the original bit. It's all derelict and no one ever goes there.

"But I needed to move around to get food and stuff, so I cut out my tracking chip. Didn't do a good job." The girl pulled up her sleeve and Luke winced at the twisted mass of scar tissue. It looked like Renie had carved a fillet from her flesh. "Got infected and I thought I was gonna die, but at least I would have died free. I weren't going to a hospital to get taken in again. Then Doc Jackson found me."

Luke was aghast. You were always told that there were no children by themselves in slavetowns. That people were only given life for really wicked crimes, like murder or rape. Weren't there foster homes for youngsters like Renie?

"Foster homes is for kids what can be fixed," she said bitterly. "Kids like you if something bad happens to your family. Not kids like me what's born unfixable. You've got a lot to learn."

Didn't he just.

He'd thought he was getting the hang of this place, and that in the club he'd found a way to fight back against its petty cruelties.

But it turned out that behind the petty cruelties were bigger cruelties. Worse ones. Did adults know that things like this went on—small children being abandoned in slavetowns—but never mention it? Or was everyone completely oblivious?

Luke wasn't sure if Renie regretted sharing all that with him, because she was subdued for the rest of the way back. When they reached that day's HQ, where Jackson and Asif were already waiting, she perched on a stack of cardboard boxes without a word. It was Luke who responded to the Doc's inquiry about their mission's success with a big thumbs-up.

"Now are you going to tell us what it was all about?" Luke asked. "Why the MADhouse now has the word 'YES' written on it in letters three yards high?"

"And Comms-1," added Asif. "He didn't tell me why, even when we were out there."

"Let's wait till Jessica and Oz get back," Jackson said with a smile. "They won't be long. And rest assured Hildy and Tildy have been busy, too."

He gestured to the boxes. They hadn't been there when the club had met earlier.

The ditcher sisters staggered through the door with one more box, then collapsed into flimsy stacking chairs. Hilda tipped her head back, staring at the ceiling, while Tilda massaged her neck with both hands. They looked knackered. Soon after, Jessica and Oz burst in. They were sweaty-faced and panting, as if they'd been running, but had triumphant grins on their faces.

"All done, Doc," said Jessica, banging a can of spray paint down on the shelf nearest Jackson.

"Now spill," said Oz. "You've got 'YES' written all over that depot—Jessie got a bit carried away—and we want to know why. Did the Overbitch ask for your hand in marriage, and this is your way of showing how much you love her?"

Even Renie, who was still looking subdued, snorted at that.

"Good guess," said Jackson wryly. "But no. And, Asif, no to your theories. All of them. Especially the one about aliens. Hilda, maybe you'd like to show everyone what the two of you have been up to?"

Hilda nodded and rose from her chair. Flipping the top off one of the boxes, she pulled out a printed sheet and held it up.

"Ladies and gentlemen," she announced, "I give you the Chancellor's Proposal: the abolition of the slavedays."

Jessica actually gasped. Even Asif stopped fidgeting.

Surely this was some kind of wind-up?

"No one has a vote on the Proposal except the Equal parliamentarians, of course," said Jackson. "And apart from maybe a handful, they'll all vote no. But I don't think they realize what they've done by even having this debate. All it would take for the slavedays to end—the loss of liberty, the abuses, the drudgery, all of it—is for a few hundred Equals to open their mouths and say 'yes.' One little syllable after the Third Debate, in the East Wing of Kyneston next spring, and everything's gone."

Jessica retied her ponytail with a brisk snap of the elastic, a gesture that reminded Luke painfully of Abi. When she spoke her tone was brisk, too. "Not to be a party pooper, Jack, but are you sure? How do you know this?"

The Doc paused for a moment, looking round the room. He's wondering if he can trust us, Luke realized.

And that was when it hit him: loyalty goes both ways.

When this all began, Luke had lost sleep over whether he could trust Jackson. Whether the club wasn't some elaborate trap. But once he'd played a few games and there'd been no visit from Kessler, no hands pulling him roughly from his bed in the middle of the night, he had forced himself to let go of a little of that fear. The Doc was for real.

But for Jackson, any one of them could betray him—at any time.

Well, not Luke. Never Luke.

"I'm in touch with someone on the outside," Jackson said eventually. "An Equal. More than that—someone close to power."

Renie rocked forward so fast it was a wonder she didn't fall off the boxes. Hilda and Tilda exchanged startled glances. Jessica put the end of her hair in her mouth and chewed like a nervous girl, not a grown woman. It was Oz who spoke.

"Crikey, Doc," he said. "Bit of a surprise you been keeping there. Care to explain?"

Jackson placed his hands palms-down on the table and stared at them for a moment.

"He sees every shadow in the House of Light," the Doc said,

as if telling them about someone he was pointing out across a room at a party. "He believes in this cause—our cause."

"And you trust him?" asked Hilda bluntly.

"I do," said Jackson. He opened his mouth as if to say more, then decided against it.

"Why has no one heard about this Proposal?" Asif asked. "Because it's too hot to handle? Media blackout?"

Jackson looked like a man trying to smile who had forgotten how you did it. "Sort of," he said eventually. "There are acts of Skill called the Silence and the Quiet. The Silence makes you forget things. At the end of the Proposal session, the Chancellor laid it on all the commoners, the Observers of Parliament. The Equal parliamentarians have submitted to the Quiet. They remember everything, but the Quiet prevents them communicating what they know to anyone who's not also an MP—even to their own families. Let's just say that we found a way around that."

The room fell silent.

Luke was appalled. The Equals could take your memories? "Silence" you with Skill? It was unthinkable. They did it in Abi's novels, of course—caddish heirs seducing girls, then making them forget all about it with a snap of their fingers. But never in a million years had Luke imagined it was true.

How could you hope to win against people who could do that?

Except Jackson must think you could, because he leaned in toward them like a general imparting battle plans to his trusted officers.

Which, Luke realized, was exactly what the Doc was. He

felt dizzy, as if he'd just downed a cocktail of one part thrill and two parts terror. Over ice.

"I'm glad you're shocked," Jackson said, looking at each of them in turn with those clear blue eyes. "It means you're all thinking about the task ahead of us. Really thinking about it. Everyone in this slavetown needs to know about this Proposal. Everyone needs to understand that abolition is so close we could just reach out and take it—if we dare. This could be the best chance we get in our lifetimes of ending the slavedays."

His eyes met Luke's, and Luke couldn't look away.

"This is the long game," the Doc said. "We need to be the winners when it ends."

# NINE

# ABI

If she wanted to discover why Luke wasn't welcome at Kyneston, Abi's only option was Jenner. But he'd warned her not to ask.

So how could she get him to tell her?

Perhaps if she could win his trust. His admiration. Maybe even his affection?

She snorted at that, and turned back to the heap of unopened mail on her desk. There might be none so daft as a clever girl in love, as Mum would say, but Abi wasn't that deluded. She wanted Jenner's affection all right, but that would be true even if Luke were at Kyneston with the rest of them.

She picked up the letter opener, a heavy silver knife bearing the Jardine family crest of the salamander embowered—a fire-breathing lizard fenced into a circular garden—and attacked the pile of envelopes.

The fourth one down had handwriting on it that she recognized. Her own.

It was the birthday card they'd sent Luke, returned unopened from Millmoor. "Inadmissible" had been stamped across it. Abi growled with frustration. It didn't even bear a censor's mark. They hadn't bothered to open it and see that it was nothing more seditious than a card, handmade by Daisy. The three-month no-communication period for all slavetown newcomers hadn't expired yet for Luke, so they'd simply sent it back.

Soon, though. She glanced at the calendar on her desk, the red ring around a date at the start of December, just days away. The three months were up then and they'd all get news on how Luke was doing, assuming he was as desperate to write to them as they were to hear from him.

Abi hoped he was being sensible and toeing the line. Surely life in Millmoor couldn't be much worse than having a rubbish job and a crummy shared flat out in the real world. Luke probably spent his days packing boxes in a factory, and had a crowd of friends already.

At least that was what Abi told herself. She tried not to think about that guard, Kessler, or the day Luke had been ripped away from them. She didn't dwell on the fact that Luke—that all of them—were just *chattels of the state* with *no rights at all*. She pushed away the image of Dad on his knees, blood streaming down his face, and Luke being prodded into the van with a baton.

Whatever it took to make Jenner Jardine bring Luke here, Abi intended to do it. She'd started with what she did best: work.

In nearly three months at Kyneston, she had already made

improvements to how the Family Office ran. She'd created a spreadsheet of the estate year, color-coded and filled with calendar alerts and reminders. She'd asked certain of the key staff—if you could call slaves that—to begin monthly audits.

She'd tried not to come across as a bossy upstart, and they'd mostly listened when she explained that better organization was in everyone's interests. Her message was that the smoother the house and estate ran, the less chance there was of Lord Jardine or Heir Gavar blowing their fuses. They'd all seen that often enough that they readily agreed. The housekeeper was particularly friendly, and Abi was always welcome belowstairs for a cup of tea and a scone. However, she knew the grizzled Master of Hounds hadn't taken kindly to this northern city girl bringing her notions to his ancient southern estate.

As for Jenner himself? Well, he was a dream.

He was sweet and funny, hardworking and thoughtful. An itemization of all the ways in which he was generally wonderful would be even longer than Abi's to-do list.

Gavar was probably the type most girls would go for, but his temper meant his buff physique was more intimidating than appealing. And the Young Master was simply too spooky even to think of in those terms. So, yes, Jenner was the only one of the three she didn't find scary. By itself this wasn't a ringing endorsement. But add in all the plus points as well, and Miss Abigail Amanda Hadley had quite a crush going on.

Could he ever feel the same? The sensible bit of Abi's brain insisted that was impossible. But the illogical bit (which was evidently bigger than she'd ever suspected) continued to hoard small moments, the way the back of her desk drawer accumulated pen lids and paper clips. A glance; an inquiry about her family; a spurious pretext for keeping her late; a hand on her arm while pointing something out.

No single action meant a thing, by itself. But taken together, could they add up to something more?

So she was disappointed to answer his summons to the Great Solar early one morning, only to find the chamber filled with what looked like every house-slave at Kyneston. One of her friends from the kitchens explained that it was the annual pre-Christmas deep clean. Everyone mucked in. Abi was reluctantly collecting a duster when Jenner appeared at her elbow.

"Not you, Miss Hadley, if I may? I was hoping you might help me in the library."

He led her there, then dithered over whether or not to shut the door. Abi wasn't much of an expert at "reading the signs," as a flirty schoolfriend had once termed it. But the situation seemed somehow promising.

To hide her confusion, Abi turned to look at what was laid out on the table. Resting on a cover of thick gray felt were three paintings and an unframed canvas, several document cases, and some custom-made book boxes.

"I thought you'd enjoy this more than dusting," said Jenner, having eventually closed the door and joined her. "With my brother's wedding to Bouda Matravers at the end of March, as well as the Third Debate, Mother suggested we show off some family treasures to our guests. It's only once a generation that the heir marries, after all. I've been digging out a few possibilities."

Abi studied the paintings, all portraits. She recognized the subjects of the largest two canvases, but had no idea about the other two sitters. One was a long-necked young woman wearing a dress the same bronze color as her hair. She petted a large lizard that nestled in her arms. The other, unframed, was a wistful, black-eyed boy aged seven or eight.

"This is Cadmus Parva-Jardine, the Pure-in-Heart," she said confidently, touching the largest picture in its gilded frame shaped like a laurel wreath. Jenner nodded.

Her fingers trailed onto the next. She knew what this man had done. Was it only that knowledge which made his likeness seem both proud and vicious, or did his deeds truly show in his face?

"Cadmus's father, Lycus Parva. Lycus the Regicide. He killed Charles the First and Last."

She shuddered. Lycus had used nothing but Skill to kill the Last King, and the histories said that Charles had taken four days to die on the scaffold at Westminster. It was written that the spectacle was so terrible that pregnant women watching miscarried, and men went mad.

"This is Cadmus's mother, Clio Jardine," Jenner said, pointing to the woman in the bronze dress. "It was painted to mark her marriage to Lycus. You see the walled garden behind her? That's the Jardine family emblem. And she's holding a salamander, the Parva heraldic device. Our coat of arms today combines both, although the Parva motto has dropped out of use. Silyen's fond of it, but it's a bit too self-effacing for Jardine tastes."

Abi looked at the painted banner. *Uro, non luceo.* "I burn, not shine." An appropriate match for the salamander, that legendary creature said to breathe fire and renew itself in flames.

Clio gazed sideways out of the canvas. Her face was framed by artful ringlets, her eyebrows painted in bold arches. Her features and coloring, though, Abi had seen before. They were like those of the young man standing beside her.

Abi looked from Clio to Jenner, and it was as if a wall as impenetrable as Kyneston's own had reared up between them. He might not have the Skill, but he had the blood. These impossible names from history books were his ancestors. His family. His great-great-greats.

Jenner hadn't noticed her reaction, and continued his tale. "Clio was the only offspring in the Jardine direct line. This was before female succession was permitted, so she couldn't inherit Kyneston. The house was due to pass to a male cousin. But when her son Cadmus's incredible Skill became apparent as a teenager, he was co-opted as the Jardine heir and given the double surname Parva-Jardine.

"Cadmus was a scholarly man and lived a quiet life. He married young, and when that first wife died he was grief-stricken and buried himself in his research. You know what happened next: the Revolution. Lycus, the father, killed the king. Cadmus, the son, restored peace. He tore down the palace and built the House of Light, in the Great Demonstration. And after becoming our first Chancellor, he married again. It was the eldest son from that marriage, Ptolemy Jardine, who next inherited Kyneston. But it shouldn't have been."

"Why not?" said Abi, mesmerized by the unfolding story. "Who should it have been?"

"Someone we never talk about," said Jenner. He pointed to the final picture. "Him."

The boy had the large black eyes of Lady Thalia and the Young Master, but none of her sparkle or his arrogance. His expression was soft and sad. The picture wasn't particularly well executed—the clothing was flat and the boy's hands were all wrong. But the artist had captured some deep sorrow in the child.

"Father won't let this one be displayed," Jenner continued, a strange note to his voice. "It would have been destroyed years ago were it not the only picture we have which was painted by Cadmus himself."

"So who is he?"

Abi was hooked by this secret that she'd never encountered in all her reading about Kyneston and the Jardines. And another, shameful part of her was thrilled that Jenner wanted to share with her this story that plainly meant so much to him.

"He's me. He's the only other rotten fruit on the family tree. The only one in our great and glorious history with no Skill— until I came along."

And what did you say to that? Abi's mind raced for an answer, but found none. She didn't do people, dammit. She did books. A world of difference.

She cast her mind back to the day they had arrived at Kyneston, Daisy opening her big gob and asking why the Young Master had let them through the gate and not Jenner. His easy, gallant response about his lack of Skill. How many years had he been practicing those lines until he could say them like that? As if they meant nothing at all, when clearly his life was poisoned at its roots by this awful, inexplicable lack.

"Take a close look," Jenner urged.

There were numerous objects displayed around the boy. An empty birdcage with the door shut. A tulip in its prime, upright in a vase but drab and gray, as if a week dead. A sheet ruled with musical staves but without notes. A violin with no strings. Abi peered at the word written at the top of the blank musical score. The nonexistent work was titled in Latin: *Cassus*.

"It means 'hollow,'" Jenner said. "'Empty.' Alternatively: 'useless' or 'deficient.' Which is to say, without Skill. All that"—he gestured at the flower, the birdcage—"that's what my world looks like, to them."

Abi still couldn't think of anything to say. Something careful.

"If he should have inherited Kyneston after Cadmus, then he must be . . . Cadmus's eldest son?"

She was rewarded with the ghost of a smile from Jenner. "I knew you'd get it, Abigail. He's Cadmus's son by his first wife. His name was Sosigenes Parva, but you won't find it in any history book."

So-si-je-knees? Even by Equal standards, the name was a mouthful.

"Doesn't exactly trip off the tongue, does it?" she said, then flushed at her own presumption. But Jenner laughed, brightening a little.

"Don't worry," he said. "I'd be the first to agree. It's a name that, if my father had his way, would never be heard again. As it is, after Cadmus's journals were lost in the Orpen fire, this little picture is the only evidence we have that Sosigenes ever lived."

Abi knew about the great fire of Orpen. It had happened before she was born, but she'd seen shaky footage captured from a helicopter flying beyond the estate wall.

Orpen Mote had been the Parva seat, where Lady Thalia Jardine and her sister, Euterpe, were born and raised. It had burned to the ground in a single night. The two sisters had been absent, but Lord and Lady Parva and their entire household had died as they slept. The shock of discovering her parents' death had plunged Euterpe into the coma in which she still lay.

But more than a house and its inhabitants had been lost. The Parvas' reputation as scholars had continued down the centuries, and Orpen Mote had held the most important collection of books about Skill known to exist anywhere in the world. That had included Cadmus's personal library. All destroyed in the blaze.

But Abi had never heard of any journals kept by the Pure-in-Heart. What documents those would be! How cruel to learn of their existence and their destruction in the selfsame instant.

Jenner was busying himself with the boxes on the table. He pulled one across and flipped back the lid. Inside was thick foam, cut to accommodate the small painting perfectly. He kept his eyes down as he talked.

"No one ever imagined there would be another Skilless child. Cadmus was so powerful, you see, that the family decided that Sosigenes's mother was to blame for her son's condition. She died in childbirth, so it was easy to conclude that she was weak. In fact, 'Sosigenes' means 'born safely,' so maybe the birth had been traumatic for him, too. It's a tidy explanation."

"Might that be true?" Abi said, unsure whether or not this was dangerous territory, but too curious not to ask. "And could a difficult birth be the answer for you, too?"

Jenner smiled again, but still didn't look at her. "Mother pushed me out in about five minutes flat, if that's what you're asking. Apparently Gavar was an enormous baby, so Sil and I came into the world very easily." He made a face. "I've never felt the need for more information on that.

"The funny thing is, no one noticed at first—about me, I mean. Some babies show their Skill very early. Silyen apparently set the nursery curtains on fire when he was just a few days old. And Nanny was constantly finding birds perched on his crib singing to him. They had to watch him every minute. But it's also perfectly normal for there to be no strong showing until the age of four or five.

"Mother swears I did a few things that resembled Skill, but they must have just been accidents, because by my fourth birthday—nothing. Nor by my fifth. Nor my sixth. Apparently, though I don't remember this, I then announced that I wasn't going to have any more birthdays. I must have understood that each one was an important milestone that I kept missing."

He had finished fussing with the box. The painting had been swaddled, the lid closed, the tape secured. Jenner's hands rested on top of the box, curled around nothing. He lifted his eyes. They were suspiciously bright.

"The wall still recognizes me, because I have the family blood. The gate appears for me, but I can't open it. It's the same for little Libby. When I was younger, there was even some hoo-ha about whether I was my father's son. As if that could ever be doubted."

Jenner pushed his fingers through his hair, the exact same color as his father's. Tugged, as if he wanted to tear a bit out and show her, as proof of his parentage. "Anyway, I know you've wondered about it all. I've seen it in your face. So now you know. No great mystery." He forced a smile. "In my own way, I'm even more remarkable than Silyen."

Abi felt like her heart had been replaced with one that was several sizes too big for her chest. She took a step closer.

"Yes, you are," she told him. "Remarkable. Amazing."

"Amazing?"

She touched his cheek, feeling guiltily grateful he didn't have Skill. If he did, he would surely blast her through the bookcases for her impertinence. But he didn't move, only raised his own fingers to cover hers, as if to confirm that her gesture was real.

Then Abi practically slapped him as she recoiled at the sound of the library door opening.

The box was knocked off the table and Jenner bent to pick it up. That left Abi, cheeks flaming like the Parva salamander, to face whoever had interrupted them.

It could have been worse—but it could have been a lot better. Lady Thalia was walking toward them, the hem of her silken housecoat swinging, while in the doorway waited Lady Hypatia Vernay.

As Lady Thalia cooed at her son over how smoothly the deep clean was progressing, the older woman stared flintily at Abi. She extended her arm and, with a sinking feeling, Abi saw that the elderly Equal's leather-gloved claw held the end of a leash.

"Girl, take this animal to the kennels," she commanded. And when Abi hesitated, *"Now."*

Abi didn't dare look at Jenner, merely bobbed a curtsey. Keeping her head down, she went to take the leash. The dog-man lay on the carpet in the corridor outside. Abi stepped out and heard the door close firmly behind her.

She'd seen Lady Hypatia's hound several times since that first day, but only ever from a distance. Being confronted with him like this almost froze her with shock.

He was crouched awkwardly, his back forced lower than would be natural for a human on all fours, as if trying to replicate the gait of a dog. His torso was emaciated, and though his legs and arms were sinewy, the muscles looked all wrong. He was entirely naked, coarse dark hair covering much of his legs, buttocks, and lower back. The hair on his head was thin and flowed down his neck in a greasy pelt. His age was entirely unguessable.

"Hello," Abi tried, when her voice was back under control. "What's your name?"

The man whined and trembled. If he really had been a dog, his ears would have been pressed flat to his skull, his tail between his legs.

"No? How long have you been like this? Why?"

His hands pattered against the carpet, the nails snagging audibly. He ducked his head and slung back his haunches, just like a dog in distress.

"Can you even speak? What have they done to you?" Abi's mouth went dry with horror.

The whining came again, louder and more urgent, almost gulping. The last thing Abi wanted was to be caught like that, as if she were the one tormenting the man. Fright made her do what reason would not and she tugged on the leash.

"Come on, then. Let's get you to the kennels."

They crossed the Solar, and Abi sensed the other slaves' heads turning to stare. She stopped by Kyneston's great front door. Even though it was closed, icy air leaked over the threshold, and she knew that outside frost lay thick on the ground. Surely the man would catch his death of cold?

She stood uncertainly, until the dog-man himself scrabbled against the door, as if begging to be let out. It hardly seemed possible, but maybe he preferred being in the kennels to the treatment he received at Lady Hypatia's hands.

The frost hadn't lifted and the cold was smothering as Abi stepped outside. When she looked back, the house was already hidden by fog, which lay over it like a giant white dust sheet. Even sounds were muted. She and Hypatia's hound could have been the last things alive.

Unnerved, Abi hurried in the direction that she thought the stables lay. The temperature wasn't much above freezing, and the man was already shivering so violently that the leash was jerking in her hand. She looked at the leather loop with revulsion. What if she just dropped it? Let him disappear and report that she'd lost him in the mist.

Except how would he escape? The wall was still there, the gate perpetually hidden without a Jardine to summon it.

Relief thawed her when they reached the cluster of outbuildings. Abi crossed the cobbled yard, then entered the long, low kennels set at an angle to the stables. It was warmer in here, and the smell of dogs was overpowering.

A figure appeared from the gloom: the Master of Hounds. He came forward to meet her with no trace of welcome.

"Well, if it isn't Miss Bossyboots," he said, sneering. He saw the dog-man. "Lady Hypatia's back, then."

Abi held out the leash, but the man made no move to take it.

"Put it in 20. I keep it separate on account of the noise it makes."

Number 20 was a metal pen, one of four in a dilapidated section of the kennels that appeared otherwise unused. It had a mesh roof and a barred door that bolted on the outside. Inside, dirty straw thinly covered the concrete floor.

Abi's hand hesitated over the collar, then she unclipped the lead and the dog-man slunk into the enclosure. He curled up on the straw and buried his head against his naked chest. The soles of his feet were cracked and filthy, and his skin was red and raw from the frosty walk.

The kennel-master came back with a couple of metal dishes, one containing water, the other a mixture of dry biscuits and a pinkish-brown jelly. Dog food. He put them both down and slid them into the pen with the tip of his boot, before dragging the door shut and shooting the bolt.

"Have you got the leash?" Abi handed it over, and he hung it on a nail. "Can't leave it with that, who knows what it'd try, eh? Not that I'd blame it, being the dog of a bitch like Hypatia."

He spat expressively over the pen. Its occupant was now drinking the water, not lifting the bowl with his hands, but crouched over it slurping as a real dog would. The Master of Hounds saw Abi watching.

"You never seen Lord Crovan's handiwork before, eh? Lord Jardine reckons the man could teach even me something about breaking in animals."

He laughed unpleasantly and Abi couldn't hide her disgust.

"Oh, don't you go looking like that, young lady. This one was Condemned, and rightly so. His mistress may be cruel, but he deserved it."

With a final rattle of the cage door to make sure it was secure, the kennel-master threaded a padlock through the bolt and clicked it shut. He took a ring of keys from his pocket and flicked to a small aluminum one, which he unpeeled and dropped into Abi's palm. Then he sauntered off, whistling. As he disappeared round the corner, the foxhound pack started up barking and whining at the return of their king.

Abi looked at the key, reluctant even to close her fingers around it. She didn't want to be this creature's keeper—this *man's,* she corrected herself. She would take the key back to the house and deliver it to Lady Hypatia. Let her do with it what she would.

Maybe the old woman would still be in the library. Maybe Jenner would be, too.

Abi gratefully let her mind fill back up with thoughts of the Skilless Jardine son. What he had shown her and what it meant. What had passed between them earlier. What might have happened, had they not been interrupted.

So when the hand seized her ankle, she screamed. The fingers were ice-cold and bone-thin, but strong. Much stronger then she had imagined.

"Shhh . . ."

The sound was almost unrecognizable as a human voice. If wolves could speak, they'd sound like this after a night of howling. It made the hairs on the back of Abi's neck prickle up. The grip on her ankle tightened, and sharp nails pierced her sock through to her skin.

The voice rasped again.

"Help me."

# TEN

# EUTERPE

He'd told her his name was Silyen.

Euterpe couldn't say for sure how long he'd been visiting her here at Orpen. But he'd been just a boy when he came for the first time.

On that day she had been sitting in a deck chair in the sunshine, looking around for Puck, who must have scampered off after rabbits again. She heard the soft sound of a violin playing somewhere nearby. It seemed like ages since she'd last seen anyone, so she had called out to the musician, inviting him into the garden. A short while later a dark-haired young boy appeared between the rosebushes, and when she gave him a wave he followed the box-hedged path to where she sat.

He'd stood there looking at her with some astonishment— and she was no less surprised by him. He was aged about ten, and his resemblance to her and Thalia was startling. It was al-

most like seeing a male version of herself. For a fleeting, confused instant, Euterpe wondered if this child was her brother.
But how could you have a brother and not know it?

A dull throbbing started up at the base of her skull—she
must have been sitting in the sun too long without her hat. But
she forgot her discomfort when the strange boy's glance flicked
past her to the house behind. His face lit up with wonder.

"Is that Orpen?" he'd asked. "Orpen Mote?"

"Yes. Don't you know it?"

She turned to follow his gaze toward her beloved home. The
sky was blue today and the moat was less water than mirror,
holding a perfect reflection of the house. Orpen's lower parts,
vanishing into the water, were solid stone; the upper half was
plastered and timbered. Small leaded windows were inset here
and there, in a crooked line. Sometimes they were stacked up
over two stories, sometimes three. The great octuplet chimney,
eight flues all in a row, loomed over the North Range. However, there was no smoke pluming from them today. In fact,
the whole place was uncharacteristically tranquil.

"But Orpen is lost," the boy said, seeming reluctant to look
away. "It's gone."

"Lost?" she said, puzzled. "Well, you appear to have found it
well enough. Did someone let you in through the gate?"

"You did," the child said, holding out his hand. "I'm
Silyen—Silyen Jardine. And you're Euterpe Parva. But you're
younger."

"Younger? I'm twenty-four, which makes me quite a bit
older than you," Euterpe told him. He really was a peculiar
child.

The boy—Silyen—scowled and looked like he wanted to

correct her, so she quickly took the offered hand and shook it. It was small and fine-boned but his grip was firm, and she felt the rasp of calluses from his violin bow.

"You're a Jardine?" she asked. "We are to be relatives, then. My sister Thalia is engaged to marry Whittam, Lord Garwode's heir."

Whittam was a beast and Garwode a bully, Euterpe thought privately, but she wasn't going to share that opinion with her Jardine visitor.

"They're not married yet?" Silyen asked. He appeared disconcerted to hear it, though he recovered his composure quickly. He waved his hand, dismissive of weddings as only a young boy could be. "It doesn't matter. We are relatives already."

And Euterpe supposed that was the truth. The Jardines and the Parvas had been connected for hundreds of years, through Cadmus Parva-Jardine himself, and his father, Lycus the Regicide. Both men had lived here at the Mote, and their likenesses still hung on the walls. Their faces were as familiar to Euterpe as those of her own sister and parents. In fact, Silyen bore a more than passing resemblance to them—much more so than to his actual family, the red-haired, green-eyed Jardines.

"Would you like to see the house?" she asked the boy. "I think you'd like some of the portraits."

His smile, unexpectedly, was just as impish as her sister's.

Silyen had been wide-eyed as they'd walked through the house, and had run his hands over everything. He'd rapped his knuckles on the armor in the hall, and picked at threads in the corridor tapestries until she'd told him off. He'd even stopped to smell the flowers she'd had cut that morning and placed in a vase in the dining room. He was clearly a clever child, and she thought she knew what room he'd like most.

When she opened the nailed-oak doors to the library, the boy had actually run in. He stood there spinning in a circle, face upturned with delight, bathed in the muted sunshine that filtered through the protective blinds. He'd gone round the room taking books from the shelves and opening them, holding them carefully by the spine. He'd turn a few pages before replacing a book and moving on to another.

She wasn't surprised when Silyen Jardine had come to visit her many times, after that first occasion. She read to him from beloved books, like *Tales of the King*. They would walk around the garden and grounds together, and Euterpe would point out plants or interesting bits of architecture. Silyen particularly liked hearing stories of her childhood, and the scrapes she was led into by her bold younger sister.

"Tell me about how you and Thalia would go skating," he'd beg.

So she'd tell again the story of their favorite pastime: midsummer ice-skating. How Thalia would appear at Euterpe's bedroom door on the hottest days of the year, holding two pairs of bladed white boots, and would drag her downstairs past their amused parents and out to the moat. There, Thalia would anchor her sister while Euterpe leaned out from the bank and dabbled her fingers into the water. A few tingling moments later it would be frozen down to its bed like thick green glass, and the girls would lace on their skates and spend the August day swooping up and down on the cooling ice.

As Silyen continued to visit, though, he stopped asking for these childish recollections. Euterpe noticed physical changes in him, too. He grew taller. During several visits his voice squeaked, then one day he spoke to her in a man's tones.

Time must be passing, and Euterpe sometimes wondered how it was that so little had happened in her own life. Her sister's marriage hadn't yet taken place, nor did her own wedding to darling Winterbourne get any closer.

She never saw anyone to ask them why that was, though. And whenever she tried to work things out herself, it all became more confused, not less. An ache would swell at the back of her head. It was simpler just to sit and enjoy the breeze, watching the butterflies and wondering where on earth naughty Puck had hidden himself.

She and Silyen fell into a routine. They would walk round the garden and moat, where it was always sunny and warm. Then they'd go indoors and her visitor would sit at the great library table going through some book or another that he'd picked from the shelves. Euterpe would settle into a window seat with a novel or sketchbook.

Her family was never around during Silyen's visits. She would have loved to present him to Thalia, who she knew would be as amazed as she was at how much this strange young man resembled them both. And it was such a shame she hadn't been able to introduce him to Winterbourne, either.

The man she had set her heart on was exceptional, gifted, she told Silyen proudly. He had been top of his year at Oxford and was now at the start of what she knew would be a brilliant legal career. Winterbourne was fascinated by politics, but as a second-born would never sit in the House of Light.

Silyen had smiled at that, and offered the observation that Winterbourne would make a fine Chancellor. And Silyen also knew—everyone did, he said—how very devoted Zelston was to Miss Euterpe.

One summer afternoon a little while after—and how long this summer had been—Silyen closed the book he was reading. He sat back in the library chair, raised his arms above his head and stretched. It was the unmistakable behavior of someone who has completed either a demanding race or a demanding book.

"Finished?" she asked.

"Finished all of them," Silyen said, flexing his fingers. Euterpe heard the fine bones crunch, like a bird in Puck's little jaws. "That was the last." He pushed the book away from him.

"The last?" Euterpe scoffed. "Not even a bookworm like you could have read everything this library contains. You're giving up. I don't blame you—that one's rather boring."

"So I gathered," Silyen said. "You only managed to get halfway through the first chapter."

Euterpe looked at him in astonishment. "How on earth do you know that?"

Silyen held up the book, open at the first page. There was the engraved frontispiece, all in Latin. It proclaimed the text an eighteenth-century Dutch treatise on the use of Skill for the conjuration of trade winds to the Indies.

It was the book that had inspired Harding Matravers's infamous voyage, Euterpe remembered. She'd thought it might be exciting, but it had proved tedious in the extreme. She'd persisted for a few pages, attracted by the author's account of the isle of Java, but had abandoned the volume once it turned technical. Her family had a reputation for scholarship, but Euterpe had never been interested in the workings of Skill. The great power she sensed in herself frightened her and she used it as little as possible.

Silyen was turning the book's pages, each covered in thick type so heavy it was deeply impressed into the paper. Then suddenly there was no more lettering, just blank, yellowing quires of paper. Euterpe blinked in surprise.

"You stopped here," Silyen said. "Page . . ."—he turned back to the last printed sheet—"twenty-three. And this one you never read at all, did you? Such a shame."

He reached across the table and pulled toward him a handsome, heavy volume bound in green leather. The lettering on the spine was in Ancient Greek—a language Euterpe did not understand, though she recognized the book itself. She had never even opened it.

"The title says it's about whether certain Greek myths are accounts or allegories of Skill," the boy said. "Sounded intriguing, but—"

He fanned open the book. There was nothing printed inside it. Every page was blank.

"All these books," he said, frustration evident in his tone. "Lost to the world once, and now lost again, to me."

What did he mean? Euterpe stood up and went to the table to examine the volume.

And that ache was back again. A compression at the base of her skull as if someone held her by the scruff of the neck, like a surplus kitten being hoicked from its indifferent mother. Euterpe rubbed her fingers there. She wished Silyen would leave; she needed some time alone, to rest.

But the boy showed no sign of leaving. He leaned back in his chair and watched her from under lowered eyelids, with those bright black eyes so like her own.

"These aren't the only books in here, are they?" he said.

"There are others, locked in a box. And you've looked through all of them, haven't you? The journals of Cadmus Parva-Jardine."

Despite herself, Euterpe's hand flew to her throat. Her fingers closed around a slender velvet ribbon tied there. At the end of the ribbon, tucked into the front of her dress so it was hidden from sight, hung a little iron key.

"How do you know that?" she asked. "There are plenty of rumors about this library and what it contains. Commoners seem to believe that half the volumes in here are written in the blood of their kind, on parchment made of human skin. But no one outside my family—not even members of your family—knows about those notebooks. They are protected by a hereditary Quiet. We Parvas can only tell our children, and only the children of the heir can pass the secret on."

Silyen looked at her for a long time before responding, as if weighing up what to say. When he spoke his tone was careful and his head tipped to one side, observing her.

"My mother told me about them."

Pain flared inside Euterpe's head. It shot sparks across her vision like the Great Hall hearth when fire finally caught and sent kindling whooshing up the chimney breast. She swayed and pressed one hand to her temples, the other clutching the key. Her breathing came fast and shallow, and she struggled to get it back under control.

A question had come into her head. A mad, foolish question, but she couldn't not ask it.

"Am I your mother?"

Of course she wasn't. How could she be? They were too close in age. She was twenty-four, and Silyen looked around fifteen. Except he had been ten when they first met, which would make her twenty-nine now—and she wasn't, she *knew* she wasn't. She was Euterpe Parva and she was twenty-four years old. Her sister was Thalia Parva. Her beloved was Winterbourne Zelston. Her Jack Russell, Puck, was the most rascally dog in the world, and she lived here at Orpen Mote with her darling parents.

And something awful had happened. Something too terrible to think about.

She staggered backward and sat down on her favorite window seat.

Don't think about it, then. Don't think about it.

Euterpe closed her eyes. She heard Silyen's chair being pushed back from the table, the creak of a floorboard as he came over to her. She felt the touch of a cool hand on her forehead—definitely not a child's hand anymore. Then an arm went around her shoulders and another scooped under her knees, and she was being lifted, carried. A door was kicked open, then another; one more. Then sunlight flooded over her skin. She heard the bees and smelled the flowers. Almost crying with relief, Euterpe Parva let sensation rinse away thought.

When she woke some time later, she was in her deck chair and she was alone.

The next time Silyen came, she led him straight to the library. There, in the middle of the table, stood the cedarwood box. She had fetched it in readiness for his visit. That wasn't a decision she had made lightly. But for some reason she didn't fully understand, it now felt terribly important that another pair of eyes should see the notebooks.

Silyen paused in the doorway. The expression on his face as he looked at the box reminded her of the boy he'd been when they'd first met. He'd gazed at Orpen Mote as if it had been conjured from a storybook. Was he feeling as Euterpe had, when Winterbourne handed her the champagne that day in the garden and she had found a diamond ring sparkling at the bottom of her glass? Silyen appeared rapt, as if gazing on the perfect fulfillment of his most secret hopes and dreams.

Euterpe suddenly missed Zelston so much it hurt.

"I wish Winter was here," she said, unable to help herself. "Or my sister. I feel like I haven't seen them for ever such a long time. I don't even remember the last time I saw my parents. You come and visit, but where are they?"

Silyen's expression was hard to read. It looked like concern, but oddly dispassionate. Like a doctor hearing a patient declare that she feels much improved, when he knows her condition is terminal.

Was she ill? The thought had crossed her mind. It would explain why she was so often confused, why she spent so much time sitting in the fresh air, left in peace and quiet. Had she been ill, and was now convalescing? Perhaps Silyen was some sort of doctor.

But no, he was a boy of fifteen, and plainly the relative he said he was. And she had something to show him. Yes.

She led him over to the box on the table, fished out the little key around her neck, and fitted it to the lock. She heard the complicated four-tongued mechanism click and slide. Lifting the lid, she carefully took them out, one by one. Eleven slim volumes bound in pale vellum, each spine thickly ridged and incised with a number filled in black. They smelled faintly of old leather, musty ink made from who knew what, and the lingering scent of cedarwood. The covers had been worn to an ivory sheen through centuries of handling.

Euterpe's were among the hands that had held these books. She'd loved them since she was a small girl. She opened one, showing Silyen. The text was written in a crabbed, curling hand. It was as if the author had tried to cram as much as possible onto one page, because he feared there wouldn't be enough paper in the world to hold every thought in his head.

Euterpe didn't understand much of what the journals described, but she cherished their connection with her famous ancestor. Loved, too, the occasional verses that Cadmus composed in memory of his dead wife, and his scribbled observations on nature and the seasons. She delighted in the vivid pen-sketches of plants and animals.

Most of all, she treasured the passages overflowing with guilty, heartsick love for his Skilless young son, Sosigenes. The boy they never spoke of, who was a secret folded up and concealed like a love letter in the bosom of their family. Sosigenes's plight drove Cadmus's relentless experimental, analytical exploration of his Skill and what it could do.

All through her childhood, Euterpe had sat in her window seat looking through the notebooks. She had empathized with her many-times-great-grandfather, and absolved him of both the acts laid at his door and the hidden things he had done. She had turned every page.

Silyen's hands were trembling, she noticed, as he finished his check of the journals and laid the last small volume down on the cloth-covered table.

"Thank you," he said, turning to her. His voice was uncharacteristically hoarse. "Thank you so much. You don't know how important this is."

And so they resumed their routine, except instead of library books, Silyen studied the journals of Cadmus Parva-Jardine.

A few other things changed, too. When they walked round the moat, it would be Silyen pointing things out and sharing anecdotes from the notebooks. He recounted scraps of family history, noted alterations to the building and garden made by Cadmus, and repeated the man's witticisms at the expense of members of other great families. Silyen's recall was prodigious, and when she teased him about it, he confessed that he was memorizing large parts of the books by heart.

He was still getting taller, though he wasn't thickening up into the muscular build of the Jardines. Euterpe thought of Whittam, her sister Thalia's betrothed, and shuddered. They must be married by now, she supposed. But if they were, why had she not been at the wedding?

After a time, she noticed that Silyen had finished reading all the notebooks. One day he sat very quietly in the library, just looking at the journals spread out in front of him. Euterpe watched him nervously from the window seat. What else could she show him, to keep him coming to Orpen?

But she needn't have worried. He merely began again, this time seeming to select the books at random. Or he'd set two or three alongside each other, flipping back and forth as if comparing, connecting.

"What are you doing?" she asked, after several visits had

passed in this fashion. "You must have read them all ten times by now."

Silyen looked up, startled. She hardly ever spoke when they were in the library.

"I'm trying to decide what he got right and what he got wrong," he said.

Euterpe scoffed, not unkindly. "Cadmus knew more about Skill than anyone who's ever lived."

"Is that so? He thought more about it, perhaps. But knew more? There's one huge thing he didn't know, that's quite plain in this record."

Euterpe stared at her friend. He clearly wanted her to ask, so with a sigh, she complied.

"Why his son had no Skill," Silyen said.

She blinked in surprise. Those were the parts of the journals that she knew best—the bits that made her cry. What had Silyen seen that she had missed? That every other Parva heir who had read them had also failed to see.

"Bit of a coincidence, don't you think," Silyen said, "that the man with the strongest Skill in all our history should sire a child with none at all."

His words hung between them. Euterpe could almost see them eddying and spinning in the resinous sunlight. Ideas trapped in amber, perfect and unchanging.

"If it's not coincidence," she said, "then what is it? Lots of Skill in one generation uses it up for the next?"

The boy would have tutted if he'd not been so well brought up. "All Cadmus's other children were perfectly normal. No, it's much simpler than that. Cadmus took it."

"Took it?" Euterpe sprang to her feet, brimming with indignation on behalf of her slandered ancestor. "Don't be ridiculous. He loved that boy more than anything. You've read his words: he was haunted his whole life by his son's lack of Skill. Besides, how can you 'take' Skill? I can't believe the hours you've spent reading, and a stupid notion like that is the best you can manage."

"You seem a little defensive," Silyen said, in that bloodless way he sometimes had. At such times the inquisitive black-eyed teenager almost disappeared, leaving only the mechanical operation of an analytical brain. "I wonder why. Your sister, Thalia: her Skill is rather paltry, isn't it? She can hardly boil tea in a cup. Which makes me wonder about you."

Euterpe couldn't bear it. She was not having this conversation. She just wasn't. She threw her sketchbook down on the floor and ran out of the library. When, some hours later, Silyen walked past her deck chair on his way to the garden gate, she pressed her lips together and did not bid him goodbye.

More time passed. Still Winterbourne did not visit. Still Thalia did not appear, a plate of scones in one hand and a jug of cool lemonade in the other. Still naughty Puck did not come bounding up, tail wagging, a scrappy bundle of feathers between his small, sharp teeth.

Euterpe's headaches became worse. The pain was bad even when she sat quite still in her chair in the garden. The buzzing of the bees was so loud as to be unendurable. She felt dizzy when she stood. She stole a glance at her own reflection in the parlor mirror one day, to see how bad she looked. But the face that stared back at her was still radiant, pink-cheeked, unshadowed, and unlined. She was still twenty-four and beautiful.

Forever twenty-four.

Fear slid down her spine like a cold key, stopping her breath.

"What has happened to me?" she asked Silyen the next time he appeared, walking down the box-hedged path from a garden gate that was always just out of sight. "Why am I not getting older? Why do I never see anyone, apart from you? It feels like it is summer always. And my head is getting worse. I can barely think straight anymore."

She studied his face; emotions passed across it, as insubstantial as cloud over sky. Then finally, like the sun, that smile— the same she'd seen the very first day all those years ago. It was Thalia's smile, no doubt about it. And it had indeed been years since Silyen had first walked into the garden. Euterpe realized that now.

Years in which he had changed from boy to man—and she had not changed at all.

Euterpe's skull felt as though it were breaking in two like an egg being cracked from within. She was terrified of whatever strange new life might come crawling out, naked and misshapen.

"This will hurt," Silyen said, holding out both hands to pull her to her feet. "But it's about time. I'm quite curious, too. Mother's told me about it, but not the whole story. And Zelston's never uttered a word."

He put his hands on Euterpe's shoulders to steady her. Then he turned her slowly around to face the house.

Orpen Mote was a charred ruin.

Her childhood home. Everything she had ever known: burnt to ashes. She remembered now. It had been an accident. An ember fallen from the hearth as the household slept.

She and Thalia had been away from home that night, at a ball at Lincoln's Inn. Winterbourne had shaken her awake in the early hours, in a cold guest room. She remembered how she had felt in that instant: breathless with longing that he had finally come to her instead of waiting till their wedding night.

Until she saw from his terrible expression that that was not why he had come at all.

Her parents had died from the smoke without ever waking, their Skill useless to save them, their slaves, or their home.

Euterpe gasped at the onrush of memory. Only Silyen's hands held her up as she swayed.

"Look," he whispered in her ear. "There."

She looked to where he pointed. Three people stood close together, a small white-and-tan dog running in circles around their feet, whining. She recognized Thalia's graceful form, the strong, dark figure of Winterbourne—and there, supported between them, herself. Tears streamed down her other self's face. Her hair was loose and unkempt, and she seemed unable to stand upright under the weight of her despair.

As Euterpe watched, the grief-stricken girl's knees buckled. Winterbourne caught her in his arms and tenderly lowered her to the ground.

Euterpe saw herself huddle facedown upon the scorched and ash-strewn earth. She heard herself let out an inconsolable cry and scrabble through the gray muck as if hoping by some miracle to unearth her parents, whole and unharmed.

Then the first bird dropped from the sky.

None of the three they were watching noticed. They were already surrounded by so much devastation. But Euterpe and Silyen saw what the trio did not.

They saw the wind whip through the still air, sending a

plume of ash gusting upward like a filthy geyser. Debris spiraled in the eddy, and a charred and blackened tree, gutted by fire, toppled to the ground.

Another bird fell heavily: a mallard, flying from the lake. The sky above the ruins of Orpen darkened, and a tangle of cloud was spun by an unseen hand into a skein of storm. Rain lashed down. More small feathered shapes plummeted to the ground.

Euterpe heard Silyen inhale sharply.

"You," he said. He sounded almost excited. "Your Skill. Incredible."

Euterpe didn't feel excited. She felt sick at heart. Her Skill terrified and disgusted her.

"Look!" the pair of them heard Thalia say, as she directed Winterbourne's gaze away from the girl in his arms. The two stared toward the water meadow on the far side of the river, the one that fed the moat.

The river had created a natural firebreak and the fields there had remained fresh and flower-filled, even as the house burned. But now the grass was bending, waving, as if under an approaching wind—and where it bent, it died.

"It's her!" Thalia cried, raising her voice to be heard above the drumming rain. "It's not something she can control; it just happens. I've seen it once or twice before, when she's been really upset. But I've never seen anything like this. We have to stop her."

Puck gave a shrill howl and huddled closer to the stricken girl's skirts. Then the breath went out of him and his legs folded. He curled up against his mistress in death, as he had in life.

From her vantage point in the garden with Silyen, Euterpe let out a choked sob. Tears rolled hotly down her cheeks.

"Stop her!" Thalia yelled at Winterbourne, looking half deranged herself now. Her hair was plastered across her face by the raging storm. Overhead, sheet lightning lit up the blackened sky. "I can't. I'm not powerful enough. But you can."

Euterpe watched her lover bend over her crumpled other self. The girl was shaking violently with the uncontrolled Skill that coursed through her, venting itself in havoc and destruction. But even so, Winterbourne gathered her up and held her to him, tight against his chest. He placed a soft kiss upon her forehead.

The words he spoke were too quiet to be heard by the watchers in the garden. But Euterpe knew them.

Remembered them.

"Hush," he told her, his voice charged with Skill. "I love you. Be still."

The girl in his arms went limp. With shocking suddenness, the storm ceased. Thalia rubbed both hands over her face and pushed back her hair. She looked in disbelief at the devastation around her, and at the clear blue sky above.

In the sun-drenched garden, Euterpe's memory cracked open. A hideous understanding crawled out.

She felt Silyen's hands upon her shoulders. The young man—her sister's child—turned her toward him, and she looked up into his face.

"So now you know," he said. "And soon it'll be time to leave this garden. They're both waiting for you. They've waited for years."

# ELEVEN

# GAVAR

Millmoor slavetown might be going up in flames, but Gavar Jardine failed to see why that was his problem. Particularly not at eight in the morning.

How could a few incidents and arrests up north necessitate an emergency convening of the Justice Council? What was important enough to drag Gavar away from Kyneston and his daughter in the days before Christmas? It was bad enough that soon there'd be the long trip to the Second Debate at Grendelsham, without this summons to London, too.

Through the leaded windows of the overheated council chamber, Gavar saw that it was snowing. He wondered if the slavegirl Daisy would be playing outside in the Kyneston grounds with Libby. Perhaps making a snowman. They'd better both be warmly dressed.

"Pay attention."

His father's whisper in his ear was like a gust of cold blown in from beyond, and it was all Gavar could do not to hunch his shoulders or turn up his collar. He shivered, and tried to focus on the speaker at the far end of the table. It would be easier if the woman's voice were not so monotonous, her face not so unimprovably plain.

". . . seditious literature," she was saying, "distributed across the city, including dormitories, workplaces, even sanitary facilities. That's toilets," she clarified.

Gavar snorted. Did the commoners think Equals never needed to use "sanitary facilities"? Though it was true that some he'd met regarded his kind as hardly human. Gavar had done nothing to disabuse them of this belief. Ignorance bred fear, as Father was fond of saying, and fear bred obedience.

Except something had gone wrong with that pithy maxim, if what the woman was saying was to be believed.

Gavar had listened carefully for the first few minutes. Word of Zelston's asinine Proposal had somehow not only leaked, despite the Silence, but had reached at least one of the slave-towns. The inhabitants of Millmoor were kicking up a fuss and demanding that parliament vote in favor of the Proposal.

It was all too ridiculous for words. What on earth did they think they'd achieve? Nothing, except years on their days. And for the ringleaders, perhaps slavelife and a generous reeducation at the hands of Lord Crovan. Anyone insane enough to risk that was probably a danger to society by default.

Crovan was an honorary member of the Justice Council, but thankfully never attended. He rarely left his Scottish castle, Eilean Dòchais, which stood on a small island in a large loch.

There he lived alone, apart from a few house-slaves—and the Condemned, the very worst of those sentenced to slavelife.

Whatever Crovan did to the Condemned (no one ever asked) kept him pretty busy. He only turned up at Westminster once a year for the opening of parliament, which was once too often in the opinion of his Equals. Even the House of Light seemed darker when he sat in it. And of course the man always attended the Third Debate at Kyneston.

When Gavar became Chancellor he would necessarily have dealings with Crovan, he thought unhappily, tuning out the droning narrative of the Millmoor Overseer. The sentence of Condemnation was always uttered by the Chancellor, before the prisoner was delivered straight to his new master.

Gavar wasn't sure when the practice of turning the Condemned over to Crovan had first begun. Had Father started it? But the man was present at every sentencing, eager to claim his new property. It was all faintly distasteful and one more reason for questioning whether the top job was all it was cracked up to be, despite Father's insistence that the Chancellorship was a Jardine family birthright.

The whole point about birthrights, Gavar thought resentfully, and not for the first time, was that they came to you automatically. You didn't have to do anything, except be who you were. To hear Father talk, the Chancellorship was just as much a Jardine prerogative as a place at Oxford's Domus College. So if it was coming to him anyway, why did Gavar have to serve this tedious political apprenticeship? Did he really have to attend endless councils, committees, and legislative debates?

His eyes roamed listlessly around the table. All the usual suspects. His future father-in-law, Lytchett Matravers, had his eyes closed in what he doubtless hoped was an expression of intense concentration, but was almost certainly trapped wind due to a rushed breakfast. Next to him was Lytchett's chum Lord Rix, who appeared every bit as bored as Gavar felt. He noticed Gavar looking and sent him a comradely roll of the eyes.

Rix was all right, but seated on his other side was Gavar's bitch-queen fiancée. She was scribbling down notes as if any of this actually mattered. Bouda had placed herself next to Zelston, at the top of the table. If Father was mistaken, and securing the Chancellorship required a modicum of effort even for the Jardine heir, Gavar felt sure his future wife could take care of greasing the wheels.

After all, there had to be some benefit to marrying a harpy like Bouda. As Father had reminded her that day Zelston dropped his little Proposal bombshell, it wasn't like they really needed the Matravers millions. And Gavar wasn't currently getting any other benefits, either. Bouda had tried to slap him when he had made a perfectly reasonable suggestion following the First Debate dinner. It was so much easier with commoner girls, when you never had to bother asking.

Not unless you actually cared about them.

Gavar clenched his fists beneath the table. He wasn't going to think about Leah. It only made him furious—and that was what had caused the whole horrendous mess in the first place.

He breathed deeply, feeling his chest strain against his crisp white shirt. Then relaxed again, rolling his shoulders.

It was easier here in London. His anger was always much worse at Kyneston. He didn't know why. Maybe it was the burden of expectation of it all. There was the house he'd inherit, the portraits of dead ancestors whom he would have to live up to. And for what? So he could watch his own heir trudge the same path he had, and in time pass on the estate to him, just as Father would to Gavar, as Grandfather Garwode had to Whittam.

It was all spectacularly pointless.

"And what can you tell us about the perpetrators?" he heard a voice say.

It was Rix. Gavar had never heard anyone sound less interested in the answer to a question they'd asked. Anything to alleviate the boredom, he supposed.

"We have one in custody," reported the Millmoor Overseer, slipping a photograph out of a fold of brown manila and sliding it to the center of the table. "He was at the scene of a sabotage of the East Sector Labor Allocation Bureau. It's believed a presently unidentified female was conducting the intrusion. However, when she was surprised by a Security patrol he made a show of force that enabled her to escape. He was subsequently subdued and apprehended."

Couldn't this peon speak plain English? The man had fought the guards to buy the woman time to get away. Under other circumstances it might have been an honorable thing to do.

Gavar glanced at the photograph. It showed a muscular black man, one of his eyes swollen shut, giving him a brutal aspect. His skin was too dark to make out any injuries, but his T-shirt was heavily bloodstained. He looked about the same age as Zelston, though this man's skull was shaved and he had none of the dandified Chancellor's fine clothes and fancy ornaments.

The accident of birth, thought Gavar, recalling another of

his father's favorite phrases. The accident of birth had given this criminal slave and the most powerful man in the land the same skin on the outside, but very different abilities within. And from that difference, their fates had diverged.

Libby had Gavar's own skin on the outside. His hair. His eyes.

He remembered the boat drifting across the lake toward them that day. Could she really have the same abilities within?

"You said 'Security patrol'?"

Bouda's officious voice broke into Gavar's thoughts. He just knew the sound of it was going to grate on him for the rest of his natural life.

The Overseer nodded, her face guarded. Bouda had clearly spotted something the woman had hoped would go unremarked.

"I presume you mean a routine patrol?" the blond girl said. "In other words, after several weeks of multiple incidents, including the defacement of your own headquarters, you have managed to catch one perpetrator—*by accident*?"

The commoner's expression turned from guarded to dismayed. Gavar almost laughed.

"You do understand"—Father sat forward in his chair, the thickly stuffed red leather seat creaking faintly—"that the authority of the Overseer's Office in Millmoor is not your own. It is *our* authority. That of your Equals and the government of this country. And therefore these attacks, which you have failed to prevent, are attacks directly upon us."

Gavar had to hand it to his father: the man knew how to make an impression. The room suddenly felt several degrees colder. He wouldn't have been surprised to see the condensation turning to ice on the inside of the windows.

"Naturally," Whittam went on, "the continuance of these outrages cannot be tolerated. Now that you have one of the perpetrators in your custody, I trust that you have taken every step to discover his associates?"

"Well . . ."

Even Gavar could have told the woman that wasn't the correct answer.

Whittam leaned back in his chair, steepling his fingers and staring over the top of them. It was a posture that, on one humiliating occasion in his childhood, had caused Gavar to wet himself. He'd never forgotten the look in Father's eyes as the hot liquid trickled miserably down his leg. It hadn't been anger, merely contempt.

Contempt for a child. No one would ever look at Libby like that. Gavar would kill them first.

Not being a five-year-old boy, the dumpy woman didn't piss her pants, but she did go pale. Then she lifted her chin ever so slightly and met Father's gaze. Maybe she had some backbone after all. The slavetowns were hellholes, from what Gavar had heard. You probably had to be tough to rise to the top of one.

"With every respect, my lord, that is precisely why I am here. The perpetrator has been questioned thoroughly, using all means at our disposal, but has so far failed to give satisfactory answers. I've come here today to seek the council's approval and assistance to implement special measures within our secure facility."

There was a noise from Gavar's left that could have been Lytchett snuffling in his sleep or a snort of derision from Rix. What were "special measures"? Gavar had no idea. But he remembered Father's injunction: "Never show ignorance." He wasn't about to show himself up by asking. Next to Zelston, Bouda was nodding sagely. It was likely she knew, but then she could have been bluffing. You could never tell with the bitch-queen.

"Special measures are not to be used lightly," came a crisp voice from opposite Zelston.

Armeria Tresco, who else? The sanctimonious old biddy was forever banging on about commoners' rights; she'd doubtless be the only person to vote in favor of the Proposal at the Third Debate. Unless her heir, Meilyr, showed up, tail between his legs. Mother and son could be pariahs together. Sweet.

"The use of Skill to break into the mind of another person is unconscionable," said Armeria. "We all know the harmful effects special measures can have. They're well documented. Some subjects have been rendered mentally incompetent for the rest of their lives. When the act is performed by one inexpert in the use of Skill for this purpose, it can even kill."

So that was what special measures were. Gavar blanched. They sounded horrifying. Or like Silyen's idea of a quiet evening's entertainment.

"Armeria," said Bouda repressively, as if speaking to a willful child. "This is a *slave* we're talking about. Slaves don't constitute legally recognized entities, thus the concept of 'harm' does not apply."

Bouda had been the star Law student of their year at Oxford. It was one of the reasons Gavar had opted to study Land Economy instead—although "study" was perhaps an overstatement.

"I don't give two hoots about whether this man"—Armeria

tapped the photograph—"is a 'legally recognized entity,' Bouda. He's a human being. If you want to talk technicalities, I would remind you that the statute governing the use of special measures states that they are only to be employed in situations liable to lead to loss of life.

"As I understand it, this man was apprehended at the scene of a rather creative hack of the Labor Allocation Bureau's network that reset everyone's status to 'Free Citizen.' He may additionally have been involved in damage to Millmoor Administration property, the escape from custody of several slaves held on sub-life crimes, and painting political slogans on Millmoor landmarks. Also the dissemination of literature stating a factually accurate truth—the nature of the current Proposal. None of these are trivial, but I see no evidence that anyone's life was put at risk as a result."

Gavar watched the exchange with some satisfaction. Wasn't it fascinating, he thought, just how quickly Bouda's milk-pale complexion could turn bright red?

"Armeria is correct," Zelston murmured donnishly, turning to Bouda. "The statute is quite clear, and it is the statute which we are required to consider *a priori*. The broader question of the status of slaves *in rerum natura* is not immediately relevant."

Whatever that gobbledygook meant, Bouda plainly didn't like it. Served her right, thought Gavar. And if she ever tried using that tone with Libby, she'd feel the back of his hand, wife or no.

"I'm not in favor of special measures," announced Rix.

Several heads swiveled to look at him with surprise. The silver-haired Equal arched an eyebrow.

"What? No one's dying in the streets, so why should one of us have to go to Millmoor to sort them out? I thought they did our dirty work, not the other way around."

Lytchett guffawed and slapped his friend on the back for his witticism. Rix smirked. Politics would be more fun, thought Gavar, if there were more in the chamber like him.

"So it seems . . ." began Zelston, looking around the table.

"It appears," cut in Father, "that further consideration is warranted. The honorable Lady Tresco cites the statute accurately: 'liable to lead to loss of life.' However, in her customary zeal she overlooks the fact that this is not about *immediate* but *eventual* loss of life. In this case I consider that eventual risk to be high."

He looked around at his peers, hands loosely interlaced and resting on the smooth tabletop. When younger, Gavar had practiced that quelling look for hours in a mirror. He'd never quite got the hang of it.

"The use of special measures saves lives," Father continued. "I think you are all aware that in my younger days I took a secondment to Joint Command of the Union States of America. This was during their years of deadlock in the Middle East. They were sufficiently desperate to turn to us and to their Confederate brothers, asking us to use our Skill in support of their military. The same Skill that they have declared an abomination—a belief for which they tore their great continent in half by civil war two centuries ago."

Lord Whittam Jardine's war stories. Gavar had heard a few over the years, usually when his father had drunk too much. The man had medals to prove the truth of them, which he kept in a box and never wore. But he had never thrown them away, either.

Gavar had once asked, when Father had been uncharacteristically confessional—which was to say, completely wasted— why he had worked with the Union Americans at all. After all, he frequently aired his contempt for the nation that had abolished slavery at the cost of outlawing Skill.

"It gave me an opportunity," Father had said, his blue-green eyes bloodshot but no less penetrating. "An opportunity to use my Skill in ways that would be frowned upon back home. I was curious. And I found that I enjoyed it."

Then he had told a detailed anecdote about exactly how he had used his Skill. It had Gavar putting down his glass of Scotch and not touching it again all night. He had never asked to hear more of Father's experiences in the desert.

Whittam didn't elaborate now, thankfully. The slaves would have been sponging the sick out of the council room carpet for days. But he had the attention of his peers as he continued.

"My role was to apply what we call 'special measures' to selected detainees. On more than one occasion, the information I secured thwarted plans that would have caused thousands of casualties and devastated civilian infrastructure. I mean cities," he clarified. "Philadelphia and Washington, D.C., to be exact.

"Sometimes, those possessed of that information were not whom you might expect: Not warlords, but teachers. Not religious leaders, but shopkeepers. All routes to knowledge should be explored by whatever means necessary. It is an error to consider anyone incapable of atrocity or above suspicion. Even the littlest child."

Gavar remembered that part of his father's reminiscences, and tasted bile in his mouth. He wondered sometimes if Lord Jardine was not a bit cracked. Wondered, too, if it was from him that he had inherited his own tendency to lose control.

To hurt people.

In fact, he sometimes wondered if he could blame every single thing that had gone wrong in his life on his father. Was that cowardly? Maybe. But it didn't mean it wasn't true.

The Equals around the table had fallen silent. The commoner woman was looking at Lord Jardine as if he were some kind of god, her mouth agape. Gavar had himself seen that look on women's faces and occasionally used it to his advantage, but mostly it just repulsed him.

"So what exactly are you proposing, Whittam?" asked the Chancellor. "Are you volunteering to go to Millmoor and see what can be obtained from this suspect?"

Zelston motioned to the photograph, but his eyes were on Lord Jardine. Bouda's gaze was darting eagerly between the pair of them. Even Rix was frowning.

"Oh, no," said Father, that smile slashing a little wider. "I'm volunteering my son and heir, Gavar."

The rest of the meeting passed in a blur.

The Millmoor Overseer transferred her hungry expression to Gavar. Rix won his gratitude by reiterating his opinion that Equals shouldn't lower themselves by going to a slavetown. But Father's intervention ensured the decision was a foregone conclusion. When the vote came, the use of special measures on the prisoner detained in Millmoor was approved. The result was eleven to one, with only Armeria Tresco dissenting.

Bouda Matravers's hand had been the first to go up.

Afterward, as Gavar followed his father down the corridor, he heard the dull tear of high heels through deep carpet as Bouda hurried after them. She placed herself in front of Father, blocking their path.

"Five minutes," she said. "We need to talk."

Father's face was unreadable, while Gavar experienced a fleeting moment of hope that she would volunteer to go to the slavetown in his place. As if. Bouda had the true politician's disinclination to get her own hands dirty.

"Very well."

Father reached past her and opened the door to a side room. Bouda started talking the minute the handle clicked shut behind them.

"How did this happen?" she said, addressing herself entirely to Father as though Gavar were not even there. "The observers are under the Silence, and we've all accepted the Quiet. How can word have got out? Zelston must have messed up. Performed the acts wrong, or just not been powerful enough."

She paused. What she'd said was so obvious, it couldn't possibly be why she had pulled Lord Jardine and his heir into a deserted room for a private conversation.

Father just watched and waited. Gavar had observed, over the years, that this often made people talk, no matter how reluctant they were to share what was in their head. Sadly, he doubted it would work if he tried it on the Millmoor prisoner.

His stomach churned again at the thought of the task he'd been assigned. What would it feel like to carry it out?

What would it feel like to fail?

He'd lived nearly two and a half decades as Lord Whittam Jardine's eldest son. They left him in no doubt as to which of those options should be more feared.

"It makes me think Zelston's not fit to be Chancellor."

Gavar stared at Bouda as her pent-up thoughts spilled out in a rush.

"This Proposal should never have been made. Zelston ought to have foreseen something like this. Even if the trouble in Millmoor ends here, it could be Portisbury next, or Auld Reekie the week after. The word is out and we can't Silence the entire country. Today, until you intervened, he didn't even have the stomach to take the necessary steps."

She paused and drew in a rapid breath. "He has another three years left in office. Right now, I'm not convinced that's in Britain's best interests."

Father watched her. "What are you suggesting, Bouda?"

"Suggesting?"

And now that she'd spoken the unsayable, Gavar saw Bouda regain her composure, wrapping it back around her as elegantly as a designer coat.

"I'm not suggesting anything. Merely sharing my little notions." She moved toward the door; opened it. "I'd better go after Daddy before he finds his way to the cake trolley. That's never pretty. Oh, and Gavar? Good luck."

The bitch!

Except he must have said that aloud, because Father rounded on him. His expression was so fierce that Gavar took a step back.

"She's twice the politician you'll ever be," said Whittam. "As is your brother. I always knew Silyen was the most Skillful of my sons, but I must account him the abler strategist, too. He has the Chancellor doing his bidding, while you and I must scurry around tidying up the consequences."

And really, Gavar wondered, had anything changed since he was five years old? Anything at all? But he was a man now—and a father himself. When would Father treat him like one? He met Whittam's eye. The man had to look up slightly at his taller son.

"Rix is correct," Gavar said. "Why should we scurry? We are Equals, of the Founding Family, not common policemen. Why should I go?"

That wasn't the right question.

"You go because the information from this slave is needful," said Whittam, stepping nearer, closing the gap Gavar had made between them. "You go because I tell you to. Because people are still gossiping about that slavegirl's death in your supposed 'hunting accident.' Doing this may be your rehabilitation. And you go because as head of this family I have the power to decide whether that bastard brat of yours is raised at Kyneston or sent to an UMUS home. At least that way your mother and I wouldn't have to look at it and be reminded each day of what a disappointment you are."

His father's face was only a few inches from his own, yet Gavar found he could barely see it. His vision swam red and black. He was five years old again. But what flowed from him now, hot and stinking, wasn't a trickle of fear and shame. It was a gush of hatred.

That wasn't the right answer, Father.

Not the right answer at all.

## TWELVE

# LUKE

Ever since Oz's capture two days before, Luke had been waiting for the tap on his shoulder, the grip round his arm. Or, just possibly, the baton to his skull.

But even when you were expecting it, your heart still half fell out of your chest when it came.

He'd just finished his shift, and had exchanged the searing heat of the components shed for the freezing streets. It was already dark, and dense flurries of sleet reduced visibility to almost nothing. He was only a few blocks from the Zone D gates when a hand tugged his sleeve. Luke's pulse exploded and he bolted.

But not so fast that he didn't hear a hissed "It's me!" behind him.

He skidded on the wet pavement and turned.

"We're getting 'im out tonight," Renie said. She was standing in the alleyway, the sleet curdling around her in the yellow lamplight. "Oz. We need a ride. One of them shuttles to the outside. I've found us one. It's in the depot for repairs. You've gotta make sure it's okay and kill its GPS tracker."

Luke boggled at her. Helping your dad fix up a vintage car didn't exactly give you the skills for that sort of thing.

"We've gotta do it," Renie said. "For 'im."

So they did.

The van was exactly like the one that had carted Luke off to Millmoor. It triggered awful memories, of both that first day and Kessler in the storeroom. He was momentarily paralyzed with fear that they'd be caught in here.

He screwed his eyes shut and willed his hands to stop trembling. Told himself he could trust Renie to keep lookout, just as she'd trusted him to anchor the rope on the MADhouse roof.

With that realization, something inside him sparked. A small but crucial connection that sent the engine of his courage sputtering into life. Then revving and roaring.

Trust was what made everything possible. Trust lent you someone else's eyes, someone else's strong arms or quick brain. Made you bigger than just yourself. Trust was how the club worked. How this whole reckless dream of abolition could work, if people could just come together and hold their nerve. Not even the Equals—not even their Skill—would be more powerful than that.

Fixing the van itself was almost easy. Details of the repairs needed were on a clipboard hung on the wall. The vehicle's key dangled from a row of hooks. The security seemed pretty lax—just a few CCTV cameras, which Renie had either navigated them past or disabled.

"Ha," she said, when he pointed this out. "It's not getting these wheels out of the depot that's the difficult bit. It's going to be getting 'em out of Millmoor. Three rings of Security and two chip-checks like what you have in Zone D."

Which made it sound impossible.

"That's where Angel comes in. She runs the Riverhead railroad. Smugglin' people outta places is her specialty. She don't normally do it like this, though. It's usually lorries, hidden compartments, trusted drivers, that sort of thing. But our pal Oz is special delivery, so Angel's comin' here herself. Tonight."

"Angel? Not an entirely reassuring name."

Renie cocked her head, amused. "It's not her real name. None of us know that. But we call her our Angel of the North. You know, like that big sculpture with wings up by Riverhead. And also—well, you'll see." The kid cackled. "Anyway, are we done here?"

They were. Luke pocketed the keys.

Renie navigated them across town to the rendezvous point—a dusty storeroom where long-dead paperwork lay coffined in archive boxes. There they found only Jackson, still and calm, and Jessie, pacing like she wanted to wear a hole in the ground that Oz could crawl through to Australia.

"Why are we still waiting, Jack? Who knows what they're doing to him?"

Jess dashed at the tears spilling from her eyes with a violence that was half fury, half despair. Guilt, too, Luke suspected, given that she had escaped while Oz had been captured. The sight of her wrung his heart.

"We all know the drill, Jessica," the Doc said. "No rescue attempts for the first forty-eight hours. Prisoners are too closely guarded and there's insufficient time to establish Security routines. Hilda's been monitoring the camera feed from the cell, so we know Oz is okay. Not great—they've been beating on him pretty hard—but nothing that won't mend. Plus, we've had to work out how to get him out. Angel will be here any minute, and then we go."

"You think she'll manage it?" sniffed Jess, her voice as raw as if she'd done a few shifts back to back in the Zone D stokeholes.

Something unreadable flashed across Jackson's face. "She's never failed anyone yet. I've not been in Millmoor a year, but she's been doing this sort of thing far longer than that. I trust her with my life, and—which is saying rather more—with the lives of all of you. Luke's sorted the vehicle, now I need you to get Angel to it. You can't stay here and I'm not going to risk you coming with us."

"I can't believe you're taking those kids and not me," Jessica burst out. "I swear, if those Security bastards have done anything to him . . ."

"Which is exactly why I'm not taking you. Sit down, Jessie. Deep breaths. This rescue is happening and we're going to get Oz out."

Squatting on the floor, listening, Luke's brain caught up with what Jessica had just said. *Taking those kids.*

The only kids in the room were Renie and Luke himself. They were the only other people in the room, full stop. Renie had told him that Asif and the ditcher sisters were doing their techno-whizzy things at separate locations, monitoring the detention center remotely. The Doc wore some kind of earpiece that crackled occasionally as they spoke to him.

Jessie slumped against a stack of boxes, head down. Apart

from her uneven breathing, the room was quiet. Jackson walked over to Luke, who was suddenly hyperaware of Renie watching them both.

"I'm not taking you anywhere you don't want to go," Jackson said. "But Jess is right. I'd like you to come with me and Renie. Oz is a big guy, and he may need help getting on his feet and moving."

Jessica stifled a sob.

"We've got to get in and out as fast as possible. I'm not going to be able to give him any medical assistance until we're away from the building. If we encounter anyone, I'll need to deal with them. Hopefully we won't, because Asif and the girls will be following the whole thing and telling us when it's clear. But this all means you'll need to look after Oz."

"Won't it look suspect, you being in there with kids—I mean, someone as young as Renie?" Luke said.

"Renie will wait at the entrance, to alert us to anything outside that the others don't catch on the cameras and comms. You're big enough to pass for Security. Renie's been clothes shopping and has a uniform that'll fit you. Luke, I won't let this go wrong."

"Don't make promises you can't keep," Jess said bitterly.

"Oh, it's not a promise," said a low, unfamiliar voice with just a hint of a Newcastle accent. "It's a fact. Hello, Dr. Jackson."

The Angel of the North.

As she joined them under the flickering strip light, Luke immediately understood the other reason for her nickname.

She was tall and blond and utterly gorgeous. Like something out of a magazine—those pictures teachers always told you were airbrushed, so normal girls shouldn't feel inadequate trying to match them. But this woman was perfect just as she was. Perfect like an angel in a church window, or a lingerie advert. A single immaculate snowflake fallen into Millmoor's filthy streets.

"Hi, Renie," said Angel, with a nod of acknowledgment. "And you must be Jessica. I know you're awfully worried about Oswald, but he's going to be safe now. And you'll be Luke. I've heard all about you."

"You're . . . Angel," Luke said, offering his hand for her to shake. And really, who knew it was possible for his palm to perspire that much in just ten seconds flat? Her touch tingled across it like electricity. "I asked . . ." He laughed nervously. "I asked Renie why they call you that. But I guess now I know."

She smiled. Luke didn't think there could be anything in the world more magical than that smile, not even Skill itself. His face heated as if he stood in the components shed. She was older than him. But not by much. Surely not by much?

No point wondering, Luke Hadley. Angel was out of his league by every measure he could possibly imagine.

If this rescue mission succeeded, would she be impressed?

If it failed, would she come and break him out?

"I was just telling the Doc that I'm ready," he told her. "And I've fixed the vehicle. For you. It'll give you no problems."

He really, really hoped that was true.

Jackson's earpiece was hissing, the lines at the corner of his eyes crinkling as he concentrated on what Asif was saying. Then he looked up.

"There's a low-footfall window in twenty-eight minutes. So here's what we're going to do."

★   ★   ★

It was nearly nine o'clock when they reached the detention center. Oz was being held separately from the others on the high-security corridor of the remand wing. That was good, because there'd be less general traffic to notice them; but also bad, because anyone they did encounter would be there for the same reason they were—to see Oz.

Renie slipped into the darkness as they reached the entrance. "Good luck," she muttered. "See ya soon."

Then they were in—just him and Jackson.

Security, like the Administration workers, weren't slaves. The architects of the system had been careful to ensure there'd be no common cause between the slaves and those keeping them in line. That meant there wasn't a gate registering the chips of those passing through. Instead, an entry team used handheld devices to check either the wrist cuffs that stored Security IDs or the flesh-embedded chips of slaves brought in as prisoners.

"There are two different scanners," Jackson had explained. "They'll see the Security uniform and use the one for the cuffs."

Luke's legs were as wobbly as that time he'd taken Daisy to an ice rink and made a fool of himself falling over. As though they might shoot in opposite directions and dump him on his backside with no warning at all. Keep it together, he thought, tensing his muscles to remind himself they were still there.

"We're here for Walcott G-2159," the Doc told the guard at the entrance, holding out his right arm for scanning. Worn by all Millmoor's free workers, wrist cuffs were attached at the slavetown's outermost entry stations as workers arrived, and removed as they left. Luke wondered how the club had acquired the two he and Jackson were wearing.

"Didn't think you looked familiar," said the guard. "You're specials from the MADhouse. What's it like servicing the glorious leader herself? Nah, don't answer that. Don't want to know." He chuckled to himself. "We had word someone was coming for Walcott. Didn't know exactly when, though. Don't reckon the Overbitch'll get much joy from him tonight, the state he's in."

The man laughed again, as if this observation was equally amusing. Did they deliberately recruit people who'd had compassion bypasses, or did doing this sort of job make you that way?

Luke obediently held up his wrist to be scanned, too. So they'd been expecting someone to come for Oz. Was the club so good that they'd already planted false authorizations in Security's system?

But it didn't seem so, because as they passed into the detention center's corridors, Jackson's face was drawn tight with concern. Luke heard him cup his hand and mutter a few words that would reach his earpiece. The crackling response had him shaking his head in frustration.

The building was sterile and pitiless. The floor was polished concrete and echoed so loudly beneath their boots that Luke cringed. His brain started up a traitorous chant in time with their footsteps: *Break. Out. Break. Out.* He was half astonished that no one else could hear it. Surely they couldn't hope to get away with this?

But no. He remembered a conversation with Asif. The guy

was a tech whiz who'd been building his own computing arrays from childhood. Technology, Asif had told him, was a simple thing that everyone had convinced themselves was complex. It was fallible, but everyone believed it to be faultless. People had delegated their better judgment—and the evidence of their own senses—to the power of technology. If you could fool the tech, you needn't worry about fooling the people.

So their uniforms and ID cuffs saw them through a second manned door, and then a third verification point. Here they had to press the bands against a panel set into the wall. The last stage was the entrance to the high-security wing.

"You lot are keen," said the guard there as he took out a set of old-fashioned keys. They unlocked two sets of double-bolted barred doors, like wild-animal cages. "Only got the final say-so ten minutes ago. So where's the lord and master—waiting back at the MADhouse with your boss, eh? Guess he decided doing it here wasn't to his liking. Too near the common folk, eh? At least using his Skill, he won't have to worry about getting blood on her carpet. Though I daresay Daddy Jardine's got enough money to pay for a new one."

Thankfully, the guy was bent over the locks as he spoke, because even Jackson's composure slipped. His eyes narrowed in concentration as he tried to make sense of what had just been said.

Luke's brain was whirring, too. The name "Jardine" had been distracting, making Luke think of Kyneston and his family, but one thing was clear from the guard's words and the Doc's reaction. They weren't the only ones coming for Oz.

The open-barred cells beyond didn't contain the stench. It was a rancid blend of everything revolting that could come out of a human body. At first Luke strained to make out the huddled shape of Oz on the floor. When he did, he really wished he hadn't. The guard aimed a flashlight so bright it was effectively weaponized straight at Oz's face. The only small mercy was that his eyes were swollen completely shut. Oz couldn't have opened them into that blinding glare even if he'd wanted to.

"Up you get," said the guard, poking Oz with his baton. "The Overseer and Heir Gavar Jardine request the honor of your company at a party for one. And you've not bothered to dress for it. Tut-tut."

Luke's fists clenched. Oz didn't move.

"Dunno if he can stand," said the guard. "Reckon you might have to drag him."

"I'll deal with this," said Jackson, stepping forward.

He crouched down by Oz. Could their friend even recognize him? Oz gave no sign. But he yielded up a sudden, almighty moan and rolled onto all fours. The Doc must have jabbed him with a shot of adrenaline.

"Get up," Jackson said, making his voice hard and indifferent. Then to Luke: "Get him moving."

Luke grabbed Oz by the back of his jumpsuit and hauled. Oz came up slowly, but at least partly under his own strength. Thank goodness. Nothing broken, then.

Apart from his nose, perhaps. Probably a cheekbone. Maybe an eye socket. There was no way Jessica could have coped with seeing him like this, in here.

"We'll be going," Jackson told the guard. "Don't want to keep our betters waiting."

The cell guard shrugged. "Good riddance to that one. He

kept quiet in interrogations—daresay he fancies himself a tough guy. But when he was by himself you'd hear him crying like a girl. Hope your boss gets more out of him than the lads here managed."

Fortunately, both of Luke's hands were clenched in Oz's coveralls, the fabric stiff and sticky, because everything in him ached to give this scumbag a pasting.

Once back out through the barred doors, Jackson and Luke supported Oz through the corridors. Oz had somehow cracked one eyelid open, and a tiny black pupil swimming in bloodshot sclera peered out at them, like the eye of a deep-sea creature fathoms down. Could he see clearly enough to recognize them? Luke hoped so.

Jackson's earpiece hissed in a different pitch than before. Renie, must be.

"Keep walking," said the Doc when the sound stopped, "and don't hesitate. On the other side of the second checkpoint, we're going to meet some people. Ignore them. You know the pickup point. We'll take Oz straight there. If I get caught up in anything, you keep going. Don't wait for me. Get him in that vehicle and away."

A fist-sized lump of dread lodged itself in Luke's throat, but he swallowed it down. He let his gaze fall slightly out of focus, in that dead-eyed way Security often had. He *was* Security. He had the ID to prove it.

At the second checkpoint Luke said nothing as he held out the cuff. Didn't let himself wince when Oz groaned as the guard grabbed his arm to run the chip-sensing device over it.

"You got the alert?" the Doc asked as he submitted his wrist.

"I think news travels faster across our network than it does on general comms. Because you really don't want to miss it. Screw up and they'd put you in this one's old cell."

Jackson gave Oz a nudge that made him stumble, and laughed nastily.

"Alert? What?" The guard screwed up his face anxiously.

"You've not heard? Rescue attempt. Seems Walcott's associates have been listening in on your piece-of-junk channel and are on their way to free him. That's why we got dispatched in a hurry. I'll be sorry to miss it. They've got some bloke posing as Heir Jardine himself. Except I guess they never checked the photos, 'cause they're trying to pass off some red-haired dude. Everyone knows the Jardines are blond."

"They are?" The man's face was ashen. He revolved the cuff on his wrist and swiped the display. "No notification. Why are we always the last to know? How am I supposed to stop them?"

"Better share it with your colleague at the entrance," said the Doc. "If I were you guys, I'd let them through, then keep them locked in. You'll have caught them all by yourself, and they'll be where they're going to end up anyway, in the max wing. Job done."

The relief on the man's face was palpable. "Yeah. Yeah, neat. Thanks."

And on they went, leaving the guard calling up his colleague on his helmet's mike. Up ahead came the bang and echo of the concrete floor. It was hard to tell how many pairs of feet were headed toward them. Three?

"We're into the general remand space," Jackson said, low and fast. "So our prisoner could be anyone. Gavar Jardine will almost certainly be with the Overseer's personal Security, so they won't know Oz on sight, either. Not that his own mother would know him, given the mess he's in. Keep walking."

They were one turn away from the entrance when the others came round the corner. And the hairs on Luke's arm lifted the minute he saw him.

Gavar Jardine was a monster of a man. Well over six feet tall, with a black leather overcoat falling from his wide shoulders to the top of his leather biker boots. Black gloves.

But the psycho outfit was the least scary thing about him. The Jardine heir could have been wearing Happy Panda pajamas, and he still would've been the most terrifying person Luke had ever seen. Abi had shown them all pictures, but no photo could prepare you for the reality of an Equal in the flesh. And there was a whole family of them. Abi worked in their office. Mum nursed one of them. Hopefully Daisy was at least keeping clear.

"We'll get in front. Eyes down," hissed Jackson.

And just like that, the groups were passing: Luke and Jackson together, Oz half shielded behind them; Gavar Jardine striding ahead. The two Security men were so intent on keeping up that they didn't spare them a second glance.

Luke's bones felt as if they'd been replaced by unsteady stacks of ball bearings. Any minute now, he'd fall apart.

But not yet. Not until he'd got Oz to safety.

The guy at the entrance was wide-eyed, ready with two scanners.

"You saw 'em?" he whispered, and the Doc nodded. "You guys were just in time. They've got some nerve, though—gotta hand it to them. Backup's on the way once they've been contained. You get the prisoner delivered."

Jackson nodded—and just like that, they were out into the freezing night.

As they crossed the road, a small shadow detached itself and followed them. They walked two streets, then Jackson propped Oz up against a wall. He took the big guy's face between his hands, ever so gently thumbed up his eyelids.

"Nearly there, big fella. You're safe now."

Jackson's very presence restored life to Oz. The puffy eyelids forced themselves open. A tongue licked at swollen, split lips. Renie put a water bottle to Oz's mouth and he gulped eagerly. His hand came up to feel his face.

"Not like I was ever pretty," Oz croaked, and Luke thought he'd never in his life been happier to hear a rubbish joke.

Then from the direction of the detention center, the muffled sound of an explosion was magnified by the hollow night.

"Take him, Luke," Jackson said. "You too, Renie. Get him to the pickup point as fast as you can. There's not a minute to lose."

"Why?" Renie was all eyes. "What was that?"

"That was Gavar Jardine."

Jackson turned and ran back the way they'd come. There was shouting behind them now. Confused noise. The wet, sleety air crackled.

"This way," Renie said. "Angel's ready with the van."

Luke had half hustled, half dragged Oz the length of one more street when he heard the sound of gunshots. Once. Twice. The second time there was an awful cry.

Luke couldn't be sure, but it sounded a lot like Jackson.

"Wasn't 'im," Renie said fiercely, pulling at Luke's sleeve. "Wasn't."

In the fourth street sat the van. As they hurried toward it, a figure came running. Jessica.

She threw herself at Oz, as if she could hold him up all by herself. She couldn't, of course. Renie pushed the messy tangle of the three of them in the direction of the van, then yanked Jessica's arm away so Luke had room to fold Oz onto the backseat. Jess gave a sob and pressed her face against his soiled jumpsuit, and from the darkness of the van a large, mangled paw reached out to pet her hair. Jessie grabbed it and kissed it.

"We've got to get moving, Jess."

Then Renie's face was lit up by a freakish glare as a plume of chemical fire shot high over buildings several blocks away. Foul, acrid smoke drifted toward them, and Luke tasted it as he heard the patter of debris raining down on a rooftop nearby.

"Time to go," said a voice from the driver's seat. "Close it up, Renie."

Angel. Luke had forgotten all about her. Looking at her face as she leaned out of the window, he wondered how that had been possible. Her blond hair was stuffed up under a beanie hat and both hands gripped the wheel.

"He's safe now, I promise. Don't worry about Jackson; he'll be fine, too. Just look out for yourselves. Split up. Go home. Take different routes—not that direction, obviously."

Angel nodded at where the smoke was still pluming upward. The sky was lit with unpleasant shades of blue and orange, resembling a fireworks show for the color-blind.

The engine was already running. As she tested the accelerator Luke stayed stupidly where he was, staring through the open cab window.

Then she reached out and—unbelievably—touched her fingers to his cheek. He felt that electric tingle again, and couldn't take his eyes from her perfect face.

"Be safe, Luke Hadley," Angel said.

She gunned the engine and the vehicle tore away into the night.

# THIRTEEN

# BOUDA

"They used Skill?"

"That's what I said."

Her future husband crossed his arms, his face reddening at her skepticism.

Bouda sighed. Was this how married life would be? Gavar getting truculent at the slightest provocation: "Was it the marmalade you wanted, darling?" *Glower.* "That's what I said." "Is your great-aunt coming for tea today, my love?" *Scowl.* "That's what I said."

She'd find out soon enough. Tomorrow was the Second Debate, at Grendelsham. They would be married at Kyneston after the Third. Three more months.

How would it have been if fate had delivered her one of the other Jardine sons: Jenner or Silyen? Jenner would have been out of the question, she supposed. If he'd been the eldest, Whittam would have disinherited him. And Silyen? Well . . . maybe there were worse things than Gavar's short temper.

And perhaps the strategies she learned for dealing with him would come in useful when they had babies.

"But I understand from your father"—she looked over at Whittam to enlist his support, and he gave a confirmatory nod—"that the escape can be explained entirely by Millmoor's own lax security protocols."

She counted off their failings on her fingers, wincing at the garish turquoise polish on each nail. Dina had returned from Paris in the small hours, spilling noisily through the door with bags of designer nonsense and exorbitantly priced cosmetics. She had insisted on giving her sister a manicure after breakfast, even though there were slaves for that sort of thing—"Because politicians can be pretty, too!" There was another fortunate accident of birth, Bouda supposed. Just imagine if DiDi had been the Matravers heir.

"The perpetrators wore valid identity bands. And because they posed as Administration Security, the fact that they were unknown to the prison guards didn't raise suspicion." She folded down two fingers, counting. "Your father has just received confirmation that they compromised the CCTV cameras, too. They were also monitoring Security's communications channels, which is how they knew you were coming.

"And above all, they held their nerve. If Walcott's escape weren't so exasperating, I'd applaud their brazenness. Walking out with the prisoner, while telling the imbeciles on duty that you were the breakout team." She folded down the last finger.

"All in all, more than enough reasons to explain how they extracted the prisoner from under the noses of such incompetents."

Gavar held his ground, looming over her where she sat on the sofa. She wasn't intimidated. They were in the snug sitting room of Daddy's little Mayfair bolt-hole. Everything here was as cozily over-upholstered as Daddy himself, and Bouda felt secure. This was home territory.

"It was more than that," Gavar insisted. "I daresay slavetown Security aren't recruited for their intelligence, but for those guards to have fallen for such a simple trick? And me? I walked straight past them. Didn't spare them a glance."

And that, thought Bouda, was the simplest thing of all in this whole farcical business. Gavar Jardine misses a breakout taking place right under his nose. And to cover his own idiocy, he starts seeing Skill at work. In a slavetown, no less. Bouda had seen how agitated Gavar was at the thought of using special measures on the prisoner. He'd probably been drinking nonstop from the moment his car left London. Everyone knew about the decanters that nestled in the Jardine Bentley's backseat.

"It's an interesting hypothesis," said Lord Whittam, who'd been leaning against the mantelpiece, observing the exchange. "But not a necessary one. The stolen vehicle was found abandoned just inside the Peak District, half submerged in a quarry. It's being recovered now, though it doesn't seem likely we'll get much from it. That isn't the sort of stratagem a Skilled person would resort to."

"Do we know who was driving the vehicle?" she asked Whittam. "The fugitive himself, or an accomplice?"

"Security ran a perimeter chip-check about five minutes after the breakout was discovered. That showed that all microchipped individuals not inside the boundary were absent with authorization, except for the prisoner Walcott. The vehicle passed through several internal checkpoints. The guards at each report that the ID was in order and the driver was a Caucasian female, though their descriptions of her are unhelpfully vague."

"Female and unchipped?" said Bouda. "His wife, is she on the outside? Free?"

"Dead," said Whittam impassively. "Breast cancer three years ago. Seems to have been what prompted Walcott to start his days."

"I'm telling you"—Gavar was clenching his fists—"it was Skill."

Bouda felt certain that the only Skill that had been used in Millmoor last night was Gavar's own. Infuriated at being trapped inside the detention center by a guard who thought Gavar himself was Walcott's rescuer, he had simply blasted his way out. The max wing of the prison had been reduced to rubble and several individuals inside were seriously injured. It was all rather excessive—albeit a well-timed reminder to Millmoor's seditionists of the power they sought to defy.

He had then pursued someone through the streets with his beloved revolver, apparently in the belief it was either Walcott or his fleeing accomplice. Gavar Jardine, the action hero. She smiled to herself. He was such a little boy.

But she didn't want Gavar throwing all his toys out of the pram at this early stage. She'd be spending the next two days with the Jardine father and son, after all. Maybe it was time to use a softer tone.

"What happened to the person you shot at? Whatever tipped you off, Skill, intuition, or a sharp pair of ears"—she sent Gavar her most mollifying smile, though he seemed sadly immune—"your instincts about the rescue attempt were correct."

"I didn't shoot *at* him," said Gavar. "I hit him. I heard him yell out."

Gavar was touchy about his marksmanship. Had been ever since word had got out about the hunting accident—the one that killed the slavegirl mother of his child. Bouda hadn't found it in her heart to be sorry about that particular incident.

"But you never found a body, or any blood indicating a wounding, where you believed your target was?"

"No." Gavar shook his head, his tone petulant. "I've already gone through all this with Father."

She saw him cast a mute look at Lord Whittam, as if appealing for support. None came. None ever did. It was almost pitiable, really.

"If Gavar hit the fugitive, well, he's gone. But if it was an accomplice, he must still be in Millmoor. The clinics should be monitored," she told her father-in-law. "The healthcare staff questioned. And even if the injury wasn't grievous and the victim is tending to it himself, managers and foremen should be instructed to keep an eye out. Residential-block staff need to watch for blood on sheets or towels."

"Good suggestions," said Whittam, and Bouda couldn't help preening under his approval.

Was it too much to hope that he might recognize how better suited for high office she was than his son? Sadly, it probably was. The only thing Whittam Jardine prized above merit was blood. Still, at least Bouda's own children would one day benefit from his single-minded devotion to his family's preeminence.

"So the facts are these," Whittam said, in the tone he used to conclude official meetings, including those at which the Chancellor was present. "The criminal Walcott broke out of the detention center with the aid of two males, possibly Skilled."

He inclined his head toward his heir in a condescending fashion. Could he not see, Bouda wondered, the resentment in his son's eyes? Gavar was like a brutalized dog that knows exactly how long its chain is and waits for the day its master forgets.

"We believe that either one of the accomplices or the prisoner was then shot and injured. We do not know the current whereabouts of the accomplices. However, the prisoner subsequently left Millmoor in a vehicle driven by an unidentified and unchipped female. Correct?"

"Whatever are you all talking about?" came a drowsy voice from the doorway. "Do you want some coffee? I've had Anna brew me some. My own silly fault for going back to bed halfway through the morning. Paris was so much fun, but I'm absolutely pooped."

It was Dina, looking rumpled. A cashmere dressing gown hung loose over her shoulders and she cuddled her unconscionable pug, Stinker. Bouda hadn't even heard her sister open the door, she'd been so focused on the discussion.

Whittam looked murderous. Bouda knew he believed Dina to be a spoiled little girl and a liability. It was unfortunate that she'd wandered into this conversation, of all the things they could have been discussing. Bouda would have to explain, yet again, that DiDi's idea of challenging the regime was to address slaves by their given names. That, and lavishing Daddy's hard-earned cash on so-called human rights organizations, which doubtless blew every penny on swanky offices and cocktail parties for the international media.

She went over to her sister and put an arm round her to steer her back toward the kitchen.

"We were just prepping for tomorrow's debate, darling, but we're done now. And yes, I'd love some coffee before we make tracks for Grendelsham."

"Stinky woke me up," Dina said, looking at her sister anxiously. "He's got a funny tummy. I guess I shouldn't have fed him so many escargots. I don't think snails agree with him. Or garlic."

Bouda looked at the dog with alarm. Stinker had earned his name ten times over in his short life. The pug looked back, its goggle eyes swiveling with unmistakable guilt.

"Why don't you put him down," she suggested. "Let him have a little run around the sitting room. I'm sure that'll help sort him out."

Bouda scooped the dog from her sister's arms and set it on the floor. She gave its belly a sharp nudge with the pointed toe of her shoe, which she hoped Dina didn't spot. It sent the pug yelping and skittering into the room where the lord and his heir stood.

Then Bouda closed the door.

After coffee and goodbyes came the long drive to South Wales and Grendelsham. Just as the First and Third Debates took place on the great equinoxes of autumn and spring, the Second Debate was held on the winter solstice, the shortest day of the year. Bouda always timed her arrival for sunset.

As the car swung round a bend, the sandy expanse of the

Gower Peninsula stretched ahead. And there atop the cliffs, bathed in the last fire of the sinking sun, was Grendelsham. It resembled a box of pure, pulsing, rosy light. Skill-built, the mansion was made entirely of glass. Gorgeous and wholly impractical, it was the first and only example of the so-called Third Revolutionary style. Nicknamed the Glasshouse, it resembled the sort of pretentious art installation that Dina liked to sponsor at the Southbank galleries. But this was a hundred times bigger and more breathtaking.

Bouda couldn't take her eyes off it. You never knew what color the Glasshouse would be: blue as the sky on a summer's day; a buttery yellow in mellow sunshine; frosty lilac at dawn. And the color was still shifting now, as the sun downed. The rosy pink deepened, darkened, became a hot fleshy red—turned, unmistakably, the color of blood.

Bouda shrank back in her seat, suddenly unnerved. With a stab at a button, she raised the tinted car window. She'd been reminded of the photograph of the Millmoor Administration building daubed with a massive scarlet *Y, E,* and *S*. The paint had been sprayed on in great slashes, as if carving the word into skin. Then there were the confiscated leaflets. "WE BLEED beneath their WHIP," one had read. Crude propagandist trash, Bouda had thought. As if anyone used whips these days.

She was glad that it was finally dark by the time the car pulled up at the house, and under the black sky Grendelsham shone brightly from within. Bouda wove through the thronging Equals, dispensing and receiving greetings and kisses as she went to find her allotted room. Grendelsham's bedrooms and bathrooms were also glass-walled (although, thankfully, curtained). The Second Debate was notorious for the indiscretions and intrigue it provoked. Bouda reminded herself to secure her door that night, in case Gavar Jardine was inspired by the house's reputation.

She summoned a slave to help her into a dress that was slashed to the small of her back. It was so narrow that Bouda had no idea how to put it on—couture brought from Paris by DiDi that she hadn't had the heart to refuse. She needn't have worried. It fell from her shoulders to the floor in a glittering spill of silver, an effect so pleasing that Bouda didn't even chastise the slave who piped up unbidden to voice her admiration.

She enjoyed the turn of heads as she went back to the reception downstairs and plunged into the press of dinner jackets and evening gowns. Her father and Rix were enjoying snifters on an uncomfortable-looking chrome-and-leather sofa. Daddy was already several sheets to the wind, while her godfather cackled over her account of the latest events in Millmoor.

"A runaway slave, eh?" Rix said, fragrant smoke from his cigar pluming down his nostrils. "Can't we set the dogs on his trail? Hypatia's one, maybe."

Bouda pulled a face. Hypatia's hound would have to be securely kenneled during the Third Debate and her own nuptials—or even better, not be at Kyneston at all. Crovan had done his work well and the thing was an eyesore. DiDi would be bound to make a fuss.

She sat between the two men at dinner, then afterward detached herself unobtrusively and began to work the room. Her favorite part of the evening.

Word of the Millmoor debacle had spread and her Equals were keen to know more. She was coy—it would all be in a little speech she had to give tomorrow, as Secretary of the Justice Council. But here and there she dropped a detail, a small seed to be watered by gossip and speculation. Along with the information went a touch of regret, of exasperation—of doubt, even. What had the Chancellor been thinking with his irresponsible Proposal, one so open to misinterpretation? And she heard the murmurs of agreement before she moved on.

What fruit might those small seeds eventually bear?

As it grew late the press of people began to thin. However, the volume of noise hadn't decreased proportionately, as those guests remaining were now rather drunk. Stonier ground for her little seeds. Time to turn in and read through her speech one final time. Perhaps a breath of fresh air first, to clear her head.

Weaving between laughing, flirting groups of Equals and the occasional Observer of Parliament, she noted any who stood particularly close together. This hour of night might not be ideal for sharing information, but knowledge could still be usefully gathered. Bouda was making for Grendelsham's massive bronze-edged door. She was close enough to see the moon-slicked beach when she was yanked backward so hard it pulled the breath from her throat.

She spun, furious, ready to lay into Gavar, having seen the red hair as she turned—and found herself face-to-face with her future father-in-law. His grip squeezed her arm to the bone as he hauled her close. Unbalanced on high heels, Bouda stumbled and fell against his chest, and his other arm went round her. The cut-glass tumbler in his hand dug into the exposed small of her back.

She smelled the whisky he'd been drinking. His face was so

close that when he spoke it was as if he breathed the words right into her, like a god animating a manikin of clay.

"You are a spectacle, in this dress."

For emphasis, Whittam dragged the glass the length of her naked spine. He stopped at Bouda's neck and brushed his thumb against her throat. She tipped her head back to avoid the touch, but it only left her feeling more exposed. There was a surging in her ears that could have been her pumping blood or the sea beyond. But they were surrounded by people. She couldn't make a scene.

"It is not appropriate"—his breath tickled her collarbone, the thumb dug in a little harder—"for a member of my family."

The slippery silver dress was treacherously insubstantial. She felt every shift of his body against hers.

When a wave of cold swept over her, she wondered if she had fainted, or if Whittam had committed the ultimate outrage of working Skill upon her to stop her struggles. But she opened her eyes—when had she closed them?—and saw that the great glass door had swung open. A dark shape stood there, a shadow pricked by a tiny hot point of light. A cigarette, she realized, as the smoke drifted toward her. Whittam's hands fell away and Bouda took a small step back.

"Is everything okay in here?"

A man's voice. Polite. Unfamiliar.

"I was merely having a word with my daughter," Whittam said easily, raising his glass to take another swig of whisky. Some of it had spilled down Bouda's back, and she felt it drying there, sticky.

"Of course, Lord Jardine. I do hope I'm not interrupting. I

simply saw Miss Matravers stumble and wondered if she might benefit from a breath of air. Though when I say 'breath of air'"—the speaker paused thoughtfully—"of course I mean 'howling clifftop gale.' The effect is quite bracing. Miss Matravers?"

The stranger pushed the door fully open, standing in the entryway as if to invite her outside, and so placing himself between Bouda and her father-in-law.

Wind gusted through and heads began to turn, voices calling irritably for the door to be shut. So she did the simplest thing and lifted the hem of her dress and stepped over the threshold. Behind her, she was aware of Whittam turning away, mingling back among their peers.

What had just happened?

Her rescuer—not that he was that, she was perfectly capable of looking after herself—let the door swing shut. They weren't quite standing in a gale, but the wind was strong and Bouda narrowed her eyes against it. It was freezing cold, and while that was no discomfort for Equals, Bouda wasn't sure if her unexpected companion was one of her own kind or a commoner. She hadn't recognized him in the doorway.

As her vision adjusted to the darkness, she studied him. Definitely not an Equal. But not an OP, either.

Then it came to her. She pursed her lips. How ignominious.

"You're Jon Faiers," she said. "Speaker Dawson's son."

"I won't hold your family connections against you"—his cigarette waved carelessly in the direction Whittam Jardine had disappeared—"if you don't hold mine against me. Anyway, I've been waiting here for ages."

"Waiting?"

She was so taken aback by his impertinence she could barely get out that one word.

"You come outside before turning in at every Second Debate, no matter what the weather. You like this place, don't you?"

He gestured at the glowing expanse of the house, and as he turned toward the light she saw his face, his cropped brown hair. His eyes were blue. She'd seen Grendelsham bathed in that very same blue, one cloudless day in summer, years ago.

"I don't blame you," Faiers continued, oblivious to her scrutiny. "It's incredible. Beautiful. Our best civil engineers couldn't build such a thing even today, and your kind did it with Skill, centuries ago."

Was he trying to be ingratiating? Yet there was an odd sincerity to his tone.

Still, what was that to her?

"You're correct, Mr. Faiers. But I really don't think this is the time and place for a discussion of architectural merit."

"Oh." Faiers turned back, his face sliding into shadow. His cigarette flared with a final deep inhalation, then he dropped it and ground it out beneath his heel. "I wasn't discussing architectural merit."

He paused, and appeared to be contemplating the view. The moon was high and full, and its radiance flared silver off the churning sea. Was this his cue to make some clumsy gallantry about her dress?

"Many of my kind—my mother, for example—think only about what you Equals take from us. Our labor, our liberty, a decade of our lives. But there are a few among us who are aware of what you give: stability, prosperity. A magnificence that other countries envy. A reminder that there is more in the world than what can be seen."

Some kind of Skill-obsessive, then? Bouda knew such people existed, commoners fixated on Skill and what it could do. Occasionally a particularly insane one attempted to ritually murder an Equal to steal their Skill—an impossibility, of course. If they weren't killed by their intended victim, they were Condemned. Then they could spend the rest of their natural lives enjoying personal demonstrations of exactly what Skill could do, at the hands of Lord Crovan.

Faiers didn't look like a madman, but you could never tell.

"You must be getting chilly out here," she said shortly. "So if you've a point to make . . ."

She'd hoped to sound repressive, but Faiers simply smiled.

"I've heard about Millmoor," he said. "And I think soon you'll be hearing about other places, too. Riverhead, or Auld Reekie. Then maybe the one after that won't even be a slave-town, just somewhere normal.

"And on that day—if not before—you might remember that there are a few of us commoners who also like this world just the way it is. Who benefit from that and who don't wish to see things change."

Faiers's glance flicked over Grendelsham's lighted interior, as if seeking out a flash of red hair among the few remaining guests. His lip curled. "Your allies aren't always who you think they are, Miss Matravers. And neither are your enemies."

Then the Speaker's son dropped a deep bow, and turned and walked away into the gusty night.

# FOURTEEN

# LUKE

The Millmoor Games and Social Club was preparing to throw the biggest New Year's party the slavetown had ever seen.

It'd be a riot.

Christmas had been less unbearable than Luke had feared. Even slaves were given the day off, and Ryan had been his guide to their dorm block's meager festivities: a lie-in, a lunch of roast chicken and soggy green veg, then a screening of the Chancellor's Christmas message in the main rec room. This was followed by movies and television specials. As the day wore on, bottles of illicit hooch were produced and passed round. Luke joined in a good-natured and occasionally life-endangering street soccer match against the neighboring block.

There were no gifts, of course. Not even a card from his family at Kyneston, because though the three months of no contact were finally up, Millmoor had been under communications lockdown since the "YES" graffiti stunt. But getting Oz to freedom was the only Christmas present Luke had needed.

The following week had brought another belated gift: the sight of Jackson, unharmed.

"We thought you were hit," said Jessica. "We heard someone yell out and assumed it was you, seeing as you weren't the one with the gun."

Jackson looked apologetic. "I was trying to draw him away from you. I'm sorry if you were worried."

"And that explosion," said Luke. "All those flames. What was that?"

"That was Skill, Luke. And just a small demonstration of what the Equals can do."

"Well, what they can't do is keep two eyes open," scoffed Renie. "That big ginger walked right past you in the slammer."

"He wasn't expecting to see us and Oz heading out," said Jackson. "So he didn't. That's how people work, Equals included. They see what they want to see. I assure you Gavar Jardine is not to be taken lightly. None of them are."

"That's 'Jardine' as in the people my family is slaving for, right?" said Luke. "He's one of them. My sister made us learn all the names."

"He is. And the plan is still to get you to their estate to rejoin your family as soon as possible. You shouldn't be here on your own, Luke."

But Luke wasn't on his own, was he? He had the club.

He had friends. And a purpose.

But he also had family. Sisters.

Suppose Daisy and Abi had to see Gavar Jardine every day? If the guy could blow up a prison with just the force of his mind—his Skill—who knew what he might do to a slave who displeased him?

No, Luke's place was with his family. But it was strange how the all-consuming need to join them had become less urgent as time went by.

"How about it, Luke?" Jackson's voice pulled him back to the present. "Shall we plan a very special New Year's party for the Overseer and her pals?"

As it turned out, "party" didn't come close.

It was remarkable, thought Luke, looking at the others seated around the table, how the Doc had managed to assemble a group of people with all the talents the club needed. As he'd come to know the others, he'd realized that behind their every-day exteriors lay some impressive abilities. Take the ditcher sisters. They'd both been police officers, but it had been a while before he'd learned exactly what kind.

"Cybercrime," Hilda had said one day, taking pity on Luke's attempts to guess.

"Catching perverts," her sister had elaborated. "Internet drug dealers. Pleasant folk like that. So we know where to find stuff and how to hide stuff on just about any system."

"Plus we've got some great jokes that your mother wouldn't approve of," finished Hilda.

So it was with the others. Jess had been a gym instructor, but had used her earnings to support a career as a semipro free runner. She'd begun her slavedays when on a protracted downer after realizing she was no longer at competition standard—

"Worst decision my ego and I ever made," she'd told him ruefully.

Asif was a recently qualified computer science teacher who'd hated the classroom. ("Kids terrify me. Imagine a room full of thirty Renies." Luke could see his point.) He'd become fascinated by the internet restriction protocols in place at the slavetowns. After spending a couple of years experimenting with hacking in, he'd decided to take on the bigger challenge of being inside and trying to hack out.

"You started your days to give yourself a challenge?" Luke asked him, incredulous.

"What can I say?" Asif shrugged. "Geeky as charged."

What did Luke bring to the team? He wasn't sure. He'd been useful fixing the getaway van, but no one could have foreseen needing his abilities there. He was also prepared to take a risk to do what was right. That had been second nature to him, though Luke had now been in Millmoor long enough to realize it wasn't the choice most people made.

So that put him in a minority. But surely only one thing about him was unique. The fact that his family was at Kyneston.

Where, despite all that he'd contributed in Millmoor, Jackson still wanted him to go.

Did the Doc have some reason why?

No answer immediately presented itself, so Luke let that thought go and threw himself into the party planning.

They sat talking and arguing for hours, until they had something that looked like an actual, honest-to-goodness day of chaos across Millmoor. Renie chewed so much gum it was a wonder her teeth weren't worn to nubbins. Jessica was looking alive again for the first time since Oz's capture. Hilda and Tilda must have drunk a bathful of tea, and Asif was jiggling in his seat, looking totally wired on nothing at all.

"I don't suppose we should involve anyone from the other slavetowns?" Luke said finally. "Like Riverhead, maybe?"

Renie caught on straightaway to this transparent pretext to see Angel again, and cackled mercilessly. Even Jess smiled.

"What?" he protested, face reddening. "Just saying. They might have some . . . awesome people, is all."

Jackson watched him squirm. "Riverhead has its own priorities," he said finally, with a grin.

"Okay, okay." Luke knew when he was beaten.

The Doc wrapped up the meeting. Now all the club had to do was bring its plans to life.

And Luke had somehow come up with the most ambitious plan of all—a daylong walkout that would shut down Zone D.

It was distinctly more daunting than his lifetime achievements thus far: getting picked for the senior soccer team, running his class project for the community festival, and nailing varial kickflips on his skateboard. He couldn't simply go asking people to join a shutdown. Security would nab him in no time. And even if they didn't, who would follow such a risky scheme, led by a seventeen-year-old boy? But Luke had an idea where to begin.

He knew his colleagues in Zone D by now. He'd noticed the ones who talked loudest in the canteen queue. The ones who always had a bunch of blokes around them, squeezing in some banter and camaraderie despite a schedule designed to make it impossible.

One of them was a guy named Declan, who had known Si's

uncle Jimmy. It was a thin connecting thread, but it would help Luke find a way deeper into the network of trust and friendship that existed among his workmates. Passed from man to man, word of an insurrection would spread.

For the first time, he was grateful for the din of Zone D, because otherwise Declan would surely hear the pounding of his heart, louder than any machinery. Luke tugged the man's sleeve as they passed near the storeroom, and drew him to one side.

"What do you think of this shutdown I keep hearing about?" Luke said. "Sounds brilliant, but scary. Are you in?"

Declan looked blank, because of course there was no shutdown, not yet, and no talk—though there would be soon. So Luke outlined his plan as if it were something he'd been told, and Declan listened with interest.

"We've not heard about it in the shakeout room," he responded. "Must be some hothead in components stirring it up. But it's a sweet idea. Teach the Overbitch a lesson for denying us even a word from our families at Christmas. Not to mention those patrols crawling everywhere these days. The third Friday, you say? Lemme check with the others."

And when Luke saw Declan next, the man reported that though none of his colleagues had heard of the shutdown, either, they'd all be well up for it.

"It's not like they can punish us all," Declan said, gripping Luke's shoulder reassuringly. "So hold your nerve and come in with us, lad."

"You know what?" Luke said, grinning. "I think I will."

The first of January came and went with no fireworks. There'd be some soon. Just not the kind the Overseer and the Equals were expecting.

Luke had a few more conversations. It wasn't long before the responses of those he spoke to began to change. They'd heard about the shutdown, too, he was told. Loads of the guys had. Everyone was up for it.

The weather was unvarying from one dreary day to the next, but by the middle of the month the atmosphere in Zone D and across Millmoor had shifted in some intangible but important way. Then the week of the club's party arrived.

Monday morning, Williams muttered something inaudible as he and Luke operated their station's clattering gears.

"Sorry?"

"Have you heard?" Williams repeated, looking like he wanted to bite off his own tongue.

"Heard what?"

Luke looked away, tracking the slow progress of the colossal piece of metal swinging over their heads. Maybe if Williams wasn't being watched, he could kid himself he wasn't actually speaking, either. Trees falling in the woods and all that.

"No-show. Friday. You in?"

"Yeah. You?"

There was a long pause. Together they unlatched the safety clasps and released the massive component into the cradle. Luke licked at the sweat that trickled along his upper lip, and tasted metal.

"Yeah."

The man sounded terrified, but Luke couldn't suppress his jubilation. Now that even a timid, trouble-averse bloke like Williams knew of the walkout, word must have gone round the whole of Zone D.

And Luke had talked it into existence.

Thinking about that made his head spin. It was almost like Skill—conjuring up something out of nothing.

"There's no magic more powerful than the human spirit," Jackson had said at the third and final club meeting. Luke was beginning to dare to hope that was true.

As he and Williams moved in smooth partnership around their workstation, Luke wondered how the others were getting on with their schemes.

Mostly, it was on-the-day stuff. They'd run through it all at that last get-together. Hilda and Tilda were going to reset the electronic pricing inventory across Millmoor's stores, so that no credit was deducted from anyone's account for purchases made. Hopefully word would spread quickly on the day and the shops would be besieged. Renie was sabotaging Security's vehicle pool—"a little knife-in-tires jobby," she'd called it— while Asif would have fun with the hated public broadcast system.

"I'll tune it to Radio Free For All," he announced, referring to an online channel believed to operate from a canal boat in the Netherlands. "Nothing like some C-pop with your agit-prop."

Luke groaned. "Just promise me you'll pull the plug if they start playing 'Happy Panda.'"

For an instant, his memory catapulted him back to last summer: Daisy and her pals prancing round the garden singing in atrocious Chinese. It was almost Luke's final memory of life before Millmoor. It was only half a year ago, but it felt as distant as the Equal history he'd been cramming that day.

If anything went wrong at the club's party, would he ever see his family again?

But no: if he thought like that, he'd never do anything. Never make a difference to all the other Daisys who didn't have an Abi resourceful enough to get them out of Millmoor.

Back to the plans, Luke.

Renie had shown Jess how to mess with the power settings on Security's stun guns, and she'd be sneaking into their gear store to reset them. The Doc had several banners prepared for landmarks around the slavetown. But the headline act would be a mass rally at the MADhouse.

Security would be distracted by the lower-level stuff: calming things down at the shops, removing the banners, maybe rounding up Zone D's workers and getting them to their stations. So hopefully they wouldn't realize what was going on at the MADhouse until a huge crowd had assembled. What happened next would be up to the crowd itself.

"You not gonna make a speech or nothing?" Renie had asked the Doc.

"Not me," he'd replied, to everyone's surprise. "This has to be something that people themselves want; it's not something we can make happen."

"Isn't that what we've just spent these last weeks doing?" said Tilda. "Making it happen?"

"Not really." Jackson scratched his beard. "We're giving people permission, if you like. Reducing the risk to any one individual by creating a mass they can lose themselves in. If anything more happens, it'll be because the people of Millmoor want it."

The people of Millmoor.

Luke was one of them now.

And something weird and terrifying had happened in the

weeks between that first planning day and now: Luke had begun to think he should stay in the slavetown.

The idea had first popped into his head, fully formed, as he'd had one of those casual conversations with a workmate that seeded the shutdown. After what he was doing right now in Millmoor, could he really go back to being just his parents' son and Abi's little brother? A dogsbody on a great estate saying "Yes, sir" and "No, sir" all day long?

Once the idea had arrived, it was strangely reluctant to leave.

It ran through his head every day as he worked alongside Williams. He had no more luck dislodging it in the nonexistent privacy of his dorm room at night. He'd resorted to the little kid's trick of pulling his blanket over his head. He tried to fool himself that if he couldn't see his roommates, they couldn't see him, either, lying there sleepless.

In the darkness, all attempts at logic overheated his brain till he wanted to rip the blanket out of pure frustration. His family down south, and his friends here. The splendor of Kyneston, and the squalor of Millmoor. Slavery there, and slavery here. But here was a chance to do something. Change something.

Maybe even change everything.

No, that was ridiculous. He was only a teenage boy. He was doing well if he changed his worn underpants for clean ones from one day to the next. His family wanted him at Kyneston. Even Jackson wanted him to go.

But if the Doc changed his mind, just said the word and asked Luke to stay . . . would he?

Luke woke on Thursday unrested, and stumbled his way through his shift no nearer to clarity. Anxiety and excitement about the next day's events lodged nauseatingly in his stomach.

Back at the dorm that evening he went to the kitchen to whip up his chef's special of *spaghetti sur toast*. But he had no appetite and just stood there staring at the rusty stove.

"All right? Thought I might find you here."

Luke turned. It was Ryan.

Sometimes the two of them met in the rec room on a Saturday night, or in the breakfast hall, and they'd natter. They didn't really have much in common—especially not now that Ryan had decided on the military route and enlisted as a mauler. His conversation was full of his training sessions and his fellow cadets. But it was nice just to have someone to joke with about the improbable glow of nostalgia that surrounded their crummy old school, Henshall.

Luke hadn't seen Ryan since Christmas. It was good timing that he'd popped down now. A bit of distraction from everything churning through Luke's brain.

Ryan pulled out a chair at one of the kitchen tables and made himself comfortable. It looked like Luke would be playing host, so he topped up the kettle and switched it on, and plucked an extra teabag out of the dusty jar.

"It's a bit like being at university, isn't it?" said Ryan, vaguely indicating the two mugs Luke had placed on the worktop. "My cousin was studying at Staffs and I went to stay with him one time. He was living in halls and they had kitchens like this."

Luke stared at Ryan. Slavery was like university? Because they had communal kitchens? Was he mad?

Or was this what Jackson had meant when he'd said that the people of Millmoor had to want to rise up? Ryan was leaning back against the wall, staring at the ceiling. He looked as likely to rise as one of Daisy's jaw-breaking cakes.

Luke made some tea and carried both mugs to the table. What he wouldn't give right now for a cookie.

Ryan seemed a bit tense, and Luke wondered what was on his mind. Maybe he'd met a girl? Some fit cadet. Lucky sod. Luke considered telling him about Angel, but knew he'd have to veil it in so many half-truths it wouldn't be worth the effort. And he'd be so terrified of letting something slip, it'd only be more stress, instead of a relief.

If only there was someone he could speak to about every-thing that was going on—someone who wasn't right in the middle of it all.

But Ryan started talking and Luke discovered it was good just to listen, to lose himself in the mundane details of someone else's life. Half his brain followed Ryan's account of his new exercise regime and something called Basic Training. The other half felt luxuriously drowsy. Maybe he'd actually get some sleep tonight.

Then adrenaline coursed through his body as if someone had jabbed a syringe of it between his shoulder blades like the Doc had with Oz, the night they broke him out.

"You what?" he said to Ryan, squinting in the fluorescent light. It didn't actually make anything brighter, just turned the room a sickly yellow.

"I said, big day tomorrow?"

And what the hell did that mean? Luke's throat closed up, but he lifted his mug of tea to buy himself time. He rested his elbow on the table in case his hand shook.

"Big day?" he said, trying to grin. "This isn't Henshall Acad-emy, Ryan. Tomorrow's only Friday—nothing big about that. My week doesn't end till Saturday night."

"Ah, yeah," said Ryan. His gaze darted around the worktop, seemingly fascinated by the meager appliances. It settled on a particularly riveting stack of saucepans. "It's just that I heard . . ."

Luke put his mug down. He was losing the struggle to keep his hand still, and tea would be sloshing over the side in a minute.

Ryan hesitated. "It's not easy here, is it? You must be angry about the fact that they transferred your family but not you."

Luke went cold. He couldn't believe it. Ryan was fishing, trying to catch him out. He was sure of it.

So what did they know—whoever they were? Did they have an eye specifically on Luke? Which would be bad, because that'd mean they'd made some connection to the club. Or had they simply got wind that something was up at Zone D? And Ryan, like a good little cadet, had volunteered to try and get something out of his mate who worked there?

*His mate.* Not anymore. The bastard.

"I'm hoping my family will get me transferred to Kyneston soon," he told Ryan. Let him think that Luke wanted out, and would therefore be toeing the line like a good boy. "I'm crossing off the days, to be honest. Who could have guessed I'd actually miss my sisters?"

Ryan huffed a weak little laugh and turned back to Luke. He looked wretched.

"So you've heard nothing out of the ordinary at work lately?" he said. "Nothing odd?"

Ryan had clearly abandoned the subtle approach. Luke's palms were sweating. Outright denial would be suspicious. Better to hide a big lie in a small truth.

"Look, I don't know what it's like where you are in maintenance, but Zone D is pretty hardcore. Moaning is about the
only way to deal with it. I hear intense stuff all the time. Blokes
talking about wrecking machinery, bunking off, or beating up
the guards. It's how they let off steam."

Ryan frowned. "You don't report any of it?"

"It's just talk, Ryan. Might as well report someone for going
to the loo or picking their nose. You know what it's like here:
grim and boring. You'll be well out of it as a mauler. Good
choice you made there. I'd do it, too, if I was sticking around."

Ryan looked down at the table. He'd drunk even less of his
tea than Luke. Maybe even none at all. Then he pushed back his
chair, looking more cheerful than he had since he arrived.
"Better turn in. Been a long week and it's not over yet. Thanks
for the brew."

He slapped Luke on the back as he went past.

Sod you. Traitor.

Luke listened to Ryan's footsteps moving along the corridor,
toward the stairs. It was hard to tell with the echo from the
stairwell and the background noise from other men moving
around and talking, but it sounded like Ryan was going down.

Not back up to his room on a higher floor, to turn in. Down
and out—to make his report?

Luke stayed at the table for a few moments, not daring to
stand till his legs stopped trembling.

What should he do? Asif was the club member closest to
him—most of Millmoor's single males were in West dorm
blocks. Had he had a late-night social call from a "friend," too?
But if anyone was keeping an eye on Luke, then going to find
Asif would be an incredibly bad idea. If they knew about the

club, it'd just confirm the connection between members. If they didn't know, it'd give them a new person of interest.

The same held for going to find any of the others.

Perhaps Renie was skulking around in the streets?

He knew she wouldn't be. She'd be away across town, slashing tires. But he so badly wanted not to be alone that he washed up the two mugs, set them on the draining board, then jogged down the corridor to go and find out.

He was nearly at the stairs before he thought of Ryan. He stopped. What if his sometime schoolmate hadn't gone anywhere to share the details of their conversation? Perhaps the person he reported to had come here, and they were talking on the pavement outside this very minute.

Besides, surely it was too late to do anything now. The men of Zone D would either turn up for work or they wouldn't. Everything else would happen as planned, or not. Luke turned in a circle considering his options, but it didn't seem like he had any.

So he went to bed.

Sleep didn't come easily. He was shaken awake just after 7 A.M. by one of his roommates who worked in the chicken sheds and caught a bus to work round the same time Luke did.

"You'll be late, sonny."

"Not well," Luke mumbled into his pillow. "Not going."

"Your funeral."

The man moved away and Luke pulled the blanket back up and tried to doze off again. Incredibly, he managed it.

He shot awake for the second time some while later—a check of his watch told him it was 9 A.M.—thanks to a horrific blaring of feedback from the public announcement system. The PA was installed in each building and at intervals along every street. As Luke rubbed his eyes, the speaker in his dorm room made a loud farting noise, then crackled into speech.

Luke recognized the voice. Had anyone warned Jessica?

"Hello there, people of Millmoor," boomed Oz. "This is Oswald Walcott and Radio Free For All wishing you all a very good morning. It's going to be an amazing day. Let's start with a special request for a friend of mine."

There was a moment's pause as if Oz was figuring out the controls, then the air filled with the unmistakable first chords of the *paopaotang* bubblegum synth.

Luke buried his face in his pillow and groaned as the familiar backing beat started up.

The music filled the room and spilled out into the corridor, where it hit a backwash of vocal cuteness issuing from other speakers throughout the dorm block. It even echoed in the streets in demented syncopation.

"It's 'Happy Panda'!" Oz's deep voice announced triumphantly. "People, let's get this party started!"

# FIFTEEN

# ABI

The evening in the Great Solar had begun, as many evenings at Kyneston did, with Gavar Jardine hurling a whisky glass into the fireplace. Perhaps it would end with him exploding one of the glass-fronted bookcases or a piece of his mother's prized porcelain—neither was a rare occurrence.

This evening Abi had not only seen Gavar smash the glass, she had been standing next to the fireplace when he did it. Jenner half rose from his chair and snapped at his brother to take better care, but Gavar only laughed contemptuously. Sitting opposite, alone on the two-seater sofa, Bouda Matravers pinched her lips together like someone watching a toddler throwing a tantrum in a supermarket.

Current probability of wedded bliss for this pair, Abi thought: about zero.

Wedding planner had been added to Abi's job description a

few hours earlier. She and Jenner were to pin down Gavar and Bouda for more specifics, given that the ceremony was now just two months away. Bouda had stalked in to the Solar after supper and sat down, smoothing her skirt, then checked her diamond-studded watch and told Jenner he had her attention until nine o'clock. Gavar had slouched in soon after.

Abi was fascinated to be in such proximity to the Matravers heir. She'd seen pictures of Bouda before, of course, in magazines. She'd even quite admired her. The young parliamentarian was always poised and polished, a cool intelligence evident in her pale blue eyes. She was a woman unapologetically making her way in a man's world. (Abi was quicker to flip through pictures of her sweet-faced sister, who was invariably papped falling out of nightclubs, accessorized with a tiny dog and a gargantuan handbag.)

Bouda Matravers in person was another matter altogether. The intelligence was there, sure enough. But it wasn't cool, it was ice-cold—the kind of cold that could burn. Not that she'd notice you were there in the first place. Bouda was one of those Equals for whom commoners were simply irrelevant. Invisible. Abi wondered, briefly, what it would take to get her attention. A jab in the leg with a sharp pencil, perhaps. She had no intention of trying.

"Ignore him," Bouda told Jenner, pointedly not looking at Gavar, who had stopped pacing and was now staring morosely into the fire. "Justice Council voted this afternoon to send him back to Millmoor tonight. Unfinished business from his last failed trip there. So he's sulking and completely sloshed already, in case you hadn't noticed."

Abi fumbled with her pencil, catching it clumsily before it dropped to the floor.

Millmoor? Why Millmoor?

Positioned to one side of Jenner's armchair, she couldn't catch his eye. But he knew how worried she was about Luke, especially because the communications lockdown meant they'd still had no news of her brother since the day he'd been taken from them. So she could have hugged Jenner when he asked, mildly, what was going on in the slavetown.

"Nothing, is what," said Gavar, rummaging through the drum-shaped drinks chest. "Rumors. A prisoner escaped just before Christmas and now there's been some new intel, so Father and Bouda have got it in their heads that something's going to kick off tomorrow. Zelston was too gutless to authorize the use of lethal force himself, so yours truly is being sent up there to"—and here Gavar turned, a rectangular green bottle gripped too tightly in one hand, and mimicked the resonant tones of the Chancellor—"*make the decision on the ground.*"

He unstoppered the spirits and drank straight from the bottle, gulping it down.

"Lethal force?" Jenner's tone was sharp, but it didn't come close to capturing Abi's fear.

Please let Luke be safe. Please.

"The only one talking any sense was Rix," Gavar muttered. He wiped his chin with the back of one hand and addressed his future wife. "Pointed out that no one's storming the estates with broom handles and kitchen knives, so why should we intervene. He's right. The people working in Security in the slavetown are all commoners. Why should it concern us if they turn on one another?"

Bouda threw her hands into the air with exasperation, then almost instantly clasped them and brought them back down to her lap. Her every gesture, every word, was controlled, Abi realized. What would it take to make Bouda Matravers crack? She didn't like to think.

"We can't tell you more," Bouda said to Jenner. "We'd fall foul of the Quiet. But let's just say that this is Gavar's chance to shine, and as usual he's doing the best he can to throw that chance away."

"Because your father really shone this afternoon," Gavar retorted. He turned to Jenner. "*Darling Daddy*"—and now he mocked Bouda's husky voice—"threw a hissy fit at Armeria Tresco for correcting some misapprehensions on the part of my future wife. Suddenly his Skill starts fizzing and he rips the council table in two. It's some mahogany monstrosity, must weigh a few tons. Never knew Lord Lard had it in him."

Bouda jumped to her feet. Her hands were up again, clutched and twisting in front of her as if one were trying to choke the life out of the other.

"Don't," she snarled. "Not my father. Don't you dare . . ."

"Or what?" Gavar's voice was singsong, taunting. He really was exceptionally drunk, Abi realized.

"Or you'll regret it," Bouda said.

And Abi saw it—saw the moment at which, with a slight clench of her fingers, Bouda Matravers stopped the words in Gavar Jardine's throat. Gavar gagged and his left hand came up to claw at his collar. His other hand let go of the bottle, which fell heavily, releasing a sickly aniseed smell as its contents spilled across the oak floor. Gavar fumbled at the mantelpiece for support, knocking to the ground a silver-framed photograph of a younger Lady Thalia and three small boys, two auburn-haired, one dark.

"Now, where were we?" said Bouda, sleeking her long po-nytail over her shoulder and sitting back down. "I know. Pink roses for my bouquet and the buttonholes, or ivory? I think pink, don't you, my love? They'll go so nicely with your complexion."

The sound that burst from Gavar Jardine was an inchoate roar. A simultaneous expulsion of sound and a sucking intake of breath.

"Bitch!" he howled.

And as Abi watched, appalled, Bouda Matravers was snatched up by nothing at all and tossed through the air. She slammed against the wall and there was a sickening crunch as her head collided with the massive gilded frame of a serene landscape of the Kyneston Pale. Abi saw a gash rip open along that white-blond hairline and bright blood well up as Bouda collapsed to the floor.

Before Abi could even yelp, the door to the Solar shattered into splinters.

Lord Jardine stood there, his arm outstretched for the door handle that his Skill and fury had rendered superfluous. His face was as red as Gavar's but his voice, when he spoke, was as controlled as Bouda's.

"What is going on here?"

Bouda rose to her feet. She should have been unconscious, surely, or at least unsteady. But not a bit of it. Blood daubed half her face red and dripped onto the neckline of her sky-blue dress, but the gash in her scalp was no longer visible.

Was no longer there, Abi realized with a start. So it was true, then. The Equals could heal themselves. How was that even possible?

"Difference of opinion about the wedding plans," Bouda said coolly. "Gavar objected to my choice of color scheme."

And could Equals kill using Skill? Abi wondered. Because Gavar Jardine ought to have been a smoldering cinder-smear on the carpet by now if they could.

"Gavar," his father said. "Why are you still here? You should be on your way to Millmoor. Go."

Lord Jardine stepped to one side of the empty doorway and gestured through it. Father and son stared at each other for a moment before Gavar gave a low growl, ducked his head, and left, kicking through the litter of splinters.

Bouda Matravers stared after him with a look of triumph. It didn't last long.

"Bouda," said her future father-in-law. "You are not to provoke him."

The blond girl opened her mouth but Lord Jardine cut her off.

"Do not argue. Gavar is my heir, until such time as I—and this family—have a better one. Your job is to manage Gavar, not rile him. I expect you to do that job better. Now come." He beckoned and Bouda went to his side.

She's not marrying Gavar at all, Abi realized, watching. She's marrying his father. His family. His house. The Jardine name. And she's giving herself to a man she despises in order to get it all.

Lord Jardine placed a hand in the small of Bouda's back and steered her toward the corridor.

"Oh, just one moment," the blond girl said, looking back over her shoulder. "While we're managing things. Don't want any belowstairs gossip about this."

Those manicured talons pinched: a falcon taking a mouse.

"No," Jenner said, stepping forward. "It's not necessary."

But Bouda Matravers's Skill was already inside Abi's skull. The Equal rammed it in like a poker and was rolling it around, burning away the memory of what had just taken place in the Great Solar, then cauterizing the loss. The shock made Abi's head recoil with such force that she bit her tongue, and her scream bubbled through the blood filling her mouth. Dark clots swam before her eyes.

Then it was over and she was sitting in the armchair, with Jenner and Lady Thalia watching her with concern. She blinked: once, twice. Her eyes stung—had she been crying?

Abi tried to stand up, but her legs trembled. She reached out to clutch at Jenner's arm and steady herself. But he lightly un-peeled each finger and transferred her hand from his sleeve to the claret upholstery of the chair. Though gentle, his action felt unmistakably like repudiation, and Abi felt the skin around her eyes prickle with shame. Her head ached terribly. The smell of alcohol hung on the air.

She looked around the room—they were in the Great Solar—but could see nothing out of place. The door was shut, the furniture neatly in position. The only items to catch her eye were an empty bottle propped against the chimney breast and the framed photograph that Lady Thalia held. Abi's notebook and a pencil were set neatly on the floor. The objects didn't add up to a coherent memory.

What had she done? Had she got drunk? Made a fool of her-self? The idea was unbearable. She wouldn't be allowed to work with Jenner anymore. Maybe they'd even send her away to Millmoor.

At the thought of the slavetown a final spasm of agony jolted through her brain and she gasped.

"What happened?" Abi asked, looking between Jenner and his mother. "I don't remember. I'm so sorry. I hope I haven't done anything wrong?"

Mother and son exchanged glances. Abi felt her insides clench, like a wave of nausea when there's nothing left to bring up.

"Of course you haven't, child," said Lady Thalia, placing the photograph back amid the Meissen figurines and jeweled gewgaws. She put her hand up to Abi's face. Her fingers were cool against Abi's cheek and her perfume was faint and floral. "You were here taking notes about my son's wedding plans. But you must have caught your foot on the fender rail or these wonky old floorboards of ours, because you took a bad tumble and banged your head. You gave us quite a fright. But you're all right now."

"I still feel a bit funny," Abi admitted. "I hope I haven't inconvenienced you?"

She looked anxiously at Jenner. His expression was miserable.

"Don't worry about that," said Lady Thalia, with a glossy smile. And Abi sensed that beneath the show of concern, she was being dismissed. "Gavar had to head off on parliamentary business, in any event. I think it would be best if you went back to your parents and had an early night. Jenner will see you home."

Under other circumstances, Abi would have been delighted to have Jenner's company for the long walk to the cottages where the slave families lived. But this evening he didn't say a word. He just dug his chin into his scarf and his hands into his pockets as they headed toward the Row, keeping always several paces in front of her. Abi had the sense of being in disgrace, though for what offense, she had no idea.

The night was cold and clear, the sky more star than dark, and their breath plumed as they walked. Abi felt her temples gingerly. She couldn't work out exactly where she'd hit her head. Perhaps Lady Thalia had healed her, she thought. Just not very well. Kyneston's mistress was only weakly Skilled, though she was a dab hand at repairing things broken by her eldest son in one of his rages.

At that thought, a fresh surge of pain seared the inside of her skull and Abi moaned, stopping where she stood. That made Jenner turn around, and when he saw her he immediately came back.

"What is it?" he asked. "What's wrong?"

And Abi couldn't help herself. He was right there next to her, so concerned. And it was such an innocent thing to do. She reached for him again.

But he stepped away. His movement was deliberate, and it wasn't done beneath the hawk eyes of his family. Abi ached with disappointment.

Jenner held his hands out as she'd seen him do to his gelding Conker, when the horse went skittish.

"Abigail," he said soothingly. The assumption that he could calm her like an animal drove a spike of fury through her distress. "Please stop this. You're a lovely girl. We make a great working team. But I think you're getting muddled up. I've seen it happen before, with other girls here. Though I can't say it's ever happened to me."

He gave a self-deprecating laugh, and even as Abi felt her

every nerve ending tingle with shame she wanted to slap him for having such a poor opinion of himself. He was the best of them all. The only truly good and kind one.

"You're a slave," Jenner continued. "I'm an Equal. Wouldn't you rather have a quick ten years in the office than be banished to the kitchen or the laundry, or sent to Millmoor, because one of my family thinks your behavior isn't appropriate?"

Was it possible to die of mortification? Abi thought it quite possibly was. She'd be a first in medical literature. They could cut her up and study her, the pathologists' metal hooks pulling out first her overlarge brain and then her small and shrunken heart. She felt hot tears running down her face and put her hand up to her forehead, wincing as if the pain were back. But it wasn't her head that hurt.

"I'm sorry, Abigail," Jenner said quietly. "But please understand, it's easier this way. I think you know where you're going from here? It's not far now."

"I know where I'm going," she confirmed. "Thank you. I'll be at my desk at eight-thirty, as usual."

Abi turned away with as much dignity as she could muster. She strained to hear the moment when he went back to the house, to at least have the illusion that he stood there and watched her go, but any footfall was muffled by the grass.

She wished people had an "off" switch, she thought as she walked. Something you could just flip to shut down thought and feeling, letting muscle memory go through the motions of putting one foot in front of the other. The confusion in her heart was beyond her brain's ability to solve. What problem in a textbook was more difficult than this? None.

The cottages of the Row were still out of sight beyond the

steep rise that hid the slave quarters from the mansion. Abi was trudging up it when something monstrous and snarling plunged down toward her from the crest. She threw herself to one side as Gavar Jardine's motorbike gouged past, the beam of its gaze dazzling her for one terrifying instant.

The heir was heading off on parliamentary business, Lady Thalia had said. So what was he doing out here? Suspicion blooming in her brain, Abi jogged up the incline.

From the top she saw the long line of whitewashed cottages, almost luminous in the moonlight. And moving toward them was a shape so large and lumpy that Abi at first thought she was mistaken, until she puzzled it out.

"Wait," she called, and her sister turned and stopped.

Daisy had put on every coat from the hallway pegs: her own, then on top of it their father's fleece and Mum's down jacket. She carried an immense nest of blankets in which the swaddled form of Libby Jardine was barely discernible.

"What are you doing out here?" Abi demanded. "It's freezing. Why did you let him drag you both outside?"

"He didn't drag me anywhere," her sister said stolidly. "It was my idea. He's being sent to Millmoor again and came to say goodbye to Libby. I said I'd bring her out and told him to wait beyond the end of the Row."

"What on earth for?"

Daisy narrowed her eyes. It would have been comical, if what she said next hadn't been so disturbing.

"I wanted to talk to him privately."

"About what?"

"Nothing." Her little sister shook her head. "Might not happen. If it does, you'll know."

Daisy wouldn't be drawn further. She bent over the blankets, fussing needlessly.

"You know what Gavar's like," Abi snapped, her frustration finally finding an outlet. "You know what Silyen told us about Libby's mother. He's not someone you should be having secret conversations with. Don't be a baby; we're not in a playground now."

Daisy glared up at her. "It's *Heir* Gavar," she said. "And he's always been good to me. I'm appreciated. Can you say the same?"

Daisy stomped off back toward the cottage, but Abi had no comeback to that anyway.

It was strange—she had been so certain that an estate would be the best way to keep her family together, safe and comfortable during their days. And yet here they were, divided and vulnerable like they had never been before: Luke in Millmoor, Daisy under the sway of Kyneston's volatile heir.

What have you managed to achieve, Abi Hadley?

Not much, she told herself. Not nearly enough.

She thrust a hand into her coat pocket and felt around. There it was, the small square of metal cold against her fingertips.

There was at least one thing she was doing that made a difference. She turned her back on both the Row and the great house, and began to walk across the frozen grass.

Inside the kennels, the man was doing push-ups, muscles bunching in his arms and across his back. The cage was too small for him to stand up in, and this was the only exercise he got. As Abi's shadow fell across him he instantly dropped to the floor, motionless. Which meant his exercise routine was covert.

Which meant that he was not entirely broken by his captivity.

"It's me," she said, edging closer. The light had been on in the Master of Hounds' rooms in the eaves, which meant that the kennels would be unstaffed, but he would be close enough to hear any disturbance.

"I've got your antibiotics. And something to help them down with."

Sinewy fingers thrust through the pen and took the palmful of pills. They ignored the offered apple. The dog-man shoved the medication in his mouth and gulped from his water bowl.

"I thought . . ." Abi hesitated, not quite able to believe what she was doing. "I thought we could take a walk. Not with the leash, I mean. Upright."

His eyes, when they looked at her, were wary.

"Yes," he rasped eventually.

"And you won't run away? Or . . . or hurt me?"

She hated herself for having to ask that. But during her visits to the kennels she had realized that whatever had been done to the dog-man—she still didn't know his name, because he couldn't remember it—had chipped away at not just his humanity, but also his sanity. Occasionally on previous visits he had snarled at her. Once he had even snapped his teeth at her hand. Shaken, she hadn't gone again for nearly a week.

Those eyes met hers. Human. Mostly.

"I won't hurt," he growled. "You. I won't hurt you."

"Anyone," Abi insisted. Her hand shook. What was she thinking? She had no idea what he had done to be sentenced in this way—to be Condemned. All she knew was what the Master of Hounds had told her: that he had deserved his punishment at the hands of Lord Crovan. And given the horror of that punishment, she didn't want to guess at the awfulness of his crimes.

"I'm trusting you," she said, fitting the little key to the padlock.

"Trust," the man rasped, before being racked by a ghastly, wheezing paroxysm.

It was laughter, Abi realized a moment later, feeling sick.

She could walk away now and leave him penned. The lock had clicked open, but it was still threaded through the clasp, holding the door shut. Her hand hovered over it.

Then she remembered Lady Thalia's veiled dismissal. Jenner unpeeling her fingers from his sleeve. The fuzziness in her head as she came to in the Great Solar. The pain, afterward, as thoughts and memories swam through her brain and tried but failed to connect.

Something had happened in that room. Something had been done to her by the Equals. What?

"Let's get you out," said Abi. She plucked off the padlock, lifted the cage door slightly on its hinge so it didn't grate across the floor, and swung it open.

For a moment, the man simply stared. Then he crept out on all fours and lay on the damp concrete. He rolled onto his back and stretched his arms above his head, straining to point his toes. He looked like a man on the rack. Every one of his ribs was visible; his abdomen a shallow dish; the hair at his groin dense and matted. His face was twisted with what could have been pain, or equally ecstasy.

Turning back onto his stomach, he hauled himself onto hands and knees. His fingers clawed their way up the side of the cage until he was kneeling upright. He paused there a moment, diaphragm ballooning. Then, with a horrible broken-boned movement, he dragged each leg into a squat.

And silently—though he must surely have wanted to howl, because what it cost him was plain on his face—the man stood.

He staggered around. It was horrible to see. Like a parody of walking performed by something inhuman. And all the while, he didn't utter a sound.

There was a scream outside, and Abi froze. Above, a window clattered open and the Master of Hounds bellowed something obscene before banging the casement shut again.

"Owl," gasped the dog-man.

Abi checked her watch. It was later than she'd thought.

"I'm sorry," she said, "but you'd better get back in the pen. I need to go home. But I'll come again soon, I promise. There must be something we can do. If they see you walking and talking, can see you recovering, they surely can't make you carry on living like this, whatever it is you've done."

The man wheezed again. That mirthless laugh. He dropped to the floor, slung back his haunches, and crawled inside. Turned.

"You're in—the pen—too." He peered through the bars, fixing Abi with glittering eyes. "Just—I see—my cage—my leash."

Abi's hands shook as she snapped the padlock shut.

# SIXTEEN

# LUKE

Luke had never imagined he'd be so thrilled to hear "Happy Panda" again. The catchy beat was still doing its *oh-wa-woah-wa-wa* in his head as he loped downstairs. Just hearing Oz's voice had put a spring in his step, and he took the stairs two or three at a time, eager to see how this day would unfold.

He pushed through the front doors. Their paint was flaking, rubbed thin by the pressure of hundreds of hands daily. Men going out to work, men coming back. Another lick of paint every few years. Another batch of men to fill the foundries and factories, to do the maintenance shifts and cart away the rubbish. Then when they were gone: more men, more paint.

Would today be a first step toward ending all that?

It was icy outside, and Luke turned up the collar of his too-thin jacket and stuffed his hands into his armpits as if trying to hold in his body heat. His jumpsuit was uncomfortably hot inside the shed, but worn outside it had been uncomfortably cold for months, though January was proving the worst. They probably designed the garment carefully for maximum thermal inefficiency in all conditions.

His breath steamed in the frigid air. The only time steam looked clean in Millmoor was when it came out of your own mouth. After a few minutes, he'd adjusted to the temperature sufficiently to lift his head and straighten his back from an instinctive, heat-conserving hunch.

Usually there wasn't much worth looking at in Millmoor, although he still did Doc Jackson's exercise of searching for details. But today was different.

Today was party day.

With a six-day workweek, Luke had never been in the streets on a Friday before. It seemed busier than when he was out and about on club business on Sundays.

Just in front of him walked a couple holding hands. The man had draped his jacket around his girl's shoulders. He must be freezing. The dark hair buzzed short at the back of his head bristled with cold, and his neck had a raw, red look. There was a slapping sound as they walked. Luke identified it as the heel of her boot, which had come loose. That wouldn't keep out much on a rainy day.

The woman stopped, uncertain, and the man's arm went around her shoulders. Somewhere up ahead was a hubbub of raised voices and angry shouts. The couple turned aside, taking a different route, but Luke thought he knew what was going on.

His feet had unconsciously carried him to the nearest shop, several streets from the dorm. It looked as if Hilda and Tilda had pulled off the unlimited-credit trick, because there must have been about fifty people gathered round the store.

Metal shutters were pulled down over the frontage and two nervous-looking blokes, not all that older than Luke, stood in front of it. They wore the uniform of Millmoor Security and were holding batons. They kept looking up and down the street as if hoping for backup, which showed no signs of coming.

One of them was trying to ignore an angry man who was shouting and gesticulating. The man's finger was stabbing at the guard's face. Kessler would have had you on your back in a second with a snapped wrist and piss-soaked pants for that, but the guard just cringed.

Two lads in their early twenties had scrounged a dustbin lid and a length of metal piping from somewhere and were attempting to prize up the shutters. A group of women were cajoling the other guard to open up. One of them was flirting in a way that wasn't exactly appealing, but was certainly distracting.

For the first time, Luke properly understood what the ditcher sisters had done. Letting people have free stuff was only a small part of it. At every store across Millmoor, the scene would be much the same. Dozens of guards would be taken up on this policing. And these younger, more inexperienced ones weren't doing a great job of looking fearsome—which might make people bolder, more willing to risk defiance. If trouble flared up at one location, hopefully Security wouldn't be able to call in reinforcements, either, thanks to Renie's busy night with her knife.

All that achieved on the ground, with just a little computer mischief. Luke let out a low whistle. Impressive.

He hurried on, keen to see more of the club's plans unfold. He'd steer clear of Zone D for now. Would the place be eerily quiet, or would people have chickened out at the last minute and shown up for work? He wasn't sure he wanted to know.

But he knew where he could admire one of Jackson's banners—his sector's Labor Allocation Bureau. The same sods who'd waved through his solo assignment to Millmoor, despite the requirement that under-eighteens could only do days with a parent or guardian. The same ones, he had learned during his months in the club, who were responsible for many more outrageous decisions.

The banner was half hanging off by the time Luke arrived. The West Sector LAB was a pitted concrete building some six stories high. It wasn't as tall as the towering accommodation blocks that ringed Millmoor's outskirts, but it still loomed over the smaller administrative buildings around it. The Doc's little message was slung across its top floor like a jaunty bandanna.

It had been detached at the top right corner, and two nervous members of Security were dangling a third guy over the edge of the roof. He must have been having even less fun. He was slashing at the fastening on the bottom corner with a blade tied to a broom handle. The banner sagged but the slogan was still clear, so neatly lettered it must have been done by Asif: "UN-EQUAL."

A small crowd had gathered to watch and a woman near the front was heckling. Her skin seemed somehow too large for her, as if she'd been a big lass before coming to Millmoor and being put on the Slavery Diet. The place had done nothing to shrink her voice, though.

"Shame on yer!" the woman bawled up at the roof. "Policin'

yer own kind. Git a proper job. You was my kids, I'd tan yer hides!"

She spat emphatically on the pavement. Several others in the crowd took up a chant of "Shame! Shame!"

Whether through fright or because he did indeed feel ashamed, the guard being dangled upside down fumbled with his pole and it slipped from his fingers. The group of onlookers scurried back to avoid the blade as it fell, then surged forward to cover it. Luke didn't see what happened to either pole or knife in the scuffle that followed. But by the time the crowd eased apart again, there was nothing on the ground.

"You wait!" the woman yelled at the roof. "You tell your lords an' masters we'll give 'em a Millmoor welcome if they ever come to visit!"

Well.

Luke knew he shouldn't be surprised. Mancunians were a feisty bunch. But when all you saw, day in, day out, was people looking knackered and hungry, you somehow forgot that.

He grinned. Decided to do a circuit through South Sector to see what else was going on.

Everywhere he turned there was something to catch his eye. He stopped short when he saw a woman standing in a dorm-block doorway with some friends.

She was wearing a dress.

She was nearly old enough to be his mum, and it wasn't a terribly nice dress. In fact, it looked like it'd been run up from bedsheets. But he hadn't seen a woman in a dress since coming to Millmoor. Mostly, ladies escaped the jumpsuits, which were for heavy labor. But trousers and tunics were the order of the day, and nonregulation wear was banned. The frock might not be much of a fashion statement, but it was a political statement all right.

One of the woman's friends noticed him staring, and pointed him out to the others with a laugh. Luke felt himself go bright red and wanted to bolt, but the lady in the dress turned round and saw him. An embarrassed but proud smile lit up her tired face, and she brushed out the creases in the skirt, which was kind of sweet.

He lost track of how far he walked after that. He'd left the areas he knew well some time ago, and was straying into unfamiliar districts. But it must have been long past lunchtime, because a sudden whiff of something delicious made his stomach cramp with hunger.

The smell was coming from a second-floor window at the back of a dorm block. It was one for "small family units," which meant single parents with few enough kids that the whole family could be housed in one room. "Few enough kids" could apparently be as many as three.

A woman stuck her head out the window, fanning steam, her brown skin glistening.

"Sorry, pet," she called down when she saw him standing below. "Coupla lil' chickens flew out the factory yesterday, but we've none spare, even for a proper lad like you."

She gave a deep, throaty laugh and disappeared back inside. Luke didn't begrudge her refusal, just stood there feasting on the aroma.

Then another face appeared at the window: a girl, maybe early teens, whose frizzy hair was barely contained by two braids. She put her finger to her lips, then held up what looked like a wodge of tissue and tossed it to him. Luke darted to catch it. It was actually toilet paper, but concealed in the middle, like an improbable prize at the end of a game of pass-the-parcel, was a hot sliver of meat speckled with salt and pepper.

Luke stuffed it in his mouth and looked up to thank the girl. But she was staring over his head at something behind him. Then she broke her self-imposed silence.

"*Run!*"

Startled, Luke looked over his shoulder.

His feet took off before his brain caught up, by which time he'd managed to get a few blocks away. He could still hear the boots behind him, though. They were going surprisingly fast given the man's size.

But Luke knew what he'd seen when he'd looked back. There was only one person in Millmoor who wore that uniform and was built like that, albeit the massive bull neck had been in silhouette. And Luke knew the voice that had roared his name just as he took to his heels.

Kessler.

Luke had to slow his pace a little. His work in Zone D might have made him stronger, and his illicit roaming around Millmoor had wised him up to the city's layout. But neither of those things had made him any quicker on his feet.

Kessler wasn't catching up just yet, though. Could he shake him off?

But the man had plainly known where he was. It would be too much of a coincidence for him to have simply run into Luke way out on the edge of South, in the depths of the family blocks. How had he known?

The chip. The bloody microchip! Luke clawed at his arm as he ran, as if he could scratch the thing out.

What did Kessler's pursuit of him mean, on this of all days? Think, Luke. Think!

Luke wondered if there was any blood in the middle part of his body at all. It would all be flowing frantically to his legs and his brain. And right now his legs were getting the lion's share.

Kessler had been looking for him. Which could mean that he hadn't succeeded in fooling Ryan last night. Or maybe Zone D had been deserted all day, and for want of any better leads they were pulling Luke in for questioning by someone who actually knew how to do it.

Or maybe they knew about the club.

The first two scenarios Luke would just have to handle. But if it was the last one, he had to warn the others. And there was only one way he could think of to do that: find Jackson.

He had to get to the Doc before Kessler caught up with him, then Jackson could get word to the others. Help them keep a low profile, somehow.

He snatched a glance at his watch. The cruddy BB digital display was hard to read, but the sky itself told Luke that the afternoon was wearing on. The rally at the MADhouse had been scheduled for three o'clock. That was where Jackson would be—even if he wasn't giving any speeches. Hopefully Luke would be able to lose Kessler in the crowd for long enough to find him.

It wasn't much of a plan, but it was all he had.

He ran through the streets as swiftly as he could without pushing himself to exhaustion. His throat and lungs began to burn. He was sucking in air that was too cold, too fast. At least Kessler wouldn't be finding it any easier. Luke couldn't hear the man behind him anymore.

He settled into a regular pace, like doing cross-country back at school, and eventually the surroundings became more familiar. Ahead he saw the agglomeration of offices that kept Millmoor functioning: Supply, Sanitation, and the vast Administration block. Off to the right was the huge, blank barracks of Millmoor Security.

The streets were strangely empty, but over the noise of his thumping heart and scraping breath Luke could hear what sounded like a cacophony of many voices.

It must have worked.

The club's plan must have actually worked. That sounded like hundreds of demonstrators. Maybe more.

As he approached the MADhouse, the streets began to fill with people. At first they were just in small groups and loosely packed knots, but ahead they thickened up into a dense crowd. And beyond that it looked as if they formed a solid wall. There were no guards here at the back of the gathering. They must all be at the front, keeping protesters away from the MADhouse and other key buildings.

Luke hurried forward, first weaving his way between people, then shouldering his way deeper, and finally pushing through.

How the hell was he going to find Jackson?

The crowd spread as far as he could see. It filled the confined area in front of the MADhouse—a meanly proportioned space never intended for public celebrations or display—and flowed into the avenues that led away from it. He revised his estimate of numbers. There must be a few thousand here. It certainly smelled and sounded like that many.

His face was squashed up against jackets and coveralls, hair and skin, as he shoved his way through. He inhaled sweat and the caustic smell of the standard-issue soap. And here and there he smelled something ranker: a whiff of moonshine alcohol, or some workplace stench that never faded no matter how long you stood under the shower.

There was something else, too. Did anger have a smell? Luke thought it might. Something that you released like phero-mones. Because the atmosphere was infused with more than words. It was composed of something greater than the catcalls, the derision, the call-and-response from one side of the crowd to the other. He could hear shouts of "UN!" and "EQUAL!," of "VOTE!" and "YES!" It was more, too, than just the raised, clenched fists and hunched shoulders, the restless press and sway of the crowd.

These weren't the sort of folk he'd met in the outer districts, being quietly subversive by wearing unapproved clothing or frying up some stolen food. No. These people were like those who'd gathered round the shop that morning and heckled the guards taking down the banner. They were angry. And deter-mined.

He was near the front now. He had seen more than a few faces he recognized from Zone D as he pushed forward. Then for the first time he had a good view of the MADhouse itself. It had had yet another paint job in the night: "UN-EQUAL" sprayed in vivid yellow right across the front.

The building was ringed by guards. These were the older guys: big, tough veterans. The head of Security stood on the small balcony above the building's stubby portico. He was a lean, hard man by the name of Grierson, who was rumored to be ex–Special Forces. Next to him was the Overbitch. Gotta hand it to the woman, she didn't look scared, just pissed off as hell.

Next to her was someone else Luke recognized.

Gavar Jardine.

The scumbag who had come to torture Oz. Who'd tried to shoot Jackson. Back for more. The heir of Kyneston stood there in his sinister leather coat, his flat blue eyes bored by the spectacle before him. Luke imagined this man giving Daisy orders, reprimanding her, and his skin crawled.

The Overbitch stepped forward.

"This is your last chance," she told the crowd. "We know the identity of everyone present." She held up a small device with a screen, presumably linked to whatever tracked the implanted chips. "Those who begin to disperse *immediately* will receive only light sanctions: an additional six months. Those who remain will face a heavier penalty."

There was some muttering at that, a few shouted curses. Luke was jostled as a number of people began to push their way back. But from what he could see, it wasn't that many. Hundreds still remained.

"As if!" yelled a man's voice from the middle of the pack. "You gonna slap us all with slavelife? Where'd you put us all?"

The Overbitch actually smiled. The effect wasn't pleasant. Luke guessed she didn't do it much.

"We can always find room," she said.

"Traitor!" came another voice, female this time. It wobbled, as if the speaker couldn't believe her own daring. "Oppressing your own people. We don't ask much. Fair day's pay for a fair day's work. Not hard to grasp."

"But contrary to the law," said the Overseer.

"Rubbish laws!" the woman called back.

"It's regrettable that you think so," said the dumpy woman on the balcony. "Now." She looked at her watch. "Fascinating though this has been, we've had quite enough. As you've shown yourself unwilling to disperse voluntarily, I can see we'll have to encourage you."

"You an' whose army?" yelled the first man. "Don't see many of your goons here."

"Oh," said the Overseer. "I don't need an army. You see, there's such a thing as natural authority in this country."

She simpered up at the redheaded freak. Luke felt fear grab him by the scruff of the neck and shake him till he trembled.

Everything happened very quickly after that.

There was a stirring in the crowd just in front of Luke. He recognized the woman who'd been heckling at the Labor Allocation Bureau. Next to her, a tall skinny bloke stepped forward with something in his hand—a pole, with a knife on the end. He launched it up at the balcony.

It struck the Overseer—only a glancing blow, by the looks, but there was blood and she screamed murder. Then Grierson strode to the edge of the balcony, lifted his rifle, and fired.

Once: at the man who had thrown the makeshift spear. Again: at the woman by his side.

He must have shot her in the head, because an arc of gore spattered across the people standing behind. Luke's eyes closed reflexively but he felt something warm splash against his cheek and gagged.

He dabbed at it with his cuff and blinked, then saw Jackson shoving his way toward the two people who'd been hit.

There was screaming now, and panic. The unity of the

crowd had ripped apart. Most were trying to turn and flee, but many were surging toward the thin line of guards around the MADhouse entrance.

They could do it, Luke thought. There were enough of them.

"At will!" Grierson yelled. "At will!"

Luke heard more shots go off and more people screaming, but still he and others kept going. This was it, he thought. They'd get no second chances after this.

"No!"

The voice had come from up above, from the balcony, and there was only one person it could belong to. It made the Overseer's threats and Grierson's commands seem as inconsequential as a child trying to overrule its parents.

But there was no more time to analyze it. Luke doubled over with the pain that slammed into him, as heavy and terrifying as his workstation hoist. He howled, and heard a stricken animal yelping in his own voice. He tried to curl up to minimize the agony, but it was everywhere, in every cell of him.

He wanted just for an instant, fervently, to die so it would end.

Then the wave of torment rolled over him and he was beached on the other side. He lay there gasping, flat on his back with tears streaming from his eyes. His abdomen was heaving as if there were an alien inside about to burst out. He coughed and it sent excruciating ripples through every part of him. He needed to spit, and turned his head as carefully as if his neck were made of glass.

From his sideways viewpoint, he realized that everyone he could see was in the same state. The square was full of fallen, writhing, groaning people. The Security guards, too, by the look of it, though his vision was too blurry to be certain.

So that was Skill, Luke thought, when he found himself able to think. The sexy, subtle magic from Abi's books. The Skill with which smoldering Equals seduced women, wove exquisite illusions for them, and punished those who tried to hurt their girl.

In reality, an agony so excruciating you wished you were dead.

How could you fight against that? How could you win against people who could do that? Not people—monsters. It didn't matter that there were hardly any of them. There didn't need to be.

Jackson was going to have to come up with a better plan than today's, that was for sure.

Luke let his head fall back onto the gritty ground. All around him he could hear people sobbing, swearing; a few throwing up.

Then in his peripheral vision—movement. A pair of black boots came to a halt by the side of his face. The toecap of one insinuated itself beneath his cheek and turned his head. He looked up into Kessler's meaty face as the man bent over him.

"Wishing you'd let me catch you earlier, Hadley?"

The tip of a long baton tapped the row of eyelets on Kessler's boots—not impatiently. Slowly. As if he had all the time in the world.

"Now, here's a funny thing," Kessler continued. "When we were trying out our stunners on a few troublemakers earlier, we found they weren't having quite the usual effect. Seems some scallywag must have been messing with the settings. But don't you worry. I can do this the old-fashioned way."

Kessler grinned, his lips going thin like a dog's. The baton stopped tapping. Luke saw the black length of it upraised above his head.

"I'm going to miss you, E-1031. But they'll take good care of you where you're going."

Luke closed his eyes before Kessler's arm smashed down.

When he came round, his head felt twice its normal size. He couldn't see. For a terrified moment he was convinced that Kessler's blow had done awful damage, detached something in his head beyond repairing. Then he thought his eyes must be swollen shut.

It was only once his vision had adjusted that he realized he was in a cramped, windowless space.

And it was moving.

# SEVENTEEN

# LUKE

He was in the back of a vehicle. A small one. So it wasn't one of Security's prisoner transport wagons—but it wasn't Angel's stolen van, either.

He was lying on what felt like folded tarpaulin, which protected his tenderized body from the vehicle's hard shell, and a couple of blankets had been draped over him. He had a bandage around his head. So someone cared about the state he was in.

But was that only so he'd be able to bear interrogation upon his arrival?

Plus, his hands and ankles were securely tied. So whoever had him thought he might try to get away.

Luke's other senses didn't have much to contribute. The wheels whirred rather than rumbled on the road surface, which likely meant they were on a motorway. This was reinforced by the fact that the vehicle wasn't making frequent changes of direction. He could hear one of the national radio stations faintly from the cab, meaning they were still in Britain. No conversation, so whoever was driving might be alone.

His nose told him nothing at all. The space around him smelled simply of van: that bloke-ish blend of metal, newspaper, and oily rags. Corners of Dad's garage had been just the same.

There was nothing more he could discover without getting free. Luke struggled with the ropes round his wrists, but the effort turned his head into a throbbing mess. He also didn't want to alert the person in the cab to the fact that he was conscious. It might give him an element of surprise when the doors were opened.

Though what was he going to do, tied up as he was? Headbutt the driver, or aim a two-footed kick at his middle? Luke was pretty sure stunts like that only worked in the movies.

Best-case scenario: Kessler was somehow linked to the club and had broken Luke out of Millmoor for a reason. That would require the man's taste for inflicting grievous bodily harm to be some sort of screwed-up deep cover, but it wasn't completely impossible. He had, after all, been the reason Luke had met the Doc in the first place. And Luke's quick recovery from their encounter in the storeroom showed that whatever he'd done that day had felt worse than it actually was. But still, that was unlikely.

Worst-case scenario: the other club members had also been rounded up and were this very minute lying hog-tied in vans. They could all be speeding to a short trial followed by a long sentence in a lifer camp. More probable. Which wasn't reassuring.

Luke's brain cycled between these two possibilities and a good few more besides. But it hadn't settled on one by the time he felt the vehicle's movements change and the speed drop.

Then they stopped.

His pulse rate shot up. He managed a sort of caterpillar wriggle toward the doors, rolled onto his back, and shuffled till his legs were bent up and his feet flat against the door panel. He heard footsteps round the side of the van; the click of the door handle. As it opened, he stamped down hard . . .

. . . on empty air and fell out of the back of the van. He landed at the feet of someone who sprang back with a yell.

Luke writhed on the ground, moaning. He hurt everywhere. It was pitch-black and absolutely freezing. He opened his eyes and looked up at a night sky filled with stars. Hundreds—thousands, must be. He hadn't seen them since going to Mill-moor.

"Who the heck are you?" a voice demanded.

A voice that apparently hadn't expected to find a trussed-up teenage boy in the back of his van.

"Was about to ask you the same thing," Luke croaked, trying to maneuver into a sitting position. "Where are we?"

He couldn't see the driver clearly. The darkness was almost total, apart from a muted glow just beyond the trees that edged the road. Was it one of those useless security lights that only went off like a beacon when a cat jumped on a fence half a mile away?

"Didn't get orders to tell you nothing," the driver said. "Didn't even know there was a 'you.' Was just told to make the drop-off here. Got a number to call when I arrived."

He pulled out a phone and there was a Post-it note stuck to

it. Squinting at the number, the man dialed and explained to whoever answered that he had made the delivery.

Luke heard him repeat back, "Leave it? You know what 'it' is, right?"

Then the conversation ended and the deliveryman began to walk back to his vehicle.

"Wait!" Luke called. "What's going on? You're not just going to abandon me? I'll freeze to death."

"Not my problem," the man said, though he pulled one of the blankets from the back and threw it in Luke's direction. It landed several yards short. Bastard.

Then he climbed into the van and drove off.

Luke waited a few moments to be sure he wasn't returning, then started casting around for anything that might cut the plastic twine binding his wrists and ankles.

The roadside verge wasn't promising, but he caterpillared his way over to the nearest tree, where he found a stone embedded among the roots. It didn't have much of an edge, but if he could work up a bit of friction he might be through by morning.

Luke didn't think he had until morning.

He'd made no headway when the light beyond the trees flared up, then died. Metal creaked and shrilled, like hinges opening. Damn. He should have bunny-hopped down the road and hidden while he could. He curled against the tree trunk and tried to make himself as small as possible.

The light shifted and he heard a muffled sound resembling horses' hooves. Two horses? Then footsteps. They came straight toward him as if they knew exactly where he was. So much for any escape.

The voice, when it spoke, was even closer than he thought.

"Hello. It's a bit late to be letting people in, but I do like having my brothers owe me."

The voice was male, the tone wry, and the accent cut-glass posh. Yet something about it made Luke want to burrow into the earth itself rather than see its owner. He pressed his shoulder blades back against the tree trunk, which was slippery with hoarfrost, and tried to control his rising panic.

The guy was Skilled. Luke could feel it in the way he spoke, just as with the Equal in Millmoor. His words could *do* stuff. Make things happen.

"Let's have a look at you, then."

A faint, cold brightness suffused the air, as if someone had turned up the starlight, and Luke found that he could see.

Cool fingers tipped up his chin. It was a proprietary gesture. Luke snarled and tossed his head, then glared at the freak who'd handled him.

He wasn't what Luke was expecting.

He was young—maybe no older than Luke himself, although taller. His hair was a mess, which saved Luke from having to see too much of his face. Luke caught a flash of dark eyes that made him shudder. It was as if someone had poked two holes right through the guy's head and the night was showing through on the other side.

Luke looked away as the Equal studied him intently. Who was this, and where were they?

"Well, I was right about one thing," said the freak, smiling in a way that was the opposite of reassuring. "You've got potential. You're also in a bit of a state, so first things first."

The guy reached out and ripped off the bandage around Luke's head. He lightly cupped Luke's skull right where Kessler's baton had hit. For a fleeting moment it was awful, then it wasn't. Luke's scalp and face tingled. His head didn't hurt anymore. In fact, nothing hurt anymore. He didn't even feel tired. The aristo was watching him carefully, wiping his fingers fastidiously on his sleeve.

"Better?" the Equal asked. "You're not going to like this next bit so much."

He didn't.

They'd all heard horror stories at school, or told them to one another late at night on camping trips when the adults were sleeping in another tent. The tales had always made Luke's flesh creep. Stories of people who woke up in the middle of operations, but were too paralyzed to raise the alarm. Backpackers who went drinking in beach bars, then came to in a bath of ice minus some vital organs. Sicko scientists who'd experimented on living, conscious prisoners during wartime.

The violation felt that deep. Like those cool fingers were inside his body—inside his soul, the existence of which Luke had never given much thought to until now. They were carefully sorting through bits of him that no other person was ever meant to see or know. He was sure he was going to throw up. He probably wasn't close enough to spatter the Equal's boots, but he'd try.

"Interesting," the freak said, in a way that even Luke could tell meant no good to anyone, least of all himself. "I wonder . . ."

The boy's eyes closed. But before Luke could experience any relief at being spared that unnerving gaze, he felt himself somehow . . . come loose. It was as if he were an engine still assembled, but with every part unscrewed.

He felt the Equal reach in and take something out of him.

Or add something? Had a new part been placed deep inside, where he'd never been aware that anything was missing? Something so essential it was impossible he had functioned without it?

He couldn't tell. And then the intrusion was gone and Luke curled into a ball on the hard-frozen ground. He gagged on his fear and let it spew all over the tree roots. The Equal just stood there watching.

"Finished?" the boy said, without a scrap of solicitude, when Luke was wiping his mouth with the back of his bound hands.

Luke wasn't going to dignify that with a reply. He knew only that he hated this freak. Hated him with a passion. No one should be able to do whatever this boy had just done to him. It was obscene that such people existed.

"Anyway," the Equal continued, as if they'd been talking about the cricket scores or last night's telly. "My brother will be over in a minute for all the usual 'Welcome to Kyneston' blah."

Kyneston.

This wasn't a Security detention facility. Not a lifer camp. It was the estate where his family lived.

The relief was so intense that Luke couldn't hold back the tears. He ducked his head, not wanting the Equal to see, and scrubbed his cheeks with the sleeve of his jumpsuit.

"How am I here?" he asked, when he'd pulled himself together.

The freak shrugged. "Thank your sister Daisy. Gavar's taken a shine to her. When we heard there'd been more trouble in the slavetown and he was going back, she begged him to get you out. Gavar is my older brother," the boy clarified. "I think you were in the audience for his little performance in Millmoor."

Gavar Jardine.

The Equal who'd blown up the prison after they'd freed Oz. Who had inflicted agony on hundreds of people like it was nothing at all. That same Gavar Jardine had spirited Luke out of Millmoor—because Daisy asked him to?

Luke shook his head, uncomprehending.

"Looks like Gavar's idea of a plan involved blunt force and a delivery van," the boy continued, smirking. "Seems about right. I'm sure Jenner will tell you all about it. I'm done here. For now."

He walked off toward what Luke realized must be the estate gate. The light flared again and Luke heard the murmur of voices. Then one set of hooves faded away at a trot and the other came slowly toward him, accompanied by a beam of light.

From a flashlight, not a freaky magical glow.

"You must be Luke Hadley," said another posh voice, which turned out to belong to a guy cursed with both red hair and superabundant freckles. He was leading a horse that snorted in the icy air. "I'm Jenner Jardine. I do apologize for all that. It's not pleasant, but it is necessary. Welcome to Kyneston. I'll take you to your family; they're going to be so glad to see you."

Jenner pulled out a penknife and sawed through Luke's bonds, then passed him the blanket, which Luke wrapped round his shoulders like a poncho. The Equal led the way through a huge fancy gate, all twirls and swirls and lit up like a Christmas tree, which was set into a faintly glowing wall.

After that, they walked across what felt like mile after mile of countryside. A vast area of England hidden from the common people, who would never walk here or even see this place. It was theft, really, Luke thought. Theft of something that should belong to everyone, locked up for the enjoyment of a few.

They skirted the edge of a wood, and Luke ducked and swore as a bat flew straight at him. Jenner laughed, though not unkindly, and explained that the creatures used the treeline to navigate. From somewhere far off came a chilling shriek, which Jenner said was an owl. Things rustled among the trees. Foxes? Or maybe weasels? It seemed like everything here was busy hunting everything else: the animals with wings and claws going after the animals with neither.

How appropriate.

They eventually arrived at a row of small cottages, all built in stone and neatly whitewashed, bright in the moonlight. It was ridiculously twee. Mum must love it.

Jenner hammered on the door and after a few moments Dad opened it, a dressing gown hanging off his shoulders. Dad did a double take and pulled Luke into his arms for a neck-cracking, back-thumping man-hug, then Mum and the girls crowded out the doorway. Briefly, brilliantly, Luke forgot that anything else existed apart from his family. They all seemed safe, well, and in bits to see him again.

The feeling was mutual.

The kitchen clock was showing nearly 1 A.M., but they talked for ages round the table. At some point a baby started crying and Daisy excused herself to soothe it. The child was Heir Gavar's daughter, Dad said, as if it were the most natural thing in the world to have the kid of a magical psychopath asleep in a crib upstairs.

Luke recalled his first sight of the heir, striding through the corridor of the detention center while he and the Doc dragged Oz to freedom. He remembered hoping that his little sister's path never crossed with Gavar's, and almost laughed at the irony.

But once his thoughts had veered hundreds of miles north to Jackson and Millmoor, then to the club and the rioters, Luke couldn't quite get back on track with the family reunion.

Mum noticed him zoning out and ordered everyone to bed, saying that he must be exhausted. He wasn't, of course. The Equal at the gate—Silyen Jardine, Abi said—had seen to that. But Luke didn't let on.

He lay awake in the darkness, trying and failing to duck the thoughts that flapped about his head. What had happened in front of the MADhouse after Kessler had coshed him? Where was the Doc? Were Renie, Asif, and the others safe? Injured? Captured? What had Silyen Jardine done to him?

And the last thought before he drifted off: what would happen to him now?

Luke spent the weekend lying in, luxuriating in the soft bed and the privacy of a room all of his own, trying to adjust to his new circumstances. Mum clucked around, bringing up bowls of soup and sandwiches. Dad told him about Lord Jardine's vintage car collection and a tricky carburetor problem he'd solved the previous week. Daisy carried in the baby to show him.

Luke wished she hadn't. Sure, the little girl looked normal enough. Cute, even. But did she have Skill? That was a creepy thought. All that power inside something so small.

Except it seemed she didn't, because the kid's mother wasn't an Equal, just a slavegirl. (And how had *that* happened? Luke thought darkly. Had Gavar Jardine seen something he liked and just taken it?)

"So where is her mum?" he asked, once the baby had been put back in her crib, out of earshot.

"Dead," Daisy said flatly.

The scenario that Luke had already conjured around Libby Jardine's origins darkened a shade further.

"Wasn't like that," said his sister. "Why is everyone so set against Gavar? He's the reason you're out of Millmoor, Luke."

Daisy being so brilliant was the reason he was out of Millmoor, and Luke told her so before pulling her into a fierce cuddle. His little sis pummeled him for squeezing her too tightly, but he didn't mind. He realized that for a while, in the slave-town and then in the van, he had genuinely believed he would never see his family again.

At breakfast on Monday, Jenner turned up and explained that Luke was going to be working as a groundsman. Abi walked into the kitchen while Jenner was there, but on seeing him she stopped short, turned, and went back out. Which was peculiar, given that she worked with him.

So Abi's relationship with Jenner joined Daisy's friendship with Gavar on the long list of things Luke worried about as he labored at his new job.

"Groundsman" meant that he was some sort of glorified woodcutter under the direction of a miserable old git named

Albert. Albert didn't talk much, which suited Luke just fine. The pair of them worked all over the estate, often miles away from the main house, which also suited Luke fine. It was cold and wet and tiring, and at the end of each day Luke was knackered, just as he had been in Millmoor. That was fine, too, because his body's exhaustion was the only way of forcing his overloaded brain to shut down each night.

He'd been at Kyneston for nine days when his bag of possessions turned up at the cottage. Did that mean the Overbitch had rubber-stamped his unscheduled departure? Luke tore the bag apart searching for a note or message from the Doc or Renie. Something sewn into the lining, perhaps? Or rolled and stuffed into the handle? But there was nothing.

He looked at the bag's pathetic contents laid out on his bed. Black socks and gray underpants, a toothbrush, a photo of himself with his classmates on the last day of term that already felt like ancient history. He had nothing to show for his half year in the slavetown. The only things that mattered—the friendships, everything he'd done and dared, the person he'd become—had all been left behind.

"How does the post work here?" he asked Abi a few days later. "Could I get a letter to Millmoor?"

When she asked why, he said he wanted to send a thank-you to a doctor who'd patched him up after an accident.

"Let him know that I'm doing okay."

Abi frowned and told him she didn't think that was a good idea, and besides, the post to Millmoor still wasn't running.

His second week at Kyneston ended. Then a third. Weeks in which, although surrounded by his family, Luke felt lonelier than he ever had in his life.

Had Jackson and the club forgotten about him already? There'd be no shortage of angry new recruits in Millmoor, so Luke could easily be replaced. But he remembered the games they'd played together: break-ins with Jessica, keeping a look-out for Asif, dangling Renie off the roof. They'd all trusted one another with their lives. You didn't simply forget about some-one after sharing such things.

There were three possibilities, he decided. His friends had been arrested. Or they planned to contact him, but hadn't been able to yet. Or they believed he was content at Kyneston with his family.

As he set about that morning's task of chopping down a rot-ten cherry tree deep in the woods, Luke tested each hypothesis. The first didn't stand up. If the club's existence and its role in the riot had been discovered, Luke would have been pulled in for questioning, too, whether or not he was at Kyneston. The second possibility was also unlikely. Jackson and Angel could break a man out of Millmoor, so they should have no problem getting a message to him—even here. That left only the third option: that the club now regarded him as out of the picture.

Which was so wrong Luke didn't know where to start. There was so much he could contribute to the cause from Kyneston. The Jardines were the most powerful family in the land, and he was right in their midst. Several of them paid slaves no more heed than furniture, creating all sorts of opportunities for eavesdropping. His sister worked in the Family Office and had a key. The Third Debate—when the Abolition Proposal would be voted upon—would be happening right here.

Frustrated, Luke whacked his ax against the shattered tree trunk, causing it to rip up out of the ground and keel over. The roots were dry and dead, as if all the life had drained out of them. He turned the stump over and began hacking off the withered tendrils one by one. It was only minimally therapeutic.

Luke had once thought that Jackson intended him to go to Kyneston. "The plan is to get you to their estate," the Doc had said at that first meeting after they'd liberated Oz.

Well, here he was. Except that was Gavar Jardine's doing, at Daisy's request. Nothing to do with any scheme of Jackson's at all.

Luke drove the ax-head down the side of the stump, swearing as the wood simply crumbled and fell to bits in his hand. He was missing something. What was it?

Here was a curious thing: Gavar Jardine had been instrumental in Oz's escape, too. He had walked right past the three of them in the prison, when it seemed unthinkable that he wouldn't have noticed them. And Jackson had doubled back toward the Equal, leaving Luke and Renie to get Oz to Angel. There'd been gunfire and a yell, but the Doc wasn't hurt. Had the two of them staged everything?

Luke remembered Jackson's shocking words on the day he told them about the Proposal. When he'd admitted that he had an ally among the Equals.

"Someone close to power," the Doc had said. "He sees every shadow in the House of Light."

Who was closer to power than Gavar Jardine? A parliamentarian. A member of the Justice Council. An heir who seemed destined for the Chancellorship himself one day.

Luke's brain raced, snatching up more clues. The man had a common-born child. He had used his Skill to strike down everyone at the MADhouse, yes, but only after that maniac Grierson had ordered open fire on the crowd. Gavar Jardine might have caused anguish, but he had saved lives.

And while it was cute to think of Gavar busting Luke out of Millmoor at Daisy's request, it wasn't very plausible that a ten-year-old—even one as cool as his sister—would have come up with that idea herself. Had the heir planted the suggestion, knowing it'd be a good cover?

Luke wasn't certain. But for now, it seemed to be the only scenario that explained everything.

Everything, except one crucial question.

What was he needed for here at Kyneston?

# EIGHTEEN

# ABI

It was all going to work out, it really was. They'd have a quick ten years.

Abi had worried about Luke initially. He'd seemed spaced out during those first weeks here. And he'd not said a lot about his time at Millmoor, beyond the easily inferred facts. One, it hadn't been much fun, and two, he didn't want to talk about it.

At least he'd arrived in one piece, despite all the rumors of unrest, and that stray mention of a doctor and an accident. More than that, Luke had done some serious growing up in Millmoor. On the awful day that he'd been torn from them, he'd displayed a strength of character she'd never suspected, and that seemed only to have deepened during their time apart. He'd filled out, too, in a way that made her glad her baby bro was safe from the clutches of her man-eating school friends.

All in all, she was one proud and relieved big sister. And now that Luke was with them, hopefully things would finally settle down and the Hadleys could get on with doing their days.

Except Jenner was still acting coolly.

And Abi still had no clear recollection of what had happened that evening in the Great Solar.

What's more, the dog-man still wouldn't tell her what he had done to supposedly deserve his humiliation at the hands of Lady Hypatia. Wouldn't, or couldn't.

The way Kyneston's other slaves seemed content to pretend the man didn't exist was frankly disgusting.

"You've got to forget about it, love," the housekeeper said, over a cup of tea one afternoon. "He's no good, and no good will come of getting involved."

When Abi demanded to know why, the answer was always the same: because he'd been punished by Lord Crovan, a fate reserved only for the most wicked. Couldn't they see they had it all backward? The severity of the man's punishment was no proof that he deserved it.

"Come with me," she told Luke one evening when they'd done the washing and wiping up. Daisy was upstairs reading as Libby settled, and Mum and Dad had gone to visit friends along the Row. "There's someone I want you to meet."

Luke had grinned, happy to humor her. Something inside him had relaxed, unwound, these past couple of weeks. At first he'd seemed agitated, almost like he missed Millmoor. She'd wondered if he'd met some girl in there and was pining for her, but he'd poured scorn on that idea. Maybe he'd just needed time to adjust.

Lady Hypatia hadn't been at Kyneston since the New Year. However, she'd be down soon with an advance party from her own dowager seat of Ide, and one from Appledurham, to get the wedding preliminaries under way. That meant the dog-man hadn't left the kennels since Luke's arrival from Millmoor. Did her brother even know he existed?

Apparently not.

"Please tell me what I'm seeing here," he said angrily, as Abi hesitated at the entrance to the kennels, wondering how to do exactly that. "Because it looks an awful lot like a naked man in a tiny cage."

Luke's voice was tight with outrage. Abi could have hugged him. She knew it was unbelievable and just plain wrong that anyone should be living like this.

"We've got to get him out," Luke said.

"It's not that simple."

Abi filled him in, speaking fast, ever mindful of the Master of Hounds in his quarters above. The kennel-keeper liked a drink, she'd discovered. So a couple of weeks ago she'd liber-ated several bottles of malt from the cellars and pretended they were a thank-you gift from the Jardines. He'd looked suspicious—plainly the Equals weren't in the habit of showing appreciation to their slaves—but had taken them anyway. Thereafter Abi breathed a little more easily when making her nighttime visits.

"If I can get him speaking, walking," she told her brother, "then maybe they'll let him do days normally like the rest of us."

"That won't happen, Abi. You know it won't. This isn't just punishment. It's too vindictive. You're thinking too small. The only way you can end this is by getting him out of Kyneston. If you want to change something, you need to think big."

His tone was earnest in a way she'd never heard from him before. He really believed what he was saying.

And the tiniest bit of fear for her brother crept into her heart. When did Luke become so . . . fear*less*?

Maybe that was what the unrest in Millmoor had been about. Perhaps Luke had heard people spouting these sorts of idealistic catchphrases. Smart words. Nice ideas. All totally impossible.

Luke plucked the key from her fingers.

"We'll take him out of these kennels for a few hours, at least. Standing up isn't enough—he needs to be able to walk around, to run. Let's head for the woods. No one will see us out there."

And before Abi could stop him, Luke was kneeling in front of the cage, lifting the door in exactly the right way. She heard him mutter in dismay as the dog-man crawled out. Was that because of the way the man looked and smelled? Or just due to the unbearable fact of him: a man twisted by Skill out of all semblance of humanity?

"I'm Luke Hadley," she heard her brother say in that new, confident voice.

"Hello—Luke Hadley," the Condemned man rasped.

"I don't know your name."

The captive's shoulders shook. That awful, empty mirth. It still made Abi shudder.

What if we've got it wrong? she suddenly wanted to call out to Luke. What if we've made a terrible mistake? What if the reason there's no humanity in him isn't because it was taken away, but because it was never there in the first place?

"Neither—do I. Your sister asks me—the same. Why not—call me—Dog."

" 'Dog'? Don't you remember your name?" Luke asked.

"I only remember—what he let me—keep. That's just—the bad things."

"He?"

"No one—you know. Someone I hope—you never meet. My jailer."

"Lord Crovan," Abi said. Luke shook his head. The name evidently meant nothing to him. "Some kind of state-sanctioned sadist," she clarified.

"Plenty of those."

Dog reared up suddenly, like an animal pulling itself effortfully onto its hind legs. Now that she had another person to compare him against, she could see that Dog must have been tall once. And strong.

Was still strong. You didn't notice when he was on all fours, but the muscles were there, clearly etched in his lean thighs and powerfully bulky along his upper arms. How many push-ups did he do in here every day?

"Clothes," said Luke. "Let's find you something."

"He can tolerate the cold." Abi didn't want her brother hunting around, disturbing the hounds or their master.

"I'm sure he can tolerate it. But three people out walking at night will be that bit more conspicuous if one of them is stark naked than if they're all, you know, *dressed*."

When did Luke get so wise? And so smart-mouthed.

No, wait. He'd always been that.

It was so good to have him back. This was how it should have been from the start.

Their nighttime outing with the dog-man—Dog, as she

supposed she should now call him, which somehow felt worse—was a success. They'd returned him to his pen without incident, and Luke was keen to make a repeat visit soon.

But that was going to become harder, because the advance wedding party had arrived. Not only Lady Hypatia, but also her eldest son and his family—the Vernays of Ide, a cadet branch of the Jardine line. Abi didn't know anything about them, beyond the fact that Ide had been the target of Black Billy's infamous, doomed revolt more than two centuries ago. With them came the bride-to-be's widowed father, Lord Lytch-ett Matravers, and his chum Lord Rix.

These two were an ill-matched pair: one a Christmas pud-ding of a man, sherry-scented and full of cheer. The other was rail-thin and suave, given to leaving pluming trails of fragrant cigar smoke in their wake. The other thing that seemed to fol-low them around was laughter, which made for a pleasant change.

Her dealings with Jenner were still distant and formal. But in every other respect, Kyneston—or was it Abi herself?—seemed to be casting off the gloom of the midwinter months. Sloughing it off like a salamander in the fire. I burn, not shine, she thought.

"You're not from round here, are you?"

Lord Rix was leaning against the paneled wall of the corri-dor. He was watching her, a slender cigarillo between his fin-gers and a smile on his lips.

Abi had been instructing a pair of house-slaves about the decorations that would transform Kyneston's East Wing from a debating chamber one day into a wedding venue the next. She tried to flatten her northern vowels. But they came out anyway when she was exasperated—as she had been, faced with two people apparently ignorant of the distinction between "bunting" and "garlands."

"No, my lord. From Manchester."

"Manchester?" Rix raised an eyebrow.

Abi couldn't remember the name of his seat, but thought it was in East Anglia somewhere. Kitchen intel had told her that Rix had lots of racehorses but no children, and was godfather to both Matravers girls.

"Aha, I know—your brother must be that lad Gavar broke out of the slavetown. Quite the daring rescue. You'll have to point him out to me one day so he can tell me all about it. Precious little else that passes for excitement round here, eh?"

Abi doubted that Luke's account of six hours in the back of a van would be as thrilling as the Equal hoped, but she nodded obediently.

"I'll tell him when I see him. But I'm afraid he's hardly ever at the house. He's a groundsman. If you're outside and see a blond teenage boy with a large ax, that'll be him."

"An ax, eh?" The Equal put both hands up in mock terror. "I guess your masters trust him not to have picked up any naughty ideas from his time in Millmoor. Ha-ha. Still, you look like a busy young lady. Don't let me keep you."

And Rix sauntered off toward the Small Solar in search of his friend.

Dismissed, Abi.

The Equal was right: she was busy. Her to-do list was long and there was one thing on it she was desperate to get to. But first she had to find yet another girl who could be spared from general duties. This one was needed to assist Lady Thalia's maid in going through her mistress's wardrobe and several trunks of Euterpe Parva's old clothes.

That was because in a few weeks' time, Kyneston's sleeper would awake. And when she did, she apparently had a wedding to attend.

Which was a medical impossibility, surely. People didn't come out of comas on a schedule.

"Medical possibility doesn't come into it," Mum had replied. "The Young Master is going to do it. And Lady Parva is in extraordinarily good shape. No loss of muscle tone that I can detect. Lady Thalia sits with her every day, and apparently uses her Skill to keep her sister strong. From a mechanical point of view, there's nothing to stop Lady Euterpe getting up from that bed and going on a five-mile walk."

Abi understood what Mum wasn't saying. Silyen Jardine might be able to restore his aunt to consciousness, but would she be in any state to function mentally? People didn't come out of twenty-five-year-long comas and just pick up where they left off.

The first-year med student that Abi would have been by now desperately wanted to see Euterpe Parva tear up the textbooks on what was possible. Curiosity about how Skill worked, physiologically, was one of the reasons she'd dreamed of doing her days in a place like this. But until she saw it with her own eyes, she wouldn't believe it.

She had no trouble finding a volunteer to spend the day mooning over ballgowns. Another job ticked off. But still there were more, standing between her and the crate in the library.

Lord Matravers was insisting on sampling all the dishes selected for the wedding banquet, so Abi negotiated a date with Cook. Housekeeping was in overdrive readying for the hundreds of guests attending the three-day debate-ball-wedding extravaganza. Delivery vans would be coming and going non-stop for the next few weeks.

In the servants' undercroft, Abi was startled to run into Luke heading out.

"I'm being roped in for the festivities," he explained. "Everyone is, each year, apparently. Even Albert, that's how desperate they are. I'll be carrying bags and serving drinks, so someone needed to measure me for a uniform. Listen, it's going to be absolutely chaotic. A good opportunity for . . . you know."

"I don't know," she said, quellingly. The effect of her best big-sister glare was only slightly undermined by the fact that she now had to look up at Luke. "We'll talk at home tonight."

And then, amazingly, her to-do list was an all-done list. So she hurried off to the library.

The room was locked, given what was temporarily stored inside. But Abi had the Family Office master keys. She checked the passageway in both directions before letting herself in, although this was a perfectly legitimate part of her duties. Okay, no one had told her to do it, but that was what being a self-starter was all about, right?

Someone had been in here before her, because it was out of its crate.

There in the library, so close Abi could touch it, was the Chancellor's Chair of the Equal Republic of Great Britain. It was brought to Kyneston each year for the Third Debate. It was both smaller and more beautiful than she had imagined.

It was turned away, facing the fireplace. Made of oak, the chair had darkened to a color and sheen resembling ebony during more than seven centuries of use.

She crept nearer. The chair had a presence almost like that of a person. Commanding. Royal.

The figures of beasts and men carved into the back had lost their sharp definition. But that didn't diminish their allure. Abi bent to study the images. A dragon. A crowned man. A winged woman holding a sword. A sun surrounded by stars. Wavy lines that could have been water, or could have been something else entirely.

She reached out a hand. Hesitated, as she had all those months ago when she'd touched the Kyneston wall, then brushed her fingertips across the lustrous wood. She smoothed her palm over the triangular top, and down to the armrest.

When she stroked her fingertips around the side of it, she received a shock that made her squeak and nearly stumble backward into the fireplace.

The chair was occupied.

"Do be careful, Abigail," chided the person sitting cross-legged and contemplative in the wooden seat. "It'd be such a nuisance to have to haul you from the flames and put you out."

Silyen Jardine was watching her mildly.

"You nearly gave me a heart attack," she snapped, startled. "What are you doing sitting there—trying it for size?"

And if there was a guide titled *How Slaves Should Never Address Their Masters,* then yes, a sentence like that would be written on page one. Abi began to blurt an apology, but the Young Master waved it away.

"That's a little farfetched, surely. I'm no heir. I'm not even a spare, although I daresay my father would prefer me over Jenner if it came to it. No, I'll never be Chancellor. But of course, this wasn't always the *Chancellor's* Chair."

To emphasize his point, Silyen unfolded his long legs and drummed the heels of his boots against the stone lodged beneath the seat. It was the former coronation stone of Britain's monarchs, broken by his ancestor Lycus the Regicide.

What was Silyen implying? Abi knew what it sounded like, but that would be bonkers, even for him.

"I presume you're not planning to restore the monarchy," she said. "I think the moment for that has passed, don't you?"

"Has my brother been giving you more history lessons?" the Equal asked. "Oh no, silly me, he's not allowed to fraternize with you anymore, is he? Just boring talk about paper clips and invoices. Mummy's orders. Well, allow me to offer a lesson of my own. I know you like history, Abigail. Remember: those who don't learn from it are doomed to repeat it. Or should that be: those who do learn from it are able to repeat it? Here."

He swung his boots and jumped lightly down from the chair.

Abi's gaze followed him, but her brain had registered only one part of what he'd said. Jenner's distancing wasn't what Jenner wanted. His mother had imposed it. A feeling fizzed in her heart that felt as magical as Skill.

Was it hope?

Silyen hadn't noticed. Hands clasped behind his back, he was peering at the carvings she'd inspected a moment earlier.

"Have you heard of the *Wundorcyning*—the Wonder King? I won't scold you if you haven't, because many of my kind don't know about him, either. He's a folk legend. A dangerous one—his story was suppressed twice over. I believe he really existed. You don't bother expunging the memory of made-up people."

Silyen stooped to trace the indistinct figure of the crowned man. "He lived during that dark gap between the Romans and when we started writing down history for ourselves. He was Skilled. The tales say he met strange and marvelous creatures, fought giants, and walked in other worlds.

"After his death—or disappearance, because there aren't any accounts of him actually dying—for some reason there was never another Skilled ruler. So legends of the Wonder King were banned by the monarchs who came after him. They had crowns, but no Skill, and I guess they didn't want to look inadequate by comparison. Since the glorious Equal Revolution, of course, our rulers have had Skill, but no crowns. So the people in power still don't want to hear about him: the one man who had both."

"But here he is," said Abi, intrigued. "Hiding in plain sight."

"Just so." Silyen smiled. "The library at Orpen Mote had the only complete copy of the oldest book, *Signs of Wonder: Tales of the King*. But here he is, I'm sure of it. On the chair. Mocking everyone who's ever sat in it—my father included."

Abi straightened. The story was fascinating. But not even talk of ancient books, lost knowledge, and a magical king could displace the one thing her brain was clamoring to hear more about.

Would the Young Master be angry if she asked? Unfortunately, she didn't really have a choice, because no one else—especially not Jenner himself—seemed willing to talk about it.

"Your brother," she began. "You said that your brother . . ."

Ugh. She was making Dog sound articulate.

"Isn't permitted to engage with you. Yes." The young Equal flapped his hand dismissively. "Mother and Father worry he's half a commoner already, so they come down hard on anything that looks like sympathy for your sort. Is 'sympathy' the best word in this case, Abigail?"

His tone was sly and Abi flushed with embarrassment. But she had to persist.

"And that's all there is to it? General disapproval? Because there's an evening I can't remember. I was worried that maybe I did something, and that's why."

"Can't remember? Someone's been doing housekeeping inside your head without your permission? How very impolite. I can take a look, if you like."

Abi hesitated. What had she got herself into? Those bright black eyes saw her uncertainty.

"Breaking into someone's memories is a dangerous and almost always damaging process, Abigail. But it's much more straightforward—at least, I think so—to discover if an act of Skill has been worked upon a person. And if so, by whom. Each one of us is unique in the way we use our Skill. It's like a fingerprint.

"Because I am this family's gatekeeper, I know the print of everyone who enters our estate. So I'll be able to tell if anyone has used Skill upon you. Look, you can even sit comfortably while I find out."

Silyen casually indicated the Chancellor's Chair. The throne of kings and queens. Her head spinning, Abi complied. She gripped the bone-smooth armrests, then screwed up her eyes until it was over.

He hadn't lied. It was nothing like as bad as what he'd done at the gate, but there was still that stomach-turning sensation of being handled. It was like Mum checking tomatoes for blemishes at the supermarket. Abi pictured Silyen looking for a spongy brown-black bit, where the sharp corner of someone's Skill had dug in and done her some damage.

"Bouda," he announced after a few minutes of this. "And my mother. Wasn't difficult to deduce. They both lack finesse. I can tell you exactly what happened, too. Bouda and Gavar had a fight, a ferocious one, which you witnessed. Bouda hates being the subject of servants' tattle, so she Silenced you. Rather brutally. I guess she was still furious with Gavar.

"You were left in a bad way, sobbing with the pain of it. So Jenner—my poor, useless, Skilless brother—went looking for me or my mother to make sure you were all right. Unfortunately for you, he found Mama first. She performed some inept healing, made another frankly pitiful effort to fiddle with your recollections, and told Jenner that you should never have been there in the first place. Then she gave strict instructions that he was to cease any unprofessional contact with you immediately. Yes. That's about it. You must have had a headache for a week."

Abi prickled all over with betrayal, though she shouldn't have expected any better from Silyen Jardine, with his weird, bright friendliness and his utter lack of scruples.

"You said you wouldn't be looking at my memories."

"Abigail, you wound me." Silyen pressed a hand to his heart—or the place where one should have been. "I didn't look at anything. I know all that because about an hour later, after walking you home, Jenner came and told me the whole story. He was practically bawling with guilt. I told him to get a grip.

I mean, it's not as though he shot you. I'm beginning to think my brothers aren't terribly good with women."

Silyen shuddered delicately, like a cat offered dog biscuits.

Abi stared at him, disbelieving. She was gripping the arms of the Chancellor's Chair so hard she might rip them off. Should she laugh—or cry?

Or should she go and find Jenner Jardine, tell him to stop being an idiot, and kiss him?

# NINETEEN

# GAVAR

Father was planning a debate. Silyen was planning a resurrection. And Gavar was planning a wedding.

There was so much wrong with that, Gavar didn't know where to start.

He rattled the ice in his glass and scowled when no footman hurried to top up his Laphroaig.

He could start with Millmoor. He'd handled that well. Even Father had said so. Soldier-boy Grierson had started shooting into the crowd, which might have put an end to that day's riot but would have stored up worse trouble for the future.

Gavar's intervention had avoided that—while giving the commoners a little reminder of who their true masters were. So there had been pats on the back from one and all when he'd returned to London, and deservedly so.

But was it childish of him to want more than that? In fact,

the only person who'd said thank you to him for anything was the slavegirl Daisy, who'd begged him to get her brother out of the place. That had been easy enough to arrange, once he'd found some brute that knew what the boy looked like.

So much gratitude from her for such a small thing, and such scant acknowledgment by everyone else for what he'd achieved: peace in Millmoor. Or quiet, at least. There had been no further incidents since that day.

Gavar took another swig of the single malt, watching the bustle in Kyneston's Great Hall from his vantage point by the massive marble hearth. He could hear the rain sheeting down outside, yet even at this late hour and in such dire weather the house was still filling up. All day long parliamentarians had been arriving. Lords, ladies, and their heirs, coming through the gigantic door without a drop upon them, while drenched slaves carried in their luggage.

There was the footman who usually supervised the drinks cabinet, sulkily heading for the service corridor, leading Speaker Dawson and her smarmy son, who was supposedly some sort of adviser to the OPs. That was one thing Dawson had learned from her Equals: the fine art of nepotism.

Gavar snorted and raised his glass as they passed, to salute her hypocrisy. The son—who was about Gavar's age—saw him do it. He didn't look chastened, though. In fact, there was something dangerously close to contempt in his pretty-boy blue eyes. Gavar's hand itched for his riding crop, though he supposed it'd be a bad start to the celebrations to thrash a guest who was barely through the front door.

Not to worry. There'd be other ways to repay the man's insolence.

At the door, Mother was doing her best to keep a smile plastered to her face as she welcomed Crovan. Gavar stepped a little closer to the roaring fire as he watched. The man's appearance might be immaculate—his hair swept back, his golden tiepin gleaming in the candlelight, the vicuña overcoat tailored to his tall, austere form—but he gave Gavar the horrors from all the way over here.

Silyen presumably had the man on the guest list for his curtain raiser tomorrow morning: the awakening of Aunt Euterpe. Crovan would find it fascinating. Maybe he'd ask for a ringside seat. Imagine waking from a twenty-five-year sleep, and the first faces you saw were Sil and Lord Weirdo. Aunty Terpy's sanity would run gibbering back to whatever cracked little corner of her skull it had been occupying all these years.

The debate and the Proposal Ball were the day after, and Crovan always voted and attended. But surely the man wouldn't then stick around for a third day, for the Wedding of the Century? The event was going to be unspeakable enough as it was.

Mother called a slave forward to take Crovan's case, and Gavar saw it was the boy he'd sprung from Millmoor. Daisy had pointed him out one day as they'd been walking with Libby, an angry-looking kid with a bag of tools slung across his back. He hadn't seemed exactly thrilled to be here. Another ingrate.

Or so Gavar had thought. But when he'd run into the boy again several weeks later, he'd had some kind of attitude transplant. The kid had looked at Gavar like he'd not only bailed him from Millmoor but had driven the van himself, then thrown a "Welcome to Kyneston" party complete with strippers. He'd offered some unfeigned thanks, and said that if there was ever anything he could do for Gavar, he would.

"Anything at all," he'd said expansively. As if there were plenty of things the heir of Kyneston might need that a seventeen-year-old slave could supply.

Gavar tipped back the last of the malt. He should go easy on it, he knew. He didn't want to end up like Father. But lately he'd been feeling the need for a little pick-me-up. He was still getting the headaches that had been plaguing him ever since Libby was born. That was one thing they never told you about fatherhood: the constant worry, and the toll it took.

Across the hall, the Millmoor kid was holding Crovan's bag. Mother looked to be describing at great length where Lord Creepypants would be staying. Probably the boy had never been inside the house before.

But then Sil came ambling out from under the west arch toward the trio, and to Mother's evident disapproval he took Crovan's bag and led their least welcome guest away. The kid watched them go, unimpressed. He actually rolled his eyes when he thought no one was looking.

Good for him. Maybe the boy had been worth rescuing.

He banged his empty glass down on the mantelpiece, where it would doubtless sit until some harried slave spotted it in the morning. He was done with his hosting duties. Three more nights left as a free man, and he intended to make the most of them. One of the border lords had recently succeeded his father, and the estate's new heir—attending her first ever debate—looked worth checking out. Gavar thought she might enjoy a rigorous induction into the big bad world of politics.

Everyone knew the Jardines were good at that sort of thing.

The girl turned out to be gratifyingly eager for his lessons. But Gavar went back to his own room to sleep, then came down early to breakfast the next morning to avoid crossing paths with her. He'd upheld the family reputation handsomely and repeatedly, but was worried she might get demonstrative. He didn't want the hawk-eyed harpy he was marrying to notice. The girl wouldn't be getting up early, Gavar was quite sure of that.

Breakfast, whenever Kyneston was *en fête,* was held in the Long Gallery. An immense table was laid down the length of it, layered with stiff linen. As Gavar entered the room, he scanned up and down. There was no sign of either his new friend (he'd have to ask Mother her name) or his wife-to-be, which was a relief.

A few heads turned as Gavar sat down. Well, let them stare. One day he'd be lord of this house, and this would be his table. Libby would be beside him in her rightful place, even if she could never be his legitimate heir.

Although, was that impossible? Gavar remembered the day, late last year, when he and Daisy had sat by the lake and the boat had drifted toward them.

Not drifted. Been drawn.

He had turned it over in his mind often since then. He had been convinced, at the time, that his daughter had summoned it by Skill. In the following weeks he had watched her avidly for further Skillful signs, but none had come. Perhaps it really had been just a chance breeze, a snap of the boat's moorings. Or perhaps it had been Gavar himself, his own Skill working unconsciously to delight his child.

But he wasn't ready, just yet, to give up the idea that it had been an early, spontaneous showing of ability. Yes, it was unheard of that a child of mixed parentage could be Skilled. But it was also unheard of that a child of Equal parentage could be Skilless, yet look at the walking absurdity that was Jenner.

If Libby was Skilled, she could inherit, illegitimate or not. Though Gavar's wife-to-be would doubtless have something to say about that.

The thought of Bouda drew him unwillingly back to the present and to the Long Gallery. Some share of the conversation up and down the breakfast table would be gossip about the wedding. But Gavar suspected most of it was speculation about this morning's opening act, for which almost none of Kyneston's guests would be present.

The audience for Aunt Euterpe's awakening—or Silyen's failure—would be small. Besides family and Zelston, there were just ten official witnesses. Half of them had known the two sisters when they were girls, and were chosen by Mother. The other half were parliamentarians, invited by Father.

Those picked for the latter group were a puzzling selection. When Gavar had asked why that five in particular, Father had told him to figure it out himself.

Slaves were hovering with trays, dishes, and napkin-covered baskets of every conceivable breakfast delicacy. Having loaded up his plate with toast and bacon, Gavar felt equal to solving the puzzle.

The five weren't Father's intimates, but they were well disposed toward him and each commanded the loyalty of a number of lesser estate-holders. It struck Gavar that they were people who could be converted from admirers into allies with a sufficiently spectacular demonstration of Jardine family power.

Such as Euterpe Parva's almost-resurrection.

Gavar frowned and called for more coffee. The slave with the silver pot couldn't have moved faster if he'd been poked with a fork, but Gavar suspected that Silyen never even had to call. The stuff was scalding, just how Sil liked it. Gavar let it sit there and cool.

Could that really be what Father was scheming? The man had some nerve. And figuring out the plan presumably proved that Gavar was worthy of being in on it. Another test.

Well, Gavar had passed this one.

He left his coffee untouched and headed back to the upper east corridor and the family quarters. Gavar hammered on the largest door and Father opened it a short way, unsmiling. His dressing gown was knotted loosely at the waist and he held a glass in his hand. A faint perfume seeped around the door.

"Worked it out, then?" Father said. "That's a relief. I would have disowned you otherwise, and I'm running out of passable sons. We're all meeting in my study at four this afternoon, after Silyen's attempt."

The door closed again. Gavar looked at it in disgust. For a moment he considered kicking it.

But no, he had a better solution these days. He'd go for a run, then swing by the slave cottages. Libby would be glad to see him and he'd released Daisy from house duty, despite Jenner's all-hands-on-deck policy. The pair of them always acted as if a visit from Gavar was the highlight of their day.

In his more ridiculous moments, he wondered if it was the highlight of his, too.

Daisy made him a cup of tea and together they watched Libby bottom-shuffle on the rug, playing with colored blocks. When Gavar realized he had to get back for Silyen's showtime, Daisy said they'd walk over to the house with him, and hurried to find a coat and carrier for Libby.

"You can't," Gavar called as he heard her rootling among the clothes pegs in the hall. "Father said she mustn't be seen."

Daisy stuck her head back round the hallway door. She looked outraged. "The pig!"

Gavar couldn't agree more. His anger had blown out several panes from the Small Solar window when Father had told him. But the man had repeated his threat to strip Libby of the Jardine name. Gavar had clenched his fists so hard he wondered if it was possible to break your own fingers, or if being an Equal meant your Skill would protect you from yourself.

He scooped his daughter up from the floor and held her close, smothering her face with kisses. The baby squirmed and giggled.

"She knows her daddy is so proud of her, though. Don't you, Libby? Daddy loves you."

"Dada," Libby agreed, reaching out a pudgy hand and patting his cheek. "Dada."

And there, thought Gavar—right there, in his child—was more magic than Silyen would ever be capable of performing.

Surprisingly, though, Sil didn't make a big production of waking Aunt Euterpe.

They'd all crowded into the bedchamber, just as arranged. Sil had indeed brought Crovan, who folded himself into the farthest corner by the window. Gavar was next to Jenner, both of them standing behind Father. Father had his hands on Mother's shoulders, every inch the supportive husband.

Gavar wondered whose perfume he had smelled that morning. Poor Aunty Terpy would have a quarter century of gossip about her sister's marital woes to catch up on.

Zelston looked like a man close to death. His whole body was trembling, and sweat stood out on his forehead. It would be ironic if the man had a heart attack the minute before his tragic beloved woke up.

What must it be like to have wanted something so much, for so long, and be finally about to receive it?

Silyen stood beside the bed, one hand steady against the table. Despite himself, Gavar watched with fascination as his brother's eyes rolled up, their blackness replaced with blank whiteness.

Silyen's relationship with his Skill was something Gavar had never understood, or recognized within himself. Gavar's own Skill felt like a barely contained force, one that blew straight through him with little or no direction or control.

He assumed that was how it was for most of them, although he'd never really asked. It wasn't polite to go inquiring about other people's ability, just as you'd never pry about the contents of their bank vault. Skill was exactly like money in that respect. You didn't need to ask, to know who had lots of it.

Except Silyen's Skill wasn't a strongroom stuffed with bullion. The boy himself was pure gold. Right now Gavar could almost see him shine.

Zelston made a noise like a wounded creature, and Gavar realized his mother was crying.

Aunt Euterpe had opened her eyes.

It all became rather embarrassing rather quickly after that.

Zelston appeared to be having some kind of full-on break-down. He'd taken Aunt Euterpe's hand. It was small and pale, cupped in his large brown palm like a tiny fledgling in the nest, too weak to fly just yet. The Chancellor's other hand was stroking her hair.

"You've come back to me, my darling," Gavar heard him say. "You've come back. And I've waited."

It seemed to Gavar that no one should be here watching this. No one but Mother and the Chancellor—the two people who'd been with Aunt Euterpe when she'd first gone under. But Father had his reasons. This wasn't only about showing off Sil. When Zelston broke apart, he wanted as many people as possible to see it.

The Chancellor was doing his best to oblige. Tears were coursing down the man's face, soaking the coverlet. Aunty Terpy's last bed bath. It looked like he wanted to get up beside her and take her in his arms and never let her go again.

A whisper came from the pillow, so faint it seemed to reach them from very far away. A quarter of a century away, he supposed. His aunt had lain asleep for Gavar's entire life. A tiny part of him envied her. Twenty-five blameless years in which she hadn't made a single mistake or disappointed anyone.

"Winter?" said a voice no louder than the rustle of sheets. "Tally? I'm sorry I've been gone so long. I'm back now. Silyen's explained everything."

Her head turned and looked for Sil. And would you believe it, he received her first smile. Something uncertain but full of familiarity, as if spotting an old friend by chance in a foreign country. Silyen smiled back.

They knew each other, Gavar realized, the back of his neck prickling. Wherever Aunt Euterpe had been all these years, Silyen had been there, too.

A few of Mother's invited guests were openly weeping. There was Lord Thurnby, who'd been a great friend of her parents, elderly now but his face full of wonder that he'd lived long enough to see this. Cecilie Muxloe, a childhood playmate of both girls, was staring at her old friend as if she were a child's beloved toy, misplaced and then retrieved long after it was believed lost.

Euterpe was struggling to sit up, and the Chancellor did rise from his seat then. He sank into the yielding whiteness of the bed and put both arms around her. Everyone in the room saw the fleeting, electrifying moment when the Skill coursed from him to her, strengthening and reviving. It was the most intimate act there was.

"I think we've all seen quite enough," someone said loudly. "We should leave them to it."

It was only when Father turned, his face purpling, that Gavar realized the speaker was him.

Father's mood had revived by the time of the afternoon meeting. No Skill was required to pep up Lord Whittam, just the prospect of conflict—and victory. All through his childhood, Gavar had thought that fights and arguments just happened around Father. It had taken him this long to realize that the man created them: one face-off after another, after another, because he knew he would win every single time.

He was going to win this one, too.

The study's glittering windows looked out across the Long Walk. But by ten to four, it was impossible to admire the view because the room was packed with people. All the usual suspects were there. Father's favored cronies, Gavar's soon-to-be wife and humongous father-in-law, their perpetual hanger-on Lord Rix, and Bouda's little clique. All five of those who had been present at Aunt Euterpe's awakening were there, too. Several more besides. Father had been a busy bee.

Gavar rested his backside against the heavy leather-topped desk and made some calculations. By his reckoning, the people gathered here were enough to carry with them the necessary two-thirds of parliament.

Father was going to pull it off.

Gavar forswore the Laphroaig that night—he wanted a clear head for what tomorrow would bring—though he did have a few more lessons for the new heiress. Rowena, wasn't it? Or Morwenna?

Then, all too soon, he awoke to his last day as a free man.

The din in the Long Gallery at breakfast was even louder than before. Equals were in high spirits, talking of an afternoon to be spent horse riding, shooting, or fishing after the Proposal had been quickly quashed. Gavar wondered how long Father's "any other business" would take.

Father was there at the head of the table, and Mother at the foot. He was magnificent; she was exquisite.

The Jardines—first among Equals.

Gavar kissed his mother's cheek, nodded acknowledgment to his father, and drew out a chair in the middle of the table. The three of them remained in place until the very last parliamentarian had eaten and departed, some two hours later.

The Third Debate was held in the East Wing, one of Kyneston's two immense glass flanks built by Cadmus the Pure-in-Heart. The West Wing was domestic. Jenner had filled much of it with an orangery. Mother liked sitting in there to read or do needlework, while Silyen had an array of telescopes assembled. But the East was used solely for social events—chiefly, the annual debate and the Proposal Ball that followed.

And tomorrow's rather special one-off: the heir's wedding.

Gavar's thoughts shied away from the occasion. As he walked in, he was relieved to see that it wasn't tarted up with flowers and white ribbons already. The slaves had worked for hours erecting tiers of seating to match the configuration within the House of Light. The message was quite clear: this, also, was parliament.

Under the household roof of the Jardines.

The glass chamber was mostly empty as Gavar took his place next to his father's seat, front and center, directly opposite the Chancellor's Chair. The great carved chair was brought to Kyneston each year, though never to Grendelsham or Esterby.

Gavar had heard all the jokes about the Jardines' favorite seat in the House. What would it feel like to sit here and see Father enthroned in it before him once again? His chest felt tight, as if his waistcoat had become two sizes too small for him overnight.

All around, Equals filed in and took their places. Here came Bouda, his not-so-blushing bride, arm in arm with her father just as she would be tomorrow. Gavar closed his eyes and tried not to think about it.

He opened them again when he sensed the chamber falling quiet. There was Crovan, stalking his way to the far end of the first tier. The heir's chair beside him was empty. At least the man was childless. The question of who would inherit Eilean Dòchais was occasionally a subject for dinner-table speculation. Personally, Gavar thought the place should be burned to the ground. And why wait till Crovan was dead to do it?

The man was mad and the rumored punishments he meted out to the Condemned were disgusting. Those who committed crimes should answer for them with their lives. A bullet to the back of the head should suffice, not a dragged-out half-life of torment and humiliation. It simply wasn't decent. Perhaps that was something else Gavar could rectify when he was Chancellor.

Assuming Father ever gave up the chair, once he'd reclaimed it.

After an uneasy moment, chatter resumed. Only a few would have marked, as Gavar did, the arrival of Armeria Tresco. Walking deep in conversation beside her was her heir, Meilyr.

The prodigal son had returned. Presumably to lend his mother's doomed cause his meager vote. Because that would make so much difference.

Wherever Meilyr had been, it hadn't done him much good. His tan had faded and he looked tired and drawn. Gavar devoutly hoped there wouldn't be any scenes with Bodina tomorrow—no noisy tears and accusations.

The chamber was almost full when Father came in, and there was a momentary hush. More noise than ever followed in his wake, voices bouncing and echoing off the glass walls and vaulted roof. Gavar checked the heavy watch on his wrist; it was five minutes to the hour.

A few belated Equals scurried in and hastened to their places. Old Hengist, slow but upright, made his way to the hammered bronze doors. High up in the cupola of the main house, the Ripon Bell rang out: eleven peals that shivered the East Wing's iron skeleton.

After the ritual knock and response, the Observers of Parliament filed in behind Speaker Dawson and occupied their benches.

There was nothing for them here, thought Gavar. Only a moment of surprise as the Silence was lifted and they learned of the Proposal, swiftly followed by disappointment as it was voted down.

Everyone was seated. A hush fell as they waited for the Chancellor.

And waited.

It was nearly quarter past by the time the trumpets sounded and Zelston appeared.

Gone was the sobbing, broken man of yesterday morning. The Chancellor was a thing exalted. The sun had come out after days of rain and the glass panes of the East Wing formed tesserae of pure light, but the brightest thing in the entire chamber was the face of Winterbourne Zelston.

The man wouldn't even care about what was to come, Gavar realized. And he felt a secret, vicious pleasure at the thought of Father being deprived of at least that small part of his victory.

With the Chancellor's introduction and the lifting of the Silence, the Third Debate commenced. When those in favor of the Proposal were invited to speak, Meilyr Tresco got to his feet. As Gavar listened, he wondered why Meilyr was so worked up on behalf of these people he had never met.

"Families of four are living in single rooms," Tresco said. "There is no educational provision whatsoever; wholly inadequate medical services; a diet devoid of any nutritional value; and six-day working weeks of often backbreaking labor, performed under the watch—and the upraised batons—of brutal supervisors.

"If this House won't vote to end the slavedays, then at least let us acknowledge our common humanity and amend them. Such cruelty is entirely needless. We Equals, who have power, should have compassion."

"Sedition," said Father, rising to his feet. "Rebellion. Arson. Destruction of property and flight from justice. This is the reality of the slavetowns. What you call compassion, I call leniency. Worse—foolishness."

Gavar craned round and looked up at Meilyr. He had once regarded him as a friend and future ally, when it had looked like they'd each be marrying a Matravers girl. Meilyr was wearing that thoughtful expression he sometimes had, and looking right at Gavar with what seemed oddly like regret.

Armeria chipped in with her usual pieties about freedom and equality. Then a resounding silence greeted Zelston's call for further contributions from the floor of the House in favor of the Proposal. He turned to the OPs' benches.

Speaker Dawson's contribution was eloquent for something impromptu, given that she'd been ignorant of the Proposal until the Silence was lifted. Probably every Commons Speaker had a diatribe against the slavedays tucked up their sleeve for just such an occasion.

Pity it wouldn't get her anywhere.

Dawson paused, perhaps to send her argument in another direction, when Gavar heard Bouda's voice cutting in. She was motioning a move to a vote. There were cries of "Hear, hear!" from her goons, and soon the entire chamber was full of catcalls and hoots of derision. Dawson looked furious, but eventually sat down, and only then did quiet return.

The vote was as unsurprising as it was overwhelming.

The Elder of the House tottered to the center of the floor. In his spindly voice, Hengist Occold announced that by a margin of 385 to 2, the Parliament of Equals had voted against the Proposal to abolish the slavedays.

Not merely a "no"—a "no chance, ever."

Gavar looked at his watch. After everything that had happened—the debates at Esterby and Grendelsham, the Justice Council meetings and his trips to Millmoor, the fugitive prisoner and the riot—the finale had taken less than half an hour. Zelston's eyes were already on the bronze doors.

Except it wasn't quite over yet.

Father rose to his feet. With slow deliberation he turned right round until his back was to the Chancellor and he faced the ranked tiers of the chamber.

"My honorable Equals," Father said. "This debate should never have happened. This Proposal should never have happened. For reasons that none of us can fathom, Winterbourne Zelston made a Proposal that has jeopardized the peace of our entire country. We of the Justice Council have weekly contended with serious unrest and disturbance. With the threat of open rebellion.

"Make no mistake, the peril to this realm has been real and substantial. It is still real and substantial. And it has been brought about by the recklessness of one man. A man who has shown himself unfit to hold office."

Father turned on the spot and pointed an accusatory finger

right at Zelston. You could always rely on Lord Jardine for a touch of the theatrics.

"I therefore lay before you a Proposal of my own: a vote of no confidence in Chancellor Winterbourne Zelston. This will remove him from office and institute an emergency administration under the guidance of the previous officeholder."

You, thought Gavar, as the chamber erupted into uproar.

You, you rotten-hearted bastard.

And he watched as one by one those who had met in Father's study raised their hands. As others followed them. As the vote was carried.

As Lord Whittam Jardine took control of Great Britain.

## TWENTY

# LUKE

From the high curve of the hill, Luke could see the whole of Kyneston spread beneath him.

A ring of illuminated windows encircled the cupola, crowning the house with light. On either side, the great glass wings stretched away. The western one was unlit and almost invisible in the twilight. The east was a blaze of candles and chandeliers, its iron frame caging a galaxy.

Should he stay here?

Should he hold fast to those few words of Jackson's, and trust that the club wanted him at Kyneston for a reason?

Or did the Doc, Renie, and the rest consider him lost to the cause? Because the only way he could prove them wrong would be by breaking his parents' hearts and ripping his family apart a second time—by escaping to Millmoor.

Luke Hadley. The only person in history to try and get back *into* a slavetown.

It felt like time was slipping away for his decision. The Proposal Ball began in less than an hour. Tomorrow was the wedding. The window of bustle and traffic in which a boy might slip away unnoticed would close soon after.

But he could make plans anyway. And whatever Luke chose, there was Dog to think about. He and Abi had argued over the man's plight. She was fair, but firm. She wouldn't be party to any escape plans until they knew what crime the man had committed.

Luke was confident he could get Dog out on his own if he had to—he'd managed rather more in Millmoor, after all. But he and his sister were in this together now. He didn't want to do it without her. And besides, she was right. They needed to know.

Dog was curled on his side in the pen. The stench was even worse than usual. There was no lavatory pail. Not even a litter tray. The man was expected to use a thin pile of straw in the corner, which didn't look as though it had been changed for days. Luke's gorge rose, but he crouched as close to the bars as he could bear.

"The guests have all arrived. I saw your jailer," he said, watching Dog's reaction. "Crovan."

"My—creator," Dog said, making that noise that sounded like the world's worst cough, but was actually laughter. He seemed to save it for the least amusing things imaginable.

"What did you do to get sent to him? Why were you Condemned? Please, I need to know."

The laughter stopped. Dog contorted himself into a bow-backed squat, the attitude of a beaten creature. He scrubbed the back of his hand over his forehead, as if trying and failing to erase the memories it contained.

"They killed—my wife."

Luke had been expecting something like that. But nothing prepared him for the pain on Dog's ravaged features. The man screwed up his face, willing the words to come more than two or three at a time.

"We wanted—a family. So we chose—an estate. At first, we were happy—so happy. She became pregnant. That's when . . ." The man's fists clenched.

"That's when—it changed. It happened. She got—confused. I saw the bruises. Thought pregnancy was—making her clumsy. It wasn't. He was—raping her. Silencing her—with Skill. Hurting her—in every way."

Dog's rasping voice dragged over Luke's skin like the unwanted touch of fingers.

"Who was he?" Luke demanded.

"He was my great-aunt Hypatia's grandson, the heir of Ide," a voice said from the doorway. "Her favorite."

Luke's entire body went cold. Terror tingled in his fingertips like frostbite. He'd been so intent on Dog's narration he hadn't heard anyone approach.

Silyen Jardine walked over to the pen, then flapped out the tails of his riding jacket and sat down on the concrete floor. Luke scrambled backward. The Equal didn't seem to notice—or didn't care, if he did.

"Do carry on," he said. "I'm sure Luke's desperate to know what happens next."

"Next," Dog said, "my wife—hanged herself." He fixed Luke with eyes that were bright with tears and shone with madness. "She was tiny but—heavy with—the baby. Nearly due. I found her. Neck snapped. Both dead. The next bit—was easy. I was a soldier—before. Before I was—a dog. I killed—him first. Then—his wife. Then—his children."

The bottom dropped out of Luke's stomach. Had he heard that last bit right? Please let him not have heard it right.

"Children?" he whispered to the man in the pen.

"Three of them," said Silyen Jardine. "All under ten. And it gets worse, because we're not talking a nice soft pillow over their faces.

"You've heard of Black Billy's Revolt, haven't you, Luke? The blacksmith who defied his masters? They made him forge the instruments of his own torture and killed him with them. Well, that all happened long ago at Ide, but my dear relatives there always kept those tools. A little memento. Let's say our resourceful canine friend found a new use for them. Isn't that so?"

Dog looked at Silyen for a long time.

"Yes," he rasped. "Worked well. Wish I—still had them."

Luke thought he was going to vomit.

This world was sicker and more rotten than he'd imagined. Who could have thought he'd be nostalgic for the days when Kessler was beating him black and blue on the storeroom floor? There was nothing like a bit of honest thuggery.

"Anyway," the Equal said, "don't let me interrupt. I doubt you were discussing a joint wedding gift for my brother and his bride. Escape plans, maybe?"

"No," said Luke. "I was just bringing him medicine."

"Because the Dog," Silyen continued, bizarrely conversational, "and you, Luke—and all our slaves—are bound to this estate. None of you can hurt us, or leave us. Not without my permission. In a nice bit of irony, Father had me devise the binding soon after the events at Ide, to ensure nothing like it could happen here."

"I'm not helping him escape," Luke said. He felt somehow, furiously, that Dog had made a fool of him. "He's a child-killer. I thought he was a victim, but I was wrong."

"That's rather narrow-minded of you, Luke." Silyen Jardine got to his feet, brushing down his jeans. "Aren't you all victims? But have it your way."

The Equal looked at Dog. "Luckily, some of us keep our promises. I'll wake the gate at 3 A.M., like I said. Wait for me in Kyngrove Hanger, the high beech wood."

Silyen Jardine reached down to the padlock that secured the cage and plucked it off. No key. No fuss. The Equal opened his fingers and a dozen broken bits that were once a padlock tinkled as they hit the floor. He nodded at Dog, then walked out of the kennel.

Luke nearly keeled over with relief that the nightmarish conversation was finished. He leaned against the adjacent pen, keeping a wary eye open.

"Silyen Jardine promised to help you escape? Why? You can't seriously believe him. It's a trap. It must be."

Dog shrugged. "Possibly. But what trap—could get me anywhere—worse than this? As for—why. Perhaps to spite—his great-aunt. Perhaps—for trouble. Perhaps just—because he can."

"I'm so sorry for what happened to your wife," Luke said

awkwardly. He stood. Dog made no move to quit the cage, which was a small mercy. "But that doesn't excuse what you did. I really did want to help you, before I knew. Anyway, it's not like you need me now. Good luck getting out."

He hoped his voice didn't betray exactly how unlikely he thought that was. Dog stared.

"You have to—hate them," the man grated out. "To beat them."

"I don't hate them enough to kill children," Luke said, with no hesitation.

"Then you don't hate them—enough."

Luke didn't have an answer for that. To the accompaniment of Dog's hoarse laughter, he ducked through the doorway and didn't look back.

He had time to shower at the cottage—he felt soiled in every way by the conversation at the kennels. Then Luke presented himself at the servants' entrance of Kyneston to begin his evening shift.

He badly wanted to be left alone to sort through whatever had just happened. Maybe they'd give him a tray full of ready-poured glasses, so he could stand in a corner like a human drinks trolley.

It wasn't quite that simple, but it was close—he was handed a silver tray with four bottles of champagne.

"We have the French: Clos du Mesnil, twelve-year vintage," the wine butler explained, peering at Luke to make sure he was absorbing the information and could relay it. "And English, from the Sussex chalk downs on the estate of Ide. They're relatives of the Jardines."

Luke eyed the cold-beaded bottle with loathing. Had the

heir enjoyed swigging some before he assaulted Dog's poor wife?

He nearly came a cropper at the outset. He emerged via a concealed service corridor and was following his ears to the din of the East Wing when he nearly tripped over a dog pattering down the hallway at speed.

It was a small, ludicrous beast with a squashed face. As Luke's feet collided with it, the creature yipped in outrage and unleashed a stomach-churning fart. Gagging, Luke hurried toward the immense bronze doors set into the glass wall ahead.

On the other side of the door was a familiar figure: Abi, in a plain navy dress. She was holding a clipboard and standing next to Jenner Jardine, both of them beside a bloke only a few years older than Luke. He was done up in the full penguin outfit of tux and tails. He wasn't prepossessing, with a dodgy haircut and cheeks full of pimples. If Luke was the grandest aristo in the land, he wouldn't put someone like that on the door, to be the first face your guests saw.

A few moments later, though, he realized the guy hadn't been chosen for his face. Just a few steps behind Luke came a middle-aged Equal in black tie, escorting a much younger girl wearing a scarlet gown gaping wide across the breastbone. Even Luke's seventeen-year-old brain thought the effect was somewhat desperate.

Jenner Jardine leaned over and whispered something in Abi's ear. Abi consulted the clipboard, then held it in front of Pimples, pointing with her pen. In an unexpectedly sonorous voice, he announced the new arrivals.

"Lord Tremanton and Heir Ravenna of Kirton."

A few guests looked up, but the entrance of lord and heir

went largely unremarked. The girl's head swiveled this way and that, searching the room, before her father gave her arm a discreet but not especially gentle tug. He led her down the few steps into the vast chamber.

The East Wing resembled an immense aviary, raucous with the squawk of conversation and the coo of a jazz singer at a microphone in one corner. It was filled from wall to wall with a multicolored flock of Equals in their finery. Black-clad slaves darted unobtrusively here and there, like some dull, inferior species released among them by mistake.

You'd never know, thought Luke, gazing around, that there'd been some kind of coup that morning. That the Chancellor had been ousted by the host of tonight's party, Lord Jardine. Was this the Equals' idea of a revolution? They'd find it no party when the people rose up.

As glasses were thrust in his face for refilling, Luke's thoughts took him to Millmoor. During the long, dull days with Albert, he'd planned every detail of how he might return. How he'd hitchhike, striking away east up the country. Then he'd travel across to Sheffield, up to Leeds, and over the top of the Peak District.

His microchip would presumably alert Security when he reentered Millmoor's perimeter. He hoped Leeds might hold the answer. In the rougher bits of the city, he'd be able to find someone who'd escaped from its notoriously lawless slavetown, Hillbeck. They'd know what to do about the implant; could maybe get it out without the sort of butchery Renie had inflicted on herself.

"You're miles away, my lad," said a voice, not unkindly.

Luke snapped back in an instant. He couldn't afford to be

pulled up on anything now. Just get through this evening. Then get the decision made.

"I'm so sorry, sir," he told the man who'd spoken to him, a dapper old dude with swept-back silver hair who smelled faintly of expensive tobacco. "Which can I get you, English or French?"

The Equal didn't bother inspecting the bottles, gesturing toward the French champagne.

"Interesting accent you have there," he said. "You're not from round here. Somewhere up north?"

"Near Manchester, sir. There you go, sir." He refilled the proffered glass.

"There's no need for all the 'sirs,' my boy. I'm Lord Rix. And you're the Millmoor lad—Luke, isn't it?"

Luke didn't like the idea of any of them knowing his name, or asking about Millmoor. Time to sidestep this nosy old cove and move on.

"We have a mutual acquaintance," Rix continued as Luke lifted the tray higher, ready to make his exit. "A certain doctor."

Luke stopped in an instant, and stared at the man.

This distinguished old parliamentarian was Jackson's contact.

Not Gavar Jardine. Thank goodness he hadn't said anything to the heir—or anything incriminating, at any rate. This was the man who saw the shadows in the House of Light. Who'd told the Doc about the Proposal.

Luke's heart soared. He hadn't been forgotten. Nor would he have to make the trek back to Millmoor, all unknowing of the reception he'd get when he arrived there. This was what he'd been waiting for.

"You've got a message for me?" he said, barely breathing. "Something for me to do? I'm ready."

Rix sipped his champagne, the epitome of patrician amusement. "Is that so?" he said, lowering his glass. "Well, I'm delighted to hear it."

Then the Equal's attention was caught by something over by the entrance and Luke reflexively followed his gaze.

And nearly dropped the tray.

His whole body trembled. It was like someone had kicked him in the back of both knees, hard, and it took everything he had not to collapse to the ground right there.

Her white-blond hair was pinned up, strands falling on either side of her face, just as they'd escaped from under her beanie hat. She'd swapped her black fatigues for a sequined gown that glittered in the light from the chandeliers. She didn't need sequins to dazzle, though.

And he stood at her side, impeccable in black tie. He'd had a haircut since Luke had last seen him, but the neat beard was the same as ever.

Jackson and Angel.

Luke was wrong. They hadn't left it all to their contact. They'd come for him, too.

Had tricked their way here, into the very center of everything they were fighting against.

They stood side by side at the top of the stairs. Luke watched, his heart throwing itself against his ribs like a wild thing maddened in a cage.

Please let them not be found out.

Please.

Abi held out the clipboard to Pimples. Pointed. Again with that showreel voice.

"Heir Meilyr of Highwithel and Miss Bodina Matravers."

And Angel and Jackson descended the steps and were swallowed up in the throng. The chatter in the room grew louder around them as they were greeted, enfolded, absorbed.

What did it mean? What disguise could be that successful? Luke's pulse thrummed at what was surely twice the normal human rate. He could feel it staccato in his fingertips against the smooth underside of the tray.

"You hadn't guessed?"

The old aristo hadn't moved away. He was studying Luke curiously.

"Well, well," Lord Rix said. "Now you see that some of us also fight. Also wish to end this abomination of slavery—by any means necessary."

Realization hit Luke like a bottle to the back of the head.

Angel was an Equal.

Jackson was an Equal.

The evidence was right there in front of him, where it had been all along.

The Doc's hands on him that first day, Skillfully healing what Luke had known were appalling injuries from Kessler, using the useless cream as a cover. Reviving Oz in the cell not with an adrenaline shot, but Skill. No heads turning as they walked Oz through a prison full of Security. Guards swallowing flimsy suggestions and fake instructions. The gunshot and

Jackson's agonized cry, with no sign of any wound a few days later.

The tingle of Angel's touch on his face. Her escape with Oz through checkpoint after checkpoint.

"How do you think we got round the Quiet?" Rix asked, watching Luke as everything swung into place, the facts heavy and irresistible. "Meilyr was in Millmoor the day of the Proposal, when Zelston laid the Quiet on us. But because parliamentarians were able to talk to other parliamentarians about it, I could tell him. And once that knowledge was with someone not bound by the Quiet, there was no limit to where we could spread it."

The shock of the truth made Luke want to double over and retch. To heave up everything he'd ever felt for the pair of them—the respect, the admiration, the longing, the *belonging*— and purge it out in a great stinking puddle at his feet till he was empty.

They weren't brave. They were Skilled. Rich young Equals who'd had fun playing at being revolutionaries, knowing they were never really in any danger—unlike Luke and the rest of the club. Unlike poor Oz, beaten to a pulp. Unlike the man and woman shot dead in the MADhouse square, and whoever else had been hurt that day before Gavar Jardine twirled the pain dial up to eleven.

Luke felt the old guy put a hand on his shoulder, and twisted his whole body to shake it off. The bottles on the tray rattled.

"They share your cause," the Equal said.

Was Rix some kind of idiot? Was he as deluded as Lord and Lady Liar, aka Jackson and Angel?

"How can any of you share our cause when you're the enemy?" he said, hearing the edge in his own voice and hating it. "You had your chance in the vote yesterday and you blew it. This isn't your fight; it's ours."

Luke could feel scalding tears spill from his eyes and course down his cheeks. Had no idea whether they were shed in fury or grief.

"Is that so?" said Rix, looking at him. The kindliness in his voice had entirely drained away. "Well, seeing as it's your fight, I'm sure you won't mind doing one last thing before we say goodbye. Once we found out where your family was, I knew this would be the perfect opportunity. And when that cretin Gavar Jardine actually brought you here, it's like it was meant to be."

He opened the breast of his dinner jacket and from a holster beneath his arm hooked out a handgun. A pistol.

"You'll be a hero, Luke."

Rix reversed the gun so he held it by the barrel, offering the grip. With his other hand, he pointed away through the crowd.

Unmistakable, in the center of the room, stood Lord Whittam Jardine.

"No," said Luke. Then again, in case the guy hadn't got the message: "No way, are you crazy?"

"That monster has been plotting his return to power for a long time," said the Equal. "I know what he intends to do now that he has it. The slavedays are nothing compared to what he'll bring. Where's the courage you had in Millmoor? I thought you'd signed up for the long game, Luke."

"I quit," Luke spat. "I'm not playing your game."

"I'm sorry to hear it." Lord Rix grimaced slightly, as if he'd just been told that his favorite restaurant didn't have an available table, or that the rain wouldn't stop in time for his round of golf. "Meilyr didn't approve of my plan, either, though I'm sure I could have persuaded my goddaughter Dina, in time. But we're all out of time. And the game is more important than any individual player. So here we go, Luke."

The sensation was extraordinary. Awful. Like being six years old and held in a neck lock by a boy much bigger and stronger, twisted this way and that.

Powerless to prevent it, Luke saw his left hand reach out and take the pistol, then disappear under the tray, concealing the firearm.

His skin prickled all over with horror. This couldn't be happening. He began to walk forward—or rather, something was walking him forward.

Lord Rix's Skill.

"Your sacrifice won't be in vain, Luke," the old Equal said, behind him now, as Luke pressed deeper into the crowd.

Panic was swelling in his throat. Luke prayed for it to choke him. To make him pass out.

Equals murmured disapprovingly as he pushed through them. One or two ordered him to stop so they could get a refill. But Luke kept moving, watching it all helplessly from behind his own eyes.

There was Lord Jardine, his cruel, craggy face unyielding as he listened to someone Luke couldn't quite see. Then the whole group came into view. Lady Thalia stood beside her husband, her sister Euterpe on her other side. The fourth figure was the Chancellor—or ex-Chancellor. And Winterbourne Zelston's impassioned speech was having no effect whatsoever on Lord Jardine.

Quite an audience for an assassination.

Equals had protective reflexes. Could heal. This would be an all-or-nothing shot. Could Luke close his eyes until it was over?

He didn't have a chance even to do that. It happened so fast it took him as much by surprise as the foursome around him.

His arm tossed the tray away, champagne spraying, bottles falling. His left hand whipped up, the pistol steady and level.

Then it was as if something were ripping him apart from the inside out, as if he were a walking human bomb. Its epicenter was where he'd felt Silyen Jardine's Skill at the gate.

He remembered Silyen's words, in the kennels: *You're bound to the estate. None of you can hurt us.*

Luke's finger was already squeezing the trigger, even as his arm jerked away from Lord Jardine as if something had pushed it . . .

. . . and the pistol discharged a burst of fire into the face and chest of Chancellor Zelston.

Pandemonium erupted and the air crackled with Skill as the Equals' defenses flared up.

From somewhere far away, Luke thought he heard a man's voice call his name. Hoarse, horrified. Was it Jackson?

He stared at the mess on the ground in front of him. It wasn't really recognizable as a man anymore. Flesh and bits that you never imagined might actually be inside a person were scattered around. The colors were unexpectedly bright. The gun slipped from his hand and fell heavily to the floor.

He could move his own body again, Luke realized. The vise-like grip of Rix's Skill was gone.

He wished it wasn't. He had no idea what to do.

"Luke!"

Jackson pushed through to the edge of the space that had cleared around the scene. His face was white and he looked stricken, like a paramedic rushing to the scene of a car crash to discover that the victim is his own child.

Winterbourne Zelston was beyond any help the Doc could give now.

Luke, too.

The scream started out quiet, almost inaudible. Keening. A bat squeak.

The woman sank to the ground beside the remains of the Chancellor. She was already spattered with gore, and her pale skirts floated on the widening pool of his blood. A crimson tideline crept up her dress.

She bent over the body. Embraced it. Kissed it.

Grotesquely tried to gather it up to cradle in her lap, but it was too far gone and the shattered chest cavity only yawned wider open as she pawed at it. She was red from head to toe now, wearing Chancellor Zelston's blood like a second skin, drying on top of her own.

She tipped her head back to howl, and the whites of her eyes were shockingly vivid in her red-painted face.

Euterpe Parva, who'd slept for twenty-five years, Luke thought numbly. Who'd woken only yesterday.

Who'd been loved by this man, and had loved him.

Her howl grew louder, became a scream. No longer a sound, but a sensation. Not pain, but pressure, building from the inside out.

To his left, Jackson had fallen to his knees. To his right, Lord Jardine was doubled over and bellowing. Everywhere, Equals were hunched and trembling.

Luke collapsed to the ground. Crouched next to him, he saw Lord Rix. The man's face was a mask of fury.

"Stupid boy—what have you done?"

The Equal reached out, pincered his fingers. Luke's brain became pure pain, as if those fingers had crushed his skull as easily as Silyen Jardine had shattered the padlock.

Stunned and weeping, half blind with agony, Luke rolled onto his back. Above him, Euterpe Parva raised a scarlet hand, fingers clawed.

The air around her seemed to twist and shudder.

And Luke felt the blood trickle hot from his ears and his nose as Kyneston's East Wing exploded in a supernova of glass and light.

# TWENTY-ONE

# ABI

Her mouth was filled with dirt and dust. It was like being buried alive. Abi blinked, and that hurt, too, grit scraping across her eyeballs until tears welled up to rinse it away. Even breathing hurt. Her nostrils, her mouth, and her lungs felt as though they'd been scratched inside with a thousand tiny needles.

Could she move? Yes.

What had happened?

The world had exploded.

Luke had shot the Chancellor.

Memory flooded back, carrying a flotsam of horror. Abi groaned and closed her eyes, letting her head fall against the ground.

She hadn't seen the moment he did it. They'd heard the gunshot, and Jenner had gone to see what was happening.

It was only when Euterpe Parva began to scream and people

started falling that Abi had seen Luke. Her brother was standing bloodstained and bewildered above a gory mess that had plainly once been Chancellor Zelston. In his hand was a gun.

The detonation of the entire East Wing had seemed like a small thing after that.

Abi coughed and sat up. Where was her brother? She had to find him.

She scrambled unsteadily to her feet and looked around. What she saw was so awful that for a few moments it displaced even Luke.

The news showed you wars in faraway places: the border between Mexico and the Confederate States, or those islands in the West Pacific that were bombarded alternately by Japanese Skill and Russian nukes. The triumphs of the Skillful regimes over their unSkilled opponents were shown in unflinching detail. But watching carnage onscreen was no preparation for finding yourself in the middle of it.

There were bodies strewn everywhere. And the East Wing of Kyneston was entirely gone.

Abi and everyone else—hundreds of parliamentarians and slaves—were exposed beneath the night sky. A fine powder was raining down. Abi thought it must be ash and looked for the fire, which was when she saw that the entire side of the stone mansion had been sheared off.

Rubble and jagged lumps of masonry bigger than a man were scattered about like Libby's building blocks. There didn't seem to be enough to add up to half a house, so some of it must have been pulverized. That accounted for both the drizzling dust and the grit that Abi could taste in her mouth.

She recoiled when she saw her clipboard a few yards away

and, close by it, an arm reaching out from under an immense bronze door, now laid not quite flat on the ground. The hand was lightly dusted with powdered stone. It could almost have been a statue toppled from the roof, were it not for a trickle of bright red blood that ran down the sleeve. The poor marshal. Abi had stood barely a yard from him throughout the evening.

The rest of her family would be safe, she knew, with a surge of relief so strong it nearly knocked her off her feet. Mum was spending the evening at a makeshift first aid station in the housekeeper's office. Dad was watching over the generator array set up some distance from the house. Daisy was back at the Row with banished Libby Jardine. Had any of them been here, they might well have been dead.

Then everyone in the world screamed all at once.

Her hearing was coming back in a rush. Abi shook her head and winced. The blast must have deafened her. In her disorientation, she hadn't even noticed till now.

The ironwork skeleton of the East Wing was shredded, its massive girders crushed by the despairing surge of Euterpe Parva's Skill. Metal lay in twisted heaps, jumbled anyhow like bones uncovered by archaeologists in some long-ago murder pit.

Beneath the ruins, here and there, were bodies—or things that had once been bodies but which were now smears and gobbets. Exposed bones that had snapped like sticks. Limbs lying without context. She saw an unmistakably female hand, curled like a hairless baby animal near the larger huddle of a man's black serving uniform.

The Equals were mostly up and walking.

Abi watched, unwillingly mesmerized, as a girl not much

older than herself surveyed her injuries. She was clad in the
tatters of a scarlet evening dress and was reaching along her legs
as if performing a sit-up. She wouldn't be touching her toes,
though, because half of them weren't there. One of her feet,
still wearing a dainty golden stiletto, lay half a yard from where
it should have been, attached only by a few stringy tendons.
The girl's other leg was slashed to the bone, plainly the work of
an ornamental iron pinnacle that lay like a bloodied dagger
nearby.

Tear tracks streaking her cheeks, the girl screwed up her face
and began to tremble all over. She was Heir Ravenna of Kirton;
Abi remembered the marshal's voice booming, a lifetime ago.

Like a ball of wool being raveled up, the stretched tendons
tightened. Heir Ravenna shook as the bone reconnected, and
her hands fluttered protectively over the injury. Beneath them,
raw flesh was knitting itself together. Finally, Ravenna's hands
dropped to brush over her skin, as if smoothing out a skirt. Abi
almost missed what happened to the girl's left leg. The skin
there drew itself together like the gaping back of a too-tight
dress pulled closed by a sympathetic pal, who zipped you up
while you held your breath.

Who knew how long it had taken. But as Heir Ravenna's
shoulders slumped, her eyelashes tarred shut by tears and mas-
cara, Abi thought that you'd never know anything had happened to her. She could just have had a few too many drinks
and a tumble off her heels.

Abi shook her head, furious with herself for becoming distracted when every second might count.

Where was Luke?

She looked round the ruined ballroom and shivered. It was

March, and now that the adrenaline had ebbed from her system the night was damp and chill. Was anyone looking after the injured slaves? Was Mum here?

Yes—there she was. Jackie Hadley was kneeling beside a crumpled figure, barking instructions at a kitchen-slave carrying a green satchel emblazoned with a white cross. The girl was fumbling inside the bag for something, which she passed across to Mum. It looked like a bandage. Mum obviously had no idea about Luke, or she would have been pulling down the rest of Kyneston looking for him.

What on earth had happened here? The last thing Abi remembered was Euterpe Parva screaming. Had Luke done something worse even than shooting Zelston? So much destruction had to have been the work of a bomb.

A crescendo of hysterical sobbing arose from somewhere to Abi's right. It was a sound that no one could hear and ignore. She hurried across, stepping carefully over shatterfalls of broken glass.

But someone was already there. Incredibly, it was an Equal, a beautiful young woman in a sequined dress. She looked vaguely familiar. Had Abi seen her picture in a magazine? The Equal's hand was pressed to the forehead of a slave who lay pinioned across the chest by a heavy iron strut.

"I can't feel my legs," the man was whimpering. "I'm so cold. Please, I've got four kids."

"Best leave out the grisly details in your next letter to them," the girl said in a husky voice, giving him a reassuring smile. "Let's get this off you, shall we?"

The fallen girder was as long as she was and must have been many times heavier. But the girl set her free hand to one end of the length of metal and, exertion plain on her pretty face, lifted it off him. When it was raised to arm's length, she flexed her elbow and shoved, sending it clattering harmlessly away.

"Still . . . can't . . ." the man gasped.

The Equal shushed him gently and moved both hands to his chest, where wetness had spread across his black uniform shirt. She laid her fingers weightlessly upon him.

"I know a doctor," she told the man, her smile softening. "He's better at this than me. I'm afraid he's busy looking for a friend of ours, but I promise I'm not too terrible. Be brave."

The Equal girl was so gorgeous Abi wouldn't be surprised if the man thought he'd died and gone to heaven already. He was gazing trustingly into her angelic face while she worked her Skill. Abi's first aid plainly wasn't needed here.

Only one person needed her right now. Where was Luke?

She searched the devastated scene once again for any clue.

Felt her breath stop in her throat as she saw the last person she would have imagined.

Dog, silhouetted against the brightness, walked to and fro across the sheared-off side of the mansion. He wore filthy coveralls and a small pack on his back, and was plainly searching for something.

He owed her a favor. And he had more reason than most to hate the Jardines. Perhaps he could help her find Luke. She started to pick her way toward him, lifting the hem of her dress over rubble and ruin.

The shattered house was a disturbing spectacle. With one wall gone, Kyneston's interior was entirely exposed, like a doll's house. Equals and slaves were visible, moving around within. If any hand was moving them, Abi didn't like to think what sort of game it was playing.

"I think I prefer it like this," said a voice right behind her. "It's much easier to see what people are up to, wouldn't you agree?"

Abi spun, knowing who it was by the shudder that ran through her, even before she saw him.

Silyen Jardine.

"Dog needs a hand," he said, looking over to where Dog had stopped to remove the knapsack. "He's about to run up against the same problem your brother did."

"What?" Abi's voice was sharp, but she didn't care. What did Silyen Jardine know about what had happened to Luke?

But the boy was already off, his long legs striding easily over the debris beneath his feet. At one point he stepped right over a whimpering slave, bleeding into the dirt. Abi murmured an inaudible "Sorry" and did the same, trying to keep up.

Silyen and the hound were already speaking by the time she reached them.

"You know the binding won't let you," Silyen was saying.

Dog stared at him. The planes of his face were etched unnaturally sharp beneath the roughly scissored hair that furred his face. His eyes burned. His leash was wrapped tight around one hand, the length of it dangling loose.

Abi glanced past the pair of them and into the ripped-apart house. In the wall-less Great Solar in a high-backed armchair, her face streaked with soot and her eyes closed to the chaos outside, sat Lady Hypatia Vernay.

"You laid it," growled Dog. "You can lift it."

"Of course I can." Silyen Jardine smiled. "But she *is* family. Why would I?"

Dog's eyes narrowed. Perhaps he was remembering his canine self and considering sinking his teeth into the Young Master. But with visible effort, he controlled himself.

"When you ask me for—a life in exchange. I'll do it. I'll owe you."

Silyen paused, seeming to consider the offer. He could probably kill someone with Skill alone, Abi thought, remembering the dead deer and withered cherry tree in the autumn woods all those months ago. But then the boy nodded. In the same instant Dog winced. It was as if a bond tying his hands had been cut, a lock inside his brain picked.

Abi wasn't sure what had just happened, but it looked a lot like permission given.

"That'll be three things you owe me," the Young Master told the man. "An escape, a life, and a name."

"A name?"

"Don't you want to know your name?"

"Not mine." A terrible longing filled Dog's eyes. "My wife's."

Silyen Jardine smiled. He leaned forward, placed his mouth close to Dog's ear, and whispered. Then pulled back.

"So I'll see you later, as we arranged. I'll be a bit busy until then."

Dog stood staring intently at Silyen with something that wasn't devotion, but wasn't hatred, either. It was gratitude, she decided—and this meant Silyen Jardine now had a larger claim on Dog's assistance than she ever would. So much for that plan.

Dog wiped his nose and face on the arm of the coveralls. He

took the other end of the leash in his free hand and wrapped it around his palm. Then he snapped both ends, testing his grip.

Without another word he turned his back on them and walked toward the house. Abi didn't want to see what came next.

"Busy night for all of us," said Silyen brightly. "I'll get to your brother later. But I've something to do here first. I think you'll enjoy it, Abigail."

"My brother?"

"May be useful to me," Silyen said, waving a hand airily. "I sensed his potential that first night at the gate. But I'd better get going. I think my audience has recovered enough to pay attention."

And the Equal was off again, walking easily through the chaos and confusion of the ballroom to its very center—to where Abi had last seen her brother, blood-drenched and shaking.

Had Luke known what he was doing? Had he done it willingly?

She didn't want to consider the idea, but if Abi was honest with herself, it was possible. Who knew what had happened to her little brother in Millmoor during the months they were all apart? The slavetown had been in a state of turmoil. She knew that much from Jenner's cryptic comments, and from snatches of conversation between Lord Jardine and Heir Gavar that she'd heard as she passed unnoticed from room to room.

Had someone there preyed on Luke's vulnerabilities? Twisted his mind and used him?

If that was how it had happened, Abi would find them out.

Would make them sorry.

The sound that interrupted her was as shining and beautiful as her thoughts were dark and discordant. A surging, chiming rush, as from thousands of bells struck all at once. Abi's eardrums tingled.

Then the effect was spoiled by a woman's terrified cry. People were pointing upward, so Abi looked. This night had already birthed more horrors than her brain could process. What was one more?

The black sky was studded with stars of glass. They hung overhead, unimaginably sharp and deadly. From jagged blades—some still edged with blood—to tiny shards and sparkling dust. Abi had read that once, thousands of years ago, people believed the heavens to be a crystalline sphere surrounding the Earth. The night sky above Kyneston now was what that might look like smashed into millions of tiny pieces, the moment before they all fell.

But they didn't fall. Instead, the galaxy of glass rotated slowly. More chimes shivered in the cold air as shards struck each other, but not a sliver broke off. Then the glittering mass curved down to the ground, encircling them all.

Abi looked at Silyen. He stood in the center of the space, arms upraised and face rapturous, like some musical prodigy conducting an orchestra only he could see.

Every piece of metal, from vast girders to lacelike ornamental tracework, rose slowly into the air. Those slaves who had been trapped beneath them and still lived groaned and sobbed. Abi flinched as a side strut lifted past her, hovered at head height, and continued its ascent.

In midair the pieces of metal melded as smoothly as Heir Ravenna's body knitting itself together. The ironwork locked like an immense skeleton, all backbone and draping wings: a roof ridge, columns and beams, rivets. The suspended glass shards contracted inward, molding to the frame.

The East Wing raised itself over them like a great metal monster with a flayed and shining hide, Equals and slaves alike swallowed in its belly.

The whole structure flared like magnesium, too bright to bear. And when Abi had blinked away the shapes seared into her retinas, she saw that the vast ballroom stood intact once more. It was as if the evening's disaster had never happened.

Silyen hadn't finished just yet. Lumps of masonry were flying back up toward the shattered stone mansion, dropping into place like some giant's version of a stacking brick game. Kyneston's sheared-off wall rose layer by layer, the people inside gradually disappearing from view as if the Young Master were walling up his family alive.

"Abigail!"

Arms seized her roughly from behind and spun her round. It was Jenner, his face so begrimed his freckles could barely be seen.

"Thank goodness you're all right." His hands cupped her face carefully as if she, too, were made of glass and had only just been glued back together.

Then he kissed her.

And for a moment she was soaring with the stars in the crystalline sphere, dizzyingly high and perfect.

She forgot her brother. Forgot Silyen. Forgot Dog making a garrotte of his leash. Forgot the marshal's broken body, and Chancellor Zelston in a pool of gore. Nothing existed apart from the urgency of that mouth against hers.

Then she was pushing Jenner away. Because although this was what she wanted—more than anything—it was too late. It was all too late. Luke was a murderer. Lord Jardine was in power. Euterpe Parva had torn open the sky. And Silyen Jardine was rebuilding Kyneston with nothing but Skill.

"It's the Great Demonstration," she said, filled with awful understanding. She pushed at Jenner even as he tried to enfold her more tightly.

"What?"

Jenner was uncomprehending. His blackened palm caressed her neck and made her shiver, and she ducked away from his hand. Couldn't he see it?

"The Great Demonstration. When Cadmus built the House of Light using nothing but Skill."

"He's just repairing the damage."

"Repairing? This isn't one of your mother's ornaments, Jenner. This is Kyneston. Look."

She pointed to the glass walls that soared above them, restored and flawless, exactly as they had been.

But they weren't exactly the same, were they? Because what she had at first mistaken for smoke, and then thought was simply shadow, was neither.

It was dim, radiant forms moving to and fro beyond the glass. Just as they did at the House of Light.

Fear filled Abi's heart. The lesson of the Great Demonstration was one that every child in Britain learned. It was the greatest statement there had ever been of the irresistibility of Skill. More powerful even than the killing of the Last King.

Cadmus's work that day had ended one world and forged

another that was wholly different, in which those without Skill were made slaves. It had ushered in Equal rule.

"What is your brother trying to prove?" she murmured.

"And what about yours?" Jenner said, gently taking Abi by the shoulders and turning her to face him. "Father has him in custody. He shot Zelston, Abigail. And Father has got it into his head that the bullet was meant for him."

"For your father? But how could Luke have missed? They were standing right next to each other."

"The binding, Abi. What Silyen does to you all at the gate. None of our slaves can hurt us. If Luke had gone for my father, he would have been compelled to deflect. And as Mother and Aunt Euterpe are family, too . . ." Jenner shrugged, at a loss to find any way of softening the blow. "Zelston was the only one left."

Abi shook her head. Could that be true?

Did it even matter? Luke had killed Zelston, whoever his true target had been.

No, only one thing mattered now. Luke was still here at Kyneston. Still rescuable.

But how?

# TWENTY-TWO

# LUKE

Luke wasn't sure what he'd been expecting. A cell? Dog's pen, perhaps.

But not this. Not a huge, sumptuous bed with a crimson silk coverlet pulled up to his chin. Someone had tucked him in like he was a little kid.

He closed his eyes with relief. So they'd realized he hadn't done it.

Because he didn't do it, he was certain. Although Lord Jardine and the other man—had it been Crovan?—seemed convinced that he had.

Kyneston's master had hauled Luke from the destroyed ballroom. Dragged him to the library and tied him to a chair. There, Crovan had dug about in Luke's skull with what had felt like knives, but was actually Skill. Digging for memories that weren't there. Memories of murdering Chancellor Zelston.

Luke remembered walking into the East Wing, four champagne bottles on a tray. He remembered the yapping dog; Abi with a clipboard; the Equal girl in the gaping gown. Then . . .

Nothing until an upraised scarlet hand and what had felt like the end of the world.

Then Lord Jardine, bloodied and dirtied and incoherent with rage. A body on the floor, that Luke only belatedly recognized as the Chancellor. Accusations he didn't understand. Terror. Pain. So much of it that he'd passed out.

But now it was over. He was safe in a soft bed. Luke snuggled beneath the coverlet. The mattress moved under him strangely. Almost rippling. He ducked his head to look.

It was too dim to see much, but he seemed to be lying in a spill of liquid. It was warm. Had a hot-water bottle burst? He snaked a hand down to check. When he drew it back up, his fingers were red.

Blood. He was lying in a pool of blood.

Panicked, he tried to throw back the coverlet to yell for help. Which was when he noticed it wasn't a coverlet at all. It was a dress. The wide floating skirts of a red dress. Or a dress that had once been some other color, but was now sopping with blood.

Luke gasped. It didn't drag nearly enough air into his lungs. Hot, salty liquid trickled down his throat. Blood. Blood everywhere.

Then he was pulled up bodily. Pulled up and out.

A voice roared in his face: "Stop it!"

He was struck so viciously he was amazed his head didn't snap right off its thin stalk of spine.

"Every five minutes," the voice continued, still shouting.

"He's doing it every five minutes. Thrashing about and yelling. I'll kill him if he does it again."

"Get your hands off my brother!"

Luke swung back and forth. He was held up by a fist bunched in the front of his shirt, like a doll in the grasp of a resentful child that wants a better toy.

"Let him go, Gavar."

A third speaker, level and calm. Who was that? Luke was released and fell heavily back onto the bed.

A hand touched his temple and lightly thumbed up one eyelid. A blurry, indistinct face loomed in his vision. Was it Abi?

"Luke? Luke, can you hear me?"

"Don't touch him. What were you thinking of, bringing her here, Jenner?"

Luke's other eyelid was pushed up gently, but Abi's tone was savage.

"He can't even tell it's me. What have your father and Crovan done to him?"

"Jenner, you know Father's orders. Get her out, or I will break your neck, then bodily throw her out. Now."

"Luke, can you hear me?"

One of Abi's hands gripped his firmly. The other tipped his face sideways.

"Blink, Luke. Focus. You'll be tried tomorrow. Lord Jardine has postponed the wedding. Instead, parliament will sit as a court. You're accused of murdering Chancellor Zelston. I know you didn't do it, Luke. But I don't know how we're going to prove that before tomorrow. Whatever happens, be strong. We'll work something out."

A trial. A court. Murder.

The words floated through Luke's head. They seemed very far away. Why wouldn't Abi let him sleep?

"He can't even follow what I'm saying," he heard Abi say, a sob catching the corner of her voice. "You can't put someone on trial in the state he's in. It's a travesty."

"It's a foregone conclusion," said Gavar Jardine. "There were five hundred people in the room when he did it. My mother was standing right next to him. You both need to go now. And Jenner—think carefully about what you're doing. We won't be able to keep her family here after this. She and her parents will be gone by the time he is."

What was any of this to do with him? Luke thought. He was in a bed—a huge, sumptuous bed. Not a cell, or a kennel. So they'd worked out he hadn't done it.

Someone had even tucked him in under a soft, crimson coverlet. And it was so warm.

Luke closed his eyes. And slept.

When he woke, everything was muted. The window was a light gray rectangle on a dark gray wall. A faint seam of light stitched the curtains together and fell across the floor. Luke's head turned to follow it.

On the far side of the room, the light traced the outline of an armchair. In which someone sat watching him.

"Good morning, Luke," the watcher said, before pausing. "Though it's not quite morning, and if I'm honest, I doubt it's going to be good."

Luke knew that voice. Was he going to get a visit from all of them—all the Jardines? Some to beat him up, some to sit by his bed. Maybe Lady Thalia would be up soon with his breakfast on a little silver tray with a tiny cup of tea.

"I thought you might appreciate the rest while you can get it," said Silyen Jardine, lowering himself casually onto the edge of the mattress. "Who knows what kind of a house Crovan keeps up at Eilean Dòchais, but I doubt he torments the Condemned with eight hours of undisturbed sleep."

"Crovan?"

And it all came flooding back. The cruel Scottish Equal and Lord Jardine digging in his head. Abi's voice in the night. Parliament. A trial.

As the confusion of his interrogation and the dark hours that followed it lifted, Luke saw with horrifying clarity what would happen next. He would be tried and Condemned for a crime he couldn't remember.

"I'm curious," said Silyen Jardine, "about who Silenced you. Because I'd wager that whoever it was could tell us a few things. For example, why you pureed the Chancellor in the middle of Mummy's ballroom."

"I didn't do it," Luke insisted, desperate to make at least one of the Equals understand.

"Oh, Luke, of course you did. But who hid your memory of doing it, and why? Who was the real target: Zelston or my father? There are other questions, too, like did you agree to it, or did they compel you? But I'm afraid no one's terribly interested in a detail like that."

"That's not a detail," said Luke. "That's the only thing that matters. I've no memory of . . . of what everyone's saying I did. There's just a gap there. A black hole where my memories should be. Someone used Skill on me. That proves I was made to do it."

Silyen Jardine actually tutted. "It proves nothing of the sort.

They could have asked you and you said yes. Then the Silence would be just a convenient way of concealing both your complicity and your co-conspirator's role."

"Who in their right mind would agree to assassinate the Chancellor with the whole of parliament looking on?"

"I can't imagine. Maybe a hotheaded teenager, angry at the system that's torn him from his family? A boy who's been radicalized in a slavetown that's been in upheaval for months? No, that doesn't sound very plausible at all."

That was when the full extent of how he'd been used sank in. He was like a gun wiped clean of fingerprints. He was merely the murder weapon—but would be punished as the murderer.

"You said you wanted to know who Silenced me. Can you do that? Can you lift it?"

"The only person who can lift a Silence is the person who laid it, Luke, as your sister Abigail could tell you—no, no, it was nothing, don't fuss." Luke's fists had clenched furiously at the thought of his sister being interfered with by this freak. "But I do have a little trick that's all my own. I can discover who did it. And sometimes, knowing who wants a secret kept is as good as knowing the secret itself."

"Do it." Luke got to his feet, stood there, arms at his side, like he was daring Silyen Jardine to hit him. "I don't care how much it hurts. After what your father and his friend did to me . . . I can take it."

"Aren't you brave?" Silyen Jardine said indulgently. "That's just as well, considering."

But it didn't hurt at all. Just that queasy combination of intimacy and insubstantiality. Luke's very self was soft sand running through Silyen Jardine's fingers. For a moment, he felt as though he didn't have a body at all. Then it dawned on him that he didn't need one.

A wave of nausea brought him back to himself again, and he was standing in front of Silyen Jardine just as the sun was breaking through the curtains.

"Well, that was unexpected." The Equal smiled. "I love it when people aren't who they seem. It makes life so much more exciting, don't you think?"

"Tell me," Luke demanded.

"Tell you? No, I'm not going to tell anyone. Secrets are like nasty vases or vintage cars, or all the other trash people like my mother and father collect. The rarer they are, the more valuable they are. I think I can get a good price for this one."

"You can't! I'll be Condemned. You've helped Dog, and he deserved his punishment. I don't deserve this, so why won't you help me?"

"Oh, Luke, it's nothing to do with *deserving,* surely you can see that? Dog is useful to me free, and you will be useful to me where you're going. And what I've just discovered will be useful, too. It's been a good night's work, even if I say so myself. And I haven't even had my coffee yet."

As Silyen Jardine turned away, Luke lashed out. But his fist never connected with a single unkempt hair on the Young Master's head. Instead he was slammed backward through the air as if struck by a collapsing gantry.

Luke crumpled against the wall, dazed by the impact and by his own fury and despair. A pair of scuffed riding boots walked slowly into view, then stopped. A moment later, black eyes met his as Silyen Jardine crouched down.

"Honestly, Luke," the Equal said. "Remember the binding? I need you to do better than that where you're going. Much better. Because I'm not done with you yet. Not by a long way."

The back of Luke's neck prickled. He shouldn't be misled by Silyen's bizarrely casual manner. This wasn't—and never would be—a fair fight.

The door opened.

"Have you learned anything, Silyen?" barked Lord Jardine. "Who moves against me?"

The Young Master straightened and turned, looking his father full in the face. And he must have a backbone of steel, thought Luke even as he seethed with hatred, to be able to lie so easily to this man.

"Nothing of use to you, Father."

"Very well. We'll speak no more of this. Whoever my enemy is, we don't want to alert them to our suspicions. Let's get this done quickly, then Crovan can apply himself to discovering what we need to know. Gavar, bring the boy."

When he was led into the East Wing, Luke wondered if he was losing his mind. Or perhaps he'd been unconscious or overwhelmed by Skill for days—or even weeks. Because he had last seen the vast structure exploding into thousands of deadly fragments.

Yet here it was, no more than twelve hours later, intact and immaculate. Outside was a bright, light-rinsed morning. High cloud was casting strange shadows on the expanse of glittering glass. The whole thing reeked of unnatural power.

Or perhaps that flowed from the people assembled here. The sight of them took Luke's breath away. Nearly four hundred Equals sat in eight ranked tiers, each lord or lady with their heir beside them. There were two empty places in the center of the front row, presumably for the Jardines. Their absence gave Luke a clear view to the seats directly behind. Sitting there was a stunning blond woman who looked strangely familiar, and a gargantuan man with a mane of ivory hair, who must be her father.

Where had he seen her before? Luke racked his brains before realizing that she was Bouda Matravers, Heir Gavar's bride-to-be. Her beautiful face was taut and angry—and no wonder, she'd been robbed of a wedding. He let his eyes roam back and forth across the first few tiers of seats. He saw curiosity in some faces, but sympathy in none. He stopped looking after that. There was no point.

Lord Jardine sat in the Chancellor's Chair. Luke stood to one side, hands clasped, head down, heart racing. Behind him, Gavar Jardine stood ready in case Luke tried to bolt.

He wouldn't be running. He knew exactly how Heir Gavar could stop him, and besides, where was there to run to?

Should he tell them that Silyen Jardine knew—or claimed to know—the identity of whoever had Silenced him? But Silyen had already denied that knowledge to his father, and would simply do so again. It would set the Jardine father and son against each other, but how would that benefit Luke?

He didn't have enough time to figure it all out. Then the cupola bell sang out a high, bright nine, and he no longer had any time at all.

Lord Jardine began speaking, and Luke realized that he wasn't here for a trial. Only a sentence.

"My own initial questioning has found no evidence of Skill-ful influence," the lord of Kyneston said, his leonine head turning to survey the assembled Equals. "Neither has examination by my fellow member of the Justice Council, Arailt Crovan. It seems likely that the boy is a lone-wolf attacker, radicalized by his time in Millmoor slavetown, incited by associates there as yet unknown."

Luke's heart roiled within him. Associates in Millmoor. They would rip apart his mind and find everything about Jackson, Renie, and the club.

His choices became clearer. Delaying tactics here at Kyneston would simply result in further Skillful interrogation by Jardine or Crovan, which would inevitably betray his friends.

If the games he'd played in Millmoor had taught him one thing, it was that action created unpredictability and opportunity. Being handed to Crovan would mean a long journey to Scotland. That would offer opportunities for escape—assuming the man didn't lead him out of Kyneston on a leash.

"The boy's guilt is beyond doubt. Almost all of us were present at his heinous murder of our former Chancellor. Many of us were unfortunate enough to witness it with our own eyes. I therefore move that the sentence of Condemnation to slavelife be passed immediately. The criminal will then be consigned to Arailt Crovan for reformation."

Lord Jardine surveyed the chamber. Luke couldn't imagine anyone being insane enough to raise their voice. There was no friend for him here, in this Parliament of Equals.

But someone spoke.

"He's innocent. You must let him go."

At the very back, someone stood up. The voice—and the face—were impossibly familiar.

"Heir Meilyr?" Lord Jardine was frowning in a way that

boded no good for the speaker. "You claim this boy is innocent?"

"I do."

The man—the Equal, Heir Something-or-other—was de-
scending from the high tier in which he had been seated. And
Luke wanted to shout at him to shut up, to sit down. To stop
saying what he was saying, because this man's identity was impossible and too awful to be true.

He wasn't an Equal. He was Luke's mentor and friend, Doc
Jackson.

"And you know this how?"

"Because I know him. For the last year I have been living in
Millmoor slavetown working as a doctor. I met this boy when
he was brought to me as a patient, following a brutal beating by
Security. Millmoor's rebellious actions over the past months
have been my doing. My attempt to show all Equals the unjust
conditions forced upon the common people—by us."

Luke couldn't believe it. He cringed away from this person
who wore Jackson's face and spoke with Jackson's voice, but
who was an Equal.

"Your attempt has failed." Lord Jardine's voice was ice. "Was
this boy your last throw of the dice? You told him to commit
this final atrocity, or he did it of his own accord under your
influence—there is little difference."

Lord Jardine's words crawled into Luke's ears. Was this what
it had all been about—the Doc's resolve that Luke should come
to Kyneston? Was this why he had been recruited for the club?
A walking weapon, ready for Jackson—this Equal—to use.

To use—and then Silence. Was it this man whose Skill Silyen Jardine had detected? The person who wasn't who they seemed?

But that wasn't the story the Doc was telling.

"Luke had no part in Zelston's murder. I can tell you exactly what he did in Millmoor: acts of kindness and deeds of bravery. There is no need for you, or that man"—Jackson turned and pointed to Crovan—"to rip up his mind for useless knowledge. The Chancellor's death must have been a personal grudge; Luke the innocent tool used by the murderer. It could have been anyone here in this chamber. Even you, my lord, who have gained most by Zelston's death."

The East Wing of Kyneston exploded for a second time in twelve hours, though only with shock this time. The uproar of Equals talking and yelling was deafening.

In the back row an older woman was on her feet, frantically calling out, "Meilyr, no! No!"

Gavar was staring at the Doc like he was seeing him for the first time.

"The detention center," Gavar said. "The escape. I knew it was Skill. That was you."

But Jackson was looking only at Luke. "I'm sorry I couldn't tell you who I was," he said, urgent and low. "And I'm so sorry this has happened. We'll make it right, just as we did for Oz. Trust me."

The Doc's face was as full of passionate sincerity as it had ever been. But how could Luke believe him now? How could you trust someone you'd never really known?

"Enough!"

Lord Jardine's voice had the same effect as his heir's Skill in the MADhouse square that day, just minus the agony and the puking. The parliamentarians were instantly subdued.

"At the conclusion of yesterday's session, you, my Equals, voted to remove Chancellor Zelston from office. A decision that, incidentally, means I have no possible motive—despite Heir Meilyr's insinuations—to wish the man dead.

"That vote also approved an emergency administration, vested in me. I remind you that emergency powers include the ability to make executive decisions on law and order. The ability to move swiftly to put down enemies of the state.

"In coming here today to pass sentence on one such enemy, we have uncovered another hiding in our midst. One who has freely confessed—should I say, boasted—of sowing sedition, violence, and open revolt against our Equal authority."

Lord Jardine turned to Crovan and beckoned him forward. Would the man be going back to Scotland with two prisoners, not one?

"You can't Condemn Equals," yelled the woman at the back, who began stumbling down the stairs toward the front of the chamber.

"Lady Tresco." Lord Jardine purred the name, but it was a lion's purr, full of teeth and blood. "How gratifying that you finally appreciate the principle of 'one law for us, and one law for them.' But I have no intention of Condemning young Meilyr. Simply correcting him.

"Arailt has been working on such an intervention for some time. Should it prove effective, your son will be able to return to Highwithel this evening having learned the error of his ways. Gavar, ensure Armeria does not interfere."

Gavar moved to intercept the woman, barring her way before she reached the bottom of the stairs.

No one else moved. In the center of the second row, the blonde leaned forward intently, her perfect face hard as marble.

"What are you doing?" asked Jackson, his voice calm.

"Doing?" Lord Jardine smiled. "Well, a dangerous beast has its claws pulled. So what to do with a dangerous Equal, hmm?"

He nodded at Crovan. The man turned to Jackson, his glasses flashing in the sunlight, and the Doc winced.

But though the Doc looked away, his grimace remained. Deepened. Twisted into a look of unmistakable pain.

"What are you doing?" he said again, in a voice clotted with horror. "No."

He staggered and dropped to one knee. One hand clutched his head. The other clenched into a fist—and the tall, immaculate form of Lord Crovan went up in flames.

Crovan gasped and slammed a hand down through the air. Jackson sprawled to the floor, felled. Still Crovan burned. Luke could feel the heat from where he stood, though there was no singeing. No smell. The man beat at his arms and legs, and where he touched, the flame died. He smoothed his fingers up his face and back through his hair, and the last of the fire was wrung out at the ends like water.

The Doc dragged himself onto all fours, the effort it cost him clear in his face. He looked up at his opponent and Luke saw tears leaking from the corner of each eye. Tears of pure gold.

The woman Gavar was restraining began to scream— harrowing, inhuman shrieks. An animal seeing its cub in a trap.

Jackson lifted one hand from the floor. The gold stuff was dripping from beneath his fingernails now. A thin line of it trickled from his eardrum to his throat. He chopped down. Everyone heard the crack as both of Crovan's legs broke and the man fell to the floor. Jackson chopped again. Another crack. Crovan screamed and writhed, his arms falling unnaturally by his side.

Luke gasped, seeing the last of the Doc Jackson he knew disappear in this desperate, unimaginably powerful Heir Meilyr. Fighting for his life. Or something more.

The Doc crawled over to where Crovan lay and wrapped both hands around his neck. And squeezed.

An airless keening escaped Crovan's lips, and for a moment, despite the horror of it all, Luke exulted. The man was getting what he deserved. Payback for Dog. Payback for whatever sick things he did behind the walls of his castle to men and women who'd defied this race of monsters that called themselves "Equals."

Then he realized it was a hiss of triumph.

The air around Meilyr burst into a fine golden mist. It sprayed up from his body as if exploding from every pore. He was too dazzling to look at. Luke put a hand to his cheek to wipe it off, whatever it was. He remembered the woman in front of him in the MADhouse square, her skull blasted apart by Grierson's rifle. The spatter and the gore.

But his fingers came away clean. The golden substance was light itself, Luke thought. Lighter than air. It rose upward, spreading, thinning. Finally gathering like a bright vapor beneath the gleaming glass of the East Wing's roof. Then with a blinding flare, it was gone.

In front of Luke, Crovan was sitting up, flexing his arms, bending his now undamaged legs.

But Heir Meilyr—Doc Jackson—was huddled in a heap. He was sobbing like his heart had been broken in two. Like his soul itself had shattered.

Like his Skill had been ripped out and annihilated.

# EPILOGUE

# ABI

The car had taken Luke in the middle of the night.

Abi's Condemned brother and his jailer, Lord Crovan, had been driven out of Kyneston's gate straight to a helicopter. By the time his family learned he was gone, Luke was already half-way to Scotland and whatever fate awaited him at Eilean Dòchais.

Jenner had brought word at breakfast, by which point the Hadleys had been sleepless for nearly twenty-four hours. Dad had crumpled at the news, and Mum had simply laid her head against his shoulder and cried. It was such a perfect nightmare that Abi was almost—*almost*—grateful for the distraction of what Jenner said next.

"Jackie, Steve, you and Abi will need to pack your bags quickly. You're being sent to Millmoor this afternoon."

"Millmoor?" Dad looked baffled.

But Mum had caught the word that Jenner hadn't said.

"Daisy, too, you mean."

Jenner looked up at the ceiling, as if the words he needed might be written along the wooden beams. They weren't, of course.

"Daisy stays here. At Kyneston."

Abi's head snapped up. She hadn't seen that one coming.

Mum roared furiously and launched herself at Jenner, battering him with her fists. Abi didn't move to help him, nor did Dad try to pull Mum away. Jenner ducked and dodged the worst of her blows, then caught both her hands in his, waiting until she'd fought herself to a standstill.

"You're taking my children," Mum sobbed, wiping her snotty nose on her dressing gown sleeve. "You're not human. You're monsters."

"It's not permitted," Abi said to Jenner, more to have the matter over and done with than in any expectation of a comforting reply. "The law says that children under the age of eighteen can only do days with their parents. Although I remember your mother forgetting that in Luke's case, too."

"Abi, my father *is* the law. He can say whatever he likes. Gavar asked, and Father agreed. Daisy will move into one of the rooms in the servants' wing, and Libby will have a nursery next door."

Daisy sat mute and motionless at the table. She twisted round to look through the kitchen door, to where Libby was bashing plastic bricks on a rug in the living room. Her expression was unreadable. She loved the little girl dearly, Abi knew. But Daisy was still a child herself, not yet eleven.

Would Gavar become a substitute family for her—a strange

combination of older sibling and parent? How would Bouda Matravers take to her husband's unorthodox household?

Daisy said nothing.

"We need regular contact," Abi rapped out. "Letters weekly. Telephone conversations whenever possible. None of this three-month waiting period; it has to happen immediately. You can ensure that."

Jenner looked chastened. "I will."

"And I need to come up to the house now. There are things of mine in the office."

"Of course. I was going to suggest that."

"Mum, Dad, get the bags packed. I'll be as quick as I can. I don't want to miss a moment with you, little sis."

Abi and Jenner were away from the Row, but not yet over the rise to Kyneston, when Jenner kissed her. For a brief, traitorous moment Abi let herself melt into him. Wondered, madly, what would happen if she begged him to beg his father to allow her to stay.

"I did ask for you already, you know," he said, somehow intuiting her thoughts. He cupped her face and looked down at her with those warm brown eyes. They were filled with the same regret he'd had when he'd warned her not to be curious, on that very first day. "I didn't want you to think that if Gavar could get permission for Daisy, that I hadn't tried."

"I believe you," she said, and stretched on tiptoe to kiss him again. She wouldn't make him say it. Wouldn't spell out what they both knew—the fact of Jenner's powerlessness. Gavar was the heir. His alliance with Lord Jardine was an uneasy, volatile one, but father and son needed each other. No one needed Jenner.

Not even me, Abi told herself fiercely. She wondered how many times she'd have to say it before she believed it. And how many more times after that before it became the truth.

The things she was after were in several spots around the office, not just her own desk. So she encouraged Jenner to look through the workbooks and databases she'd set up, to make sure he understood them. While he was occupied, she moved around opening drawers, unlocking cabinets, occasionally announcing what was where, for Jenner's benefit.

She asked him not to walk her back to the cottage, and they said their goodbyes there in the Family Office. Jenner wound his fingers in her long hair as if he never wanted to untangle them again, and she pressed her face to his chest and breathed him in.

"I want this," she announced, tugging at his scarf when they separated. He knotted it round her neck, kissed her cheek, and watched her go.

The Hadleys' final hours together were subdued. They didn't discuss Luke. His absence was too awful to speak of just yet. Mum and Dad held Daisy desperately, trying to remember every inch of her. By the time they saw her again, their baby would be a grown woman of twenty.

"It's not uncommon for kids Daisy's age to be away from their parents," Abi tried to console their dad. "It'll be like she's at the world's most exclusive boarding school."

"Only with no one checking my homework," Daisy chipped in. "And I'm the one doing the teaching."

Dad laughed, then halfway through the laughter turned into excruciating weeping. For the millionth time Abi cursed herself for talking them into applying to Kyneston. If it weren't for her, they would all have been in Millmoor: underfed, poorly housed, bored out of their minds—and together.

Jenner came back just after lunch and led the four of them to the wall, where the Young Master was waiting on his black horse. The gate shimmered into existence. Abi hated that its appearance was every bit as miraculous as it had been the first time. There was a car visible on the other side, another silver-gray Labor Allocation Bureau vehicle.

The gate swung open. Four of them walked up to it, but only three walked through. Daisy stood and waved, Libby Jardine cradled to her chest in a harness. Then, just like that, the gate was gone and so was she. Kyneston's wall stretched away, an unbroken and unbreachable barrier, furred with moss and glowing faintly with Skill-light.

"You've not got much," said the driver as Abi tossed her half-empty duffel into the trunk on top of Mum and Dad's bags.

"I know how the slavetowns work," said Abi. "My brother was at Millmoor. They don't let you take much in."

She slid into the backseat of the car, Mum beside her, Dad up front. The driver tried to make small talk for the first few minutes, then gave up on them all. Abi watched the roads as the car turned. They'd be cutting west across to Bristol, then north up the M5 all the way to Manchester—and Millmoor.

She shoved her hands into her coat pockets, willing down the queasiness in her stomach.

"I'm sorry," she blurted, a short while after. "I don't travel well. I think I'm going to be sick."

"What?" The driver looked over his shoulder and scowled.

"Those trees over there. Please." Abi put a hand up to her mouth to cover a hiccup. "Can you pull over?"

She didn't dare do more than squeeze Mum's fingers as she got out, leaving the door open.

She moved a short way into the trees, turning her back on the car and doubling over. Her retching sounds would be plainly audible. She coughed, and moved a little deeper into the woods.

Then once she was out of sight, she took off at a sprint.

The map in her pocket batted against her leg as she ran. The map she'd taken from the Family Office, and studied as she walked back to the cottage by herself. She knew exactly where she was. Just a short way from here was a small A-road that led west, down to Exeter. Someone would stop quickly for a teenage girl on her own.

From there she'd get a train to Penzance, the last city in the southwestern tip of England. All the money she could possibly need was zipped into her coat. She'd emptied the office petty cash box, and needless to say the Jardines' idea of a float was more than most people earned in a month.

She could buy a change of clothing, or hair dye. It'd be wise to change her appearance, as alerts about her fugitive status would go out soon. On her side was the fact that they'd have no idea where she was headed. They'd probably guess Manchester. Or maybe even Scotland.

From Penzance she could get a ferry. Or a helicopter. Or talk or bribe her way onto a fishing boat or yacht.

She could be in the Scillies by the day's end. Nestled at the heart of the archipelago was an island estate. An estate that belonged to the only people who might help rescue her brother: Lady Armeria Tresco and her now Skilless son and heir, Meilyr.

Abi ran on. She intended to be at Highwithel by nightfall.

# ACKNOWLEDGMENTS

My agent: Robert Kirby, for believing in me and making it happen.

My international agents: Ginger Clark and Jane Willis, for making it happen all over the world.

My editors: Bella Pagan and Tricia Narwani, for making it the very best it can be.

My international editors: Eva Grynszpan, Marie-Ann Geissler, and many others, for loving this ever so British book.

My PanMac and Del Rey teams: Lauren, Phoebe, Kate, Jo, Emily, David M, Keith, Thomas, Quinne, David S, Julie, Loren and colleagues, for being an absolute professional pleasure.

My #TeamUA: Kate, Kat, and Yasmin, for having everything covered.

My family: Mum, Jonathan, and Dad, for filling my childhood with books and for always letting me read.

My old friends: Hils, Giles, Tanya, John, and far too many to mention, for always believing that one day you'd hold my book in your hands.

My new friends: Debbie, Taran, Tim, and Nick, for inspiring me and cheering me all the way.

My telly people: Mike, Jacques, Fiona, and Jay, for enabling my great escape.

My first responders: Gav who featured me, Amy who pulled me from the slushpile, and Winchester Library who gave me a writing prize at age eight. Early belief is everything.

My Wattpadres: for being there from the beginning.

My Homies: for buying me drinks along the way.

My Goldies: for believing that creative and intellectual endeavor belong together.

My Swankies: for not letting me do this alone.

# ABOUT THE AUTHOR

VIC JAMES is a current-affairs TV director who loves stories in all their forms. Her programs for BBC1 have covered the 2016 U.S. presidential election and Britain's EU referendum. She has twice judged *The Guardian*'s Not the Booker Prize. *Gilded Cage* is her first novel, and an early draft of it won a major online award from Wattpad for most-talked-about fantasy novel. She has lived in Rome and Tokyo, and currently lives in London.

vicjames.co.uk
Facebook.com/VicJamesAuthor
@DrVictoriaJames